O9-ABF-827

**Praise for the novels of #1 *New York Times*
bestselling author Debbie Macomber**

"Macomber is a skilled storyteller."
—*Publishers Weekly*

"It's easy to see why Macomber is a perennial favorite:
she writes great books."
—*RomanceJunkies.com*

"Debbie Macomber writes characters
who are as warm and funny as your best friends."
—*New York Times* bestselling author Susan Wiggs

"Macomber's storytelling sometimes yields a tear,
at other times a smile."
—*Newport News*, VA, *Daily Press*

"[Debbie Macomber] demonstrates her impressive skills
with characterization and her flair for humor."
—*RT Book Reviews*

"When God created Eve, he must have asked
Debbie Macomber for advice because no one does
female characters any better than this author."
—*Bookbrowser Reviews*

"Debbie Macomber is one of the most reliable,
versatile romance authors around. Whether she's writing
light-hearted romps or more serious relationship books,
her novels are always engaging stories that
accurately capture the foibles of real-life men and women
with warmth and humor."
—*Milwaukee Journal Sentinel*

"Popular romance author Debbie Macomber
has a gift for evoking the emotions that are
at the heart of the genre's popularity."
—*Publishers Weekly*

September 2014

Dear Friends,

One question I'm almost always asked is: What's your inspiration? Generally I joke and answer, "Two house payments." That's all the inspiration I need! The truth is ideas come from everywhere.

It all started when Wayne and I used part of my advance for a short vacation trip to Mexico in the 1980s. For the first ten years that Wayne and I were married we didn't leave the state of Washington—we were too busy having babies. Our children were a bit older at this point, and my parents were excited to have them for a week, so Wayne and I headed out with our best friends, the Frelingers. And what a fabulous time we had! It was while we were in Mazatlan that I came up with the idea for *Shadow Chasing*.

For All My Tomorrows was one of the first opportunities I had to write a longer story, and I chose a subject that had touched my heart. The summer before I wrote the book, a Seattle policeman had been killed in the line of duty. The evening news showed the grieving widow. I remember watching that scene with tears in my eyes as she gathered her children close to her side. I wanted to take this kind of tragedy and, as much as possible, show that there is a way through grief and that life does continue.

Now you know where I got the idea for these two books, which I hope you'll enjoy. I've refreshed them to reflect current times, so if you're reading along and everyone's cell phone is in need of a charge, you'll know why. (When I wrote these books there were no cell phones and if they were available, they were the size of shoe boxes.)

Hearing from my readers is one of the many joys I receive as a writer. You can find me on Facebook, Twitter (@debbiemacomber) or Instagram. You can also reach me through my website, debbiemacomber.com, or even by letter at P.O. Box 1458, Port Orchard, WA 98366.

Thank you for your ongoing encouragement and support.

Debbie Macomber

DEBBIE MACOMBER

To Love and Protect

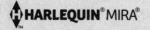
HARLEQUIN® MIRA®

ISBN-13: 978-0-7783-1645-9

TO LOVE AND PROTECT

Recycling programs for this product may not exist in your area.

Printed in U.S.A.

www.Harlequin.com

Also by Debbie Macomber

To Norm and Sharon Frelinger with thanks for all the wild, fun adventures we've shared through the years.

CONTENTS

SHADOW CHASING

One

"You're kidding." Carla Walker glanced at her friend suspiciously. "What did they put in that margarita, anyway? Sodium pentothal?"

Nancy Listten's dark eyes brightened, but her attention didn't waver from the mariachi band that played softly in the background.

"I'm serious," Nancy replied. "This happens every vacation. We now have seven glorious days in Mazatlán. What do you want to bet that we don't find a man to flirt with until day six?"

"That's because it takes awhile to scout out who's available," Carla argued, taking a sip of her drink. The granules of salt from the edge of the glass felt gritty on the inside of her bottom lip. But she enjoyed the feel and the taste.

"Exactly my point."

Nancy took off her glasses and placed them inside her purse. That action said a lot. Her friend meant every word. She was dead serious.

"We spend at least two days trying to figure out who's married and who isn't."

"Your idea isn't going to help," Carla insisted. "The next two men who walk in here could be married."

"But imagine how much time it'll save if we *ask*. And"—Nancy inhaled a deep breath—"have you noticed how picky we are? We always act like our choices are going to improve if given enough time. We've simply got to realize that there're no better candidates than whoever walks through that door tonight."

"I don't know…" Carla hesitated, wondering if there was something wrong with her drink, too. Nancy's idea was beginning to make sense. "What if they speak Spanish?" That was a stupid question, and the look Nancy gave her said as much. They each had a phrase book, and Carla had watched enough *Sesame Street* when baby-sitting her nieces to pick up the basics of the language. She groaned inwardly. She'd begun this vacation with such high hopes. Seven glorious days in one of the most popular vacation spots in the world. Men galore. Tanned, gorgeous men. And she was going to end up introducing herself in *Sesame Street* Spanish to the next guy who walked through the door. Even worse, the idea was growing more appealing by the minute. Nancy was right. For two years they'd ruined their vacations looking for Mr. Perfect. Not only hadn't they ever found him, but as their time had grown shorter, their standards had lowered. The men they'd found marginal on day one looked like rare finds by day six. And on day seven, frustrated and discouraged, they'd flown back to Seattle, having wasted their entire vacation.

"I think we should establish some sort of criteria, don't you?"

Carla nodded. "Unencumbered."

"That goes without saying." Nancy gave her a classroom glare that Carla had seen often enough to recognize. "They should walk in here alone. And be under thirty-five." Nancy's eyes sought Carla. "Anything else?"

"I, for one, happen to be a little more particular than you."

"All right, add what you want."

"I think they should order a margarita."

"Carla! We could be here all night if we did that."

"We're in Mazatlán; everyone orders margaritas," Carla countered. Well, a tourist would and that was what she wanted. No serious stuff, just a nice holiday romance.

"Okay," Nancy agreed.

Their eyes focused on the two entrances. Waiting.

"Have you noticed how all the cocktail lounges are beginning to look like furniture showrooms?" Carla commented, just to have something to say. Her hands felt damp as she stuidied the entry to the nightclub.

"Shh...someone's coming."

A middle-aged couple walked through the door.

They both relaxed. "We'd better decide who goes first."

"You," Carla returned instantly. "It was your idea."

"All right," she agreed, and straightened, nervously folding her hands on her lap.

Carla pulled up the spaghetti strap of her summer dress. Normally a redhead couldn't wear pink, but this shade, the color of camellias, complemented the unusual color of her hair.

"Here comes a single man."

Two pairs of intense eyes followed the lumbering

gait of a dark-haired Latin-American who entered the lounge and took the closest available love seat.

"He's in a cast," Nancy observed in a high-pitched whisper.

"Don't panic," Carla said in a reassuring tone. "He doesn't look like the type to order a margarita."

Nancy opened her purse and put on her glasses. "Not bad-looking, though."

"Yes, I suppose so," Carla agreed, although she thought he looked too much like a movie star, smooth and suave to suit her. His toothy smile looked bright enough to blind someone in broad daylight. For Nancy's sake, she hoped the guy was into wine. "You can back out if you want," Carla said, almost wishing Nancy would. The whole idea was crazy.

"Not on your life."

"The guy's in a cast up to his hip. I'd say he was encumbered, wouldn't you?"

"No," Nancy replied smoothly. "You're doing it again."

"Doing what?"

"You know."

"All right, I'll shut up. If you want to be stuck with a guy who leaves a funny trail in the sand, that's fine with me."

"Look," Nancy whispered, "your fellow's arrived."

Quickly, Carla's attention focused on the lounge entrance at the other side of the room. She recognized him immediately as someone from the same flight as theirs. Not that she'd found him particularly interesting at the time. He'd sat across the aisle from Nancy and read a book during the entire trip.

"Hey, he was on the plane with us," Nancy pointed out.

"I know," Carla answered evenly, trying to disguise her disappointment. Secretly, she'd been hoping for someone compelling and forcefully masculine. She should have known better.

Both girls sat in rigid silence as their eyes followed the young cocktail waitress, who delivered two margaritas, one to looker, and one to the bookworm.

"You ready?" Nancy whispered.

"What are we going to say?" Carla's hand tightened around her purse.

Nancy gave another of those glares normally reserved for her pupils. "Good grief, Carla, we're mature women. We know what to say."

Carla shook her head. "Mature women wouldn't do something like this."

They stood together, condemned prisoners marching to the hangman's noose. "How do I look?" Nancy asked with a weak smile.

"Like you're about to throw up."

Her friend briefly closed her eyes. "That's the way I feel."

Carla hesitated.

"Come on," Nancy hissed. "We aren't backing out now."

Carla couldn't believe that calm, level-headed, left-brained Nancy would actually suggest something like this. It was completely out of character. Carla was the impulsive one—creative, imaginative, right-brained. That was why they were such good friends: their personalities complemented each other perfectly. Right-brained, left-brained, Carla mused. That was the problem. Each of them had only half a brain.

She studied the man from the plane. He wasn't any-

one she would normally have sought out. For a light romance, she wanted someone more dynamic. This guy
was decidedly—she searched for the right word—un-
dashing. He was tall, she remembered, which was lucky.
At five nine she didn't look up to many men. And he
was on the lanky side. Almost reedy. He wore horn-
rimmed glasses, which gave him a serious look. His
sandy hair, parted on the side, fell carelessly across his
wide brow. His tan was rich, but Carla mused that he
didn't look like the type to use a tanning machine or
lie lazily in the sun. He probably worked outdoors—
maybe he was a mailman.

He glanced at her and smiled. Carla nearly tripped
on the plush carpet. His eyes were fantastic. A deep
gray like the overcast winter clouds with the sun beaming through. A brilliant silver shade that she had never
seen. Her spirits brightened; the man's eyes, at least,
were encouragingly attractive.

"Hello," she said as she stood in front of his deep
cushioned chair. "I'm Carla Walker." She extended her
hand. Might as well be forthright about this.

He stood, dwarfing her by a good four inches, and
shook hands. "Philip Garrison."

He looked like a Philip. "We were on the same flight,
weren't we?"

He pushed his glasses up the bridge of his nose with
his index finger. The action reminded her of Clark Kent.
But Carla wasn't kidding herself—Philip Garrison was
no Superman.

"I believe we were," he said with a smile that was
surprisingly compelling. "Would you like to sit down?"

"Yes, thank you." Carla took the chair beside him.

Hoping to give an impression of nonchalance, she crossed her shapely legs. "Are you from Seattle?"

"Spokane."

"On vacation?"

His smile deepened. "In a way. My parents have a condominium here that needs a few repairs."

Carla smiled absently into her drink. So he was a carpenter. The occupation suited him, she decided. He was deceptively lean and muscular. And he had a subtle, understated appeal, something she found refreshing.

"Would you like another margarita?" he asked as he glanced at her empty glass.

"Yes. Thank you."

He raised his hand to get the waitress's attention. The lovely olive-skinned girl acknowledged his gesture and indicated that she would be there in a moment. Service here was notoriously slow, but right now Carla didn't mind. She looked around for Nancy and discovered that her friend was chatting easily and seemed to be enjoying herself. At the moment, this crazy scheme appeared to be working beautifully.

"Is this your first visit to Mazatlán?" Philip asked, and took a sip of his drink.

Carla noted the way the tip of his tongue eased the salt from the bottom of his lip. She dropped her gaze, finding his action disturbingly provocative. "Yes, my first time in Mexico, actually. To be honest, I didn't expect it to be this beautiful."

The waitress arrived, and Carla handed the girl her empty glass. She had noticed that the waitresses spoke only minimal English. Although her Spanish wasn't terrific, the urge to impress Philip with her knowledge of the language overpowered her good sense, so, proudly, without the hint of a foreign accent, Carla asked for another drink.

The waitress frowned and glanced at Philip, who was obviously trying to contain his laughter. He delivered a crisp request to the girl in Spanish, who nodded and smiled before turning away.

"What's so humorous?" Carla could feel herself blushing.

Philip composed himself quickly. "You just told the waitress that Big Bird wants a drink of water."

Carla closed her eyes and did her best to laugh, but the sound was weak and revealing. She would never watch *Sesame Street* again, she vowed, no matter how desperate she was to entertain her two nieces.

"How long will you be staying?" he asked pleasantly, deftly changing the subject.

"A week. My roommate, Nancy, and I are on a discount vacation package for teachers."

"You teach preschool?"

It was a logical assumption. "No, I'm a surgical assistant."

One thick brow arched with surprise. "You don't look much older than a student yourself."

"I'm twenty-five." And old enough to know better than to make a fool of myself like this, she added silently.

Their drinks arrived, and Carla restrained the urge to gulp hers down and ease the parched feeling in her throat. Gradually she relaxed as they spoke about the flight and the weather.

After a half hour of exchanging pleasantries, Philip asked her if she was available to join him for dinner. The invitation pleased her. Since her faux pas with the waitress, she'd imagined he'd wanted to be rid of her as quickly as he could manage to do so without appearing impolite.

"Yes, I'd like to have dinner with you." To her surprise, Carla discovered it was the truth.

He took her to a restaurant named El Marinero. The view of the harbor was excellent, as was the shrimp dinner. Philip spoke to the waiter in Spanish, then quietly translated for Carla. It was a thoughtful gesture. She would have felt excluded otherwise. Not once did he try to overwhelm her with his wit and charm. He was who he was, quiet and a little reserved, and apparently he saw no need to change because he'd been approached by her.

"I can't believe I ate that much," Carla groaned as they left the restaurant. The air was still sultry but much cooler than when they'd arrived.

"Would you like to walk along the beach? It'll be less crowded outside the hotel."

"I'd love to." Her blue eyes looked fondly into his. "But can we? I mean, it's all privately owned, isn't it?"

"Not in Mexico. The beaches are for everyone."

"How nice," Carla murmured, thinking she was beginning to like Philip more with every passing minute.

They rode back to the hotel in an open-air vehicle that resembled a golf cart—a hot-rod golf cart. The driver weaved his way in and out of lanes with complete disregard for pedestrians and traffic signals.

Philip took her by the hand and led her through the lobby, around the huge swimming pool in back of the hotel and to the stairs that descended to the beach. The strip of white sand stretched as far as the eye could see. So did the array of hotels.

"I don't suppose you've been in the ocean yet."

"No time," Carla confessed. "The first thing Nancy and I did was take a shower." The heat that had greeted them on their arrival had been suffocating. They'd stepped from the air-conditioned plane into one-hundred-degree weather. By the time they'd arrived at the hotel room, their clothes had been damp from the humidity and clinging. "I couldn't believe that death trap of a shuttle bus actually made it all the way to the hotel."

Philip grinned in amusement. "I think the same thing every time I visit."

"Do you come often?" Carla asked as they sat in the sand and removed their shoes. Philip rolled up the tan pant legs to his knees.

"Once or twice a year."

He stood and tucked her hand into the crook of his arm.

"I think there's something I should tell you," Carla said as an ocean wave gently lapped up to her bare feet. The warm water was another surprise.

"You mean that you don't usually pick up men in bars," Philip said with a chuckle. "I already knew that."

"You did?" Carla was astonished.

"What made you do it this time?"

Carla kicked idly at the sand with her big toe. "You aren't going to like hearing this," she mumbled.

"Try me."

She took a deep breath, then exhaled slowly. "It happens every vacation. Nancy and I spend the entire time waiting to meet someone. This time we decided that instead of wasting our vacation, we'd take the initiative ourself. To make the decision easy we decided we could find someone on the first day. One problem is that we're too picky so we decided to be a bit more spontaneous. You came in alone. You're under thirty-five, and you ordered a margarita."

The pleasant sound of his laughter blended with a crashing wave that pounded the beach. "I almost asked for a beer."

"I'm glad you didn't." The words were automatic and sincere. It surprised Carla how much she meant them.

The sun became a huge red ball that slowly descended to meet a blue horizon. Carla couldn't remember ever seeing anything more spectacular. She glanced at Philip to see if he was also enjoying the beauty of their surroundings. He wasn't the chatty sort, she realized, which was fine—she could do enough talking for them both. His laugh was free and easy, and the sound of it warmed her.

"What were you reading so intently on the plane?" Carla asked, curious to know more about him.

"The latest book by Ann Rule, she's—"

"I know who she is," Carla interrupted. The talented Seattle author was a policewoman turned reporter turned writer. Ann's books specialized in true crime cases. Her novel on serial murderer Ted Bundy was a national bestseller. "My father worked with Ann before she took up writing," Carla explained. "She's from Seattle."

"I read that on the cover flap. What does your father do?"

Carla swallowed uncomfortably. "He's a cop," she murmured, not looking at Philip.

"You sound like it bothers you."

"It does," Carla replied vigorously. "Half the boys

in high school wouldn't ask me out. They were afraid I'd tell my father if they tried anything, and then he'd go after them."

"Your father would arrest them for making a pass?" Philip sounded incredulous.

"Not that." She tossed him a defiant look. It was obvious that Philip, like everyone else in her life, didn't understand. "It's too hard to explain."

"Try me."

Carla felt a tightening in her stomach. Although she'd held these feelings deep inside since childhood, she had never verbalized them. She wasn't sure she was capable of expressing them now. "A good example of what I'm saying happened when I was about ten. Our family went to a friend's wedding reception. Everyone had been drinking, and an uncle had given some of the teens spiked punch. The minute Dad walked in the room the temperature dropped fifteen degrees."

"Were they afraid he was going to make a scene?"

"I don't know. But I do recall how uncomfortable everyone was."

"Including you?"

She hesitated. "Yes."

"But that's not all, is it?" he asked gently.

"No," she admitted. "It was far more than that. I can count on one hand the number of Christmases Dad spent home. It was the same thing every holiday. And we were lucky if he was there for our birthdays. It got so that I'd dread it every time the phone rang, because I knew he was always on call. It was his job."

"I don't blame you for resenting that."

Once started, Carla discovered she couldn't stop. "He worked with the scum of the earth: pimps, prostitutes, muggers, murderers, drunks and derelicts. Then there were the sick people, dying people, dead people, wife beaters and child abusers. Sometimes he'd come home at night and…" She stopped, realizing that everything had come out in one huge rush. When she'd caught her breath, Carla continued. "I'm sorry, I didn't mean to unload on you like this."

"You didn't," Philip said, and casually draped his hand over her shoulder. "You've never told your father any of this, have you?"

"No. What was the use? Dad loves his work." Philip's hand cupped her shoulder. He was comforting her, and in a strange way Carla appreciated it. Never before had she voiced these thoughts, and the fierce intensity of her feelings had surprised her.

By unspoken agreement, they turned back toward the hotel. The sky had grown dark now, and the lights from the long row of hotels dimly lit the beach. Other couples were walking along the sandy shores. A few flirted with the cresting ocean waves.

"Philip." Carla stopped and turned toward him. "Thank you," she whispered.

"What for?"

Their eyes met in the moonlight, and Carla was trapped in the silvery glow of his gaze. Those beautiful, warm gray eyes held her as effectively as the arms that had slipped around her waist and brought her into his embrace.

"I may never drink anything but margaritas again." His whisper was husky, but he didn't make a move to do anything more than hold her. His arms pressed her gently as he rubbed his chin across the top of her head. A mist-filled breeze off the ocean had ruined her carefully styled hair; now it fell in tight ringlets around her oval face.

Her hair was another thing that endeared her to Philip. Not once had he mentioned its color. Men invariably teased her about it, asking if her temper matched the color of her hair. The only time it did was when someone made tiresome remarks about it. Not red and not blond, the shade fell somewhere in between. Red oak, her mother claimed, like her grandmother's. Like russet potatoes, her brother suggested. The color of her hair and her fair complexion had been the bane of Carla's existence.

"Would you like to go for a swim?" Philip asked, dropping his arms and taking her hand. They continued walking toward the hotel.

"In the ocean?" She'd have to get her suit.

"No, the current's too dangerous. I meant the pool."

The hotel's swimming pool was the most luxurious Carla had ever seen. A picture of the massive pool area at the hotel had been the determining factor in their decision to book their holidays at the El Cid. Blue, watery channels stretched all around the hotel, with bridges joining one section to another.

"I'd love to go swimming," Carla replied enthusiastically. They reached the short flight of stairs that led to the hotel from the beach. "Give me ten minutes to change and I'll meet you back here."

"Ten minutes?" Philip arched one brow. Carla had noticed him do that a couple of times during the evening. It seemed to be Philip's way of expressing mild surprise.

"Ten minutes—easy," Carla confirmed confidently. She knew exactly which corner of her suitcase held her swimsuit. It wouldn't take her more than five minutes to change, so she figured she'd easily have five minutes to spare. But what she hadn't counted on was that Nancy had neatly stored their suitcases under the beds. Carla spent a frantic five minutes tearing their room apart, certain that they'd been robbed. Finally, she found it. She should have remembered her friend's penchant for neatness.

Fifteen minutes later, a chagrined look pinching her face, Carla met Philip at poolside.

Pointedly he glanced at his watch.

"I couldn't help it," she told him breathlessly, and offered a sketchy explanation as she placed her towel on a chaise longue. The pool was empty, which surprised Carla until she removed her wristwatch and noted that it was after midnight.

She tugged the elastic of the forest-green maillot over her thigh and tested the water by dipping one foot into the pool. Warm. Almost too warm.

"Are you one of those women who gets wet by degrees?" Philip asked as he took off his glasses and tossed them on his towel.

"Not me." She walked to his side, stretched out her arms and dived in. Her slim body sliced into the water. Philip joined her almost immediately, and together they swam the width of the pool.

"Do you want to race?" he called out.

"No," Carla answered with a giggle.

"Why not?"

"Because I was on my college swim team, and I'm fast. Men can't stand to lose."

"Is that a fact?"

"It's true."

"I'm not like most men."

Carla had noticed that. But this was turning out to be a promising relationship, and she didn't want to ruin it. Floating lackadaisically on her back, she paddled rhythmically with her hands at her side. Carla decided to ignore the challenge in his voice.

Philip joined her, floating on his back as well. "If you don't want to race, what would you like to do?"

"Kiss underwater." She laughed at the surprised look on his face as he struggled to a standing position. Philip looked different without his glasses, almost handsome. But not quite.

He stood completely still in the shoulder-deep water. "I'm not that kind of man."

He was so serious that it took Carla a moment to realize he was kidding.

"I'm not easy, you know," she said, flirting. "You have to catch me first." They were acting like adolescents, and Carla loved it. With Philip she could be herself. There wasn't any need to put on sophisticated airs.

Laughing, she twisted and dove underwater, surfacing several feet away from him. He came after her, and Carla took off with all the energy she'd expend for an important race. Using her most powerful strokes, she surged ahead. When his hand groped for her foot, she kicked frantically and managed to escape. That he'd caught up with her so quickly was hard to believe.

She was even more amazed when his solid stroke matched hers and he gripped her waist and pulled her to the side of the pool.

"You're as slippery as an eel."

"You're good," she countered. "Who taught you to swim like that?"

"My mother." They were hidden under the shadow of a bridge that crossed a narrow section of the pool.

Carla slipped her arms around his neck. She wanted him to kiss her. She could tell he was attracted to her; she'd seen it in his eyes when they were on the beach. That look had prompted her flippant challenge about kissing underwater.

He pushed the wet strands of hair from her face. The silver light in his eyes darkened. He moved closer, but Carla assumed it was because he couldn't see her clearly without his glasses. She liked his eyes. They were so expressive. She liked the way they darkened when he was serious and how they sparkled when he was teasing. Tiny lines fanned out from the edges, and Carla recognized that this man laughed and enjoyed life. Her feelings for him were intensifying every minute they were together.

His hand rested on either side of her face, pressing her against the side of the pool. "I'm going to kiss you," he whispered. He released one hand and encircled her waist to pull her gently but firmly toward him.

Slowly, lengthening each moment, each breath, he lowered his mouth to hers. Carla felt herself relax, felt her body, her heart, opening to him. Wanting to touch him, needing to, she ran her hand along the side of his face, twisting her head so that when he found her lips their mouths slanted across each other's. The kiss was gentle and soft, gradually building in intensity until Carla melted against him.

Philip let go of the side of the pool, and they sank just below the surface. Their legs entwined, and Carla opened her mouth to him. His tongue sought hers, forcing her mouth to open farther under its exploring pressure. Carla felt as if she were drowning, but the sensation was exquisite.

They broke the surface of the water together and drew in deep, shaky breaths. Her body remained tucked in his embrace. His chest pressed against the softness of her breasts, and a crazy dizziness overcame her.

The pressure of his embrace backed her against the side of the pool, and he kissed her again. Carla gloried in the wonderful, inexplicable sensations that overwhelmed her.

Their breathing was ragged when Philip buried his face in the side of her neck.

"My word," she murmured breathlessly, "who taught you to kiss like that?"

Philip responded with a weak laugh. "Carla." Philip hesitated and wiped the moisture from his eyes. "I wish I could see you better."

"I'm glad you can't," she replied happily. "You might get a swelled head if you could see how much I like you."

"Carla." His voice grew strong, serious.

"What's wrong?" She placed a hand on each of his shoulders, liking the feel of her body floating against his.

"There's something you should know."

"What?" He was so serious that her heart throbbed. She didn't want anything to ruin this. If he told her he was married she wasn't sure what she'd do.

"Carla, I'm a policeman for the city of Spokane."

Two

Carla woke just as the sun crested the horizon and bathed the beach in a flashy glow of color. Nancy had been asleep by the time Carla had returned last night, which was just as well. She hadn't felt much like talking.

Philip Garrison had taught her a valuable lesson. She should have trusted her instincts. From her first look at Philip, she'd felt he wasn't her type. At the time, she hadn't realized how true that was. True, his kisses had been… She couldn't find a word to describe them. Pleasant, she mused. All right, very pleasant. But that certainly wasn't enough to overcome *what* he was.

Drat. Drat. Drat.. She'd liked him. In fact she'd liked him a lot. He was sensitive, sympathetic, compassionate, kind, caring… Carla placed the pillow over her head to drown out her thoughts. She wouldn't allow herself to think about him again. This crazy idea of Nancy's had been ridiculous from the beginning. She'd put the episode behind her and get on with her vacation.

Throwing back the covers of her bed, she stood and

stretched. Nancy grumbled and curled into a tight ball. Typical of Nancy, who hated mornings.

"What time is it?" she demanded in a growling whisper.

"Early, the sun just came up."

"Sun!" Nancy's eyes popped open. "I forgot to set the alarm."

Carla smiled as she sat in the middle of the single bed and ran a brush through her hair to tame the wild array of red curls. "Don't worry about the time. We're on vacation, remember?"

With an uncharacteristically hurried movement, Nancy threw back the sheets. "But I promised to meet Eduardo on the beach at dawn," she cried out. "Oh, good grief, how could I have been so stupid?"

For Nancy to forget anything was surprising by itself. But to have her friend show this much enthusiasm in the morning was astonishing.

"I take it you and…Eduardo hit it off?"

Nancy's head bobbed energetically. "What about you?"

"Not so lucky," Carla returned with a wistful sigh.

Nancy's most attractive summer dress slid over her hips as she turned her back to Carla in an unspoken request for her to do up the zipper. "What went wrong?"

"You don't have time to hear," Carla said with forced cheerfulness.

"He looked nice."

Nice was only the beginning, Carla thought. "Looks are often deceiving." That much was true. Who would have imagined that Philip Garrison would turn out to be so appealing? "If I'm not mistaken, I'd say you and Eduardo got along famously."

"He's fabulous. I can't remember a night I've enjoyed more." Nancy paused, and a dreamy look replaced the hurried frown that had marred her smooth features.

"His cast doesn't bother you?" Carla couldn't help asking.

"Good grief, no. I hardly thought about it."

That was saying something.

"He's taking me on an all-day tour of Mazatlán. You don't mind, do you?"

"Mind? Me? Of course not." Carla's mouth formed a tight smile. Now she'd be forced to spend the entire day alone. "Have a good time," she managed without a hint of sarcasm. No need to ruin Nancy's fun.

"Thanks, I will." Always practical, Nancy grabbed a hat to protect her from the sun, tucked her credit cards in a secret flap in her purse and was out the door in a rush.

Carla flopped back on her bed and stared at the shadows on the ceiling. This vacation was rapidly turning into a disaster. Day two and already she wished she were back in Seattle.

After an unhurried shower, Carla decided to head for the pool. With her skin color, she wasn't able to stay out in the sun long, and morning was generally the best time for her to sunbathe.

The pool area was filling up with early sun worshippers, and Carla chose a chaise longue near the deep end. That way she could dive in and cool off whenever necessary. This afternoon she'd do some shopping at the Mazatlán Arts and Crafts Center. She'd heard about the center almost immediately after her arrival. With twenty-eight shops to explore, she was certain to find souvenirs for her family. But even shopping had lost its appeal, especially since she'd be doing it alone. If she was lucky, she might meet someone at the pool—preferably someone male and handsome. She spread her towel out as a cushion for the longue and lay on her stomach, facing the pool. With her arms crossed she pressed her cheeks against her forearm. Boring, she admitted regretfully. Day two and she was bored to death. The turquoise bikini she wore was modest, especially when compared to the daring suit on the luscious, curvy creature across the pool from her. Carla guessed that if she had a body like that, she might be tempted to wear the same thing. She'd heard of string bikinis, but this one was hardly more than threads. The woman was attracting the attention of almost everyone at poolside. When Philip moved into her line of vision, Carla's eyes widened. He smiled, and his gray eyes twinkled. It didn't bother her that his smile wasn't directed at her. For all the attention he'd given her, he obviously hadn't noticed that she was across the pool from him.

Carla chose to ignore him, but her heart leaped just seeing him again. He wasn't muscular or strikingly masculine, but he was compelling in a way she couldn't describe. If she hadn't spent yesterday with him, she wouldn't have given him a second look today. But she'd felt the lean hardness of him against her in the water. She'd tasted the sweetness of his kiss. She'd experienced the gentle comfort of his arms. Her eyes refused to move from him, and when he looked her way, she shook herself from her musings and lowered her cheek against her arm, pretending not to see him.

Her heart was racing and that angered her. One look from Philip was no reason for her pulse to quicken. Although Carla refused to pay attention to him, she could feel Philip's gaze on her. She smiled as she imagined the satisfaction in his gaze, the look of admiration that would dominate those smoky-gray eyes of his. How she loved his expressive eyes! Unable to resist, she raised her head a fraction to catch a glimpse of his approval. To her dismay, Carla discovered that Philip wasn't studying her at all. His concentration was centered on the daring blond beauty at the other side of the pool.

Carla expected the woman to treat Philip like a pesky intruder. But she didn't—in fact, she seemed to encourage his attentions. Grudgingly, Carla admitted there *was* a certain attraction to Philip, and an aura of quiet confidence that was…well, masculine. His sandy hair had a tendency to curl at the ends, she observed, and most men would have styled it into submission. But not Philip; professionally groomed hair wouldn't be on his list of priorities.

After several minutes of what appeared to be light conversation, Philip dived into the pool and did a number of laps. Carla couldn't help admiring the way his bronze body sliced through the water. Anyone would. A rush of pink colored her cheeks as she recalled their antics last night. Yes, Philip Garrison was indeed gifted.

When Philip came out of the pool, he maneuvered himself so that he "accidentally" dripped water on his scantily clad acquaintance. The luscious blonde sat up to hand him a towel and laughed lightly when more drops of water splashed on her bare midriff.

Forcefully, Carla directed her gaze elsewhere. For a full five minutes she refused to allow herself to turn their way. When curiosity got the better of her, she casually glanced toward Philip and the other woman, who were an unlikely match. To her dismay she found that they were laughing and enjoying a cocktail. One side of Carla's mouth curved up sarcastically. One would assume a dedicated police officer would know better than to consume alcohol at such an early hour.

Pretending that the sun was burning her tender skin, Carla made a show of standing and draping a light terry-cloth wrap over her shoulders. She tucked her towel and tanning lotion in the oversized bag and walked down the cement stairs that led to the beach.

The beach wasn't nearly as crowded as the pool area. Carla had just settled in the sandy mattress when she was approached by a vendor carrying a black case. He knelt in front of her and opened the lid to display a large number of silver earrings, bracelets and rings. She smiled and shook her head. But the man persisted, telling her in poor English that he would sell jewelry to her at a very good price.

Politely but firmly, Carla shook her head.

Still the man insisted, holding out a lovely silver-and-turquoise ring for her to inspect. His eyes pleaded with her, and Carla couldn't refuse. The ring was pretty.

Someone spoke in Spanish from behind her. It didn't take Carla two seconds to realize it was Philip. His words were heavy with authority, although he hadn't raised his voice. Resenting his intrusion, she tossed him an angry look.

"Do you like the ring?" He directed his comment to her.

"Well, it's more than I wanted to spend—"

She wasn't allowed to finish. Philip said something to the vendor, who nodded resignedly, took back the ring and turned away.

"That wasn't necessary, you know," she told him stiffly.

"Perhaps not, but you could buy the same ring in the hotel gift shop for less than what he was asking." Philip spread out his towel a respectable distance from her. "Do you mind?" he asked before he sat down.

"It's a public beach," she returned coolly, recognizing it wouldn't do any good to object. "Just leave enough space between us so no one will assume we're together." She suspected that Philip would only follow her if she got up and moved. "What happened with Miss String Bikini?" Carla had hoped to resist any hint of acid in her query.

Philip chuckled. "Unfortunately, Miss is a Mrs., and hubby looked like the jealous type."

Now it was Carla's turn to laugh. She was sorry to have missed the scene of Philip meeting the irate husband. "I'll admit, though, she had quite a body."

"Passable," Philip admitted dryly as his eyes swept over the beach.

Passable! Carla's mind echoed, wondering what he considered terrific.

"Where's your roommate?" he asked breezily.

"With…Eduardo. They seem to have hit it off quite well."

"We did, too, as I recall. I wonder what it would take to get you to agree to have lunch with me."

"Forget it, Garrison," Carla said forcefully.

"You know what a good time we could have," he prodded softly.

"I'm not interested," Carla replied without looking at him. She felt a twinge of regret at how callous she sounded, and recalled how cold she'd been to him after he'd told her his occupation. She wouldn't have been so unfeeling, she suspected, if she hadn't previously expressed her resentment about her father being a policeman. Later, unable to sleep, she decided she was glad she'd told him. It had saved an unnecessary explanation. As it was, she'd pushed herself from his arms and swum to the opposite side of the pool. "It was a pleasure meeting you, Philip Garrison," she'd said tersely while toweling dry. "But I have one strict code regarding the men I date."

"I think I can guess what that is," he'd replied with a control that was frightening. "You realize I didn't have to tell you. We could have had a pleasant vacation together without you ever being the wiser."

"Perhaps." Carla hadn't been in any mood to reason. "But you saved us both a lot of trouble." With the damp towel draped over her neck, she'd hurried back to her room. Not until she'd changed out of her swimsuit had Carla realized how miserable she was. Disappointed in herself and disappointed in Philip. He might as well have admitted to being married; he was as off limits as if he had a wife and ten children.

"Nice-looking brunette to your left," Philip pointed out, breaking her train of thought.

"It doesn't look like she's sporting a jealous husband, either," Carla said jokingly.

Philip's laugh was good-natured. "I'll use my practiced routine on her. Care to watch me in action?"

"I'd love it," Carla answered with open delight. "At least with you out of the picture some handsome tourist can make a play for me."

"Good luck," he called as he stood and loped lazily down the beach.

Handsome tourist; Carla almost laughed. At the rate things were going, the only men she'd be fighting off would be persistent vendors.

Carla watched with growing interest as Philip carelessly tossed his towel on the beach close to the girl and ran into the rolling surf. She'd remember to ask him later about swimming in the ocean. Last night he'd told her the tide was too dangerous, yet he was diving headlong into it without a second's hesitation.

After a few minutes, which he apparently thought suitable for a favorable impression, he stood, wiped the water from his face and walked out of the ocean. He squinted and rubbed his eyes, giving the impression the water was stinging. The way he groped for his towel made Carla laugh outright. Again by an apparent accident, he flicked sand on the tanning beauty. The girl sat up and brushed the offending particles from her well-oiled body. Philip fell to his knees, and although Carla couldn't hear what he was saying, she was sure it was some practiced apology. Soon the two of them were talking and laughing. Spreading out his long body, he lay beside the brown-haired beauty. His technique, tried and true, had worked well. Rolling his head, Philip caught Carla's gaze and winked when she gestured with two fingers, giving the okay sign.

For the first time in recent memory, Carla wished that she were as good at acting as Philip. For a moment she toyed with the idea of following his lead and blatantly approaching a man. Carla's devil-may-care system should work as well on the beach as in the cocktail lounge. But a quick survey of the area didn't turn up a single male she cared to flirt with. There wasn't anyone she particularly wanted to meet. Maybe Nancy was right, maybe she had become much too picky lately.

Ten minutes later, Carla stood, brushed the sand from her skin and picked up her things. After lunch she'd do some shopping.

Philip gave her a brief wave, which she returned. At least one of them had been successful. At least one of them was having a good time.

The oppressive afternoon heat eventually brought Carla back into the air-conditioned cocktail lounge. Sipping a pina colada, she surveyed the growing crowd of tourists. A couple of times men had asked if they could buy her a drink, but she'd declined. Men who used tanning machines, wore gold chains around their necks and left their shirts open to their navels didn't interest Carla. Her spirits were low, and she hated to think she'd be fighting this depression the entire week. If she wasn't careful, she'd get locked in a state of self-pity.

The room was filling up rapidly, and when Philip entered Carla pretended an inordinate amount of interest in her drink.

"Hi." He sauntered to her side. "Do you mind if I join you, or will I be distracting any potential margarita drinkers?"

"By all means join me," she said with a poor attempt at a smile. "I don't exactly seem to be drawing a crowd. How about you? I expected you to stroll in here with Miss September."

He cleared his throat and took the plush seat beside her. "That didn't work out."

"Was there a Mr. September?"

"No." Philip cleared his throat a second time. "Things didn't work out, that's all."

"Philip," she moaned impatiently, "come on, tell me what happened. You can't leave me in suspense like this." Something perverse inside her wanted to know about Philip's latest rejection. Maybe she needed to salve her pride at his expense, which was childish, Carla thought, but shared misery beats the solo kind.

He ignored her while he raised his hand to attract the waitress's attention. "What's that you're drinking?"

"Pina colada," Carla answered quickly. "Out with it, Garrison. Details, I want details."

The waitress came to take his order. Carla had lost the desire to impress him with her vast knowledge of the Spanish language. As it was, the waitress eyed her warily, as if she were afraid Carla were a loco gringo.

"No margarita tonight?" His eyes mocked hers as a smile touched the corners of his mouth.

"Don't change the subject."

"I'll tell you over dinner." He raised both thick brows suggestively.

"Do you think bribing me is going to work?"

He smiled faintly, rather tenderly, at her. "I was hoping it would."

This was the best offer she'd had all day. And she wasn't about to refuse. "All right, as long as we understand one another."

"Of course we do," he replied formally. "You don't want to date cops, and with good reason."

"With a very good reason," she repeated emphatically.

The waitress delivered their drinks and brought a plate with two tacos, or what Carla assumed were tacos. She'd noticed that a sign outside the lounge stated that anyone buying a drink between four and five would receive a free taco. But this fried corn tortilla that had been filled with meat and rolled didn't resemble anything she'd call a taco. No lettuce, no cheese, no tomato.

One nibble confirmed that it didn't taste anything like one, either. "What's in this?"

Philip eyed her doubtfully. "Are you sure you want to know?"

"Of course I do."

He shrugged. "Turtle."

Carla closed her eyes and swallowed. "Turtle," she repeated. "It tastes more like week-old tuna fish to me."

"You don't have to eat it if you don't want."

She set it back on the plate. "It's something to tell my friends about, but it's nothing I'd recommend."

"It'll grow on you," Philip commented.

"I certainly hope not," Carla said with a grimace. "Have you ever examined the skin on those things?"

Suddenly they were both laughing as if she'd said the most uproariously funny thing in the world. "Come on." His hand reached for hers. "Let's get out of here before they throw us out." He laid several bills beside their uneaten turtle tacos. Together, hand in hand, they practically ran out of the cocktail lounge.

Not until they were in a golf cart/taxi did Carla ask where they were headed.

"Senor Frog's," Philip shouted, the wind whipping his voice past her.

"No." She waved her hand dramatically. "Not if they serve what I think they do."

"Not to worry." Philip placed an arm around her shoulder and spoke close to her ear. "This is a famous tourist trap. The food's good, but the place is wild. You'll love it."

And just as he'd promised, Carla did love it. After almost an hour's delay, they were ushered through the restaurant doors only to be led to a cocktail lounge. The music and boisterous singing were so loud that Carla couldn't hear herself speak when she leaned over to ask Philip something. He bent closer but finally gestured that they'd have to talk afterward outside.

Two hours later, well fed and singing softly, Carla and Philip left the restaurant with their arms wrapped around each other.

"That was wild."

"I knew you'd like it," Philip said, smiling tenderly at her.

"But there's a method to your madness."

"How's that?"

"With all the noise, you weren't able to tell me about Miss September."

"All right, if you must know."

"I must," she replied firmly. "I hope you realize I baked in the hot sun while I waited to see how you did. Honestly, Philip, your approach could have been a little more original."

The look he gave told her that he was offended. "I thought my technique was one of a kind."

Carla looked at the darkening sky and rolled her eyes, but refrained from comment. "I'm surprised that you didn't go up to her and ask if you'd met someplace before."

Philip shifted his weight onto the other foot. "To be honest, that occurred to me, too."

Laughing, Carla slipped her arm through his. "You, my dear Philip, are refreshingly unimaginative."

He made a funny little noise that sounded as if he

was clearing his throat. He seemed to be studying the cracks in the sidewalk on which they were strolling. He didn't appear to have any clear direction.

"Now, will you spill the beans about Miss September? I'm dying to know what happened."

He was quiet for a few moments. "You prefer not to date policemen, and I have a thing about flight attendants."

Most men had a "thing" about flight attendants, too, but it wasn't to avoid them. It wasn't one of her more brilliant deductions to guess that Philip had once loved a flight attendant and been hurt. "Do you want to tell me about her? I make a great wailing wall," she murmured sympathetically.

"Not if I can avoid it." He looked at her and smiled. "Tell me about your afternoon. Any success?"

"No one," she said dejectedly, and shook her head for emphasis. "Unless you count guys in gold chains who enjoy revealing their chest hair."

"Some women like those kind of men."

"Not me."

Philip hesitated, then asked, "I wonder if I could interest you in a short-term, no-obligation, strictly regulated, but guaranteed fun relationship."

Carla's mouth curved wryly. She'd had a better time with Philip tonight than the entire day she'd spent alone. Her mind was flashing a bright neon "NO" in bold red letters. If she had any sense whatsoever, she'd shake her head and decline without another word.

"Well?" he urged.

"I don't know," she answered truthfully. Five days, what could possibly happen in five days? She'd come to

Mexico looking for a good time. She knew who Philip was and, more important, *what* he was.

The silence lengthened. "I think I should make one thing clear. I have no intention of treating you like a sister."

He could have lied. But again, he'd chosen to be straight with her. She appreciated that.

"I don't want anything more than these five days. Once we leave Mazatlán it's over."

"Agreed," he said, and a finger tenderly traced the outline of her jaw.

A tingling sensation burned across her face, and she closed her eyes against its potency. She'd be safe. She'd walked into this with her eyes wide open. He lived in Spokane. She lived in Seattle. A light flirtation was what she'd had in mind in the first place. Knowing what he was should make it all the easier to walk away next Saturday. But it hadn't lessened the attraction she felt for him—and that appeared to be growing every minute.

"I…haven't agreed yet." Her pride demanded one last stand.

"But you will," Philip said confidently.

"How can you be so sure?" Carla returned, piqued by his attitude.

"Well, for one thing, you're looking at me with 'kiss me' eyes."

Embarrassed, Carla shot her gaze to the ground. "That's not true," she denied hotly, and was ready to argue further, but Philip cut her off.

"Do you agree or not?" He held out his hand for her to shake.

"I have a feeling I'm going to regret this," she said, and placed her hand in his.

Philip didn't argue. But when his arm closed around her shoulders, she didn't object. She liked the idea of being linked with this man, even if it was only for a few days.

"How about a ride on an araña?" he suggested, his mouth disturbingly close to her ear.

"I don't know what you're suggesting, Philip Garrison, but that doesn't sound like something nice girls do."

His laughter filled the night. "That's a two-wheeled, horse-drawn cab."

"Sounds romantic." Knowing Philip, Carla was willing to bet he'd instruct the driver to take the long way back to the hotel through scented, shady boulevards. She was in the mood for a few stolen kisses, and so was Philip, gauging by his look.

"If we can't find one, we can always jog back to the hotel," he said seriously.

"With a name like Walker you expect me to run?"

"What's the matter with running? I thought you'd be into physical fitness."

She laughed softly. "I swim, and that's the entire repertoire of my athletic abilities."

"You mean you weren't in track? With those long legs of yours, I'd think you'd be a natural."

"So did my high school coach—until the first practice. He had to time me with a calendar. Running's out."

"Walking?" Philip suggested.

"Good grief, if we can't find a carriage, what's the matter with those golf-cart things that we've been taking lately?"

"You mean the pulmonias?" His gray eyes were dancing with amusement, and Carla struggled not to succumb to the invitation in their smoky depths.

"Whatever," she replied, pleased with herself now for agreeing to this crazy relationship. She honestly enjoyed this zany man.

"If you insist," Philip said blandly, and flagged down a passing taxi when it became obvious that finding an araña would take longer than they were willing to wait.

Back at the hotel Carla mentally chastised herself for being so easily swayed by Philip's direct approach. She really ought to have played harder to get.

"There's a band playing at the—"

"I love to dance," she interrupted enthusiastically. "My feet are itching already."

Philip smoothed the hair at the side of his head. "Tell me, why was I expecting an argument?" He was regarding her with a look of amused surprise.

"I don't know." Carla laughed gaily, happiness bubbling over.

"If you're not into sports, what kinds of things do you like to do?" With his hand at her elbow, he escorted her toward the lively sounds of the mariachi band.

"Play checkers," Carla responded immediately. "I've won the King County Park and Recreational checker championship three years running. It's a nice friendly game, and I've got a terrific coach I'll tell you about sometime."

Carla felt relaxed and happy as they stood in line outside the lounge. They seemed to be waiting in a lot of lines tonight, not that she minded.

Philip studied her intently; his eyes narrowed slightly as if he had trouble assimilating the fact she was non-athletic.

"No sports, you say?"

"Just checkers." Carla's gleaming eyes didn't leave

his. "Knowing that I'm a champion, Philip, would you have any trouble jumping me?" She was teasing, but the responding look in Philip's eyes was serious.

"I'd consider it," he murmured, "but I think I'd probably wait until after the game."

Three

Golden moonbeams softly lighted a path along the beach. The gentle whisper of the ocean breeze was broken only by the sound of the waves crashing against the smooth white shore.

Philip slipped his arm around Carla's shoulders, and she brought her hand up so that they could lace their fingers together.

"Why didn't you tell me you could dance like that?" he murmured against her hair. "I've seen card sharks with slower moves."

Enjoying his surprise, Carla smiled softly to herself. "All I do is swing my hips a little."

"Yes, but I felt the least I could do was try to keep up with you. I'm dead."

"And I thought you police officers had to be in top physical condition." Not for a minute would she admit that she was as exhausted as Philip.

"I'm in great shape," he argued, "but three hours on the dance floor with you is above and beyond the call of duty. Next time I think I'll suggest checkers."

"You'll lose," Carla returned confidently.

"Maybe, but I have a feeling my feet won't hurt nearly as much."

Philip had been the one to suggest this stroll. But it wasn't a walk in the moonlight that interested him; Carla was convinced of that. He was seeking a few stolen kisses against the backdrop of a tropical night. And for that matter, so was she. Every time they met, Philip astonished her. One look the day on the plane and she'd instantly sized him up as dull and introspective. But he was warm, caring and witty. There wasn't any man who could make her laugh the way Philip did.

"I enjoyed myself tonight. You're a lot of fun." She felt compelled to tell him that.

"You sound surprised." Philip moved his chin so it brushed against the crown of her head. The action was strangely comforting and erotic.

"Surprised is the wrong word," she said softly, struggling to express herself. "Leery, maybe. I don't want to like you too much. That would only complicate a nice, serene relationship. We're having a good time, and I don't want to ruin it."

"In other words, you don't want to fall in love with me?"

"Exactly." Carla hated the heartless way this made her sound. Already she recognized that falling for Philip wouldn't be difficult. He was many of the things she wanted in a man. And everything she didn't.

He expelled his breath in a half-angry sigh, but it was the only indication he gave that she had displeased him.

Closing her eyes, Carla felt an unexpected rush of regret settle over her. One evening together and she was already doubting that this arrangement was going to work. Spending time with Philip might not be a good idea if they were both going to end up taking it seriously. All she wanted was a good time. And he'd claimed that was all he was looking for too. This was a holiday fling, after all, not a husband hunt.

"Don't you think you're overreacting just a little to the fact I'm a policeman?" Philip asked, his voice restrained and searching.

"Haven't we already been over this?" she answered hastily. "Besides, you have your own dating quirk. What if I'd been a flight attendant? You said yourself you prefer not to go out with them."

"But in your case I'd have made an exception."

"Why?"

"It's those lovely eyes of yours—"

"No," she interrupted brusquely, reacting with more than simple curiosity. "Why don't you like flight attendants?"

"It's a long story, and there are other things I have in mind." Clearly he wasn't interested in relating the details of his experience, and Carla decided she wouldn't push him. When he was ready to tell her, if he ever was, she'd be pleased to listen. She found it interesting that after only a few hours' acquaintance with Philip she had released a lifetime full of bitterness about her father and his occupation. Apparently, she hadn't generated the same kind of response in him. It troubled her a little.

"You're quiet all of a sudden." His lips found her temple, and he kissed her there lightly. "What are you thinking?"

Tilting her head back, she smiled into those appealing smoky-gray eyes of his. "To be honest, I was mulling over the fact that you'll tell me about your hang-ups in time. But then it occurred to me that you might not."

"And that bothers you?" He studied her with amused patience.

"Yes and no." In a way that she didn't understand, Carla suddenly decided she didn't want to know. Obviously Philip had loved and presumably lost, and Carla wasn't sure she wanted the particulars.

"The curious side of you is eager to hear the gory details—"

"But my sensitive side doesn't want to have you dredge up unhappy memories," she finished for him.

"It was a long time ago."

Carla slipped an arm around his waist and laid her head against his shoulder. "And best forgotten."

They continued walking along the moonlit beach in silence. Carla felt warm and comfortable having this man at her side. The realization wasn't something she wanted to explore; for now she was content.

"It's been six years since I broke up with Nicole," Philip said after a time.

Twisting in his embrace, Carla turned and pressed the tips of her fingers against his lips. "Don't," she whispered, afraid how she'd react if she saw pain in his eyes. "It isn't necessary. There isn't a reason in the world for you to tell me."

His jaw tightened, and memories played across his face. Some revealed the pleasant aspects of his relationship with Nicole, but others weren't as easily deciphered.

"I think you should know," he said, and his eyes narrowed to hard points of steel.

Carla wasn't sure which was troubling him more: the past or the sudden need to tell her about his lost love.

"Let me simplify things by saying that I loved her

and asked her to marry me. But apparently she didn't care as deeply for me as I thought."

"She turned you down?" Carla murmured.

"No." His short laugh was filled with bitter sarcasm. "That's the crazy part. She accepted my ring, but she refused to move out on the guy she was living with. Naturally niether one of us knew about the other."

Carla struggled not to laugh. "If you want my opinion, I think you made a lucky escape. This Nicole sounds a bit kinky to me."

Philip relaxed against her. His hands found the small of her back, arching her closer to him. "I don't know, there's something about me that attracts the weird ones. Just yesterday some oddball approached me in the bar with a lunatic story about me being her date for the night because I ordered a margarita."

"A real weirdo, no doubt." One brow arched mockingly.

"That's not the half of it." His head lowered with every word, so that by the time he finished, his lips hovered over hers.

"Oh?" Breathlessly she anticipated his kiss.

"Yes." His low voice was as caressing as his look. "The thing is, I'd been watching her from the moment I walked into the lounge, trying to come up with a way of approaching her."

Before she could react to this startling bit of news, Philip brought her into his embrace. Slowly his mouth opened over hers, taking in the softness of her trembling lips in a soul-stirring, devouring kiss. Carla stood on the tips of her toes and clung to him, devastated by the intensity of her reaction. This had happened the first time he'd kissed her. If Philip's lovemaking had been hard or urgent, maybe she could have withstood it. But he was incredibly gentle, as if she were of exquisite worth and as fragile as a rosebud, and that was irresistible.

When his tongue outlined the fullness of her mouth, Carla's willpower melted, and she couldn't pull herself away from the fiery kiss. Desire shot through her, and when she broke away, her breathing was irregular and deep.

"I… I think we should put a limit on these kisses," she proposed shakily.

Philip didn't look any more in control of himself than she felt. His eyes were closed as he drew in a husky breath and nodded in agreement. Only a short space separated them, but he continued to hold her, his hands running the length of her bare arms.

"Let's get you back to your hotel room."

"Yes."

But they didn't move.

Unable to resist, Carla rested her head against his muscular chest, weak with the wonder of his kiss. "I don't understand." She was surprised to hear the words, not realizing she'd spoken out loud.

"What?" Philip questioned softly.

She shrugged, flustered for a moment. "You. Me. If you had come up to me yesterday and asked to buy me a drink, I probably would have refused."

He flashed a crooked grin. "I know. Why do you think I didn't?"

"Obviously you recognized that I was about to take the initiative," she said jokingly to hide her discomfort.

Together they turned and headed back toward the hotel, taking leisurely steps. Carla's bare toes kicked up the sand.

"What would you like to do tomorrow?" she asked, not because she was especially interested in their itinerary, but because knowing she would be seeing him in the morning would surely enhance her dreams tonight.

"Shall we get together for breakfast?"

"I'd like that."

Outside her door, Philip set a time and place for them to meet in the morning, then kissed her gently and left.

Carla walked slowly inside the room and released a long, drawn-out sigh. For such a rotten beginning, the day had turned out wonderfully well.

"Is that you, Carla?" The question came from the darkened interior of the room.

"No, it's the bogeyman," Carla teased.

"I take it you met someone?" Nancy's voice was soft and curious.

"Yup."

"Tell me about your day." The moonlight silhouetted her roommate against the wall. Nancy was sitting on the side of the mattress.

"It's the guy I met yesterday." Carla couldn't disguise the wistful note in her voice.

"What happened? When I asked this morning, the looks you gave me said you didn't want to have anything to do with him."

"That was this morning."

Fluffing up her pillow, Nancy positioned it against the headboard, leaned against it and put her hands behind her head. "I'm glad things worked out."

"Me too." Carla moved into the room and began to undress."

"I can't believe how much I like Eduardo," Nancy said pensively as she stared dreamily at the ceiling. "I can't even begin to tell you what a marvelous day we had."

Carla slipped the silk nightie over her head. "The funny part was, I had no intention of seeing Philip again."

Nancy sighed unevenly and slid down so her head rested in the thick of the pillow. "He gave me a tour of Mazatlán that will hold memories to last a lifetime. And later tonight when he kissed me I could have cried, it was so incredibly beautiful."

"But then Philip was there, and I'd been so miserable all day, and he suggested we have dinner, and not for the life of me could I refuse."

"I've never felt this strongly about a man. And I've barely known Eduardo more than twenty-four hours."

Carla pulled back the bedcovers and paused, holding the pillow to her stomach. "I'm meeting Philip first thing in the morning."

"Eduardo says he can't believe that someone as beautiful as I would be interested in him. And just because he broke his leg. He keeps assuring me he really isn't a klutz. As if I'd ever think such a thing."

"I don't know if I'll be able to sleep. Every time I close my eyes I know Philip will be there. I don't know how to explain it. To look at him you'd be unimpressed. But he's the most gentle man. Tender."

"I can't sleep. Every time I try, my heart hammers and I wonder if I'm going crazy to feel like this."

The sheets felt cool against Carla's legs as she slipped between the covers and yawned. "I guess I should get some sleep. Night, Nance."

"Night," Nancy answered with a yawn of her own.

"By the way," Carla asked absently, "how'd your day go?"

"Fantastic. How about you?"

"Wonderful."

"I'm glad. Good night."

"Night."

Philip was already seated in the hotel restaurant when Carla arrived. Her gaze met his, and she smiled. She enjoyed the way he was watching her. The sleeveless pink-and-blue crinkle-cotton sundress was her favorite, and she knew she looked good. She'd spent extra time with her makeup, and one glance from him confirmed that the effort had been well spent.

"Morning." Philip stood and pulled out her chair. "Did you sleep well?"

He leaned forward and kissed her cheek lightly. "Like a baby. How about you?"

Setting the large-brimmed straw hat on the empty seat beside her, Carla nodded. "Great."

The waiter appeared and handed them each a menu, but they didn't look at them. "What would you like to do today?"

"Explore," Carla replied immediately. "Would you mind if I dragged you to the arts and crafts center?"

Philip reached for her hand and squeezed it gently. "Not at all. And tomorrow I thought we'd take an excursion to Palmito de la Virgen."

Carla blinked. "Where?"

"An island near here. It's a bird-watcher's paradise."

The only bird Carla was interested in watching was Philip, but she didn't say as much.

"And Thursday I thought we might try our hand at deep-sea fishing."

"I'm game," she said, and giggled. "No pun intended."

"My, my, you're agreeable. Are you always like this in the mornings?"

Carla reached for the ice water, keeping her eyes lowered. "Most of the time."

"I'd like to discover that for myself."

The waiter arrived with his pen and pad, and Carla glanced up at him guiltily, realizing she hadn't even looked at the menu.

After breakfast they rode a pulmonia to the Mazatlán Arts and Crafts Center, and Philip insisted on buying her a lovely turquoise ring. Carla felt more comfortable purchasing her souvenirs from these people and not from the beach vendors. Here the price was set and there wasn't any haggling.

Tucking their purchases into a giant straw bag, Carla took off her hat and waved it in front of her face. Most of the shopping areas were air-conditioned, but once they stepped outside, the heat was stifling.

"Would you like something cool to drink?" Philip asked solicitously.

Smiling up at him, Carla placed a hand over her breast. "You, my dear man, know the path to my heart."

Unexpectedly, Philip's hand tightened on the back of her neck until his grip was almost painful. He dropped his hand and took a step forward as if he'd forgotten her completely. Surprised, but not alarmed, Carla reached for his arm. "What's wrong?"

"There's going to be a fight over there." He pointed to a group of youths who were having a heated exchange.

Although Carla couldn't understand what was being said, she assumed from the angry sound of their words that they would soon be coming to blows. Her gaze was drawn to Philip, and she was witness to an abrupt change in roles taking place within him. After all, she was a policeman's daughter. And Philip was an officer of the law. Once a cop, always a cop. He may be in Mazatlán, but he would never be entirely on vacation.

Philip's jaw hardened and his eyes narrowed with keen interest. Briefly he turned to her. "Stay here." The words were clipped and low and filled with an authority that would brook no resistance.

Carla wanted to argue. Everything inside urged her to scream that this was none of his business. What right did he have to involve himself with those youths? Mexico had its own police force. She watched as Philip strode briskly across the street toward the angry young men. He asked them something in Spanish, and even from this distance Carla could hear the authority in his voice. She hadn't a clue of what he was saying, but it didn't matter. It was the law-enforcement officer in him speaking, anyway, and she didn't want to know.

Only one thing prompted her to stay. If the situation got ugly and Philip needed help, she could scream or do something to get him out of this mess. But he didn't need her assistance, and a few minutes later the group broke up. With an amused grin, Philip jogged across the street to her side.

"That was—"

"I don't care to know, thank you," she announced frostily. Opening her large bag, she took out the several small items he'd purchased during their morning's outing.

"What's this?" He looked stunned.

"Your things," she answered without looking up. "You couldn't do it, could you?"

"Do what?"

Apparently he still didn't understand. "For once, just once, couldn't you have forgotten you're a cop? But no, Mr. Rescue had to speed to the scene of potential danger, defending truth and justice."

His face relaxed, and he reached for her. "Carla, couldn't you see—"

She sidestepped him easily. "You bet I saw," she shot back angrily. "You almost had me fooled, Philip Garrison. For a while there I actually believed we could have shared a wonderful vacation. But it's not going to work." Her voice was taut with irritation. With unnecessary roughness, she dumped the packages into his arms. "Not even for a few days could either of us manage to forget what you are. Goodbye, Philip." She spun and ran across the street, waving her hand, hoping to attract a pulmonia driver. At least she could be grateful that Philip didn't make an effort to follow her. But that was little comfort...very little.

A pulmonia shot past her, and Carla stamped her foot childishly. She wished she had paid closer attention to the Spanish phrase Philip called to get the driver's attention.

Already she felt the perspiration breaking out across her face as she walked along the edge of the street. The late-morning sun could be torturous. Another driver approached, and Carla stepped off the curb and shouted something in Spanish, not sure what she'd said. With her luck, she mused wryly, it was probably something to do with Cookie Monster. But whatever it was worked because the driver immediately pulled to the curb.

"Hotel El Cid," she mumbled, hot and miserable.

"*Sí, señorita,* the man already say."

Man? Tossing a look over her shoulder, Carla found Philip standing on the other side of the street, studying her. He'd gotten the driver for her. If she hadn't been so blasted uncomfortable, she'd have told him exactly what he could do with his driver. As it was, all Carla wanted to do was escape. The sooner the better.

Her room was refreshingly cool when she returned. She threw herself across the bed and stared at the ceiling. Tears might have helped release some of her frustration, but she was too mad to cry.

After fifteen minutes, the hotel room gave her a bad case of claustrophobia. From her carryall Carla pulled the book she'd been reading on the airplane and opened the sliding glass door to the small balcony. A thorough inspection of the pool area revealed that Philip was nowhere in sight. Stuffing her book in her beach bag, Carla quickly changed into her swimsuit, slipping a cotton top over that and put on the straw hat. Not for anything was she going to allow Philip Garrison to ruin this vacation.

Carla was fortunate to find a vacant chaise longue. The pool was busy with the early-afternoon crowd. Several vacationers were in the water eating lunch at the counter that was built up against the pool's edge. Smiling briefly, Carla recalled her first glimpse of the submerged stools and wondered what this type of meal did to the theory of not swimming after eating.

Spreading out her towel, Carla raised the back of the lounger so that she could sit up comfortably and read.

Her sunglasses had a tendency to slip down the bridge of her nose, and without much thought she pushed them back up. Philip's glasses did that occasionally. Angrily, she wiped his image from her mind and viciously turned the page of her suspense novel, nearly ripping it from the book.

An older man who was lying beside her stood, stretched and strolled lackadaisically toward the bar, apparently seeking something cool to drink. He was barely out of sight when a familiar voice spoke in her ear.

"Is this place taken?"

Carla's fingers gripped the page, but she didn't so much as acknowledge his presence. Without lifting her eyes from her book, she replied, "Yes, it is."

"That's fine, I'll just sit on the edge of the pool and chat," he replied casually.

Clenching her jaw so tight her teeth hurt, Carla turned a page, having no idea of what she had just read. "I'd appreciate it very much if you didn't."

Forcefully, Philip expelled his breath. "How long are you going to be unreasonable like this? All I'm asking is that you hear me out."

"How long?" Carla repeated mockingly. "You haven't got that much time. Never, as far as I'm concerned."

"Do you mean it?" The question was issued so low Carla had to strain to hear him.

Idly, she turned the next page. "Yes, I meant it," she replied.

"Okay." He took the towel, swung it around his neck and strolled away.

Carla felt a deep sense of disappointment settle over her. The least he could have done was argue with her!

One would assume that after yesterday she meant more to him than that. But apparently not.

Without being obvious she glanced quickly around the pool area and discovered that Philip was nowhere in sight. Ten minutes later she did another survey. Nothing.

Tucking the book inside her beach bag, Carla settled back in her seat, joined her hands over her stomach and closed her eyes. A splash of water against her leg was more refreshing than irritating. But the cupful of water that landed on her upper thigh was a shock.

Gasping, she opened her eyes and sat up to brush the offending wetness away.

"Did I get water on you?" came the innocent question. "Please accept my apology."

"Philip Garrison, that was a rotten thing to do!" Inside she was singing. So he hadn't left.

"So was that last, untruthful remark."

"What remark?"

"That you never wanted to talk to me again." He lay down beside her on the chaise that had been previously taken by the older sunbather. "Obviously you did, or you wouldn't have made two deliberate inspections of the pool to see if I had left."

She should have realized Philip had stayed and watched her. That was a rookie's trick. And clearly Philip was a seasoned officer. Rather than argue, she lifted her glasses and turned toward him with a smug look. "I told you that place was taken," she said and re-positioned herself so that the back of one hand rested against her brow. "And I don't think he'd take kindly to you lying in his place when he returns."

"Sure he would," Philip murmured confidently. "Otherwise I wasted ten very good dollars."

Struggling between outrage and delight, Carla sat up. "Do you mean to say you bribed him?" Her eyes widened as he nodded cheerfully. "What do you think you're doing, Officer Garrison? First…first you spy on me and…then…and then…" She sputtered. "You bribe the man in the chair next to me. Just how low do you plan to stoop?"

Philip yawned. "About that low."

Carla did an admirable job of swallowing her laughter.

"I suspect you aren't as annoyed as you're letting on," Philip commented.

The humor died in her eyes. "What makes you suggest that?"

"Well, you're still here, aren't you?"

Standing up, Carla pulled the thin cotton covering over her head. "Not for long," she replied, and dived into the pool.

It felt marvelous. Swimming as far and for as long as she could under the aqua-blue water helped relieve some of her pent-up frustration. Finally she surfaced and sucked in a large breath of fresh air. In the glint of the sun, her hair was decidedly red. Carla had hoped to avoid having Philip see it wet. Like everyone else, he was sure to comment on it. Swimming at night was preferable by far.

She'd barely caught her breath when Philip surfaced beside her. Treading water at his side, she offered him a tremulous smile. "I really was angry this morning. I behaved childishly to run off like that. Thank you for seeing that I got a ride back to the hotel."

Their eyes met, and he grinned. "I know how angry you were; that's why I didn't follow you. But given time,

I figured you'd forgive me." His arms found her waist and brought her close to him. Their feet kicked in unison, keeping them afloat.

"I'll forgive you on one condition," she stated firmly, and looped her arms around his neck. "You've got to promise not to do that again. Please, Philip. For me, leave your police badge in your room. We're in Mexico, and they have their own defenders of justice."

Philip went still, and she could feel him become tense. The sparkle faded from his eyes as they darkened and became more intense. "Carla, I'll do my best, but I can't change who or what I am."

Her grip around his neck relaxed, and with a sense of defeat she lowered her eyes. "But don't you see? I can't, either," she murmured miserably, and her voice fell to a whisper.

His hold tightened as he brought his body intimately close to hers in the water. "But we can try."

"What would be the use?"

"Oh, I don't know," he said softly, and brushed aside the offending strands of wet hair from her cheek. "I can think of several things." His lips replaced his fingers, and he blazed a trail of infinitely sweet kisses along her brow and eyes, working his way to her mouth.

For an instant, Carla was caught in the rapture of his touch, but an abrupt noise behind them brought her to her senses. Breaking free, she shook her head. "I... I don't know, Philip. I want to think on it."

"Okay, that sounds fair."

He didn't have to be so agreeable! At least he could have argued with her. With a little sigh, Carla turned away and said, "I think I'll go to my room and lie down for a while. The sun does me in fairly easily."

She started to swim away, then rapidly changed direction and joined Philip. "I almost forgot something," she murmured as she covered his mouth with hers and kissed him thoroughly.

Obviously shaken, Philip blinked twice. "What was that for?" he asked, and cleared his throat.

"For not mentioning my frizzy hair or the color."

He cocked his head, and a puzzled frown marred his brow. "There are several other things I haven't mentioned that you may wish to thank me for."

"Later," she said with a small laugh.

"Definitely later."

Four

Amazingly, Carla did sleep most of the afternoon. She hadn't realized how exhausted she was. The sun, having taken its toll, had faded by the time she stirred. A glance at the clock told Carla that it was dinnertime. Although she hadn't made any arrangements to meet Philip, she knew he'd be looking for her.

Dressing quickly, she hunted for her sandals, crawling on the floor. Finally she located them under the bed and was on her way into the bathroom to see what she could do with her hair when something stopped her. The faint sound of someone singing in Spanish drifted in past the balcony door that had been left ajar. Those deep male tones were unmistakable.

After eagerly parting the drapes, Carla opened the sliding glass door farther. The music and voice grew stronger, and the lovingly familiar voice sang loudly off key.

"Philip!"

Standing below, playing a guitar and singing at the top of his voice was crazy, wonderful Philip. A band of curious onlookers had gathered around him. Now, however, they focused their attention on her.

"You idiot," she cried. "What are you doing?"

"Serenading you," he shouted back, completely serious. "Do you like it?"

"I'd like it a lot better if you sang on key."

He strummed a few bars. "Can't have everything. Are you hungry?"

"Starved. I'd eat turtle tacos."

"You must be famished. Hurry down, will you? I think someone might arrest me."

Stuffing her hair under her straw hat, Carla bounded down the stairs. She paused on the bottom step, straightened her dress and took a deep breath. Then, feeling more composed, she turned the corner and found Philip relaxing on a chaise longue.

"Hi," she said, fighting the breathlessness that weakened her voice.

He rose to his feet with an ease many would envy. "I must have sounded better than I thought."

"What makes you think that?"

A grin played at the edges of his mouth as he dug inside his pocket and pulled out a handful of loose change. "People were obviously impressed. Soon after you went back inside, several started throwing coins my way."

Fighting back the bubbling laughter, Carla looped her arm around his elbow. "I hate to disappoint you, Philip, but I have the distinct feeling they were paying you *not* to sing."

The sound of his laughter tugged at her heart. "Where are we going for dinner? I wasn't teasing about being hungry."

"Anyplace you say." Tucking her hand more securely

in the crook of his arm, he escorted her through the hotel to the series of stairs that led to the busy street below.

"Anyplace I say," she repeated. "My, my, you're agreeable all of a sudden."

"With a beautiful girl on my arm, and my pockets full of change, why shouldn't I be?"

She smiled, pleased by the compliment.

"Then dinner wherever the lady chooses."

"Well, I suppose I'd better choose a restaurant where I won't have to take off my hat. I didn't wash my hair after our dip in the pool this afternoon, and now it resembles Raggedy Ann's."

"Then it's perfect for what I have in mind," he said with an enigmatic toss of his head. Sandy locks of hair fell across his brow and he brushed them aside.

"Well, are you going to tell me, or do I have to guess?" she asked with a hint of impatience. She noticed that Philip had a way of arousing her curiosity, then dropping the subject. Her father did the same thing, and Carla briefly wondered if this was a common trait among policemen. They didn't want to give out too much information—keep the world guessing, seemed to be their intent. Other things about Philip reminded her of her father. He was a kind, concerned man. Like her father, he cared when the rest of the world didn't want to be bothered.

"Ever hear of La Gruta de Cerro del Creston?" Philip asked, snapping her out of her musings.

"He was some general, right?"

"Wrong," he responded with a trace of droll tolerance. "It's a cave where, it's rumored, pirates used to store their treasure. Stolen treasure, of course. It's only accessible at low tide, but I thought we might pick up a picnic lunch and eat along the beach. Later, when the tide is low, we can explore the cave."

Carla's interest was piqued. "That sounds great."

"And of course there's always the advantage of having you to myself in a deep, dark cave."

"Honestly, Garrison, cool your hormones," she joked.

One of the hot-rod golf carts Philip enjoyed so much delivered them close to the lighthouse near the heart of the city. Holding her hat, Carla climbed out from the back of the cart. Her senses were spinning, and she doubted if she'd ever get used to riding in those suicidal contraptions. The short rides weren't so bad, but anything over three miles was like a death wish.

A drop of rain hit her hand. Carla raised her eyes to examine the darkening sky and groaned inwardly. A storm would ruin everything. Besides, if Philip saw what happened to her hair in the rain, she'd never live it down. The frizzies invariably gave her a striking resemblance to the bride of Frankenstein.

"Philip?"

Preoccupied for the moment, Philip paid the driver and returned the folded money to his pocket. "Something wrong?"

"It's raining."

"I know."

Twisting the strap of her purse, she swung it over her shoulder and secured the large-brimmed straw hat by holding it down over both ears. "Maybe we should go back to the hotel."

"Why?"

She swallowed nervously. "Well, we obviously can't

have a picnic in the rain, and if…my hat should come off…well, my hair—"

Suddenly, the sky opened up and the earth was bombarded with heavy sheets of rain. Giving a cry of alarm, Carla ran for shelter. Mud splashed against the back of her legs, and immediately a chill ran up her arms.

Philip caught up with her and cupped her elbow. "Let's get out of here."

"Where?" she shouted, but he didn't answer as they raced down a side street. After two long blocks, Carla stopped counting. Placing one foot in front of the other was all that she could manage in the torrent that was beating against her.

Philip led her into a building and up two flights of stairs.

Leaning against the hallway wall, Carla gasped for breath. "Where are we?"

"My parents' condo."

Vaguely, she recalled Philip mentioning that the condo was the reason he was in Mazatlán. He'd said something about repairs, but Carla didn't care where they were as long as it was dry.

"Let's get these wet things off," Philip suggested, holding the door open for her and leading the way into the kitchen.

The condominium looked surprisingly modern, and Carla hurried inside, not wishing to leave a trail of mud across the cream-colored carpet. The washer and dryer were behind a louvered door. Philip pulled his shirt from his waist and unbuttoned it. "We'd better let these dry."

Wide-eyed, her mouth open, Carla watched him toss

his drenched shirt inside. He paused and glanced expectantly at her.

"You don't honestly expect me to parade around here in my underwear, do you?"

"Well, to be honest," he said with a wry grin, "I didn't expect it, but I was hoping. Hold on and I'll get you my mom's robe."

By the time he returned, Carla had removed her sandals and found a kitchen towel to dry her feet. When she heard Philip approach, she straightened and continued to press her hat—still secure despite everything—down over her ears.

"Here." He draped the cotton robe over a chair. "I'll start a fire. Let me know when you're finished."

Shivering, Carla slipped the dress over her hips and tossed it inside the dryer. Another towel served as a turban for her hair and hid the effects of the rain.

She tied the sash of the robe and took a deep breath. Self-consciously, she stood just outside the living room. A small fire was crackling in the fireplace, and Philip was kneeling in front of it adding one stick of wood at a time.

He seemed to sense that she was watching him. "How do you feel?" He stood and crossed the room, joining her. Placing a hand on each shoulder, he smiled into her eyes. "Mother's robe never looked so good."

"I feel like a drowned rat." The turban slipped over one eye, and Carla righted it.

His hands found the side of her neck, and his touch sent a warm sensation through her. "Believe me when I say you don't look like one."

They continued to study each other, and Carla's heart began to pound like a locomotive racing against time.

In some ways she and Philip were doing that. There were only a few days left of their vacation, and then it would be over. It had to be.

"Come in and sit down," Philip said at last, and his thumb traced her lips in a feather-light caress. "The fire should take the chill from your bones."

"I'm…not really cold." Not when you're touching me, she added silently.

"Me neither."

Carla was convinced his thoughts were an echo of her own.

"Hungry?"

"Not really." Not anymore.

"Good."

Together they sat on the plush love seat that was angled to face the fireplace. Philip's arm reached for her, bringing her within the haven of his embrace.

Resting her head against the curve of his shoulder, Carla let her fingers toy with the dark hairs on his bare chest. Her body was in contact with his chest, hips and thighs, and whenever they touched, she could feel a heat building. She struggled to control her breathing so Philip wouldn't guess the effect he had on her.

"I poured these while you were changing," Philip murmured, his voice low and slightly husky. He leaned forward and reached for the two glasses of wine sitting on the polished oak coffee table.

Straightening, Carla accepted the long-stemmed crystal glass with a smile of appreciation and tasted the wine. It was an excellent sweet variety with a fragrant bouquet.

Removing the glass from her unresisting fingers, Philip set it aside. As he leaned back, his jaw brushed

her chin, and his warm breath caressed her face. The
contact stopped them both. He hadn't meant it to be
sensual, Carla was sure of that, but her heart thumped
wildly. Closing her eyes, she inhaled a quivering breath.

"Philip?" she whispered.

His mouth explored the side of her neck, sending rapturous shivers up and down her spine. "Yes?"

"Did you arrange for the rainstorm?" Carla couldn't
believe how low and sultry her voice sounded.

"No, but I'm glad it happened."

Carla was, too, but she wouldn't admit it. She didn't
need to.

Gently, Philip pressed her backward so that her
head rested against the arm of the sofa; then his mouth
claimed hers. His kiss was slow, leisurely and far more
intoxicating than potent wine.

Drawing in a shaky breath, Philip diverted his attention to her neck, nuzzling the scented hollow of
her throat. His hands wandered over her hips, artfully
arousing her so that she shifted, seeking more. She
wanted to give more of herself and take more at the
same time. Her restless hands explored his back, reveling in the tightness of his corded muscles. This man
was deceptively strong. Her fingers found a scar, and
she longed to kiss it.

Gradually, the heat that had begun to flow through
her at the tenderness of his touch spread to every part
of her, leaving her feverishly warm. But when Philip's
hands slid across her abdomen, she tensed slightly. He
murmured her name, and his mouth lingered on her
lips, moving from one side of her mouth to the other
in a deep exploration that left her weak and clinging.
Philip turned her so that she was sitting half-upright. As

he did so, the towel that was covering her hair twisted and fell forward across her face. Gently, Philip lifted the offending material off her face, but her desperate hold on it prevented him from tossing it aside.

"Can we get rid of this thing?" he asked gently.

"No." She struggled to sit completely up. Both hands secured the terry-cloth towel.

"Your hair can't be that bad," he coaxed.

"It's worse. Turn around," she demanded as she leaned forward and rewound the turban. "I… I don't want you to see it."

Expelling his breath, Philip leaned against the back of the sofa and closed his eyes. "Would you feel better if you showered and dried those precious locks?"

She nodded eagerly.

"Come on, I'm sure Mom's got something in the bathroom that should help."

Carla followed him down a long, narrow hallway that led to a bathroom. Investigating the vanity drawers, he managed to come up with a blow-dryer and curling iron.

"I think my sister gave this to her for Christmas last year."

Carla's heart sank. "But I can't use this. The package isn't even open."

With a crooked grin, Philip tore off the cellophane. "If it bothers you, I'll tell her I used it."

Carla giggled delightedly. "I'd like to hear her answer to that."

Removing several fluffy towels from the hall closet, Philip handed them to her. "While you're making yourself beautiful I'm going to make us something to eat."

Hugging the fresh towels, Carla gave him a grateful smile. "Thank you, Philip. I honestly mean that."

He shrugged and pushed his glasses up the bridge of his nose. "Are you sure you don't need someone to wash your back?" he asked in a low, seductive voice.

"I'm sure." But the look he gave her as he turned toward the kitchen was enough to inflame her senses. Never had she felt this strongly about anyone after such a short time. Maybe that was normal. They had only a week together, and already three of those precious days had been spent. All too soon the time would come when she'd say goodbye to him at the airport. And it would be goodbye.

The water felt fantastic as it sprayed against her soft skin. When she'd finished showering, she put the robe on and opened the bathroom door to allow the steam to escape.

"Your dress is dry if you want me to bring it to you," Philip called to her from the kitchen.

"Give me a minute," she shouted back. Carla's russet-red curls were blown dry and tamed with the curling iron in record time. Her face was void of makeup, and she knew she looked much paler than usual, but one kiss from Philip would correct that.

Tying the sash of the robe as she walked across the living-room carpet, Carla sniffed the delicate aroma drifting from the kitchen.

"Mushrooms," she announced, and picked one out of the sizzling butter with her long fingernails and popped it into her mouth.

"Canned, I'm afraid."

"No problem, I like mushrooms any way they come." She lifted out another and fed it to Philip. His shirt was dry and tucked neatly into his waistband. Her dress, she'd noticed, was hanging off a knob from the kitchen cabinet.

Peeking inside the oven, she turned around delightedly. "I don't suppose those are T-bone steaks under the grill?"

"Yup, but they'll take time. I had to get them out of the freezer." Philip set the cooking fork beside the skillet and reached for her. His hands almost spanned her waist. "But then we have lots of time."

But not nearly enough, her heart answered.

Hours later, after they'd consumed an entire bottle of wine and eaten their fill, they washed and dried the dishes. Soft music played romantically in the background.

"Philip?" Carla tilted her head as she released the plug from the sink to drain the soapy water.

He looked at her expectantly. "Hmm?"

"There's a scar on your back. I don't think I'd noticed it before. What happened?" she asked curiously.

"It's nothing." He stooped down to place the skillet in the bottom cupboard.

"It didn't feel like it. It's long and narrow, like… like…" She stopped cold. A painful sensation in the pit of her stomach viciously attacked her, and she leaned weakly against the counter. "Like a knife. You were stabbed, weren't you?"

Lifting up the frames of his glasses, Philip pinched the bridge of his nose. He muttered something she couldn't quite hear under this breath.

"You didn't want me to know. Well, I do now," she said, and gestured defiantly with her hand. "What happened? Did you decide to step in and break up a gang war all by yourself? You were willing to try your hand at that this morning." Her voice shook.

"No, it wasn't anything like that. I was—"

"I don't want to hear. Don't tell me." She searched frantically for her hat, moving quickly across one room and into the other.

"First you demand to know, then you claim you don't. I hope you realize how unreasonable you sound," he said with a low growl.

"I...don't care what I sound like." Her hat was beside her purse in the other room, and she practically raced to it. "One look at you and I should have known you were bad news. But oh, no, I had to follow this crazy scheme of Nancy's and make a complete idiot of myself. It's not going to work, Philip. Not for another day. Not for a week. Not at all. I'm going back to the hotel."

"Carla, will you listen to me?" Philip stuffed his hands into his pants pockets, and his face hardened with a grimness she hadn't expected to see in him. "It's working, believe me, it's working."

"Maybe everything is fine for you. But I don't want to get involved. Not with you."

"You're already involved."

Defiantly, she crossed her arms in front of her. "Not anymore." Mentally and emotionally, she would have to block him out of her life before the pain became too great.

"That's twice in one day."

"Don't you see?" she cried as if shouting helped prove her point. "All right, all right, I conceded the point. I could like you very much. It probably wouldn't take very much to fall in love with you, but I just can't. Look at me, Philip." Tossing her head back, she held out her hands, palms down, for his inspection. "I'm shaking because already I care enough for you to worry about a stabbing that happened before we even met."

"Being knifed is the only thing that's ever happened to me. I was a rookie, and stupid...."

"This is supposed to reassure me?" she retorted, jamming her hat on top of her head.

He followed her to the front door and pressed a shoulder against the wood to prevent her from opening it. "Carla, for heaven's sake, will you listen to reason?"

Hands clenched at her side, she emitted a frustrated sigh. She didn't expect him to understand. "It was hopeless from the beginning."

"I'm not letting you leave until you listen to me."

Carla exhaled, her lungs aching from the effort to control her emotion. "Philip, I like you so much." Of its own volition, her hand found and explored the side of his jaw. She could feel his muscles tense as her fingertips investigated the rough feel of his day-old beard. "I won't forget you," she whispered shakily.

His hand captured hers and moved it to his mouth so that he could kiss the tender skin of her palm. As if he'd burned her, Carla jerked her fingers free.

"Come on, I'll take you back to the hotel." His quiet determination convinced her to let him escort her back. She knew him well enough to realize arguing would do little good.

Philip didn't say a word on the entire trip back. They passed a horse-drawn carriage, and Carla wanted to weep at the sight of the two young lovers who sat in the back with their arms entwined. What a perfect end to a lovely day such a ride would have been. Philip gave

her a look that said he was reading her thoughts. They
could have been that couple.

Bowing her head, Carla studied her clenched hands,
all too aware that Philip thought she was overreacting.
But she couldn't ask him to be something he wasn't,
and she couldn't change, either.

His hand cupped her elbow as she climbed the short
series of stairs that led to the hotel lobby. Halfway
through the lobby, Carla paused and murmured, "I'll
say goodbye here."

"No, you won't. I'll take you to your room."

When they reached her door, Carla's fingers nervously fumbled with the purse latch. Her hand closed
around the key, and she drew in a deep, shuddering
breath.

"I know you're angry," she said without looking up.
Her gaze was centered on the room key. "And to be honest, I don't blame you. Thank you for today and yesterday. I'll never think of Mexico without remembering
you." The brittle smile she gave him as she glanced up
took more of an effort than he would ever know.

Philip's mouth drew faintly upward, and Carla
guessed that he wasn't in any more of a mood to smile
than she was.

Her hand twisted the doorknob.

"What? No farewell kiss. Surely I deserve that
much."

Carla meant only to brush her lips over his. Not to
tease, but to disguise the very real physical attraction
she felt for him. But as she raised her mouth, his hand
cupped the back of her head and she was crushed in his
embrace. Where Philip had always been gentle, now he
was urgent, greedily devouring her with a hunger that

left her so weak she clung to him. She wanted to twist away but realized that if she struggled, Philip would release her. Instead, her arms crept around his neck. Philip groaned aloud and gathered her as close as physical boundaries would allow, his arms crushing her.

A trembling weakness attacked her, and Philip altered his method of assault. He kissed her leisurely, with a thoroughness that made her ache for more. He didn't rush but seemed to savor each second, content to have her break the contact.

She did, but only when she thought her lungs would burst.

"Goodnight, Carla," he whispered against her ear, and opened the door for her.

Carla would have stumbled inside if Philip hadn't caught her. With as much dignity as possible, she broke free, entered the room unaided and closed the door without looking back.

The cool, dark interior contained no welcome. The taste of Philip's kiss was on her mouth, and the male scent of him lingered, disturbing her further.

Pacing the floor did little to relieve the ache. Desperately, she tried watching television and was irrationally angry that every station had programs in Spanish.

After her long afternoon nap she wasn't tired. Nor was she interested in visiting the party scene that was taking place in the lounge and bars.

Her frustration mounted with every second. Standing on the balcony that overlooked the pool area, she noted again that there wasn't anyone around. A gentle breeze stirred the evening air and contained a freshness that often follows a storm. The first night she'd arrived and met Philip they had gone for a swim. And the pool had been fantastic.

Laps would help, and with the heavy tourist crowds that filled the pool during the day, it would be impossible to do them in the morning. Besides, if she tired herself out, she might be able to sleep.

Determined now, she located a fresh suit in the bottom of her carryall and hurriedly undressed. Tomorrow would be filled with avoiding Philip, but she didn't want to think about that now.

The water was refreshingly cool as she dived in and broke the surface twenty feet later. Her arms carried her to the far side, and the first lap was accomplished with a drive born of remorse. There wasn't anyone to blame for this but herself. She'd known almost from the beginning what Philip was. He hadn't tried to disguise it.

Her shoulders heaving as she struggled for breath ten long laps later, Carla stood in the shallow end and brushed the hair from her face.

"I didn't think you'd be able to stay away," Philip said, standing beside her. "I couldn't either."

Five

Carla froze, her hands in her hair. Philip was right. When she'd come to the pool, the thought had played in the back of her mind that he would be there, too. For all her self-proclaimed righteousness, she didn't want their time together to end with an argument.

The worst part was that she'd overreacted, and like an immature child, she'd run away for the second time. It was a wonder he hadn't given up on her. "I'm sorry about tonight," she murmured in a voice that was quivery and soft. "But when I realized how you'd gotten that scar, I panicked."

Philip turned her around so that they faced each other standing waist deep in the pool's aqua-blue water. "You don't need to explain. I know."

The moon's gentle radiance revealed a thin film of moisture glistening on his torso. Carla longed to touch him. "Turn around," she requested softly, and when he did, she slid her arms around his waist, just below the water line, and pressed her cheek against the curve of his spine. Almost shyly, her fingers located the scar, and she bent down and kissed it gently. The next time,

Philip might not be so fortunate; such a blade could end his life. The thought was sobering, and a chill raced up Carla's arms.

"We agreed to a week," Philip reminded her as he twisted around and looped his arms over her shoulder. "This vacation is for us. Our lives, our jobs, our friends are back in Washington state. But we're here. Nothing's going to spoil what we have for the remainder of the week." He said it with a determination she couldn't deny.

Nothing will ruin it, Carla's heart responded. Everything was already ruined, her head shouted.

They swam for an hour, making excuses to touch each other, kissing when the time seemed right. And it often seemed right.

The night had been well spent when they made arrangements to meet again in the morning. Silently, Carla climbed into the bed across from her sleeping friend. A glance at her watch told her it was after two. This time she had no trouble falling into a restful slumber.

The early-morning sounds of Nancy brushing her teeth and dressing woke Carla when the sun was barely up. Struggling to a sitting position, Carla raised her arms high above her head and yawned. "What time is it?"

"Six," Nancy whispered. "Eduardo and I are flying to Puerto Vallarta. I probably won't be back until late tonight."

Carla nodded and settled back into her bed, hugging the thick pillow.

"And before I forget, I have an invitation for you and…your friend."

"Philip," Carla supplied.

"Right." Nancy laughed lightly. "Who says my head isn't in the clouds? Anyway, you're both invited to dinner with Eduardo and me Saturday evening."

Carla's eyes remained closed, and she nuzzled the covers over her shoulder. "Sounds nice, I'll mention it to Philip." Her lashes fluttered open. "That's our last day here."

"It's really going by quickly, isn't it?" The sad note in Nancy's voice couldn't be disguised. "We've got only three more days."

"Three days," Carla repeated sleepily.

"But you have to admit, this has been our best vacation."

And our worst, Carla mused. Every year she hoped to have a holiday fling. But not next year. Her heart couldn't take this. Of course, not everyone would affect her the way Philip had, but she wasn't game to have her hopes dashed every year.

"By the way, did you hear the gossip that was going around the hotel yesterday?" Nancy didn't wait for Carla's answer. "Some crazy American was standing by the pool serenading a girl with love songs. Apparently, she's staying at the hotel."

For the third time that morning, Carla's eyes opened. A faint color began an ascent up her neck to her cheeks. "Some crazy American?"

"Right, an American. Isn't that the most incredibly romantic thing you've ever heard? Women would kill for a man like that."

"I think you're right." Carla's interest was aroused as she sat up. "Allow me to introduce you to some crazy American Saturday night."

"Philip?"

"You got it." Carla blinked twice. "And it was romantic, except that everyone at the pool was staring at us."

Nancy sighed and sat on the end of Carla's mattress. "Eduardo's romantic like that." She smoothed a wrinkle from her white cotton pants as she crossed her legs. "He says the most beautiful things to me. But half the time I don't know whether to believe him or not. The lines sound so practiced, and yet he appears sincere."

"In instances like that only time will tell," Carla said without thinking.

"But that's something we don't have. In three days I'll be flying home, and I bet I never hear from Eduardo again."

Carla searched her friend's coolly composed face, interpreting the doubts. "But I thought we were only looking for a little romance to liven up our holiday."

Nancy sighed expressively, and her eyes grew wary. "I was, but you know what? I think there's something basically wrong with me. For years now, you and I have had this dream of the perfect vacation. We've been to Southern California, Vegas, Hawaii and now Mazatlán. Every year we plan one week when we can let down our hair and have a good time." She paused, and her shoulders sagged in a gesture of defeat. "We do it so that when we get back to Seattle and our neat, orderly lives, we'll have something to get us through another year."

"But it's never worked out that way. Our vacations are as dull."

"I know," Nancy agreed morosely. "Until this year, and all of sudden I discover I'm not the type for a one-week fling. I'll never be the 'love 'em and leave 'em' type. I like Eduardo, and as far as I can tell, he likes me. But I could be one of any number of women he escorts during the course of a summer. He sees a fun-seeking American on vacation, and I doubt that he'd recognize the hardworking high school teacher that I really am." Nancy sighed and ran her fingers through her hair in frustration. "The funny part is that after all these years this was exactly what I thought I wanted. And now that I've met Eduardo I can see how wrong I've been. When I meet a man I want a meaningful relationship that will grow. Not a one-week fling."

Carla wasn't surprised by her friend's insights. Nancy often saw things more clearly than she did, whereas she, Carla, often reacted more to her emotions. Remembering last night and the way she'd panicked at the knowledge that Philip had been stabbed produced a renewed sense of regret. With Philip her emotions had done a lot of reacting lately.

Later, when they met for an excursion to the Palmito de la Virgen, the bird-watchers' island in the bay, Carla mentioned Eduardo's invitation to dinner. Philip was agreeable, as she knew he would be.

The following morning, Philip and Carla went deep-sea fishing at the crack of dawn. Philip managed to bring in a large tuna, but all Carla caught was a bad case of seasickness.

"It wasn't the boat rocking so much," she explained later, "but the way the captain killed that poor fish, cut him up and passed him around for everyone to sample—*raw*."

"It's a delicacy."

"Not to me."

On their last afternoon together, while Carla stood terrified on the beach, Philip went para-sailing. With her eyes tightly shut, his glasses clenched in her hand, she waited until he was in the air before she chanced a look. Even then her heart hammered in her throat, and she struggled to beat down the fear that threatened to overcome her. Philip had to be crazy to allow his life to hang by a thin line. The only thing keeping him airborne was a motor boat and a cord that was attached from the boat to the parachute.

Her fear was transmitted as an irrational form of anger. The worst part was that Carla realized she was reacting to her emotions again. She wanted Philip to behave like a normal, safe and sane male. Who would have believed that a lanky guy who wore horn-rimmed glasses defied death every day of his life?

Carla was exactly where Philip had left her when he returned. His glasses had made deep indentations in her fingers, and she didn't need to be told she was deathly pale.

Exhilarated, Philip ran to her side and took his glasses from her hand. "It was fantastic," he said, wiping the sea water from his face with a towel and placing it in her beach bag.

She gave him a poor imitation of a smile and lied. "It looked like fun."

"Then why do you resemble a Halloween ghost?"

"It frightened me," she admitted, and was grateful he didn't mention that she looked as if she were going to throw up.

"Carla, I was watching you from up there. You were more than frightened. You looked like a statue with your eyes closed and your teeth clenched, standing there frightened out of your wits."

"I thought you couldn't see without your glasses," she responded, only slightly piqued.

"My vision is affected only close up. I saw how terrified you were."

"I told you before, I'm a conservative person." She didn't enjoy being on the defensive.

"You're more conservative than a pin-striped suit," he growled. "There's nothing reckless in para-sailing."

"And that's your opinion." Impatiently, she picked up her beach towel, stuffed it in her bag and turned away.

"The most daring thing you've done since we arrived is eat chicken in chocolate sauce," Philip insisted, rushing up beside her.

If he wanted to fight, she wasn't going to back down. "What do you want from me, anyway?" she cried.

He slapped his hands against his sides. "I don't know. I guess I'd like for you to recognize that there's more to life than self-actualization through checkers."

Her hand flew to her hip, and she glared at him with a fierceness that stole her breath. "You know, I really tried to be the good sport. Everything you've wanted to do, including risking my life in that…that ocean surf." She waved her finger at the incoming tide. "Deep-sea fishing…everything. How can you say those things to me?"

"For heaven's sake, people come from all over the world to swim in this ocean. What makes it so dangerous for you?"

Several moments passed before she'd gained enough control of her voice to speak. "The very first day we arrived you warned me that the current was too strong for swimming."

"It was." He pointed to a green flag beside the lifeguard station. "The flag was red."

"Oh." Carla swallowed and forged ahead, weaving

her way around the sunbathing beauties that dotted the beach. "Why didn't you explain that at the time?" she demanded.

Curious stares followed her as she ran up the concrete steps that led to the hotel's outdoor restaurant. Not waiting for Philip, she pulled out a chair and sat down, purposely placing her beach bag in the empty chair beside her.

Philip joined her, taking his short-sleeve shirt out of her bag and impatiently stuffing his arms into the sleeve.

"And I suppose you're going to make a big deal out of the fact I didn't want to eat raw fish or dance on my hat," Carla cried, incensed. "I'll have you know—"

Before she could finish, the waiter came for their order. To prove a point, Carla defiantly asked for the hotel special, a hollowed-out coconut filled with a frothy alcoholic concoction. Philip looked at her in surprise, then ordered a cup of coffee.

"Carla," he said after the waiter had left, "what are you doing? You'll be under the table before you finish that drink. There must be sixteen ounces of booze in that coconut."

Gritting her teeth, Carla slowly shook her head. "Everything I do is wrong. There's no satisfying you, is there? If you find me so dull and boring, why have you insisted we spend this week together?"

"I don't find you dull." The paper straw he was fingering snapped in half.

"Then…then why are you so angry with me? What have I done?"

Philip ran a hand across his eyes. "Because, , I know what's coming. We're leaving in the morning, and when we arrive in Seattle it's goodbye, Philip. With no regrets and no looking back."

"But we agreed—"

"I know what we agreed," he growled. "But I didn't count on…Listen Carla, I didn't mean for any of this to come out this way. I think I'm falling in love with you."

Carla felt the air rush out of her. "Oh, Philip, you can't make a statement like that after only knowing me a week."

"Six days," he corrected grimly, and stared at her. His annoyance was barely in check, even now, when he'd admitted his feelings. "I'm not all that versed in love," he said stiffly. "Nicole was evidence of that. And if the truth be known, I thought for a long time afterward that there'd never be another woman I'd care about as much. But what I feel for you grows stronger every minute we're together. We have something special, Carla, and your cautious, conservative fears are going to ruin it."

Philip stopped talking when the waiter approached with their drinks. Carla stared at her drink. Normally she didn't drink during the day, but Philip's accusations hurt. She took a tentative sip from the alcohol-filled coconut and winced. Philip was right; she was a fool to have ordered it.

"I can see what's going to happen," he continued. "And I don't like it."

Confusion raced through her. Philip was saying the very things she'd dreaded most—and most she longed to hear. "Don't you attribute this attraction to the lure of the forbidden?" She sought a sane argument. "You knew from the beginning how I feel about men in law enforcement…and maybe in the back of your mind you thought I would change."

"No," he answered starkly. "Maybe the thought flitted through my mind at one time. But I felt that chemistry between us before you ever told me about your father."

"That soon? Philip, we'd only just met."

Her answer didn't appear to please him. "Don't you think I've told myself that a thousand times?"

The silence stretched between them, tight and unbearable. Carla shifted and pushed her drink aside. Tonight was their last night, and it seemed like they were going to spend it fighting. She was more than half in love with him herself, but she couldn't let Philip know that, especially since she had no intention of continuing to see him after they returned to Washington state. What was the use? He wouldn't change, and she couldn't. There was no sense in dragging out the inevitable.

"I think I'll go up and get ready for tonight," she said, struggling to keep her voice level.

Philip didn't try to stop her as she stood, reached for her beach bag and walked away. Tears had filled her eyes by the time she reached her room. Pressing her index finger under her eye helped stop the brimming emotion. Somehow, with a smile on her face, she'd make it through tonight and tomorrow. When the time came, she'd thank Philip for a marvelous week and kiss him goodbye. And mean it.

A careful application of her cosmetics helped disguise the fact that she'd spent a good portion of the afternoon fighting back emotion. Carla thought she'd done a good job until Nancy came into the room to change, took one look at her friend and declared:

"You've been crying."

"Oh, darn!" Carla raced to the bathroom mirror. "How'd you know?"

"It was either the puffy red eyes or the extra makeup. Honestly, Carla, with a complexion like yours you can't help but tell."

"Great. Now what am I going to do?"

Nancy inspected her closet, finally deciding on a pale-blue sleeveless dress with spaghetti straps. "The same thing I'll probably end up doing. Smile and say how much you're going to miss Mexico and how this has been the best vacation of your life." She turned and laid the dress across the bed. "Now that's what you're supposed to tell everyone else. What you say to me is the truth."

"Philip claims he's falling in love with me," she declared, and sniffled loudly. Fresh tears formed, and she grabbed a tissue and forced her head back to stare at the ceiling, hoping to discourage any new tear tracks from ruining her makeup.

"And that makes you cry. I thought you really liked Philip."

"But there's something I didn't tell you. Philip's in law enforcement. He's a cop." She didn't need to say another word.

"Good grief, Carla, how do you get yourself into these things?"

"I don't know," she lamented, pressing the tissue under her eyes. "Philip was so open and honest about it when he didn't have to be, and when he suggested that we enjoy this week I couldn't turn him down. He's wonderful. Everything about him is wonderful."

"Except that he's a policeman."

"And he's amazingly like my dad. It doesn't matter where either one of them is, the badge is always on. Even when we were shopping, Philip stopped and broke up a potential fight. Worse, Philip's been stabbed once because he was careless."

"Your dad was hurt not long ago, wasn't he?" Nancy asked from her position on the end of the bed.

"Once. He was chasing a suspect, fell and broke his arm."

Nancy nodded. "I remember because you were so furious with him."

"And with good reason. Dad's too old to be out there running after men twenty years younger than he is."

"Take my advice and don't tell him that." Nancy's comment was punctuated with a soft laugh.

Carla decided that Nancy knew her father better than most people did. "Don't worry, Mom said it for me."

An abrupt knock on the door caused them both to glance curiously at one another. Carla's watch told her it was forty-five minutes before they were scheduled to meet the men.

Since she was ready, Carla answered the door. "Philip!" she exclaimed. How good he looked in a suit and tie! And his eyes were the deepest gray she could remember seeing. One glance at her, and their color intensified even more.

"I thought you might be ready," he said stiffly.

"Yes... I am."

"Would you have a drink with me in the lounge? Nancy and Eduardo can join us there."

He sounded as if he were preparing to read Carla her rights. "Sure," she replied, and tossed a look over her shoulder to Nancy. "We'll meet you in the lounge."

Nancy arched both brows expressively. "See you there."

Philip didn't say a word until after they'd ordered their drinks. "I owe you an apology."

Carla's smile wavered only slightly as she reached for his hand. "You can't be any sorrier than I am. I wish I could change, and if there was ever a man I'd do it for, it would be you. But you've seen how I am. I just don't want our last hours together to be spent arguing."

Philip took her hand and squeezed it tightly. "I don't either. We have tonight."

"And tomorrow," she murmured. But their flight was scheduled for the morning, and they'd be in the air a good portion of the day. Once they landed at Sea-Tac International Airport, Philip would catch a connecting flight to Spokane. They would be separated by three hundred and fifteen miles that might as well have been three thousand.

"I have something for you," he announced casually, and pulled a small wrapped package from his coat pocket.

Astonished, Carla raised questioning eyes to Philip. "We must think alike. I've got something for you, too. I'd planned on giving it to you tomorrow. I didn't want you to forget me."

"There's little chance of that," he said with a wry twist of his mouth. "Go on, open it."

Eagerly, Carla tore off the ribbon and paper and was surprised to discover it was a jewelery box. Lifting the black velvet lid, she gasped in surprised pleasure. An exquisite turquoise necklace and matching earrings lay nestled in a bed of plush velvet. The ring he'd given her earlier matched the set. "Oh, Philip, you shouldn't have." Fresh tears misted her eyes, and she bit her bottom lip in an effort to forestall their flow. "They're beautiful. I'll treasure them always."

"Would you like me to help you put it on?"

"Please." She moved to the edge of the chair, turned and scooped up her hair with her forearm. Deftly, Philip placed the turquoise necklace against the hollow of her throat and fastened it in place. Carla managed the earrings on her own.

When she'd finished, she searched through her purse for a tissue to wipe away the tears that clouded her vision. She had to be crazy to walk away from the most wonderful man in the world. Crazy and stupid.

"Here comes Nancy and Eduardo," Philip announced, and stood as the introductions were being made.

The four sat together, and Carla was surprised to discover that Eduardo wasn't anything like she recalled. Her first impression had been all wrong. The Latin good looks were in evidence, but there was a natural shyness about him, a reserve that was far more appealing than his striking good looks. When he spoke English, his Spanish inflection was barely noticeable. Carla guessed that Eduardo had traveled extensively in the United States or had lived there. But more than anything else, Carla noted the way Eduardo watched Nancy. Each time his gaze swung to her friend, the dark eyes brightened and his masculine features would soften noticeably.

Conversation between the four flowed smoothly. When it came time to leave for dinner, Eduardo told them that the hotel's most expensive restaurant had a dining area designated especially for small private parties. The room resembled an intimate dining room, and had been reserved for them. A friend of his owned the hotel, Eduardo explained, and had given his permission for them to use this room. He led the way.

"It's lovely," Carla observed at first glance, impressed with the Aztec decor.

"I chose the menu myself," Eduardo explained. "I hope you will find it to your liking."

"I'm sure we will," Carla murmured. If the meal was anything like the room, this would be a dinner she'd remember all her life.

Eduardo continued by naming the dishes that they would be sampling. Carla understood little Spanish and appreciated it when Eduardo translated for her. "The food in Mexico is a combination of indigenous Indian dishes and Spanish cuisine with some Arabic and French influences."

Carla quit counting after six courses. Replete, she settled back in her chair, her hands cupping a wineglass. "And to think none of us would be here if you two men hadn't ordered a margarita that first night." Almost instantly Carla realized that she'd said the wrong thing. Nancy's eyes widened in warning, and Carla averted her gaze to the wineglass in her hand. Apparently, Nancy hadn't explained their game to Eduardo, and Carla had just stuck her foot in her mouth.

"I'm sorry?" Eduardo questioned, and a curious frown drew his thick brows together. "I don't understand."

"It's nothing," Nancy said quickly.

"Carla said something about Philip and me ordering margaritas the day we met. I'm confused."

"Really, it's nothing," Nancy insisted, a desperate edge to her voice.

An uneasy silence filled the room. "Please explain," Eduardo said stiffly. "A man doesn't like to be the only one not in on a joke."

"It wasn't a joke." Nancy avoided meeting Eduardo's probing gaze. "It's just that Carla and I never have any luck finding decent men, and we decided… Well, you see, we were sitting in the cocktail lounge and…" She tossed Carla a frantic glare. "You explain."

Carla's eyes rounded mutinously. "Nancy—I mean… we…" Good grief, she wasn't doing any better! Silently she implored Philip to take up the task.

To Carla's relief, Philip did exactly that, explaining at length in Spanish. Three pairs of eyes studied Eduardo, and it was easy to see that he was furious.

"And whose idea was this game?" His accent became thicker with every word.

"Mine," Nancy replied, accepting full responsibility. "But it wasn't like you think. I would never have—"

Pushing back his chair, Eduardo stood. "This has been an enjoyable time with my American friends, but I fear I have a business engagement and must cut our evening short."

Nancy stood up as well. "Eduardo, you can't leave now. We must…"

Philip leaned over to Carla.

"Let's leave these two alone to sort this out," he whispered in her ear, and they stood.

"How could I have said anything so stupid?" Carla moaned as they left the restaurant.

"You didn't know."

Philip's words did little to soothe her. "Didn't you see the look in Nancy's eyes? She'll never forgive me, and I don't blame her." Carla felt like weeping. "I've betrayed my best friend."

"Carla," Philip said, and placed an arm around her shoulder. "You can't blame yourself. Nancy should have said something to Eduardo before this."

"The bad part is that Eduardo honestly likes her, and I've ruined that.." She kicked at a loose pebble. "I always did get a loose tongue when I drink too much wine."

Philip cleared his throat. "I hadn't noticed."

"And you're not helping things."

"Sorry." But his smile told her he wasn't. "You shouldn't worry. If Eduardo cares for Nancy, he'll give her the opportunity to explain."

"But I feel rotten."

"I know you do. Come on. Let's walk off some of that fantastic dinner." His arm tightened around her waist, and she propped her head against his shoulder.

The beach was possibly even more beautiful than it had been any night that week.

"Do you remember the first time we were here?" Philip asked, his voice low as he rubbed his chin along the top of her head.

Carla answered with a short shake of her head. "I remember thinking that you wanted to kiss me."

"I did."

"And at the time I was afraid you were the type of guy who would wait until the third date."

"Me?" He paused and pushed his glasses up the

bridge of his nose. "And I was wondering what you'd do if I did make a pass."

A gentle breeze off the ocean carried Carla's soft laugh into the night. "No wonder you had a shocked look when we went swimming and I asked you to kiss me under water."

"I thought I'd died and gone to heaven."

The laughter faded and was replaced by a sadness born of the knowledge that within a matter of hours they would be separating. "This has been a wonderful week."

"The best."

Absently, Carla fingered the turquoise necklace. "I don't ever want this to end. This is heaven being here with you. Reality is only a few hours away."

"It doesn't have to end, you know." Philip stopped walking and turned her in his arms. His smoky-gray eyes burned into hers. "I love you, Carla."

"Philip, please," she pleaded. "Don't."

"No, I'm going to say it. Believe me, I know all the arguments. One week is all we've had, and there are a thousand questions that still need to be answered. I want to get to know you, really know you. I want to meet your family and introduce you to mine."

A bubble of pain and hysteria threatened to burst inside her. "You and my dad have a lot in common."

Philip ignored the sarcasm. "You're a beautiful, warm, intelligent woman."

"Don't forget conservative."

"And conservative," he added. "Have you ever thought how beautiful our children could be?"

"Philip, don't do this to me." She had thought about it. Blending her life with Philip's had been on her mind all afternoon. But no matter how appealing the imagery,

Carla couldn't see past the police uniform and badge. "I… I think I should go back and check on Nancy. And I still have my packing to do."

Philip pinched his mouth tightly closed when he delivered her to the hotel room. "I'll see you in the morning," she promised, not meeting his gaze.

"In the morning," he repeated, but he didn't try to kiss her. Carla couldn't decide if she was grateful or not.

A muffled sound could be heard on the other side of the door. "Good night," she murmured miserably, and slipped inside her room.

Nancy was lying across the bed, her shoulders heaving as she wept. "Oh, Carla," she cried, and struggled to sit up. "Eduardo wouldn't even listen to me. He was barely polite."

Nancy and Carla looked at each other, and both burst into tears.

Six

The sun had barely crested the ocean, its golden strands etching their way across the morning beach, when Carla woke. Her roommate remained asleep as Carla slipped from the bed, quickly donning washed-out jeans and a warm sweatshirt. It wouldn't seem right to leave Mazatlán without one last walk along the water's edge.

Rushing down the concrete steps that led to the countless acres of white sand, Carla scanned the deserted area. Her spirits sank. This last stroll would have been perfect if Philip were here to share it with her.

Rolling up the jeans to her knees, she teased the oncoming tide with her bare feet. The water was warm and bubbly as it hit the shore. She vividly recalled the few times she'd swum in the surf with Philip. When the salt water had stung her eyes and momentarily blinded her, Philip had lifted her into his strong arms and carried her to shore.

With a wistful sigh, Carla strolled away from the water's edge, kicking up sand as she walked. Every memory of this vacation would be connected with Philip. She'd be a fool to think otherwise.

"Carla!"

Her heart swelled as she spun and waved her hand high above her head. Philip.

His shoulders were heaving by the time he ran the distance and joined her. "Morning." He reached for her and looked as if he meant to kiss her, then dropped his hands, apparently changing his mind.

"Morning. I was praying you'd be here."

"I thought I saw you by the pool."

The salty breeze carried her laughter. "I was there waiting for you to magically reappear."

"Poof. Here I am."

"Like magic," she whispered, and slipped her arm around his waist. They turned and continued strolling away from the hotel. The untouched morning beach meandered for miles in the distance.

"How's Nancy?"

Carla shrugged. "Asleep. But for how long, I don't know," she said as a reminder to them both that she couldn't stay long. "I guess Eduardo wouldn't let her explain that picking him up in the lounge never was a game. Not really."

"His attitude is difficult to understand, since Latin men are usually indulgent toward their women."

"Are you as indulgent toward your women?" Carla inquired with rounded, innocent eyes, determined to make this a happy conversation. She'd never be able to tell him all the things in her heart.

"I must be, or you would have shared my bed before now."

Forcing her gaze toward the sea, Carla struggled to maintain control of her poise. "You sound mighty sure of yourself, Philip Garrison," she returned. If he'd said that for shock value, he'd succeeded. The evening in his parents' condo had caught her off guard. The atmosphere had been intimate, and the wine had flown too freely.

"I don't think I'm being overconfident," Philip replied. "You wanted me as much as I did you. But whether you're willing to admit it is something else."

Carla understood what he was saying and flushed.

"What were you thinking when I called you just now?" Philip asked, breaking the uneasy silence that had settled over them. "I can't remember ever seeing you look more pensive."

"About Mexico and what a wonderful time I've had," she said, and smiled up at him. "That's mostly your doing. In my mind I'll never be able to separate the two."

"Me and Mazatlán?"

She answered with a short nod.

Her response didn't seem to please him. He glanced at his watch and applied a gentle pressure to the small of her back as he turned them around and headed for the hotel. "I'll take you back before Nancy wakes."

They didn't speak as they walked toward the El Cid. Then, Carla said somberly, "I was hoping you'd be here. My beach bag's up ahead. Your gift's inside." The handcrafted marlin carved from rosewood had been expensive. Carla had seen Philip admire it the day they'd gone shopping at the arts and crafts center and had purchased the hand-rubbed wood sculpture for him while he had been talking to some Canadians.

Now her eyes shone with a happy-sad expression as Philip unwrapped the gift. He peeled back the paper and glanced at her wordlessly. Delight mingled with surprise as his eyes looked almost silver in the light of the morning sun.

"Thank you," he said simply.

"No," she replied, and swallowed against the hoarseness building in her throat. "Thank you. I'll never forget you, Philip, or this week we've shared. The reason for the marlin is so you won't forget me." She kissed him then, her hands sliding around his middle as her lips met his. It was meant to be a simple act of appreciation, but this kiss soon took on another, more intense significance. This was goodbye.

Philip's arms locked around her narrow waist, lifting her off her bare feet. Bittersweet memories merged with pure hunger. Mouths hardened against one another in a hungry, grinding demand. Their heads twisted slowly from side to side as the kiss continued and continued until Carla thought her lungs would burst. Incredibly, she couldn't give enough or take enough to satisfy the overwhelming passion consuming her resolve.

When they broke apart she was weak and panting. Her legs were incapable of holding her as she pressed her cheek to the hard wall of his chest and gloried in the thundering, erratic beat of his heart. Her shaking fingers toyed with the hair that curled along the back of his neck. But the comfort and security of his embrace was shattered when he spoke.

"Carla, I'm only going to ask you once. Can I see you once we're home?"

"Oh, Philip," she moaned, caught in the trap of indecision. He was forcing her to face the very question she dreaded most. Her lips felt dry, and she moistened them. She couldn't tell him "yes," although her heart was screaming for her to do exactly that. And "no" was equally intolerable. Bright tears shimmered in her eyes as she stared up at him, silently pleading with him to understand that she couldn't say what he wanted to hear.

"Listen to me, Carla," he urged gently. "What we found in Mazatlán is rare. But two people can't know if they're in love after seven short days. We both need time to discover if what we've found is real." His hand smoothed the red curls behind her ear. "What do you say? Spokane isn't that far from Seattle, and meeting would be a simple matter of a phone call."

"Oh, Philip, I'm such a coward." Her long nails made deep indentations in her palms, but she hardly noticed the pain.

"Say 'yes,'" he urged, his fingers gripping her shoulders.

Carla felt as if she were standing on the edge of the Grand Canyon looking down. She knew the pitfalls of loving Philip, and the terror of it gripped her, making speech impossible.

Trapped as she was, she couldn't agree or disagree. "I wish you wouldn't," she murmured finally.

The gray eyes she had come to adore hardened briefly before he dropped his hands to his side. "When you're through letting your fears and prejudices rule your life, let me know." Abruptly he turned, leaving her standing alone in the bright morning sunlight.

"Philip." Her feet kicked up sand as she raced after him. "We can talk more at the airport."

"No." He shook his head. "All along you've assumed I was booked on the same return flight as you. I won't be leaving for another two days."

"Oh." She was forced to continue running to keep up with his long strides. "Why didn't you say something?"

"Why? If you can't make up your mind now, flying back together shouldn't make any difference."

He stopped and caressed the underside of her face. "Goodbye, Carla." His eyes were infinitely sad, and he looked as if he wanted to say something more, but changed his mind. Without another word he turned and left.

Alone and hurting, she stood on the beach with the wind whipping at her from all directions.

"Phone. I think it's Cliff," Nancy announced on her way out of the kitchen.

Before Mexico the news would have been mildly thrilling. But Carla couldn't look at Cliff Hoffman and not be reminded of Philip. Not that the two men were anything alike. Cliff was the current heartthrob of half the medical staff at Highline Community Hospital. Carla had been flattered and excited when he'd started asking her out.

Unhooking her leg from the arm of the overstuffed chair, Carla set her book aside and moved into the kitchen, where the phone was mounted on the wall.

"Hello."

"Carla, it's Cliff."

"Hi." She hoped the enthusiasm in her voice didn't sound forced.

"How was Mexico?"

The question caught Carla off guard, and for one terrifying moment she couldn't breathe. "Fine."

"You don't sound enthusiastic. Don't tell me you got sick?"

"No...no, everything was fine." What a weak word "fine" was, Carla decided. It couldn't come close to describing the most gloriously wonderful, exciting vacation of her life. But she couldn't tell that to Cliff when she sounded on the verge of tears.

"I expected to hear from you by now. You've been back a week." She could hear an edge of disappointment in his voice, but suspected it was as phony as her enthusiasm. From the beginning of their nonrelationship, Cliff had let it be known she had plenty of competition. Philip had once asked her if there was anyone special waiting for her in Seattle. At the time, mentioning Cliff hadn't even crossed her mind.

"It's been hectic around here...unpacking and all." No excuse could have sounded more lame.

"I was thinking we should get together soon." Cliff left the invitation open-ended.

If he expected her to jump at the opportunity to spend time in his company, he was going to be disappointed. "Sure," she agreed without much enthusiasm.

"This weekend?"

Why not? she mused dejectedly. She wouldn't be doing anything by moping around the apartment, which was exactly what she and Nancy had been doing since their return. "That sounds good."

"Let's take in a movie Saturday night, then."

"Fine." There was that word again.

Five minutes later, Carla returned to the living room and her book.

"These arrived while you were on the phone." A huge bouquet of three dozen red roses captured her attention. Philip. Her heart soared. That crazy, wonderful man was wooing her with expensive flowers. It was exactly like him. She'd phone him and chastise him for being so extravagant, and then she'd tell him how miserable the last week had been without him.

Nancy sniffled and wiped the tears from her cheeks. "Eduardo sent them."

"Eduardo?"

"He sent the flowers in hopes that I'll forgive him for his behavior our last night in Mazatlán."

Carla felt like crying, too, but not for the same reasons as her roommate. "I'm really happy for you." At least one of them would be lifted from the doldrums.

"You might still hear from Philip."

"Sure," Carla said with an indifferent shrug. If anyone did anything to improve the situation between her and Philip, it would have to be she. And she couldn't, not when seeing him again would make it all the more difficult. As it was, he dominated her thoughts.

Fifteen minutes later the phone rang again. Carla's immediate reaction was to jump up and answer it, but Nancy was sitting closer to the apartment telephone and for Carla to rush to it would be a dead give away. Although Carla pretended she was reading, her ears were finely tuned to the telephone conversation. When Nancy gave a small, happy cry, Carla's interest piqued. Eduardo, it had to be, especially since Nancy was exclaiming how much she loved the roses. She told him how sorry she was about the mix-up and how everything had changed since Mexico.

When her friend started whispering into the receiver, Carla decided it was time to make her exit. "I think I'll go visit Gramps," she said, reaching for her bulky knit sweater and her purse.

Nancy smiled in appreciation and gave a friendly wave as Carla walked toward the door.

The sky was overcast, and Carla swung a sweater over her shoulder as she walked out the front door. Summer didn't usually arrive in the Pacific Northwest until late July.

"See you later," Nancy called with a happy lilt of her voice.

Carla's Grandpa Benoit was her mother's father. He lived in a retirement center in south Seattle not far from Carla's apartment. Whereas Carla had always felt distant from her mother, she shared a special closeness with Gramps. Grandpa Benoit loved cards and games of any kind. From the time Carla could count, he had taught her cribbage, checkers and chess. The three essential C's, Gramps called them. It was because of Gramps that Carla had won the checkers championship through the King County Parks Department.

Pulling into the parking lot, Carla sat in her car for several minutes. If she showed up again today, Gramps's questions would only become more probing. From the day she'd returned to Seattle he'd guessed something had happened in Mexico. At first he hadn't pried; his questions had been general, as if her answers didn't much concern him. But Carla knew her grandfather too well to be tricked by that. Yesterday, when she'd stopped by on her way to work, they'd played a quick game of checkers, and Carla had lost on a stupid error.

"I guess that young man from Mexico must still be on your mind?" His eyes hadn't lifted from the playing board.

"What young man?"

"The one you haven't mentioned."

Carla ignored the comment. "Are you going to allow me a rematch or not?"

"Not." Still he didn't lift his gaze to hers. "Don't see much use in playing when your mind isn't on the game."

Carla bristled. She'd lost plenty of games to Gramps over the years, and it was unfair of him to comment on this one.

"Seems you should have lots of things you'd rather be doing than playing checkers with an old man anyways."

"Gramps!" Carla was shocked that he'd say something like that. "I love spending time with you. By now, I'd think you'd know that."

His veined hands lifted the round pieces one by one and replaced them in the tattered box. "Just seems to me a woman your age should be more interested in young men than her old Gramps."

Carla started picking up the red pieces. "His name's Philip. Does that satisfy you?"

The blue brightened on his ageless face. "He must be a special young man for you to miss him like this."

"He is special," Carla agreed.

Gramps hadn't asked anything more, and Carla hadn't voluntarily supplied additional information. But if she were to show up again today, Gramps wouldn't let her off as lightly.

Backing out of the parking space, Carla drove to a local Hallmark shop and spent an hour reading through cards. She selected two, more for the need to justify spending that much time in the store than from a desire for the cards.

That evening, as a gentle drizzle fell outside, Carla sat at the kitchen table and wrote to Philip. The letter seemed far more personal than an email. It was probably the most difficult of her life. Bunched-up sheets littered the tabletop. After two hours, she read her efforts with the nagging feeling that she'd said too much—and not nearly enough.

Dear Philip,
You told me to let you know when I was ready to let go of the fears that rule my life. I don't know that I'm entirely prepared to face you in full police uniform, but I know that I can't continue the way I have these last two weeks. Nothing's the same anymore, Philip. I lost a game of checkers yesterday, and Gramps said I shouldn't play if my mind isn't on the game. The only thing on my mind is you. The moon has your image marked on its face. The wind whispers your name. I can't look at the ocean without remembering our walks along the beach.

I'm not any less of a coward than I was in Mazatlán. But I don't know what to do anymore.

I used to be happy in Seattle. Now I'm miserable.

Even checkers doesn't help.

Once a long time ago I read that the longest journey begins with a single step. I'm making that first attempt. Be patient with me.
Carla

The letter went out in the next morning's mail. Since she didn't have Philip's address, Carla sent it to him in care of the Spokane Police Department. His return letter arrived four torturous days later.

Dear Carla,

My first reaction was to pick up the phone and call, but if I said everything that was going through my mind, I'd drive you straight to Alaska and I'm afraid you'd never stop running.

My partner must have thought I was crazy when the watch commander handed me your letter. I've read it through a thousand times and have been walking on air ever since. Do you mean it? I never dreamed I could take the place of checkers.

Carla, I don't know what's been going through that beautiful head of yours, but with every minute that passes I'm all the more convinced that I'm in love with you. I didn't want to blurt it out like this in a letter, but I'll go crazy if I hold it inside any longer. Get used to hearing it, love, because it feels too right to finally be able to say it.

You asked me to be patient. How can I be anything else when that first step you're taking is on the road that's leading you back to me?

Hurry and write. Your last letter is curling at the edges from so much handling.

I love you.

Philip

P.S. I can tell I'm going to like your grandfather.

If Philip claimed to have read her letter a thousand times, then Carla must have doubled his record. Her response, a twelve-page epic, went out in the next day's mail.

Monday evening the phone rang. Nancy called Carla from the kitchen. "It's for you. Cliff, I think."

Carla was tempted to have her roommate tell him

she wasn't home. Their date Saturday night had been a miserable failure. The movie had been a disappointment, and their conversation afterward had been awkward. But the problem wasn't Cliff, and Carla knew as much. Nothing was wrong with Cliff that substituting Philip wouldn't cure.

"Hello."

"Who the hell is Cliff?"

"Philip," Carla cried, and the swell of emotion filled her breast. "Is it really you? Oh, Philip, I've missed you so much." Holding the phone to her shoulder with her ear, she pressed her fingertips over her eyes. "Good grief, I think I'm going to cry."

"Who's Cliff?" he repeated.

"Trust me no one important." How could he even think anyone meant half as much to her as he did? "We went out last Saturday night, and I think he was thoroughly pleased to be done with me. I'm rotten company at the moment." Her laugh was shaky. "It seems my thoughts are preoccupied of late."

"Mine, too. Jeff's ready to ask for a new partner. I haven't been worth much since I got back."

Carla stiffened, and her hand tightened over the receiver. If Philip was being careless, he could be stabbed again. Or worse.

"What's wrong? You've gone quiet all of a sudden."

"Oh, Philip, please be careful. If anything happened to you because you were thinking about me, I'd never forgive myself."

"Carla, I can take care of myself." The tone of his voice told her he was on the defensive.

Carla paused, remembering that he'd already been

stabbed once. "I… I just don't want anything to happen to you."

"That makes two of us."

"I'm so glad you called," she said, and leaned against the countertop, suddenly needing its support. "I've never felt like this. Half the time I feel like I'm living my life by rote. Every day I rush home and pray there'll be something in the mail from you."

"I do, too," he admitted, his voice low and husky. "Listen, Carla, I've got two days off next Thursday and Friday. I'd like to come over."

"Philip, I'm scheduled in surgery both days."

"Can you get off?"

Carla lifted the hair from her forehead and closed her eyes in frustration. "I doubt it. This is vacation time and we're shorthanded as it is." Their mutual disappointment was clearly evident. "Don't be upset," Carla pleaded softly. "If it was up to me, I'd have you here in a minute. What about the weekends? Unless I'm on call I'll be free."

"But I won't."

"Right." She sucked in an unsteady breath. For a moment she'd forgotten that he didn't work regular hours. His life had to be arranged around his job. Even love came in a poor second to his responsibility to the force.

The awkward stillness fell between them a second time.

"Now you're upset?"

"No." The denial came automatically. "I understand a lot better than you realize. I can remember how rare it was to have Dad home on a weekend. Nothing has changed to make it any easier for you."

"You're wrong." Philip's voice dropped to a husky

timbre. "Everything's changed. My life is involved with this incredible person who fills every waking thought and haunts my sleep."

"Oh, Philip."

"The worst part is that I get discouraged. You asked me to be patient and I promised I would be. I guess I'm looking for you to make leaps and bounds and not small steps."

Her throat tightened and she struggled not to give into tears. "I'm trying. Really trying."

For a long moment he didn't speak, but when he did, his voice was ragged. "Please, Carla, don't cry."

"I'm not," she lied, sniffling. "I wish I could be the kind of woman you want. . . ."

"Carla—"

"Maybe it would be better if you quit wasting your time on me and found someone who can adjust to your life style." Her voice shook. "Someone who doesn't know the score…someone who doesn't understand what being part of the police force really means. Believe me, ignorance is bliss."

"Maybe I should," Philip said sharply. "There's not much to be said about a woman who prefers to live with her head buried in the sand."

Carla placed her hands over her eyes. All this time they'd been fooling themselves to think that either of them could change.

"I think you're right," she whispered in voice that was pitifully weak. "Goodbye, Philip."

He started to say something, but Carla didn't wait to listen. Very gently, very slowly, she replaced the receiver. She expected a flood of tears, but there were none—only a dry, aching pain that didn't ease. In some ways Carla doubted that it ever would.

Ten minutes later the phone rang again. Carla didn't answer it, knowing it was Philip. The phone was silent for the remainder of the evening.

Carla found two messages on the kitchen counter when she returned home from work the following afternoon. PHILIP PHONED. CLIFF DID, TOO.

Carla returned Cliff's call. They made arrangements to go to dinner Thursday night. Carla wasn't particularly interested in continuing her non-relationship with Cliff. But not for the world would she let someone—anyone—accuse her of burying her head in the sand. That comment still hurt. Most girls should consider themselves lucky to be going out with Cliff. Obviously there was something about him she was missing. Thursday she'd make a determined effort to find out what it was.

Two days later a letter arrived from Philip, and Carla silently cursed herself for the way her heart leapt. She managed to make it all the way into the apartment, hang up her sweater and pour a cup of coffee before she ripped open the envelope.

Dearest Carla,
I promised myself I wouldn't rush you, and then I do exactly that. Can you find it in your heart to forgive me? At least give me the chance to make it up to you.
Be patient with me, too, my love.
Philip

Carla read the letter twenty times nonstop. Never had any two people been more mismatched. Never had any two people been more wrong for each other. But right or wrong, Carla couldn't ignore the fact that she'd never felt this strongly about a man. If this was what it meant to love, she hadn't realized what a painful emotion it could be.

Dear Officer Garrison,
It's been brought to my attention that two people who obviously care deeply for one another are making themselves miserable. One has a tendency to expect overnight changes, and the other's got sand in her eyes from all those years of protecting her head. I'm writing to seek your advice on what can be done.
Carla
P.S. I'll be more patient with you if you're still willing to stick it out with me. P.P.S. I've got a date with Cliff Thursday night, but I promise not to go out with him again. Maybe I should cancel it.

Two days later Carla got a phone call from Western Union.

"Telegram from Mr. Philip Garrison for Miss Carla Walker."

She had never received a telegram before, and her heart leapt to her throat as she searched frantically for a pencil. "This is Carla. Will I need a piece of paper?"

"I don't think so. There are only two words: 'Break date.'"

Seven

Early Thursday evening Carla rushed home from the hospital. "Did Philip call yet?" she asked breathlessly as she scurried inside the apartment.

Nancy looked up from her magazine, happiness lighting up her face. "Philip didn't, but Eduardo did. He's in Colorado on a business trip and wanted me to hop in the car and join him."

"You're joking?"

"No," she countered, "I'm totally serious. Obviously he had no idea how far Seattle is from Denver. We did have a nice talk though."

From the look on her roommate's face, Carla could see that the conversation with Eduardo had been satisfying. Fleetingly, she wondered where the relationship would go from here. It was obvious the two were strongly attracted to each other. For Eduardo to have swallowed his pride and contacted Nancy, revealed how much he did care.

"So Philip hasn't phoned?" Disappointment settled over Carla. Everything was going so well with Nancy that she couldn't help feeling a small twinge of envy.

"Not yet. But it's a little early, don't you think?"

Carla had already kicked off her shoes and was unbuttoning the front of her uniform. "It's not nearly early enough. I guess I can wait a few more minutes." In some ways, she'd been waiting a lifetime for Philip.

"What makes you so sure he's going to phone?" Nancy asked, following her down the hallway to the large bedroom they shared.

Carla laughed as she pulled the uniform over her head. "Easy. He'll want to know if I broke the date or not."

"And did you?"

"Of course. I'm not all that interested in Cliff anyway."

Nancy released a sigh of relief. "I'm glad to hear that."

"Why?" Carla turned to her roommate as she slid pale blue cotton pants over her slender hips.

"Because he asked me out."

Carla was shocked. "Cliff did? Are you going?"

Nancy's eyes were evasive. "You don't mind, do you?"

Carla couldn't have been more shocked if Nancy suddenly had announced that she'd decided to date a monkey. Her roommate had practically jumped for joy because Eduardo had phoned her, yet she was going out with Cliff. It didn't make sense.

"I don't mind in the least. But…but why would you want to? I thought you'd really fallen hard for Eduardo."

"I have," Nancy admitted freely, "maybe too hard. I want to know if what I feel is real or something I've blown out of proportion. We were only together for six days. And although I've been miserable without him ever since, I need to test my feelings. Eduardo's culture is different from ours, he thinks and reacts to things completely opposite of the way I do sometimes and that frightens me."

Nancy revealing she was frightened about anything was a shock. Of the two roommates, Nancy was by far the more stout-hearted. But she was the type who would be very sure before committing herself to Eduardo and once she did, it would be forever.

"But why date Cliff?" Carla wondered aloud.

"To be honest," she said a little shyly, lowering her eyes, "I've always been attracted to him, but you were seeing him and I'd never have gone out with him while you were."

"You like Cliff?"

Nancy nodded, indicating that she did. "But if it troubles you, I'll cancel the date."

"Don't," Carla said without the least hesitation. "As far as I'm concerned, Cliff is all yours."

The doorbell chimed and Nancy glanced at the front door. "That must be Cliff now. You're sure you don't mind?"

"Of course not. Enjoy yourselves, I'll talk to you later."

Too excited to bother eating dinner, Carla brought in a chair and placed it beside the phone. As an afterthought, she added a pencil, some paper and a tissue box in case she ended up crying again. Satisfied, she moved into the living room to watch the evening newscast.

When the phone rang, she was caught off guard and glanced at her wristwatch before leaping off the sofa.

"Hello," she answered in a low, seductive voice that was sure to send Philip's heartbeat racing.

There was a lengthy pause on the other end of the line. "Carla?"

"Mom." Embarrassed, Carla stiffened and rolled her eyes toward the kitchen ceiling. "Hi… I was expecting someone else."

"Obviously. Is it someone I know?"

"No, his name's Philip Garrison. I met him in Mazatlán." She briefly related the story. "I thought he might be phoning tonight." Take the hint, Mom, and make this short, Carla pleaded silently.

"You and…Philip must have hit it off for you to be answering the phone like a seductress."

"I like him very much," was all Carla would admit.

"Since you're so keen on this young man, when do your father and I get to meet him?"

Clenching a fist at her side, Carla struggled to hold on to her temper. She resented her mother for asking these questions, and she wanted to get off the phone in case Philip was trying to get through to her. "I don't know. Philip lives in Spokane."

"Spokane," her mother mused aloud. "Your father and I knew some people named Garrison. Delightful folks—"

"Mom," Carla interrupted, "would you mind if we talked later? I really do need to get off the phone."

"No, that'll be fine. I just wanted to know if you could come to dinner tomorrow night."

"Sure." At this point she would have agreed to anything. "What time?"

"Seven."

"I'll be there. Talk to you later."

"Goodbye, dear. And Carla, it might help if you're a little more subtle with…what's his name again?"

"Philip."

"Right. I'll see you tomorrow. And, Carla, do try to be demure."

"Yes, Mother, I'll try."

After hanging up, Carla took several calming breaths. She had never gotten on well with her mother. Over the years, Rachel Walker had admirably portrayed the role of a docile wife, but Carla had always thought of her as weak-willed: there were too many times when she'd witnessed the anger and hurt in her mother's expressive eyes. She had wanted to shout at both her parents. Her father should have known what his career was doing to the rest of the family. Her mother should have had the courage to speak up. Carla had tried at sixteen and had been silenced immediately, so she'd moved away from home as soon as possible, eager to leave a situation that made her more miserable every year. And now... here she was following in her mother's footsteps. A knot tightened in the pit of her stomach. Dear heavens, what was she getting herself into with loving Philip? Again and again she'd tried to tell herself that what they shared was different—that she and Philip were different from her parents. But their chances of avoiding the same problems her parents had dealt with were slim— likely nonexistent. With stiffening resolve, Carla vowed she would never live the type of life her mother had all these years. If that meant giving up Philip, then she'd do it. There wasn't a choice.

The phone rang again a half hour later. Carla stared at it as if it were a mad dog, her eyes wide with fear. Chills ran up and down her spine. This was Philip phoning—the call she'd anticipated all day.

Trembling, she picked up her purse and walked out

the door. A movie alone was preferable to listening to the phone ring every half hour. If she let Philip assume that she had gone out with Cliff, then maybe, just maybe, he'd give up on her and they could put an end to this misery. Her instincts had guided her well in the past. Now, more than at any other time in her life, she had to listen to her intuition—for both their sakes. Philip deserved a woman who would love him for his dedication to law and order and his commitment to protect and serve. He needed a wife who would learn the hazards of his profession a little at a time. Carla knew too much already.

Nancy wasn't back when Carla returned to the dark, lonely apartment. And within five minutes the phone rang. She ignored it. Coward, she taunted silently as she moved into the bedroom. But if she was behaving like a weakling, it shouldn't be this difficult. It wasn't right that it hurt this much.

Nancy was still asleep when Carla dressed for work the following morning. She penned her roommate a note and left it propped against the sugar bowl on the kitchen table: *If Philip contacts you, please don't tell him I didn't go out with Cliff last night. I'll explain later. Also, don't bother with dinner. I'm going to my parents'. Am interested in hearing how things went with Cliff. Talk to you tonight.*

Carla's first surgery was an emergency appendectomy, a teenage boy who was lucky to be alive. Carla had witnessed only a handful of deaths in the last couple of years. She didn't know how the rest of the staff dealt emotionally with the loss of a patient, but each one had affected her greatly.

When she had finished assisting with the appendectomy, she found a message waiting for her. She waited to read it until she was sitting down, savoring a cup of coffee in the cafeteria. Call Nancy, it read. A glance at the wall clock confirmed that there wouldn't be enough time to call until after lunch. When she phoned at one-thirty, however, there wasn't any answer, so Carla assumed it couldn't have been that urgent. She'd wait to talk to Nancy at home.

Three hours later Carla headed for the hospital parking lot, rubbing the ache in the small of her back to help relieve some of the tension accumulated from a long day on her feet. Dinner with her parents would only add to that tension. And eventually she would have to talk to Philip—he'd demand as much. But she didn't want to think about that now. Not when her back hurt and her head throbbed and she was facing an uncomfortable dinner with her parents.

Carla was soaking in a tub full of scented water when Nancy knocked on the bathroom door. "Carla."

"Hmm," she answered, savoring the luxurious feel of the warm, soothing water.

"I think you should get over to your grandfather's as soon as possible."

Carla sat up, sloshing water over the edge of the bathtub. "Why? What happened?"

"I can't explain now, I'll be leaving any minute. Cliff's on his way. He's taking me to the Seattle Center for the China Exhibit."

"Is anything wrong with Gramps?" Carla called out frantically. Already standing, she reaching for a thick towel to dry herself.

"No, nothing like that. It's a surprise."

"What about you and Cliff? Things must be working out if you're seeing him again." Carla could feel Nancy's hesitation on the other side of the bathroom door.

"They're working out, but not as I'd expected. I'm giving it a second chance to see if it's any better the second time."

"Oh?" Carla hoped that Nancy wasn't going to make her ask that she explain that.

"Cliff's all right, I guess."

Behind the closed door, Carla smiled smugly. That was how she felt about Cliff. He was fine, but he wasn't Philip, and now apparently he wasn't Eduardo either.

"Does Eduardo know? I mean did you tell him you were seeing another man?" Carla hated to think what would happen if he discovered Nancy was dating Cliff. Eduardo's male pride was bound to cause him to overreact.

"I…I told him yesterday."

"And?"

"Oh, he understands. In fact, he encouraged me to see Cliff again. I told him he should do the same thing and you know what he said? He said he didn't need to see another woman to know how he feels about me. He mentioned something about me flying to Mexico City to meet his family, but I didn't let him know one way or the other." As if regretting she'd revealed that much, Nancy added hastily, "Listen, Carla, I promise that you'll like your surprise. I'd hurry if I were you."

The doorbell sounded and was followed by a clicking sound that told Carla she wouldn't get any more information from her friend. A surprise! Presumably this was why Nancy had contacted her at the hospital.

Dressing casually in cotton pants and an antique

white blouse with an eyelet collar, Carla hardly bothered with her hair. A quick application of lip gloss and a dab of perfume and she was out the door.

Her heart was hammering by the time she arrived at the retirement center. Her shoes made clicking sounds as she hurried inside, pushing open the double glass doors with both hands. She took the elevator to Gramps's room on the third floor, thinking it would be faster than running up the stairs.

Gramps's door was closed. Carla knocked loudly twice and let herself inside. "Gramps, Nancy..." The words died on her lips as her startled eyes clashed with Philip's. He was sitting opposite her grandfather, playing a game of checkers.

"Philip." She stood there, stunned. "What are you doing here?"

Gramps came to his feet, using his cane to help him stand. "Nancy brought your young man over to meet me."

"I asked her to," Philip added. "Your grandfather was someone I didn't want to miss meeting."

"Mighty fine young man you've got yourself," said Gramps, his blue eyes sparkling with approval.

"He could be saying that because he beat me in checkers," Philip explained, grinning.

Gramps's weathered face tightened to conceal a smile. "Leave an old man to his peace. Knowing my daughter, she'll have your hide if either of you is late for dinner."

"Dinner," Carla repeated with a panicked look.

"Yes, your mother was kind enough to include me in the invitation."

"My mother."

"Something's wrong with my hearing aid," Gramps complained, tapping lightly against his ear. "I'm hearing an echo."

Philip chuckled and cupped Carla's elbow. "Nice meeting you, Gramps," he said as he led the way out the door and into the hallway.

"Philip Garrison, what are you doing here?" Carla demanded. Her hands rested defiantly on her hips. Oh my, he looked good. His sandy-colored hair was combed to the side, and a thick lock fell carelessly across his wide brow. His appealing gray eyes were dark and intense as they met hers. To Carla he had never looked more compelling. Staying out of his arms was growing more difficult every minute.

"Are you trying to drive me crazy? Because you're doing a mighty fine job of it. Why wouldn't you answer the phone?"

"I…couldn't." She wouldn't lie outright, but she had no compunction about letting him believe she'd been out with Cliff.

"And while we're at it, you can explain this." He took Carla's note to Nancy from his pocket. "'Don't tell Philip I didn't go out with Cliff,'" he read with a sharp edge in his voice. "It seems to me we've got some explaining to do."

"Y-yes…yes, I guess I do."

"Then let's go back to your place. At least there we can have some privacy." He flashed a look down the wide corridor.

They rode back to the apartment in silence.

"How'd you get here?" Carla asked shakily as she pulled into her assigned parking space.

"I flew in at noon. Nancy picked me up at the airport."

"When are you going back?"

His gaze cut into hers, and one thick brow arched arrogantly. "Can't wait to be rid of me, is that it?"

"No…yes…I don't know." She replied, her voice trembling.

Her hands were unsteady as she unlocked the apartment and stepped inside. Philip had come all this way because she hadn't had the courage to talk to him last night. She'd been foolish to believe he wouldn't find out why. "Would you like a cup of coffee?" she asked, hanging her purse over the inside doorknob of the coat closet.

Gently Philip settled a hand on each shoulder and turned her around so that he could study her. Carla's gaze fell to the floor.

"Carla, my love." Philip's voice was low, sensuously seductive. "You know what I want."

She did know. And she wanted it, too. "Oh, Philip," she groaned, and slipped her arms over his shoulders, linking her fingers behind his neck. "It's so good to see you."

His mouth claimed hers in a series of long, intoxicating kisses that left her weak and trembling. Philip was becoming a narcotic she had to have; his touch was addictive.

His hands roamed over her back, pulling her soft form against his muscular frame. A warmth spread through her limbs, and she turned her head when his lips explored the smooth curve of her shoulder and the hollow of her throat.

Taking a deep breath to keep the room from spinning, Carla pushed against his chest, leaving only a narrow space between them.

"How can you refuse to speak to me, deceive me by letting me think you'd gone out with this other guy, and then kiss me like that?" Philip asked in a voice husky with emotion.

Melting against him, she explored his earlobe with her tongue as her fingertips caressed his clenched jaw. "I think I'm going crazy," she murmured at last. "I want you so much my heart's ready to pound right out of me."

"Then why?" he groaned against her ear. "Why are you running from me so hard I can barely keep up with you?"

"I'm so scared." Her low voice wavered. "I don't want to be like my mother."

"What's that got to do with anything?" He continued to nibble the side of her neck, making it impossible for her to think clearly.

"Everything," she cried desperately. "I'm not the right person for you."

"But I won't want anyone else."

"Philip, be reasonable."

"You're in my arms. I can't think straight." He bit gently at the edge of her lips. "Carla, I'm going crazy without you. I want you to marry me. I want to share my life with you, because heaven knows I can't take much more of this."

Carla's eyes shot open. "How can you talk about marriage?" she asked, struggling to break free of his hold.

"It's the normal process when two people feel as strongly about one another as we do."

"But I don't want to love you," she cried. "When my husband leaves for work in the morning I don't want to worry about him risking his life on the streets of the city."

"Carla—"

"And when he comes home at night I don't want him to drag his job with him. I want a husband, not a hero—"

His mouth intercepted her words, muffling them until she surrendered to his kisses, arousing her until she clung to him, seeking a deeper fulfillment. "Kissing me won't settle a thing," she murmured, breaking free with her last reserves of strength.

"I know, but it keeps you from arguing."

"When you're holding me like this," she admitted shyly, "there's not much fight in me."

"Good. All I need to do for the next seventy years is keep you at my side. Agree, and I'll whisk you to a preacher so fast it'll make your head spin."

"You're incorrigible."

"I'm in love." His hands were linked at the small of her back and slipped over her buttocks, arching her backside, lifting her up to meet his descending mouth. The kiss was shattering.

"Can we talk now?" Every minute in his arms made it more difficult to think clearly.

"Okay, explain what happened yesterday," he said as they sat in the living room. "Why wouldn't you talk to me last night?"

"I already told you why," she said, and exhaled slowly. "I don't want to be like my mother."

"Carla." Philip captured both her hands in his and kissed her knuckles. "That doesn't make any sense. You're who you are, and I'm me. Together we'll never be like anyone else."

Shadow Chasing

Carla bowed her head, and her lashes fluttered until they closed completely. "Mom and I are a lot alike. You'll understand that when you meet her later. But she's weak and afraid and never says what she's really thinking. And Philip, I'm trying so hard to be different."

"That still doesn't explain why you wouldn't talk to me."

Carla swallowed uncomfortably. "Mom called just before you did, and everything she said reminded me how unhappy she's been all these years."

"Ah," Philip said, and nodded thoughtfully. "And the note to Nancy?"

"I...I was thinking that if you assumed I was still dating Cliff, you'd give up on me."

He tucked his index finger under her chin and lifted her eyes to his. "I think there's something you'd better understand. I'm not giving up on you. Never. I love you, Carla."

"But loving someone doesn't make everything right," she argued. "We're different in so many ways."

"I don't see it like that. We complement each other. And although it seems like I'm the one who's asking you to make all the changes, I'm not. When we're married I promise that you and our family will be my first priority. Nothing will ever mean more to me than you."

"Oh, Philip." She felt herself weakening. "But it's more than that."

"I know, love." Slowly, deliberately, his eyes never leaving hers, he pulled her toward him. His mouth sought her lips, exploring their softness as if he would never get enough of the feel of her.

"Philip," she groaned, her voice ragged. "We have to leave now for my mother's."

"Your mother's," he repeated as if he needed something to bring him back from the brink.

"You'll be meeting my dad," she said softly, teasing his neck and ear with small, biting kisses.

"Mom and Dad, I'd like to introduce Philip Garrison." Carla stood just inside her parents' living room. "Philip, my mom and dad, Joe and Rachel Walker."

Joe stepped forward and shook Philip's hand. "Nice to meet you, Philip."

Carla felt the faint stirrings of pride. Her father, although graying, was in top physical condition. Over the years he hadn't lost the lean, military look of his younger days. Intuitively, Carla knew that in twenty years Philip wouldn't, either.

"It's a pleasure to have you join us," Rachel added warmly. "Carla said you live in Spokane."

"Yes, I flew in this afternoon."

The four of them sat in the large living room, and Philip immediately took Carla's hand in his. The action didn't go unnoticed by either of her parents. Rachel's blue eyes sought Carla's, and she gave her daughter a small wink, indicating that she approved of this young man. Maybe Carla should have been pleased, but she wasn't. Having her family like Philip would only complicate her feelings.

"And when will you be leaving?"

Carla was as interested in his answer as her parents.

"Tonight; I'd like to stay longer, but I'm on duty tomorrow morning."

"Carla said that you two met in Mazatlán."

"Yes, the first day she arrived." Philip looked at Carla, and his dark eyes flickered with barely concealed amusement.

Her eyes widened, silently warning him not to mention *how* they'd met. Then flustered, she cleared her throat and said, "Philip helped me out with my Spanish."

"You speak Spanish?" Joe asked, but his narrowed gaze studied Carla. Her father was too observant not to recognize that there was a lot going unsaid about her meeting with Philip. Fortunately he decided not to pursue the subject.

Rachel glanced at her gold wristwatch. "Excuse me a minute."

"Can I help, Mom?" Carla asked, and uncrossed her long legs.

"No, everything's ready, I just want to check the corn. Your father's barbecuing chicken tonight."

"You're in for a treat," Carla told Philip proudly. "I've been telling Dad for years that when he retires he should open a restaurant. He makes a barbecue sauce that's out of this world."

"It's an old family recipe that's been handed down for generations."

"He got it out of a Betty Crocker cookbook," Carla whispered, grinning. Then before her father could open his mouth, she stood. "I'll see what I can do to give Mom a hand." Although her mother had refused her offer, there was undoubtedly something she could do to help.

Rachel was taking a large bowl of potato salad from the refrigerator when Carla came through the swinging kitchen doors. "I like your young man," she announced without preamble.

Carla couldn't hold her mother's gaze. She should have been surprised; Rachel had disapproved of most of the men Carla dated. Her excuses were usually lame ones—this boy was careless, another boy was lazy. By the time Carla moved out, she had stopped introducing her dates to her parents. Somehow, though, she'd known her mother would approve of Philip.

"He's clean-cut, polite and he has a nice smile."

Carla bit into a sweet pickle from the relish tray. "And his eyes are the most incredible gray. Did you notice that?" Naturally they wouldn't discuss any of the important aspects of her relationship with Philip.

"You two make a nice couple."

"Thank you," Carla answered with a hint of impatience. She opened the silverware drawer and counted out forks and spoons. "I'll set the table."

Philip was holding a beer, watching her father baste the chicken with a thick coating of pungent sauce, when Carla joined them on the sunny patio. He slipped an arm over her shoulder. His thumb made lazy, sensuous forays at the base of her neck.

Annoyed, she shrugged her shoulder and Philip dropped his hand to her waist. She didn't want him to make this kind of blanket statement to her family about their relationship. *He* was serious about her, but she had yet to deal with her feelings about him. When she stepped free of his hold, Philip firmly but gently cupped her shoulder.

"Philip," she groaned in an irritated whisper. "Please don't."

His eyes sparkled as he leaned toward her. "I told your father outright that I'm going to marry you."

"You didn't!" she cried in angry frustration.

Joe turned aside from the barbecue. "Hand me a spoon, would you, Carla?" he requested, and his gaze followed her as she moved to the picnic table and brought back a spoon. "Problems, Princess?"

"No." She shook her head, the red curls bouncing with the action. "I'm just sorry that Philip made it look like we're more serious than we are."

"He was rather forthright in his feelings."

Carla swallowed. "I know."

"But aren't you sure?"

"I won't marry a cop." Years of self-discipline masked any physical reaction from her father.

"I can't say I blame you for that," he said after a long moment. Some of the brightness faded from his eyes as he concentrated on his task.

"I love you, Dad, you know that. But I won't live the life Mom has."

With practiced skill he turned the chicken over with a pair of tongs. "She's never complained."

"Oh, Dad," Carla said with a rush of inner sadness. She respected and admired her father and had never thought of him as oblivious of the stress his career had placed on their family. "Are you really so blind?"

His mouth tightened, and the look he gave her was piercing. "I said she's never complained. It takes a special kind of woman to love a man like me."

Carla lifted her gaze to Philip, who was examining the meticulously kept flower beds, and her father's words echoed in her mind. Carla didn't know if she could ever be that special kind of woman.

Rachel appeared at the sliding glass door. "Carla, would you help me carry out the salads?"

"Sure, Mom." Carla followed her mother into the kitchen.

Rachel stuck a serving spoon in the potato salad,

handed it to Carla and turned away. "Philip mentioned that he had to be back tomorrow because he's on duty. You did say he was a doctor, didn't you?" Her voice was unnaturally high, and her hands were busily working around the sink.

"No, Mom." She'd wondered how long it would take for her mother to pick up on that. "Philip's a police officer."

A glass fell against the aluminum sink and shattered into little pieces. Rachel ignored it as she turned, her face suddenly waxen. "Oh, Carla, no."

Eight

"Your flight will be boarding in a minute." Carla stood stiffly in the area outside of airport security. The lump in her throat was making it hard for her to talk. The crazy part was that she didn't want Philip to leave and at the same time she couldn't bear to have him stay.

The meal with her parents had been an ordeal. As she had suspected, Philip and her father had gotten on like soul mates. They were alike in more ways than Carla had first suspected. Their personalities, ideas and thoughts meshed as if they were father and son.

Rachel had remained subdued during most of the meal. Later, when Carla had helped clear the picnic table and load the dishwasher, a strained tension had existed between them. Her mother had asked a few polite questions about Philip, which Carla had answered in the same cordial tone.

"I don't think it would be a good idea for you to become too serious with this young man," Rachel said as they were finishing. Her casual attitude didn't fool Carla.

Fleetingly, Carla wondered what reason her mother

would give. Philip wasn't the careless type, and even the most casual observer could see he wasn't lazy. She was bound to say everything but what was really on her mind.

"Why not?" Carla implored. "I thought you said you liked him."

"I do," Rachel replied quickly in a defensive tone. "But he's too much like your father, and I'll love that man to my death." The poignant softness of Rachel's voice cracked the thin wall that stood between mother and daughter.

"And you," Rachel continued with a wry grin, "are too much like me: vulnerable, sensitive, tender-hearted. Our emotions run high, and when we love, we love with a fervor. Philip could hurt you, Princess."

Her mother so rarely called her by that affectionate term that Carla lifted her head in surprise.

"There are plenty of men in this world who will make life a thousand times easier for you than someone involved in law enforcement."

"But you married Dad," Carla argued, studying her mother intently. This was as close as they had ever come to an open conversation.

"Your father joined the force after we were married."

"I...I didn't know that."

"Something else you may not know is that Joe and I separated for a time before you were born."

Shocked, Carla's mouth dropped open. "You and Dad?"

Rachel busily wiped off the kitchen counter, then rinsed out the rag under the running faucet. "There are certain qualities a policeman's wife should have. I...I've never been the right woman—" She stopped in mid-sentence as Philip and Joe sauntered into the kitchen.

Mother and daughter had been unable to finish the conversation, but Carla had felt a closeness with her mother she had never experienced. She realized now that they had always been too much alike to appreciate each other.

"Carla?"

Philip's voice brought her back to the present, and to the reality of his leaving.

"You're looking thoughtful." His fingers caressed the gentle slope of her neck, trailing down her shoulder. "I expect a kiss goodbye, one that will hold me until I see you again."

A smile briefly touched Carla's eyes. "I don't think that kind of kissing is allowed in public places."

"I don't care." His voice was low and husky as he ran his hands up and down the length of her silken arms. "Seeing each other again has only made things worse, hasn't it?"

"No," she denied instantly. "I think it's been good for us both."

"Good and bad," he growled, and the frustration and longing in his eyes deepened. "Good, because holding you lessens the ache I feel when we're apart." His hands gripped the back of her collar, bringing her closer into his embrace. "And bad, because I don't know how much longer it'll be before I hold you again."

Their gazes met and held, and Carla felt as if she were suffocating. His eyes, steel-gray and narrowed, slowed the torment within him, and Carla realized hers were filled with doubt. Her lips started quivering, and she pressed them tightly together.

Philip's hands tightened on Carla's blouse, and he dipped his head forward so that their foreheads touched. "I hate this."

Her arms slid around his waist, and she pressed her face to his shirt. "I do, too." Her voice was scratchy and unnaturally high as she swallowed hard, determined to be strong. "You should go," she said, and gave him a brave smile.

"Not until the last minute. Not until I have to." His voice wasn't any more controlled than her own. "Carla" —he breathed in deeply—"I want to do everything right for you. You need me to be patient and wait; then I'll do that."

"Oh…Ph…Philip. How can you love me? I'm so wrong for you."

"No one has ever been more right," he insisted, his words muffled against her hair. "I love you, and someday we'll have beautiful redheaded children."

"With warm gray eyes."

"Tall," he added.

"Naturally," she said, and offered him a shaky smile.

"Does this mean that you've reconsidered and will marry me? Because let me warn you: if it does, I'll make the arrangements tomorrow."

She couldn't answer him. Something deep and dark in her soul wouldn't allow her to speak. Instead she blinked her eyes in an effort to hold back the emotion that threatened to overtake her.

Disappointment, regret, pain and several other emotions Carla couldn't name played across Philip's face.

"Soon?" he asked in a whisper.

Carla forced a smile. "Maybe."

"That's good enough for now. Just make it soon, my love. Make it very soon."

Philip waited until the very last minute before going through security. Carla waited and once he was through, he tossed an impatient glare over his shoulder and disappeared down the corridor, rushing to make his flight. His kiss had been short, but ardent. As she watched him go, Carla pressed four fingers to her lips and closed her eyes.

She didn't leave the terminal until the plane was out of sight and her tears had dried. Her spirits were at an all-time low as she headed to the airport parking lot, fighting back questions that tormented her from all sides.

Philip's letter arrived in Saturday's mail.

My dearest love,
It's been only a few hours since I left you in Seattle. I couldn't sleep, and it's too late to phone. As I flew back tonight I couldn't drop the picture of you from my mind. This week is hectic, but I'll phone you Tuesday night. I'm involved with three other friends from the force in a canoe race—don't laugh. Ever hear of the Great Soap Lake Canoe Race? Well, yours truly is captain of the motley crew. We're planning to arrive in Soap Lake Friday afternoon. The race begins early Saturday morning. The others have their own cheering squad. I have only you. Tell me you'll come. I want to introduce you to my friends and their wives. And for all the trouble I've been giving Jeff Griffin, my partner, since Mexico, he claims

he has a right to meet you. Let me warn you now
that you shouldn't believe everything he says. Jeff
likes to tease, and believe me he's had a lot to kid
me about the last few weeks. I want you to talk
to Jeff's wife when you come. Sylvia is pregnant
with their first child. I know you'll like her. Please
tell me you'll be there.

This is torment, Carla. I can feel your kiss on
my lips, and the scent of your perfume lingers, so
all that I need to do is close my eyes and imagine
you're with me. And, my love, don't ever doubt
I want you with me. I'm praying that this feeling
can hold me until Friday.
I love you.
Philip

Carla read his letter again and again, savoring each
word, each line. Several times she ran her index finger back and forth over his declaration of love. Philip
sounded so sure of things. Sure that they were right for
each other. Sure that she could put her insecurities behind her. Sure that she would eventually marry him.

And Carla felt none of it. Every day the list of pros
and cons grew longer. Philip, like her father, was an ide-
alist. Carla wasn't convinced that being in love made
everything a rose garden.

As for his invitation to have her come and root for
him in the canoe race, Carla was sure that the real reason was so she could meet his friends. And she didn't
need to be told that policemen usually socialized with
other policemen. Her parents had few friends outside
the force; the same undoubtedly held true for Philip.
Friday was only a few days away and finding some-

one willing to trade work days would be difficult with half the staff scheduled for vacation time. It was a convenient excuse until she made up her mind what to do.

"Have you decided what you're going to tell him?" Nancy asked Tuesday evening as she carted her luggage into the living room. After her last date with Cliff, Nancy had returned convinced she knew what she was feeling for Eduardo. When he'd pressed the invitation for her to meet his family she hadn't hesitated.

"No," Carla answered dismally. "I'm afraid that I'll be dragged into his life little by little until we're married and I don't even know what happened."

"I think Philip's counting on that."

"I know." Carla nibbled on her bottom lip. Philip would be phoning later, and she still didn't know what she was going to tell him. If she told him outright that she wouldn't come, he'd accuse her of burying her head in the sand again. And he'd be right. But if she did agree, Carla realized that things would never be quite the same again. He had come to Seattle and invaded her world. He'd played checkers with Gramps and had dinner with her parents. She didn't feel safe anymore. Inch by inch he was entwining their lives until it would be impossible for her to escape.

A happy, excited Nancy had left for Mexico by the time Philip phoned. Carla stared at the phone for five long rings before she had the courage to answer.

"Hello." As hard as she tried, she couldn't disguise her unhappiness.

"Carla, what's wrong?" She wanted to cry at the gentle concern that coated his voice. "You aren't coming," he said before she could answer.

"I...I don't know. Friday's a busy day at the hospital, and finding a replacement—"

"You don't want to come," he interrupted impatiently.

"It's not that." Carla leaned her hip against the counter and closed her eyes in defeat. "It's too soon for this sort of thing. I don't think I'm ready."

"For a canoe race!" Carla could feel his anger reverberate through her cell. "You said you'd give me time and then you immediately start pushing at me. You're not playing fair, Philip Garrison. Don't force me into something I'm not ready to deal with yet."

"You mean to say you can't handle a social outing with my friends?"

"I don't know," she cried.

An unnatural, tension-filled silence followed. Carla struggled for some assurance to give him and found none. Maybe Philip was seeking the same. A full minute passed and neither spoke, yet neither was willing to break off the connection.

Carla heard Philip take a deep breath. "All right, I won't push you. I said I'd be patient. When you decide if you're going to come, phone me." From the tone of his voice, she knew that he was hurt and discouraged. "I'll be out most of the week—practicing with the rest of the team." Apparently he wanted her to realize why he wouldn't be available. "If you can't reach me, I'll be waiting at the B and B Root Beer stand in Soap Lake from seven to nine Friday night. It's on the main road going through town. You can't miss it. If you don't come, I'll understand."

"I'll call you before then." The lump in her throat made her voice sound tight.

"I'd appreciate that."

Again there was silence, and again it was obvious neither of them wished to end the conversation.

"I...I have some good news about Nancy," Carla said at last. "She's flying to Mexico City to meet Eduardo's family. From the way things have been progressing I wouldn't be surprised if Nancy returned wearing an engagement ring."

"You could be too." Philip told her in a tight voice and Carla regretted having said anything. It'd been a mistake to bring up the subject of Nancy and Eduardo in the light of their own circumstances.

"I know."

"But you're not ready? Right?"

"Right," Carla returned miserably.

The strained silence returned until Philip finally spoke, his voice devoid of anger. "Eduardo's a good man."

So are you, Carla mentally added.

"So you think Nancy may marry Eduardo."

"It wouldn't surprise me," Carla said, forcing an air of cheerfulness into her voice. "Nancy's a lucky girl." The second the words were out, Carla desperately wanted to take them back. "Philip," she said contritely, and swallowed. "I didn't mean that the way it sounded."

"The problem is, I believe it's exactly what you mean. I'm not a good-looking, Latin American who's going to impress your friends." His words were as cold as a blast of wind from the Arctic.

"Philip, you're everything I want in a man except..."

"Except...I've heard it all before. Goodbye, Carla, if I see you Friday, that's fine. If not, that's fine too."

The phone clicked in her ear and droned for several moments. The entire conversation had gone poorly.

She'd hoped to at least start off in a lighter mood, and then explain her hesitancy about meeting him for the weekend. But she'd only succeeded in angering Philip. And he'd been furious. She knew him well enough to realize this type of cold wrath was rare. Most things rolled off him like rain water on a well-waxed car. Only the important matters in his life could provoke this kind of deep anger. And Carla was important.

She still hadn't decided what to do by the time she joined her grandfather after work on Thursday for their regular game of checkers. Carla hoped he wouldn't try to influence her to go. She'd taken Gramps out to dinner Sunday afternoon, and he had done little else but talk about what a nice young man Philip was. By the end of the day, Carla had never been more pleased to take him back to the retirement home. She prayed today wouldn't be a repeat of last Sunday.

"Afternoon, Gramps," she greeted him as she stepped into his small apartment.

Gramps had already set up the board and was sitting in his comfortable chair waiting for her. "The more I think about that young man of yours, the more I like him."

"Philip's not my young man," she corrected more tersely than she had intended. Carla had suspected this would happen when Philip met her family. Gramps and her dad had joined forces with Philip—it was unfair!

"'The lady doth protest too much'—Shakespeare."

Carla laughed, her first real laugh in two days. She and Gramps played this game of quotes occasionally. "'To be is to do'—Socrates," she tossed back lightly as she pulled out the rocking chair opposite him and sat down.

Gramps's eyes brightened and he stroked his chin, deep in contemplation. "'To do is to be'—Sartre." He nodded curtly to Carla, and the set of his mouth said he doubted that she could match him.

"'Do be do be do'—Sinatra," she said, and giggled. For the first time in recent memory she'd outwitted her grandfather. Soon Gramps's deep chuckles joined her own, and his face shone with pride. "I'm going to miss you, girl."

"Miss me?" She opened the game of checkers by making the first move.

"When you and Philip marry you'll be moving to Spokane to live with him."

Miffed, Carla pressed her lips tightly together and removed her hand from the faded board. "Did he tell you that?"

"Nope." Gramps made his return move.

With her fingers laced together in her lap, Carla paused and looked up from the checkers. "Then what makes you think I'm going to marry him?"

"You'd be a fool not to. The boy clearly loves you, and even more obvious is the way you feel about him."

Carla returned her gaze to the checker pieces, but her mind wasn't on the game. "He's a cop, Gramps."

"So? Seems to me your daddy's been a fine officer of the law for twenty-odd years."

"And Mom's been miserable every minute of those twenty-odd years."

"Your mother's a worrier. It's in her blood," Gramps countered sharply. "She'd have fretted about your dad if he was the local dogcatcher."

"But I'm afraid of being like Mom," Carla declared vehemently. "I can't see myself pacing the floors alone at night when Philip's called on a case, or when he isn't and just goes away for a while to settle things in his head. Don't you have any idea of how much time Mom spends alone? She's by herself when she needs Dad. But he's out there"—she pointed to the world outside the apartment window—"making the city a better place to live and forgetting about his own wife and family." Her voice was high and faltering as she spewed out her doubts in one giant breath. "Gramps, I'm afraid. I'm afraid of loving the wrong man." Her fists were tightly clenched, and her nails cut painfully into her skin.

"And you think Philip is the wrong man?"

"I don't know anymore, Gramps. I'm so confused."

His gnarled hand reached across the card table and patted her arm. "And so in love."

Talking out her fears with Gramps had a releasing effect on her, Carla realized as she walked around the lonely apartment hours later. Only a few days ago Philip had been sitting on that couch, holding her as if he'd choose death rather than let her go.

Her gaze was drawn to her cell. She'd promised to call him by now and let him know if she was coming. Her heartbeat accelerated at the thought of hearing his voice. With trembling resolve, she reached for her phone, and waited for the electronic bleeps to connect their lines.

Philip answered on the first ring with a disgruntled "Yes?"

"Do you always answer your phone like you want to bite off someone's head?" Just hearing his voice, unwelcome and surly as it was, had her heart pounding erratically.

A long pause followed. "Carla?"

"The one and only," she answered. Her voice throbbed with happiness. She'd pictured him lying back in an easy chair and relaxing. Now she envisioned him sitting up abruptly and rolling to his feet in disbelief. The imagery produced a deep smile of satisfaction.

"You called!" This time there was no disguising his incredulity.

"I said I would," she murmured softly.

"You've decided about the canoe race?"

"Yes."

"And?"

"First, I need to know if you're wearing your glasses."

"Good grief, Carla, what's that got to do with anything?"

"Do you have your glasses on or don't you?" she demanded arrogantly.

"Why?"

Carla was learning that he could be just as stubborn as she. "Because what I'm about to say may steam them up, so I suggest you remove them."

Washington was known as the Evergreen State, but there was little evidence of any green in the eastern portion of the state—and none at all in the sagebrush, desert-like area in which Carla was traveling. Divided by the Cascade mountain range, Washington had a wet side and a dry side. In Seattle, summers and winters were less extreme—for example, although it was already mid-July, there had been only a handful of days above eighty-five degrees.

Carla shifted in the driver's seat of her compact car, hoping to find a more comfortable position. She'd been on the road for almost four hours and was miserably hot. Her bare thighs stuck to the seat of her car, and rivulets of perspiration trickled down the small valley between her breasts. Even Mazatlán hadn't seemed as hot.

Exiting off the interstate freeway at the town of George, Carla gassed up her car at Martha's Inn and paused to read over the map a second time. Within an hour or so she would be meeting Philip. They'd been apart only six days, yet it felt more like six years. Carla didn't know how she was going to endure any long separations.

As he'd said he would, Philip was sitting at a picnic table in front of the B and B Drive-In. Carla savored the sight of him and did a quick self-inspection in her rearview mirror. Instantly, she was sorry she hadn't stopped at a service station outside of town to freshen her makeup.

As she pulled into the drive-in's parking lot, she noticed that Philip had spotted her and was heading for her car. Carla's throat was dry, and she couldn't think of a thing to say.

"Hi." Philip opened the driver's side and gave her his hand, his face searching hers all the while as if he couldn't quite believe she wasn't an apparition. The hand gripping hers tightened. "How was your trip?"

"Uneventful," was all Carla could manage.

Lightly, Philip brought her into his arms and brushed her cheek with his lips. Their eyes met as they parted, and still he didn't smile. "You really came," he said hoarsely.

She answered with a short nod. Philip had known without her fully explaining what her coming meant.

The doubts, her determination to fight this relationship, were slowly dissolving. And coming here to meet his friends was a major step on her part.

"Jeff and Sylvia will be by in a few minutes." He led her to a picnic table. "Sit down and I'll get you something cool to drink."

"I can use that." Now that she was outside the car, the heat was even more sweltering.

Philip returned with two cold mugs of root beer. He set them on the table and sat opposite her. "I can't believe this. My heart's beating so fast I feel like an adolescent out on his first date."

"I feel the same way." She lowered her gaze to the root beer. Her fingers curled around the mug handle, and she took her first long drink. "I noticed in your note you said that you wanted me to talk to Sylvia."

Philip's hand reached for hers. "I think you two will have a lot in common."

"Does she feel the same way about Jeff's job as I do?" Carla asked tentatively.

"No." His voice was gently gruff. "But you're about the same age."

"Didn't you say she was pregnant with their first child?"

"Very." He said it with an odd little smile. "You'll be beautiful pregnant."

Carla could feel herself blushing. "Honestly, Philip," she murmured, her eyes looking troubled. "I wish you wouldn't say things like that."

"Why not? Last night after we finished talking I was so happy that I lay in bed thinking I could run ten miles and not even feel it. But I didn't run. Instead I lay there and closed my eyes, picturing what our lives would be like five years from now."

"And?" She was angry with herself for going along with this fantasy, but she couldn't help herself.

"You were in the kitchen cooking dinner when I walked in the back door. A little redheaded boy was playing at your feet, banging pots and pans with a wooden spoon. When you turned to me, I saw that you were pregnant. I swear, Carla, you were so beautiful I went weak. My heart stopped beating and my knees felt like putty. I don't think anything's ever affected me like that. I've never made any pretense about wanting you, and I'm not going to start now."

Carla busied herself by running her finger along the rim of her mug, and when she lifted her gaze, their eyes met. "That's beautiful," she said, and was shocked at how low her voice was. The closeness she felt with him at that moment was beyond anything she had ever known. But she wished he wouldn't say such things to her. It only made her more miserable.

Silence fell between them, but Philip seemed content to watch her. Her hands trembled as she lifted the mug for another long drink. "Philip," she moaned, finding his continued scrutiny uncomfortable, "please stop looking at me like that. You're embarrassing me."

Immediately he dropped his gaze. "I didn't mean to. It seems I do everything wrong where you're concerned. I thought I'd play it cool today when you arrived. And the minute I saw you every nonchalant greeting I'd practiced died on my lips."

"Mine too," she confessed shakily.

"I'm still having trouble believing that you came."

"We both need to thank Gramps for that."

"I think we should name our first son after him."

Carla shook her head. "He'd never forgive us for naming a boy Otis."

"All right, we'll name him after your dad."

"He'd like that." Good heavens, the sun must have some effect on her mind. Here they were discussing the names of their children, and Carla wasn't even convinced she should marry Philip!

"Jeff and Sylvia are here," he announced, and his expression became sober. Carla turned and noticed a sky-blue, half-ton pickup kick up gravel as it pulled into the parking lot.

A lanky fellow with a thick patch of dark hair jumped down from the driver's seat and hurried around to help his obviously pregnant wife.

Sylvia, a petite blonde with warm blue eyes, pressed a hand to the small of her back as she ambled toward them. Carla guessed that Jeff's wife must be seven or eight months pregnant.

"Hi, you must be Carla." Jeff held out his hand, not waiting for an introduction.

"Hi. You must be Jeff."

Sylvia offered her a gracious smile. "I'm glad you could make it."

"The whole team's ecstatic she could make it. Philip hasn't been worth a damn since he got back from Mexico. I certainly hope you're going to put this poor guy out of his misery and marry him."

Carla's startled eyes clashed with Philip's. This was exactly what she'd feared would happen. She didn't want to have to answer these kinds of questions. They were bad enough coming from Philip and Gramps.

"I…I'm not sure what I'm going to do," she answered stiffly, her eyes challenging Philip.

Nine

The warm sun had disappeared beyond the horizon, and the sun-baked land cheerfully welcomed the cool breath of evening. The flickering flames of a campfire licked at the remaining pieces of dry wood.

Sylvia and Carla were the last to remain by the dying fire. The other women were busy tucking their little ones into bed, and the sound of their whispers and hushed giggles filled the still evening air. Carla and Sylvia glanced at each other and grinned. Next year Sylvia would be joining the other young mothers. And next year Carla... She closed her eyes and shook her head. She didn't know what she'd be doing.

Jeff, Philip and the rest of the ten-man relay team were meeting to plan their strategy for the coming race. An air of excitement drifted through the campgrounds. The Great Soap Lake Canoe Race had dominated the conversation all afternoon. This was the first year the Spokane Police Department was competing, and their cheering squad held high expectations. For the last couple of years, the eighteen-and-a-half-mile course had been won by a two-man marathon team in the amazing time of two hours and thirty minutes. Philip's team-mates seemed to think that ten men in top physical condition could easily outmaneuver two. The most incredible fact, Carla thought, was that every team that had ever entered this outrageous competition had finished. "Carla?" Sylvia's voice broke into her reverie, and she looked up.

"Hmm?"

"Jeff didn't mean to put you on the spot this afternoon—about marrying Philip, I mean," Sylvia said shyly. "It's just that we all like him so much."

"I…like Philip, too." The toe of Carla's sandal traced lazy patterns in the dirt. "In fact, I love him."

"You didn't need to tell me that. It's obvious."

A sad smile played at the edges of Carla's mouth. She liked Sylvia. She'd discovered that she liked all of Philip's friends. They had welcomed her without hesitation and accepted her as a part of their group, going out of their way to include her in the conversation and activities. One of Philip's friends had worked in Seattle for a short time and remembered Carla's father. Perhaps that was the reason she was accepted so quickly, but Carla didn't like to think so.

"The natural thing to do when two people love one another is to get married," Sylvia suggested softly.

"Not always," Carla answered with an emotional tremor in her voice. "Oftentimes there are… extenuating circumstances. My father's a policeman."

"I heard." Sylvia slipped her arms into the sleeves of the thin sweater draped over her shoulders and leaned back against the folding chair. "I can understand your hesitancy. Being a policeman isn't the kind of work I would have chosen for Jeff. There are too many worries, too many potential dangers that affect both our lives. But Jeff's career is an important part of who he is. It was a package deal, and I've had to learn to accept it. Each police wife must come to grips with it sooner or later."

"Philip's got to be the most patient man in the world to put up with me."

"He loves you." Sylvia smiled. "I remember the first week after Philip returned from Mexico. Jeff complained every night." She paused and laughed softly. "A lovesick Philip took us all by surprise. We just didn't expect him to be so human. He's been as solid as a rock, and we were shocked to discover he's as vulnerable as the rest of us."

"He was in love with a flight attendant a few years back. Did you ever meet Nicole?"

"No." Sylvia shook her head slowly. "That was before I married Jeff. But I can remember him mentioning how hard Philip took it when they split up. I think Jeff's worried the same thing is going to happen again."

Rather than offer reassurances she didn't have, Carla said, "Philip's like that. Everything is done full measure."

"Everything," Sylvia agreed.

"Nicole was a fool to let him go." Carla paused and sucked in her breath, realizing what she'd just said. She'd be a fool to allow her fears and inhibitions to ruin her life. Yet something within her, some unresolved part of herself, couldn't accept what Philip was. The other wives had come to terms, appreciating their men for what they were. Carla hadn't honored Philip's commitment to his career, just as her mother had never been able to fully respect her father's dedication to his. The thought was so profound that it caused Carla to straighten. Maybe for the first time in her life she needed to talk with her mother.

"Would you like some help out of that chair, Mommy?" Jeff asked as he stepped behind his wife and lovingly rested his hand on her shoulder.

"Next time, I'm going to let him be the one to get pregnant," Sylvia teased, and extended her hand, accepting her husband's offer of assistance.

With their arms wrapped around each other, Jeff and Sylvia headed toward their tent.

"Night, Carla," Sylvia called back with a yawn. "I'll see you in the morning."

"Night."

"Are you tired?" Philip asked as he took the chair Sylvia had vacated.

"Not yet." Not when she could spend a few minutes alone with Philip. Not when they could sit undisturbed in the quiet of the night and talk. There were so many things she wanted to tell him. But in the peaceful solitude by the campfire, none of them seemed important.

"It's a beautiful night," he murmured as he leaned back and stared up at the sky. "In fact, tonight reminds me of Mexico and this incredibly lovely woman I once held in my arms."

"If I close my eyes, I can almost hear the surf against the shore," Carla responded, joining his game. "And if I try, really try, I can picture this incredibly wonderful man I met in Mexico sitting across from me."

Philip's chuckle was deep and warm. "How hard do you need to try?"

"It's not so difficult, really."

"I should hope not." Philip smiled and moved his chair so that they were sitting side by side. When he sat back down and reached for her hand, Carla glanced at him. His strong face was profiled in the moonlight, his look deep and thoughtful.

"Have you got your strategy all worked out, Oh master of the canoe race?" she asked lightly. His pensive look troubled her. She didn't want anything to ruin these few minutes alone together; this wasn't the time to discuss her doubts or find the answers to nagging questions.

"Pretty much." He grimaced and quickly disguised a look of pain.

"Philip, what's wrong?" Her voice was unnaturally high with concern. "You're not feeling well, are you?" Immediately she knelt at his side and touched his brow, which was cool and revealed no sign of a fever.

"It's nothing." He tried to dispel her worry with a wide grin. "Nerves, I think. I'm always this way before a race."

Returning to her chair, Carla nodded. "I had the lead in a play when I was in the eighth grade, and I was deathly sick before the first performance. I know what you mean."

"Have you and Sylvia decided where you're going to position yourselves to cheer us on?"

Apparently Philip didn't want to talk about his nerves, this Carla understood and could sympathize. "At the finish line. Sylvia isn't in any condition to go running from lake to lake with the rest of the team. So we've decided to plant ourselves there and wait for our dedicated heroes to bring in the trophy."

"You may have a long wait," Philip said wryly and grimaced again.

Carla decided not to comment this time, but she was

concerned. "Five lakes, Philip. Are you guys honestly going to canoe across five lakes?"

"We're going to paddle like crazy across each one, then lift the boat over our heads and run like madmen to the checkpoint. From there the next two-man team will take the canoe and the whole process will start again."

"Which lakes?" Carla had heard them mentioned only fleetingly.

"Park, Blue, Alkaline, Lenore and Soap."

"I think you're all a little nuts."

"We must be," Philip agreed soberly. "But to be honest, I'd swim, hike, canoe and run a lot farther than a few miles for an excuse to have you with me." He raised her fingers to his lips and kissed the back of her hand.

He studied her in the moonlight, and, feeling wretched, Carla lowered her eyes. "I don't know how you can love me," she murmured.

"Patience has its own rewards."

"I do love you." But a declaration of love, she knew, was only a small part of what he wanted from her.

"I know." He stood and offered her his arm. "I think we should both turn in. Tomorrow's going to be a full day." His voice was bland, almost impersonal, but his tone was at odds with the look in his eyes. Carla would have sworn he was hiding something from her and it was a whole lot more than nerves.

Philip's kiss outside her tent was brief, as if he were more preoccupied with the race than he was with having her near. It could be nerves, but they'd only seen each other twice since Mexico and she'd thought he'd do a whole lot more than peck her cheek when it came time to say goodnight. A hand on her hip, Carla tipped her head to one side and flashed him a confused glance as he turned toward the tent he was sharing with another officer. Carla didn't know what was troubling Philip, but she'd bet hard cash it had nothing to do with her or the race. But whatever it was, he wasn't going to tell her. That hurt; it seemed to prove that Philip didn't feel he could discuss his problems with her. He wanted her to share his life, but there was a part of himself he would always hold back. The same way her father had from her mother.

Carla didn't know there were this many people in all Eastern Washington. The start of the race was jam-packed with participants, friends, casual observers and cheering fans. Some of the contestants wore identifying uniforms that would distinguish themselves as being looney enough to participate in such a laughable race.

Everyone had been laughing and joking before the race, but when the gun went off, the competition began in earnest; each team was determined to win.

Jumping up and down with the others and clapping as hard as she could, Carla was caught up in the swirl of craziness that seemed to have engulfed the entire city of Soap Lake.

Three hours later, when Philip and Jeff crossed the finish line, placing a respectable fifth, Carla and Sylvia had cheered and laughed themselves weak.

Dramatically throwing themselves down on the grass, both men lay staring at the cloudless blue sky, panting.

Jeff spoke first. "Next year," he managed breathlessly, "we'll go after the trophy."

Sitting around the picnic table at the campgrounds later that afternoon, Philip positioned himself by Carla's side and casually draped his arm over her shoulder. "Do you think we should compete again next year?"

Carla lowered her hot dog to the plate. "It'd be a shame not to. You were only twenty minutes off the best time, and with a little practice you're bound to improve. Don't you agree?"

"On one condition. That you promise to be on my cheering squad again next year." His eyes searched hers, seeming to need reassurance.

Confidently, Carla placed her hand on his. "You got it." The sun beamed off the gold band of her watch, and Carla noticed the time and groaned.

"What's the matter?"

"I've got to leave."

"Now?"

Sadly, she shook her head. "Soon. In order to have Friday afternoon free, I traded days with another girl who's on call tomorrow."

"Which means?" His eyes narrowed.

"Which means I have to be back tonight by midnight in case there's an emergency."

Standing, Philip tossed his paper plate in the garbage can. Carla dumped the remainder of her lunch away and followed Philip to a large oak tree, where he stood, staring at the ground.

"It was hardly worth your while to make the trip. I'm surprised you came."

"I'm glad I did. I enjoyed meeting your friends, especially Sylvia and Jeff."

He pursed his lips, and Carla studied him suspiciously. He looked as if he wanted to argue and she couldn't understand why. Planting herself in front of him, her legs braced slightly apart, she stared at him until he met her gaze "It's not going to work, you know."

He frowned. "What's not going to work?"

"Starting an argument. I refuse to react to your anger. I wish I could stay. If it was up to me, I would. But circumstances being what they are, I've got to leave this afternoon." She paused and drew a long breath. "Now. Will you walk me to the tent and spend the next few minutes saying goodbye to me properly, or are you going to stand here and pout?"

Philip bristled. "I never pout."

"Good." She smiled and reached for his hand. "Then let's escape for a few minutes of privacy before someone comes looking for us."

The sun was setting, whisking back the splashes of warm, golden rays, by the time Carla pulled into her apartment parking space. After emerging from the car, she stretched, raising her arms high above her head and yawning. The trip back had been leisurely and had taken the better part of four hours. Philip had promised to connect as soon as he was back in Spokane. That brooding, troubled look had returned when he'd kissed her goodbye. Carla didn't know what was bothering him, but she guessed that it had nothing to do with her. Already he was acting like her father, afraid to tell her something he knew could upset her. If she was going to consider being his wife, she didn't want him treading lightly around information she had a right to know. She'd ask him about it Monday night.

Sunday afternoon, while on call at the hospital, Carla drove to her parents' house.

"Hi, Mom," she said as she let herself in the front

door. Rachel Walker was sitting on the worn sofa, knitting a sweater.

"Who's this one for?" Carla asked as she sat across from her mother, admiring the collage of colored yarn. Rachel was constantly doing something—idle hands led to boredom, she had always said. She was a perfectionist housekeeper, and now that Carla and her brother had left home, she busied herself with craft projects.

"Julianne," her mother replied without a pause between stitches, her fingers moving with a skill that was amazing. "She'll need a warm sweater this fall for first grade. She's six now, you know."

"Yes." Both her nieces had always been special to Carla, and she'd missed them terribly since her brother and his wife had moved to Oregon.

"Where's Dad?"

Briefly a hurt look rushed across her mother's face. "He's playing on the men's softball team again this year." The Seattle Police Department had several teams, and Carla's father loved to participate, but her mother had never gone to watch him play, preferring to stay at home. What Joe did outside the house was his business, because it involved the police force—and Rachel had never had anything to do with the force.

"Actually I'm glad Dad isn't here, because I'd like to talk to you alone."

"To me?" Momentarily, Rachel glanced up from her handiwork.

"I'm in love with Philip Garrison," Carla announced, and closed her eyes, preparing for the backlash that was sure to follow.

"I think I already knew that," her mother replied

calmly. "In fact, your father and I were just talking about the two of you."

"And?"

"We agreed that you and Philip will do fine. What I said to you the other night isn't altogether valid. We are alike, Carla, in many ways, but in others we're completely different."

Carla marveled at the way her mother could talk so frankly with her and at the same time keep perfect pace with her knitting.

"Joe pointed out that your personality is stronger than I've given you credit for. You're not afraid to say what you feel or to speak out against injustice. Your work at the hospital proves that…" Rachel paused and after taking a shuddering breath, she bit her bottom lip.

Carla moved out of the chair and kneeled at her mother's side. Rachel tossed her yarn aside and leaned forward to hug her daughter as she hadn't since Carla was a child. "I would have chosen another man for you, Princess. But I can't hold against Philip the very things that make me love your father. Be happy, baby. Be happy."

"I love you, Mom," Carla murmured. She'd never thought she'd feel this close to her mother. Philip had done that for her. He had given her the parent she had never thought she'd understand—the closeness every daughter yearns to share with her mother.

Carla laughed and said, "It's not every day your only daughter decides to get married. Could we do something together? Just you and me."

Leaning back in the cushioned sofa, Rachel reached for a tissue and blew her nose. "What do you want to do?"

"Can we go to Dad's softball game?"

For a second Rachel looked stunned. But gradually a smile formed at the edges of her mouth. "I've been waiting twenty years for an excuse to do just that."

Monday afternoon, on her way home from the hospital, Carla stopped off to visit Gramps, but she stayed just long enough for a single game of checkers and to tell him she'd made a decision about Philip.

"So you've come to your senses and decided you're going to marry him?"

"If he'll have me."

"No worry there," Gramps said with a chuckle. "The problem, as I see it, is if you're ready to be the right person for a man like Philip."

Carla didn't hesitate. "I know I am. Philip is a policeman, and I should know what that means. After all, I've been a policeman's daughter all my life."

His eyes beamed with pride as he slowly shook his head. "I see you've come to terms with that. Now I pray that you'll be as good a wife as your mother has been all these years."

"I hope I can, too," Carla added soberly.

The phone rang just as she she let herself into the apartment. Carla dumped her purse on the kitchen table and grabbed her cell.

"Hello."

"Carla. Thank heaven I caught you. Where have you been? This is Jeff, Philip's partner."

Carla felt the blood rush from her face. Jeff would be phoning her only if something had happened to Philip. Her knees went weak, and she leaned heavily against the counter. "We aren't allowed to keep our phones with us while on duty. What is it?"

"Apparently you didn't check your messages either. Philip's in the hospital. I think you should get here as soon as possible. I checked with Alaska Airlines, and there's a flight leaving Seattle in two hours. If you can be on it, I'll pick you up in the patrol car and take you directly to him."

Ten

"What happened?" Somehow Carla managed to get the words past the bubble of hysteria that threatened to overtake her.

"We were on patrol and… It was my fault., I should have known what was happening. With all the medical training I've had, I can't believe I didn't know what was going on. But I got him to the hospital in record time. Listen, Carla, I can't explain everything now. Just get here. Philip asked for you when he came out of surgery. I want to tell him that you're coming."

"Yes…of course, I'm on my way now. And Jeff." Her hand tightened around her phone. "Thanks for letting me know."

Unable to move, Carla felt an almost tangible fear move through her body. Her senses reeled with it. Her mouth was dry, her hands were clammy, her knees felt weak. Even the rhythmic beating of her heart slowed. It seemed unfair that once she had reconciled herself to who and what Philip was, her newfound confidence should be severely tested this way. With a resolve born of love, Carla had thought she could face anything. Now

she realized how wrong she was. She would never come
to terms with losing Philip.

By rote, she reached for her phone and contacted her
parents.. "Mom," she cried, not waiting for a greeting,
"Philip's been shot." Carla heard her mother's soft gasp
and fought her own rising panic. "He's just out of surgery and I'm flying to be with him. Call the hospital
and explain that I won't be in. And let Gramps know."

"When's your flight."

Carla ran her hands through her hair. "In two
hours…. There's a flight on Alaska but I…I"

"You pack," her mother said, taking over. "I'll call
the airport for you. Your father will be there in ten minutes to drive you. Don't worry, Princess, Philip will be
fine." Her mother hadn't any more information than
Carla, but the gentle reassurance gave her the courage
to think clearly.

Yanking clothes off the hanger, Carla stuffed them
in an overnight case. After adding her toothbrush, curling iron and a comb, she slammed the lid closed. She'd
be fine if only she could stop shaking. Pausing, she
forced herself to take several deep, calming breaths.
The shock of Jeff's call prevented tears, but she knew
those would come later.

The doorbell rang, and Carla rushed across the living room to open the door.

"You ready?" Her father looked as pale as she did,
Carla realized, but she knew he was far too disciplined
to display his emotion openly.

She gave an abrupt nod, and he took the small suitcase out of her hand and cupped her elbow as they hurried down the flight of stairs to the apartment parking
lot. During the ten-minute drive to Sea-Tac Interna-

tional Airport, Carla could feel her father's concerned scrutiny.

"Are you going to be all right, Princess? Do you want your mother with you?"

No, I'm fine," she said, and with a sad smile amended, "I think I'm fine. If anything happens to Philip, I don't know that I'll ever get over it."

"Cross that bridge when you come to it," he advised. "And phone as soon as you know his condition."

"I will," she promised.

Jeff was nervously pacing the tiled airport floor when Carla spotted him just minutes after stepping off the plane. Without hesitation she ran to him and gripped his forearm. "How's Philip?" Her eyes pleaded with him to tell her everything was fine.

"There weren't any complications. But apparently I misunderstood him. He said he *didn't* want you to know."

"Didn't want me to know?" she echoed incredulously. If that bullet didn't kill him, she would. Philip was lying on a hospital bed wanting to protect her from the unpleasant aspects of his occupation. It infuriated her, and at the same time she felt an overpowering surge of love.

"Just before I left, the doctors told me it would be several hours before he wakes."

Carla weighed Jeff's words carefully. "Take me to the hospital. I want to be there when he wakes."

A smile cracked the tight line of Jeff's mouth. "As the lady requests. Tell him the decision was yours and I'm not responsible."

"I'll tell him," she said and winked.

"Great." He looked at his watch. "I'm afraid I can't

take you to the hospital personally; I'm still on duty. But another friend of ours will get you there safely. If you like, I can take your things and drop them off at Philip's condo."

"Yes…that'll be fine."

Jeff introduced Bill Bower, a ruddy-faced officer Carla didn't recognize from the previous weekend. Bill nodded politely, and after saying goodbye to Jeff, the two of them headed for Bill's car.

"Can you tell me what happened?" she asked Bill when they were on the freeway. During the flight she had prepared herself to hear the details of what exactly had gone wrong. In some ways Carla realized that she didn't want to know. It wasn't important as long as Philip was alive and well. There would be time for explanations later when Philip could make them himself. But knowing that he would make light of the incident, she'd hoped to get a fuller version of the story on the way to the hospital.

"I wasn't there," Bill stared matter-of-factly, "so I don't know how it happened. But apparently Philip was in tremendous pain, and Jeff may have saved his life by getting him to the hospital as quickly as he did."

Carla paled at the thought of Philip in agony. He'd be the type to suffer nobly. Her lips felt dry, and she moistened them.

The stoic-faced offer must have caught her involuntary action. "I wouldn't worry. Philip's healthy and strong. But he's bound to be in a foul mood, so don't pay any mind to what he says."

"No, I won't," she replied with a brave smile.

The hospital smelled faintly of antiseptic. Carla was admitted into Philip's room without question, which surprised her. Seeing him lying against the white sheets, tubes coming out of his arms, nearly undid her. She sank gratefully into the chair beside his bed.

"The doctor will be in later, if you have any questions," the efficient nurse explained.

"I'll be leaving now," added Bill. "If you need anything, don't hesitate to call. Jeff will be back later tonight."

"Thanks, Bill."

"All the thanks I want is an invitation to the wedding."

"It's yours." She tried to smile, but the effort was painful.

Still wrapped in the warm comfort of sleep, Philip did little more than roll his head from one side to the other during the next two hours. Content just to be close to him, Carla did little more than hold his fingers in hers and press her cheek to the back of his hand.

"Carla?"

Forcing herself to smile, Carla raised her head and met Philip's gaze.

"Is it really you, or is this some befuddling dream?"

"If I kiss you, you'll know for sure." Gently she moved to the head of his bed and leaned forward to press her lips to his. Philip's hand found her hair, and he wove his fingers through its rusty curls.

"Oh, Philip, are you going to be all right?" she moaned, burying her face in the side of his neck.

"Stay a while longer, and I'll prove it," he whispered against her temple.

He lifted his gaze to hers, and the intense look in those steel-gray eyes caught her breath. A muscle worked in his lean jaw as his gaze roamed possessively over her face. "I didn't want Jeff to contact you."

"I know, but I'm here now and nothing's going to make me leave." Her hand clasped his as she took the seat beside the bed.

"What did Jeff say when he phoned? He has a high sense of theatrics, you realize."

"You warned me about that once before. He said that you'd just come out of surgery and had asked for me."

"What I asked was that he not contact you. I didn't want you worrying."

"Philip Garrison, if you think you can keep something like getting shot from me"—she tried to disguise the hurt in her voice—"you've got a second think coming, because I can assure you, wild canoe racers wouldn't keep me away from you at a time like this."

"Shot?" His breath quickened as he raised his head slightly to study her. "Jeff told you I was shot? I'll kill him."

"Well, good heavens, something like a gunshot wound is a little difficult to keep from me. Just how were you planning to tell me about it? 'Carla, darling'" she mimicked in a deep rumbling voice, "'I guess I should explain that I got scratched while on duty today. I'll be in the hospital a week or so, but it's nothing to worry about'"

"Carla…" His voice was a husky growl. "If I told you I'd been shot, paranoia would overtake you so quickly that I'd never catch you, you'd be running so fast."

"It's a high opinion you've got of me, isn't it?" she asked in a shaky voice. "You're missing the point. I did learn what happened, and I'm here, because it's exactly where I want to be."

"Only because Jeff made it sound as if I were on my deathbed."

"He said you asked for me—that's all."

"And I hadn't."

Sitting became intolerable, and she stood, pacing the floor with her arms gently wrapped around her to ward off the chill in his voice.

"As it is, you've wasted a trip. There won't be any deathbed scene. I was never in any danger from a gunshot wound. I had my appendix out."

Carla pivoted sharply and her mouth dropped open. "Your appendix out?"

"If you need proof, lift the sheet and see for yourself."

She ignored the heavy sarcasm lacing his voice. "Then why did Jeff—" What kind of fool game was Philip's friend playing anyway? Did he feel he needed to fabricate stories to convince her to come?

"That's exactly what I intend to find out."

Silence hovered over them like a heavy thundercloud.

"I don't mean to be rude, but I'm not exactly in the mood for company, Carla."

She'd thought he'd been shot and all the while it was his appendix. To her humiliation, she sniffled and her soft breath became a hiccuping sob. Frantically, she searched for her purse, needing to get out of the room before she humiliated herself further.

"Carla. Don't go," he groaned in frustration. "I didn't mean that. I'm sorry."

"That's all right," she mumbled shakily, wiping the tears from her pale cheeks. A kaleidoscope of emotions whirled through her—shock, relief, hurt, anger, joy. "I understand."

"This is exactly what I didn't want. If it had been up to me, you wouldn't even have known I was in the hospital. I don't want you worrying about me."

"You didn't even want me to know you were in the hospital?" Carla closed her eyes. She didn't want to think about the life they'd have if Philip insisted on shielding her from anything unpleasant. She wondered how he'd feel if the tables were turned. By heaven she was going to get Jeff for this. She'd arrived expecting something far worse and he'd let her believe it!

"I may be out of line here, but didn't you ask me to marry you not long ago?" she reminded him.

Philip looked at her blankly. "What's that got to do with anything?"

"Doesn't a wife or a fiancée or even the woman in your life have a right to know certain things?"

His hand covered his weary eyes. "Do you mind very much if we discuss this at another time? Go back to Seattle, Carla. I'll call you when I'm in a better frame of mine and we can discuss it then."

Placing four fingers at her temple, she executed a crisp military salute. "Aye aye, Comandant."

Carla couldn't tell whether the sound Philip made was a chuckle or a snort, and she didn't stay long enough in his room to find out.

Luckily, Jeff was due to arrive at the hospital within a half hour. Her anger mounted by the time Philip's partner arrived. The minute he appeared she stood, prepared for battle.

"That was a rotten trick you pulled," she declared with clenched teeth.

"Trick?" Jeff looked stunned. "I didn't pull any trick."

"You told me Philip had been shot."

Jeff looked all the more taken aback. "I didn't."

"You implied as much," she returned, barely managing to keep her voice even.

"How could you have thought he'd been shot? Especially since he was feeling so crummy during the canoe race. Saturday night someone suggested it could be his appendix and…" Jeff swallowed, looking chagrined. "That's right, you left early. Phil was feeling even crummier later and I think we all should have known what was wrong. Listen, I apologize, I thought you knew. You must have been frantic. I wouldn't have frightened you had—"

"It's all right," Carla accepted his apology with a wry grin. Obviously she had read more into his comments than he had intended. The misunderstanding hadn't been intentional.

"I'd better explain to Philip," Jeff said with a thoughtful look. "He's probably mad as hops."

"It's best to let the beast rest for now. If you want you can explain later."

One glance at Carla was apparently enough to convince him that Carla knew what she was talking about. The ride through Spokane seemed to take forever and when Jeff stopped at a traffic light, Carla couldn't hold back a giggle.

"What's so funny?" Jeff glanced at her curiously.

"I don't know…just my thoughts, I guess. I assumed that someone as wonderful as Philip would be a good patient. I thought he'd be the type of man to suffer silently…and he's terrible. Just terrible."

"Give him a day or two," Jeff advised good-humoredly. "He'll come around."

Philip's condominium was located in the heart of the
city near the Spokane River. "Here are the keys to his
car," Jeff said, handing them to her after unlocking the
front door. They stood just inside the entryway. "Bill
dropped it off on his way home tonight. Listen…" Jeff
paused and ran his hand along the side of his short-
cropped hair. "Sylvia called and said she was feeling
strange. I don't know what that means, but I think I
should head home. I have this irrational fear that the
baby is going to come into this world without me coach-
ing, and I'd hate to think that all those classes would go
to waste. Call if you need anything, all right?"

"Sure. Go on, and give Sylvia my best."

"I will. Thanks."

Jeff was out the door, and Carla turned to interrupt
Philip's orderly life even more by invading his home.
Maybe he was right; maybe she should take her things
and head back to Seattle. No, she wouldn't do that.
Things between them had to be settled now.

The first thing that caught Carla's attention was the
hand-carved marlin that she'd given Philip. He'd set it
on the fireplace mantel. A photo of them together in
Mexico sat on his dresser. Carla was smiling into the
camera as the wind whipped up her soft russet curls.
Philip's head was turned and his eyes were on her. There
was so much love in his expression that Carla breathed
a soft sigh as she examined the framed photo.

Her letters to him were stacked on the kitchen table.
Each one had been read so many times that the edges
had begun to curl. Carla took one look and recognized
again that there wasn't any man on earth who would
love her as much as Philip. And more important, there
would never be anyone she could love as much.

After a reassuring phone call to her parents, she took a long shower and slept fitfully.

She waited until noon the next day before venturing outside the condominium. Driving Philip's car to the hospital proved to be eventful. Twice she got lost, but with the friendly help of a local service-station attendant, she finally located the hospital.

A nurse on Philip's floor gave her a suspicious look as she walked down the wide corridor carrying a guitar.

One loud knock against his door was all the warning she gave.

"Carla."

She suspected it was relief she heard in his voice, but she didn't pause to question him. Instead she pulled out the chair beside his bed, sat at an angle on the cushion and strummed one discordant chord. With that she proceeded to serenade him in the only song she knew in Spanish.

He started to laugh but quickly grimaced and tried to contain his amusement. "Why are you singing to me the A, B, C's?"

"It's the only Spanish song I know all the way through. However, if you'd like to hear parts of 'Mary Had a Little Lamb,' I'll be happy to comply."

Extending a hand to her, he shook his head. "The only thing I want is you."

"That's a different tune than you were singing yesterday."

"Yesterday I was an unreasonable boor." He pulled her closer to his side. "I'm glad you're here. Today I promise to be a much better patient."

"Once we're married I suspect I'll have ways of helping you out of those irrational moods."

The room went quiet as Philip's eyes sought hers. "Once we're married."

"You did ask me, and you better not have changed your mind, because I've already given my two-week notice at the hospital."

"Carla." His gray eyes reflected an intensity she had rarely witnessed. "Do you mean it?"

"I've never been more serious in my life. But I won't have you holding out on me. If I'm going to be your wife, I expect you to trust me enough not to try to shield me from whatever comes our way. I'm stronger than I look, Philip Garrison."

"Far stronger," he agreed as his hand slipped around her waist. "You've already convinced me of that. I love you, Carla Walker—soon to be Carla Garrison."

Tenderness surged through her as she slipped her arms over his shoulders. "But not near soon enough," she said with a sigh of longing as her mouth eagerly sought his.

* * * * *

FOR ALL MY TOMORROWS

Prologue

The mournful sound of taps cut through the coarse gray afternoon. Lynn Danfort stood tall and proud before her husband's casket, refusing to release the emotion that clawed at her chest. Her two children were gathered close at her sides, as though she could hold on to them tightly enough to protect them from the reality of this day.

Seattle's police chief, Daniel Carmichael, assisted by Ryder Matthews, neatly folded the American flag that rested atop the polished casket and calmly presented it to Lynn. She tried to thank the police chief, but realized she couldn't speak. Even nodding was more of an effort than she could make.

When they'd finished, Pastor Teed spoke a few solemn words, and then slowly, in coordinated movements, Gary Danfort was lowered to his final resting place.

Lynn repressed a shudder as the first shovelful of dirt slammed against his casket. The sound reverberated in her ears, magnified a hundred times until she yearned to cover her head and scream out for them to stop. This was her husband…the father of her children…her best friend…and Gary Danfort deserved so much more than a cold blanket of Washington mud.

Shot in the line of duty. Pronounced dead at the scene. At first Lynn had refused to believe her husband was gone.

The thick dirt fell again, and Lynn believed.

The tightening in her chest worked its way up the constricting muscles of her throat and escaped on a sob as the shovel was handed in turn to the men and women who had so proudly served with Gary. The trembling increased as each dull thump echoed like a somber edict in her tortured mind.

Hope was gone.

Dreams destroyed.

Death the victor.

Tears welled like hot liquid in the corners of her eyes, her first for that day. She'd wanted to be strong—it was what Gary would have wanted—but now she let them fall. The moisture seared crooked paths down her ashen cheeks.

A voice violated her pain. "It's time to go."

"No."

"This way, Mrs. Danfort."

Again she shook her head. "Please. Not yet."

Her strength was depleted, and for the first time since she'd learned of Gary's death, she needed someone—someone she loved, someone who had loved Gary. She looked around for Ryder. Her friend. Gary's partner. Godfather to their children.

Her gaze scanned the crowd until she found him, standing in front of Chief Carmichael.

A protest swelled in her throat as she watched him

pull his badge from his wallet and place it in the police chief's palm.

Ryder turned to her then, his pain and grief as strong as her own. She could see that Chief Carmichael was trying to reason with him, but Ryder wasn't listening. His gaze reached over the crowd of mourners until it found Lynn. Their eyes met and locked.

Lynn pleaded with him not to leave her.

His gaze told her he must. Regret clouded the harsh features as his eyes shifted to Michelle and Jason, her children.

Then, silently, Ryder Matthews turned and walked away.

One

"Lynn, there's a call for you on line one."

"Thanks." She reached for her phone and pressed it against her shoulder, securing it with her ear. "Slender, Too, this is Lynn speaking."

"Mom?"

Lynn released a silent groan and rolled her eyes toward the ceiling. It wasn't even noon and this was the fifth phone call she'd received from the kids. "What is it, Michelle?"

"Jason ate the entire box of Cap'n Crunch cereal. I thought you'd want to know so you could take appropriate action."

"I didn't take it all." Jason's eight-year-old voice echoed from the upstairs extension. "Michelle ate some, too."

"I didn't."

"Did, too."

"Didn't."

"Michelle! Jason! I've got a business to run!"

"But he did, Mom, I swear it. I found the empty box stuffed in the bottom of the garbage. And we all know who put it there, so don't try to lie your way out of this one, Jason Danfort. And, Mom, while I've got you on the phone, I think you should have a serious discussion with Jason about his Super Heroes Club."

Lynn closed her eyes and prayed for patience. "Michelle, this conversation will have to wait until I'm through here. Where's Janice?"

It was the third week of June. School had been out for a grand total of five days, and already Michelle and Jason were at each other's throats. The high-school girl, whom Lynn was paying top dollar to look after the kids, had revealed all the maturity of an eleven-year-old, which was Michelle's age. One child responsible for two more. This wasn't working, and Lynn's options were limited.

"Janice is checking the garbage to see what else Jason's hiding in there."

"Mom, you can't expect me to live like this," her son interjected. "A man is a man. And a man's got to do what a man's got to do."

"Right," Lynn responded without thinking.

"You're agreeing with him?" Michelle's shrill voice echoed her outrage. "Mom, your son is stealing food and you seem to think it's perfectly all right."

"I'm going out on a mission," Jason cried in self-defense. "I could be gone three or four hours doing surveillance. I'll need nourishment, but if you're so concerned about your stupid cereal, I'll put it back."

"Can you put a hold on this war until I get home?" Lynn demanded of the two.

Silence.

Lynn mentally calculated a list of effective threats that had worked in the past. Regrettably her mind came up blank. She was a strong, effective businesswoman, but when it came to her children she was at a loss as to how to deal with them—especially in matters such as stolen Cap'n Crunch cereal.

"Lynn." Sharon Fremont, her assistant, stuck her head around the door. "Your aerobics class is ready and waiting."

"Listen, kids, I've got to go. *Please* don't fight and don't call me at work unless it's an emergency."

"But, Mom…"

"Mom!"

"I can't talk now—I've got a class waiting." Lynn checked her watch. "I'll be home by four. Now be good!"

"All right," Michelle muttered. "But I don't like it."

"Me, either. If I'm not home when you get here," Jason whispered into the phone, "you know where to find me."

"You think you're so smart, Jason Danfort," Michelle whined, "but I know your hiding place—I have for weeks."

"No, you don't."

"Yes, I do."

"*Kids*, please!"

"Sorry, Mom."

"Yeah, sorry, Mom."

Lynn replaced the phone. Michelle and Jason claimed they were sorry. Somehow she doubted that.

The house was suspiciously quiet when Lynn let herself in at three-forty-five that same afternoon.

"Michelle?"

Silence.

"Jason?"

More silence.

"Janice?"

"Oh, hi, Mrs. Danfort."

The fifteen-year-old appeared as if by magic, and every aspect of her peaches-and-cream complexion spelled guilt. The teenager rubbed her palms back and forth and presented a forced smile.

"Where are Michelle and Jason?" Lynn asked, and slipped the sweatband off her forehead. She hadn't taken time to shower, preferring to hurry home dressed in her turquoise spandex leotards and top, in an effort to deter yet another world war.

"They're both gone," Janice announced, her eyes avoiding Lynn's. "That's all right, isn't it?"

"It's fine."

"Oh, good."

Lynn reached for the mail, shuffling through the pile of bills and setting them back down on the counter unopened.

"Jason's with his Super Hero friends, and Michelle's over at Stephie's."

"That's fine. I'll see you tomorrow morning then."

"Sure," Janice said and was through the door before Lynn could figure out why she wore the look of a cat burglar caught with a bagful of goodies.

Mulling it over, Lynn traipsed over to the fridge and took out a cold soda—her carbinated drink-for-the-day. This was a family rule—no one drank more than one can a day, otherwise her children would go through a 12-pack by noon.

She sat, plopped her feet on the chair across the

table from her and took a sip, letting the cool liquid revive her.

"Mom," Michelle called, as she raced through the front door. She stopped abruptly when she found Lynn in the kitchen.

"Hi, sweetie," Lynn answered and smiled. "Did you ever solve the Cap'n Crunch caper?"

"Jason pulverized it into sand and poured the entire bag into his canteen." She raised her eyes toward the ceiling in mute testimony to what she thought about her brother's odd ways. "You've got to do something about him, Mother. That cereal was half mine, too, you know."

"I know…I'll talk to him."

"You say that, and then nothing ever happens. He should be punished. That boy has no sense, and you're not helping. He honestly thinks he's the Incredible Hulk. Any other mother would put a stop to it."

"Michelle, please, I'm doing the best I can. Wait until you're a mother…there are just some things you have to make judgment calls on." Lynn couldn't believe she'd said that. It was like an echo from the past, when she'd battled with her younger brother and her mother had said those identical words to her.

"At least let me decide Jason's punishment," Michelle cried. "I know that boy better than anyone. Let me give him what he deserves."

"Michelle…"

"Mom." The screen door burst open and Jason roared into the kitchen, dressed like his hero, his shoulders arched forward as he knotted his fists and puffed out his chest to dispay his muscles. He let loose with a scream that threatened to crack the walls.

Michelle plugged her ears and cast her mother a look that spoke volumes.

"Jason, please," Lynn pleaded, placing her fingertips to her temple. "If you're going save the world do it outside."

"Okay," he answered with a grin, and cheerfully lowered his weapon.

Her son was dressed in his camouflage pants and a grimy green sweatshirt. His face was smeared with green coloring. His knees were caked with mud, and he looked as if he'd battled long and hard all afternoon.

"So how's the war going?"

"We won."

"Naturally," Michelle said in a know-it-all voice that caused Jason to slowly turn in her direction, and gave her the evil eye.

"Not in the house," Lynn reminded him.

"Right," he answered slowly, baring his teeth at his sister.

Michelle placed her hand over her flat chest. "I'm shaking in my boots with pure terror at the thought of you coming to get me."

Jason's eyes narrowed into menacing slits. "You better do something about her, Mom, or she's going to suffer a slow, painful death."

"Jason, I don't like you talking like that."

"Answer me this," he cried with indignation. "Does Edward Norton have to put up with a big sister like this one?"

"You're not Edward Norton."

"Not yet," he said forcefully. "But someday I'm going to be."

Lynn prayed this was a stage her son was going

through because, like Michelle, she'd about had it with Jason's antics.

"When are we leaving for the picnic?" Michelle asked, glancing toward the bulletin board.

"Picnic?" Lynn echoed. "What picnic?"

"The one Dad's ol' police buddies invited us to—the one with the notice on the bulletin board."

Lynn dropped her feet and whirled around to check her calendar. "Is today the twentieth?"

Both Michelle and Jason nodded.

"Oh, great," Lynn muttered. "I'm supposed to bring potato salad."

"Do what you always do," Jason suggested. "Buy it at the deli. Why should today be any different?"

Lynn reached for her drink and hurried toward the stairs, taking them two at a time. She stripped off her top and reached blindly toward the shower dial when she noted the bathroom counter. Something stopped her, but she didn't know what. Something wasn't quite right.

In a flash, she recognized what was different. Reaching for a towel to cover her torso, she stormed out of the bedroom. "Michelle. Jason. Front and center—pronto."

Both kids came racing into her bedroom.

"All right," she said, her voice wobbling, "which one of you got into my makeup?" Her gaze narrowed, and what she saw on her son's face answered her own question. "Jason...that's my green eye shadow all over your face! My *expensive* green eye shadow."

"Mom, your shower's running," Jason said, pointing in that direction. "You're wasting precious liquid, and you always say how we should conserve water. Remember the drought a couple of years ago—you wouldn't want to start another one, would you?"

"He used my eye shadow," Lynn announced to her daughter, while she returned to the bathroom to turn off the shower. The day had started off badly. First Michelle and Jason had found every excuse known to mankind to call her at the office, and now this!

"If you look real close, you'll note the black under his eyes looks a lot like *your* eye liner, too," Michelle said once Lynn reentered the room.

"My eyeliner, too?"

A look of betrayal crossed Jason's young features. "Okay, Michelle, you asked for this. I wasn't going to tell, but now you're forcing my hand."

Michelle stiffened. "You wouldn't dare," she whispered.

Jason squared his shoulders. "Michelle and Janice were in your room this morning, Mom. I felt it was my duty to find out what they were doing—"

"Jason…" Michelle's frail voice rose an octave, pleading.

"They were trying on your bras. The real fancy lace ones."

"Oh, my goodness." Lynn sank onto the foot of her bed. Nothing was sacred anymore. Not her makeup. Not her underwear. Nothing. And worse, she was paying a teenage neighbor girl to snoop through her drawers.

"Mom," Michelle moaned. "I need a real bra…you haven't seemed to notice, but I'm filling out my training one." She paused and turned to face her traitor brother. "Get out of here, Jason. This is woman talk."

"Trust me, Mom, she doesn't need anything. She's as flat as—"

"Jason!" Lynn and Michelle cried simultaneously.

He jerked up both hands. "All right, all right. I'm out

of here. I felt you needed to know the truth…I was only doing my duty as your son and as Michelle's brother."

Lynn's fingers were trembling as she ran them through her thick brown hair. She reached behind her head and released the clip that held her hair neatly in place.

"You and Janice aren't allowed in my bedroom, young lady," she said. "You know that."

Michelle buried her chin in her shoulder blade, looking miserable.

"I can't have you sorting through my things while I'm at work."

"I know…I'm sorry," Michelle murmured, still not looking at her mother. "We didn't mean to try them on, but they looked so pretty and Janice said you'd never know, and I didn't think it would hurt until Jason—"

"This just isn't working," Lynn whispered. "You and Jason are constantly bickering. Janice is fifteen, going on ten. I can't stop running my business just because you kids are out of school. It may be summer, but we still have to eat!"

"It won't happen again," Michelle promised. "I'm really sorry."

"I know, honey." But that didn't change things. Janice was too immature to be watching Michelle and Jason, and the children were too young to stay on their own.

Michelle straightened her shoulders. "What are you going to do to Jason for getting into your makeup? I know I shouldn't have tried on your bras, but Jason shouldn't have gotten into your things, either."

"I don't know yet," Lynn answered.

"Hey, are we going to the picnic or not?" Jason demanded from the other side of the bedroom door.

"He was listening," Michelle whispered with righteous indignation. "I bet you anything, he had his ear to the door and the minute we started talking about him, he broke in."

"We're going to be late for the picnic if you two don't stop this," Lynn commented, eager to change the subject.

She hated to think what Michelle and Jason would do once they learned she was putting them in a day-care center. They were going to hate it, but she didn't have a choice.

After what had happened today, her mind was made up.

Two

Toting the carton of potato salad in one hand, and with a blanket tucked under the other, Jason marched across the park lawn with crisp military precision. With his head held high and proud, he angled toward the assigned picnic area at Green Lake. Lynn and Michelle, holding the handles of the picnic basket between them, followed.

Lynn's smile was forced as she raised a hand to greet the men and women who had once worked with her husband. She remained good friends with several of the other wives on the force, although there were lots of new faces these days.

"I'm so pleased you could make it," Toni Morris called out, walking toward Lynn. "It's good to see you, stranger!"

Lynn let go of the basket and hugged her friend, who was a former policewoman. She didn't see nearly enough of Toni these days and treasured the few times they could be together. "It's good to be here."

"How's everything?"

Lynn knew that pert and practical Toni would easily see through a false smile and a cheerful facade. This summer had gotten off to a rotten start, and she was troubled. With the other police wives, she could grin and nod and claim her life was a bed of rose petals and because they wanted to believe that, they wouldn't question her.

But not Toni, who had married an officer of the law herself and who was well aware of life on both sides of the coin.

"Life's so-so," Lynn answered honestly. Afternoons like this one made her feel she'd failed as a mother. Like so many other women, she wore two hats—one for work and another at home. Michelle and Jason came first in her life, but she *had* to earn a living. What Slender, Too, didn't drain from her energy tank, the kids did. She felt stretched to the limit, and there was only so much elastic in her.

Toni slipped her arm around Lynn's waist, glanced in Michelle's direction and pointed toward a picnic table with a red checked cloth spread across the top. "Michelle, go ahead and set your stuff next to mine. Kelly's getting her feet wet at the lake. Go on down and surprise her—she's dying to see you."

"Oh, good! Wait until she sees my hair, she's going to flip," Michelle announced, and raced like a speeding freight train, taking the basket with her.

"Okay," Toni murmured, looking thoughtful. "Tell me what's wrong?"

For lack of a more precise answer, Lynn shrugged. "Nothing's working out this summer the way I hoped it would. Michelle and Jason are constantly bickering. The babysitter is snooping through my drawers. Jason's into this Super Hero stage and is slowly driving me bananas. He doesn't seem to make the connection between what happened to Gary and the war games he plays with his friends."

"He doesn't," Toni assured her. "He's a perfectly normal eight-year-old, and this thing with the war games is just a stage he's going through. Both Michelle and Jason are perfectly normal kids."

"I don't know if they'll ever get used to me working. I swear they use every excuse in the book to phone me at work. Michelle wanted me to know Jason used the ink up in my felt-tip pen. And Jason was convinced Michelle hid his army canteen from him. And then there was a fiasco over the Cap'n Crunch cereal. Honestly, Toni, how can I be expected to supervise them and run a business, too?"

Toni's look was sympathetic.

"It's as if they feel the need to compete for my attention," Lynn added. "I don't know what to do anymore."

"Who's watching them this summer?"

"A neighbor girl, and I think that's a major part of the problem. Michelle's at that transitional age when she's too young to stay by herself and yet resentful of having someone look after her. I'd hoped to solve that by hiring a neighborhood girl, but it simply isn't working."

"Can you find someone else?"

Lynn shrugged again. "At this late date? I doubt it. And the programs at the 'Y' filled up so fast it made my head spin. Parents register months in advance for summer day care."

Toni studied her a moment longer. "It's more than problems with the kids and summer vacation, though, isn't it?"

Lynn had to stop and think about that. Toni was right—she usually was. For the past several months

Lynn had been experiencing a restlessness that came from the deepest part of her inner self. She hadn't been sleeping well and often awoke feeling depressed and out of sorts, without understanding why.

"You're not taking care of yourself," Toni said, after a thoughtful moment.

Lynn blinked, not sure she understood her friend. She'd never been more physically fit—in fact she looked as good, if not better, than she had as a twenty-year-old bride. Her hair needed to be cut, but finding the time was the biggest hangup there.

"You can't always be the perfect mother *and* an astute businesswoman," Toni went on to say. "You need time to be you."

"Me?" Lynn repeated. She wasn't exactly sure who *she* was anymore. There'd been a time when her role in life had been clearly defined, but not anymore. Since Gary had died, she viewed herself as a quick-change artist who leaped through hoops—some small, others large—in an effort to make it to the end of the day or the end of the week. She felt as if she'd been cast adrift in a lifeboat and she was the only one strong enough to man the oars.

"Be good to yourself," Toni continued. "Splurge. Take a whole day and relax at the beach or shop to your heart's content."

"Good idea," Lynn whispered, feeling a nearly overwhelming urge to cry. "I'll do exactly that the next time I find the time."

"When did you last go out on a date?"

"I haven't in months, but don't try to convince me that's the problem," Lynn said, her voice sharp and strong. "It's a jungle out there, with lots of lions and tigers roaming about, After my last hot date with a forty-year-old mechanic who lives with his mother, I decided I'd let Mr. Right find me. I'm done with the dating scene. Finished. Kaput."

"The mechanic was a tiger?" Toni gave her a look that suggested therapy was sure to help.

Lynn sighed. "Not exactly. He was more of a wart-hog."

"And exactly what type of beast interests you? A cheetah? Gorilla?"

"Tarzan interests me," Lynn said, and laughed. Soon Toni's chuckles mingled with her own.

"Come on now, Lynn, you're not really serious about refusing to date anymore? You're too young to resign yourself to life alone."

"I'm not interested in remarrying—at least not for now." There'd been a time, albeit short, when Lynn had seriously considered re-marrying and making a new life for the kids and herself. She hadn't expected Prince Charming to come charging into her living room atop a white stallion, but she hadn't been prepared for all the court jesters, either. Soon after she'd reentered the dating world, she'd discovered how shockingly naive she was and exited with a speed that convinced her friends she hadn't tried nearly hard enough. Her friends, however, were married or involved in satisfying relationships. They weren't the ones forced to mingle with warthogs and court jesters.

"There's something you should know," Toni announced, tossing a glance over her shoulder.

"Don't tell me you've got someone here you want me to meet. Toni, please, don't do that to me."

"No, not that."

"What, then?"

"Someone's here all right, but I didn't bring him."

"Who?" Her friend had seldom looked more serious. Lynn had been aware the entire time they were talking how Toni had kept her on the outskirts of the group. Sensing that whatever her friend had to say was important, Lynn met her look, feeling Toni's anxiety.

"Ryder Matthews stopped by," Toni announced. "In fact, he's here now."

"Ryder," Lynn echoed, her voice little more than a hoarse whisper. Emotion circled her like smoke rising from a campfire, twirling around her, choking off a reply. Lynn wasn't exactly sure what she felt. Relief mostly, she decided, but that was quickly followed by resentment that flared, then vanished as fast as it came. Ryder had turned his back and walked away from her— literally and figuratively. A week after Gary's funeral a letter with a Boston postmark had arrived from Ryder. He'd told her he'd had to leave the force, and asked her forgiveness for leaving her and the kids when they needed him most. He promised her that if she were ever to need anything, all she had to do was let him know and he would be there. Lynn didn't doubt his word, but she never asked—and Ryder had never come. He promised to keep in touch, and true to his word, he'd faithfully remembered Michelle and Jason on their birthdays and Christmas, but he never directly wrote Lynn again.

And now Ryder was back. Ryder Matthews. She loved him like a brother, but she couldn't help resenting the way he'd abandoned her. She didn't want to have anything to do with him, but she'd needed him at one time and then had gone about proving exactly the opposite. Her thoughts were as knotted and twisted as pine wood.

"Are you going to be all right?" Toni asked.

"Sure. Why shouldn't I be?" But she wasn't. Lynn felt as though the world had been briefly knocked off its axis. She squared her shoulders and stiffened her spine, mentally and physically preparing for whatever was to follow. She'd waited a long time to talk to Ryder and now she hadn't a clue about what she would say.

"Apparently he just moved back to Seattle," Toni added.

Lynn nodded, not knowing how else to respond.

"He's an attorney now and recently joined some prestigious uptown law firm. He kept in touch with several of the guys, but his return surprised everyone."

Lynn knew that Ryder had been accepted into law school following graduation from college but had grown restless after the first year, eager to make a more concrete contribution to society. After he dropped out, he'd applied and was accepted into the police academy, where he'd met Gary.

"Well," Toni urged her. "Say something."

"What's there to say?"

"I don't know," Toni admitted. "But every time Joe's talked to him the last couple of years, all he does is ask about you and the kids."

"Wh-what did he want to know?"

"How you were. How the kids were doing. That sort of thing. He may have stayed away from you, but I know for a fact that you were never far from his thoughts."

"He could have asked me himself."

"Yes, he could have," Toni agreed. "I'm sure he's

going to want to later. I just felt you should know he's here so it won't come as a shock."

"I appreciate that," Lynn said, although she wasn't sure there was anything to say to Ryder. There had been once, but not now.

Ryder Matthews spotted Jason first. Gary and Lynn's son had sprouted like a weed, and just catching a glimpse of the boy produced an involuntary smile. He looked like a miniature commando, with his face painted...was that green? He was dressed in fatigues with a green sweatband strapped across his forehead as though he planned to stalk through a jungle at any minute.

Ryder's gaze left the youth to scan the picnic area. He located Michelle next. The preteen was standing by the lake, talking to another girl. She'd changed, too. The girlish features had disappeared, and the promise of a special beauty shone from her sweet oval face. Her hair was shorter now, the pigtails and bright ribbons replaced with carefully styled curls. The eleven-year-old was several inches taller, too, as was Jason. Ryder smiled, pleased with the changes he noticed in them both.

A couple of minutes later, he allowed his gaze to search for Lynn. Gary's Lynn...*his* Lynn. When he found her, talking to Toni Morris in the picnic area, a rush of air left his lungs as though someone had playfully punched him in the stomach. She was everything he remembered and more. Only heaven knew how he'd managed to stay away from her so long. He'd never forgotten her face, or the athletic grace with which she moved. The sunlight had always seemed to bounce off her hair, and the one way he could think to describe the husky sound of her voice was smoky molasses. He recognized every line of her creamy smooth face, which was dominated by high cheekbones, a stubborn chin and that wide, soft mouth.

Lynn's hair was much longer now, the thick dark length woven in a single braid that gently fell against her back. She wore fashionable white shorts and a pink tank top that showed off her golden tan. She carried herself with such pride and grace that it humbled him just studying her. Ryder watched as she smiled and waved to another friend, while standing with Toni. She paused and glanced in his direction. Although Ryder was fairly certain she hadn't seen him, he felt the physical impact of her smile halfway across the park. He'd always found Lynn attractive, had admired her from the first, but the years had matured her elegant beauty.

Just looking at her caused his heart to swell with pride. Everything he'd learned about her revealed an inner fortitude. She was strong, stronger than he'd realized. She'd walked through the valley in the shadow of grief and destruction and come out the other side, confident and strong.

Ryder loved her for it.

The need to talk to her burned in his chest. There was so much that had to be said, so much he needed to explain. It had taken him three long years to surface from the tragedy of Gary's death. Three years to come to grips with himself.

For the first year, he'd submerged himself in his classes, preferring to bury his head in books and study until all hours of the night. Anything but sleep, because sleep brought with it the nightmare he longed to forget. Law school had given him a purpose and an excuse.

There wasn't time to think, and for the next twelve months school anesthetized him from painful memories he longed to forget.

The second year had been much the same, until the anniversary of Gary's death had arrived. He hadn't been able to sleep that night, playing back the details in his mind over and over again until his heart had started pounding so violently he could hardly breathe. He knew then that he would have to deal with the emotions surrounding his partner's death, or they would haunt him for the rest of his life unless he sought professional help. That second year had been the most draining; it had been the time he'd dealt with his feelings for Gary and, perhaps even more importantly, his feelings for Lynn.

It happened unexpectedly, when he was the least prepared to deal with it, following a conversation with Joe Morris, Toni's husband. Joe had told Ryder that Lynn had started to date a mutual friend, Alex Morrissey. At first, Ryder was pleased because he longed for Lynn to find a new life, but he wasn't thrilled with her choice of men. Lynn could do better than Alex. He was relieved when he called Joe a few weeks later and found out that Lynn had stopped seeing Alex but had accepted a date with Burt, another mutual friend. But Ryder didn't like Burt any better—he was downright irritated about the whole matter. Burt would make a terrible stepfather and Alex wouldn't be much better. In fact, Ryder couldn't think of a single man worthy of Lynn and Michelle and Jason.

Then it came to him so sharply that he was left stunned by the shock. He was in love with Lynn and had been for years. When Gary was alive, the three of them had been inseparable—the very best of friends.

He hadn't realized his feelings for her then, hadn't been honest enough with himself to have been able to face it.

It had been an old joke between them, the way Ryder had drifted in and out of relationships. Little wonder! Every woman he ever dated simply couldn't compare to Lynn. He may have been close to acknowledging what was happening, because he'd started thinking about returning to law school long before Gary's death. But after the tragedy, his love for Lynn had been so repressed it had taken two years for him to even recognize his feelings for her.

Knowing what he did, the third and final year of law school had been sheer hell. Ryder's greatest fear was that Lynn would find someone to love and remarry before he could get back to her.

Now he was back, ready to build bridges with the past, ready to start life again. Everything hinged on Lynn. Not a day went by that he didn't think about her and the children. Not a night passed that he didn't plan their reunion.

For the first time in years, Ryder felt a strong urge to reach for a cigarette. Years of habit directed his hand to his empty shirt pocket. A momentary sense of surprise was followed by a chagrined pat against his chest. He'd given up the habit before joining the force, and that had been a lifetime ago. How odd that he would feel the need for a smoke now, after all these years.

"Toni," Lynn asked without looking up from the table where Michelle had set their picnic basket. "Have you seen Jason? He disappeared the minute we arrived." She sliced a pickle in half and added it to the pile on the plate. "Knowing him, he's probably doing surveillance, checking out the area for enemy agents." She paused and licked the juice from her fingertip, and reached for another dill pickle. It was then that she realized she was talking to thin air. Toni was standing across the picnic area from her.

"Has he found any yet?"

The strong male voice froze her fingers, and slowly Lynn raised her eyes to meet Ryder Matthews. "Found any?" she asked, hardly able to speak. Just seeing him again brought a throb of excitement.

"Enemy agents?" Ryder asked.

She shook her head. The weight of his gaze held her prisoner. Instinct told her to go back to the task at hand, act nonchalant, friendly. "Hello, Ryder," she managed finally when her heart had righted itself. "It's good to see you."

"Hello, Lynn." His voice was warm and husky. It felt like a warm blanket wrapped around her shoulders on a cold winter night.

"Toni mentioned that she saw you earlier," she said, taking pains to keep her voice even.

"I thought she might have." He stepped closer to the picnic table.

"Want a pickle?" It seemed crazy that she hadn't seen Ryder in three years and all she could think to do was offer him something to eat.

"No, thanks."

Her fingers trembled slightly and she slipped the knife through the cucumber and added the slices to the plate. "She also said she'd heard something about you passing the bar."

"She heard right."

"Then congratulations are in order." Once more

she struggled to keep her voice and emotions on an even keel.

"Lynn…" He paused and rubbed the back of his neck as if weighing his words. "It's time we talked," he said slowly, thoughtfully.

The silence that followed screamed at her. She expelled her breath and dropped her hands to the table. "That isn't really necessary. I know why you're here."

Three

"You know why I'm here?" Ryder echoed, his frown darkening.

Lynn closed her eyes and nodded. She'd known almost immediately why Ryder had left her alone the day of the funeral. She also knew why he'd found it essential to resign from the police force. Seeing him confirmed it. Even the most casual study of his features revealed that the years had weighed heavily upon him. Although they were close to the same age, Ryder looked several years older. She'd forgotten how tall he was—well over six feet, with wide shoulders and a powerful torso. His hair was as dark as his eyes, and his features had a vividness that drew her gaze to his face as effectively as a puppet's string. A soft smile touched her mouth as she pictured him standing in front of the jury box delivering the final argument to an important case. She was pleased with the image that formed in her mind. Ryder would do well as an attorney, but then Ryder Matthews was the type of man who would succeed at whatever he set out to accomplish.

When Toni had announced Ryder was at the picnic,

Lynn's feelings had been ambivalent. Her instinct had been to lash out at him, hurt him the same way he'd hurt her, but she realized now how senseless and immature such thoughts were. She couldn't do that. Ryder had suffered, too, perhaps even more than she had. He hadn't left her because he'd wanted to—he'd gone because the pain had been too overwhelming to allow him to stay. Law school had just been a convenient excuse.

"Probably more important," Lynn told him, smiling sadly, her heart aching for them both, "I know why you went away."

"Lynn, listen—"

"Please, this isn't necessary." Her long nails pressed against the underside of the picnic table as she leaned her weight against it. "You've blamed yourself, haven't you? All these years you've carried the guilt of what happened to Gary."

Ryder didn't answer her, but pain flashed in and out of his eyes like a flickering light until he regained control.

"Don't. Gary loved his job. It was his life—what he was meant to do. He knew the risks, accepted them, thrived on them. I knew them, too." She had to keep talking, had to say what needed to be said before she succumbed to the emotion welling inside her throat and choked off her voice. Ryder had lived with the regrets and the guilt long enough; it was time for her to release him so he could make peace with himself. It was the reason he'd come to her, and she could do nothing less for the man she'd once considered family.

Ryder looked away and then slowly shook his head. "I was the one who told him to walk around the back of that house. It was my decision, my choice, I—"

"You couldn't have known," she said, cutting him off. "No one could possibly have guessed. It wasn't your fault—it wasn't anyone's fault. It happened. I'm sorry, you're sorry. The entire Seattle Police Department is sorry, but that isn't going to bring Gary back."

Time had done little to erase the memory of the tragic incident that had led up to her husband's death. Everything had been so routine, so mundane. Gary and Ryder had been called to investigate the report of a suspected prowler. The two men had arrived on the scene and split up. Ryder went to the left, Gary to the right. A crazed drug addict, desperate for another fix, had been waiting. He panicked when Gary stumbled upon him, and frantic, the addict had turned and quickly discharged his weapon. A wild shot had gone through Gary's head, killing him instantly.

"It should have been me." Ryder's words were harsh and ground out, each one a breathless rasp.

"No," she countered. "I can't blame you, and I know in my heart that if Gary were standing here right now, he wouldn't fault you, either."

"But—"

"How he loved working with you." Her voice cracked and she bit into her lower lip until she'd composed herself enough to continue. "The best years he had on the force were the ones spent as your partner. The two of you were more than fellow officers, you were friends. Good friends. Gary loved his job because you were such a big part of it."

Ryder lowered himself onto the bench beside the picnic table, leaned forward to brace his elbows against his knees and clasped his hands. "He trusted me, and I let him down."

"You trusted him, too. It wasn't you who fired that gun. It wasn't you who turned on him. Fate did, and it's time you accepted that. I have. There's no bitterness left in me. I couldn't go on—couldn't be a good mother, if my life were marked with resentments."

Ryder was silent for so long that Lynn wondered what he was thinking. His brow was creased in a thick frown, his eyes dark and unreadable. He held himself so completely still that she feared he'd stopped breathing.

"We should have had this discussion long before now," he murmured.

"Yes, we should have," Lynn returned. "But you've corrected that. You're free now, Ryder, truly free. Nothing's going to hold you back any longer—your whole life is about to start again. It's your time to soar."

Slowly he rose to his feet, his frown intact. He studied her closely, as though he didn't know how to respond to her.

"I wish you the best, Ryder. You're going to do well as an attorney. I know it—I can feel it in my blood." She felt the urge to hug him but suppressed it. Instead she made busywork around the picnic table. "It really was good to see you again." She could feel the weight of his eyes on her, demanding that she look at him.

"I'm back now," he said. "I intend to stay."

"I…heard that. I'm happy for you and proud of everything you've managed to accomplish." She lifted the container of potato salad Jason had carried from the car and set it in the middle of the picnic table.

"I'd like to see you again."

Lynn fiddled with the paper napkins. "I suppose that will be inevitable. The precinct tries to include the children and me in their social functions. We attend when we can. I imagine you'll receive the same invitations."

"I didn't mean that way. I want to take you to dinner, spend time getting reacquainted...date."

Lynn's gaze, which she'd so carefully trained on the checkered tablecloth, shot upward. She was sure she'd heard him incorrectly. Was Ryder talking about a date? It would be like having dinner with her own brother. He couldn't have surprised her more had he suggested they climb a tree and pound their chests like apes. She opened her mouth, then closed it again when no fleeting words of wisdom surfaced to rescue her. In addition to everything else, Lynn was well aware of Ryder's dating habits. He never went out with any woman for long. It used to be a big joke between her and Gary how Ryder used to drift from one relationship to another. The longest she could ever remember him dating one woman was a couple of months.

"I'd like to gain back that closeness we once shared," he elaborated.

"We already know each other, in some ways probably better than we know ourselves."

"And there are ways we haven't even begun to explore."

Lynn watched as his gaze gently fell to her lips. They stood so close that she could see gold flecks in his dark irises. Doubt was there and mingled with another emotion she couldn't identify. The desire to ease his pain welled inside her. She longed to wrap her arms around him and absorb the hurt and let him soak up hers. Once more she resisted, attributing these strange feelings to the closeness they'd once shared.

"Well?" he asked, though not impatiently. "Can I pick you up tomorrow night for dinner?"

She shook her head. "I'm flattered, Ryder, but no."

"No?" he echoed, surprised.

"I could give you any number of reasons, but the truth of the matter is I simply don't have much time for a social life right now. I bought a business, and the kids keep me hopping, and frankly, I don't think it would be a good idea for us to form that kind of friendship—there are too many ghosts."

"Because of Gary?" he asked. "Or is it because I walked away from you?"

"Yes...no...oh, heavens, I don't know." She glanced at her watch and was shocked to see that her hand was trembling. "I have to round up the kids now, so if you'll excuse me."

His eyes narrowed, and Lynn could see that he was debating on whether or not he should argue with her. Apparently he'd decided against it, and Lynn was grateful. Instead he reached out and gently touched the side of her face. A warmth radiated from his light caress, and Lynn blinked, having difficulty sorting through the sensations that bolted through her. Her stomach muscles constricted, and her heart shot into her throat. A brother shouldn't make her feel this way. A lover maybe, but not a brother. Something was wrong with her, terribly wrong.

"I want you to think about it." He dropped his hand and removed a business card from his wallet. "Give me a call when you change your mind...or if you need anything. I'm here for you now."

Lynn picked up the card and read his name and

phone number, searching the words as though they could reveal what was happening to her.

"I mean it, Lynn."

For the past year, Ryder had planned this first meeting with Lynn, going over and over it in his mind, practicing what he was going to say until he'd memorized each line, each bit of dialogue. Yet nothing had gone as he'd planned, nothing had happened the way he'd hoped. Lynn had assumed he'd been crippled by guilt and that was what had kept him away all these years. Until she started to speak, Ryder hadn't realized how many unresolved feelings he still harbored for his late partner.

Everything had been so clear in his own mind. He knew what he wanted and knew what he had to do in order to get it. It shouldn't come as any big surprise that it wasn't going to be easy to escape the ghosts from the past. But then, Ryder realized, obtaining anything of value rarely came without effort.

He was so deep in thought that he didn't notice the boy who stood in front of him until the lad spoke. The dark brown eyes studying Ryder were wide and serious.

"You're Uncle Ryder, aren't you?"

Ryder was astonished, Jason hardly seemed old enough to remember him.

"My mom has a picture of you and my dad on the fireplace," Jason explained, before Ryder could question him. "You send me something for my birthday every year and Christmas, too. You buy real good gifts. I wanted to send you a list last year, but Mom wouldn't let me."

Grinning, Ryder asked, "So you recognized me from my picture?"

Jason nodded. "Except you've got a different color of hair on the side of your head now."

Ryder smiled at that. "I'm getting old."

"You used to be my dad's best friend, didn't you?"

"We were partners."

"Mom told me that, too." Jason paused and removed a canteen from his belt loop. With a good deal of ceremony, the eight-year-old opened the lid and poured a granulated pink-and-wheat-colored substance into the palm of his hand. When he'd finished, he lifted the canteen to Ryder in silent invitation. Without knowing what it was that Jason was eating, Ryder held out his open palm. When Jason had finished, Ryder sampled the mixture and decided that whatever it was, it didn't taste bad.

"It's cereal," Jason explained. He was silent for a moment, frowned and then asked, "Do you have any older sisters?"

"One."

"Yeah, me, too. They can be a real pain, can't they?"

"At times." Ryder finished licking up the last of the crumbs, then brushed his hands free of the granules. "But trust me, Jason, girls have a way of improving with age."

"That's what my grandpa says, but personally I can't see it. The Incredible Hulk doesn't have anything to do with them, except to save their lives."

"Your dad saved mine once."

Jason's eyes brightened. "My dad saved your life? Really?"

Ryder nodded, regretting bringing up the subject of Gary, but it was too late now. "More than once actually."

"Can you tell me about my dad? Mom talks about

him and you a lot—or at least she used to before she bought Slender, Too. She told me she doesn't want me to forget him, but to tell you the truth, I hardly remember anything about him, even when I try real hard. My mom talks to me about the mushy things he used to do, like getting her roses on their anniversary, but she never talks about the good stuff."

Now that he'd fallen into the trap there wasn't anything to do but continue. Jason was hungry for information about his father, and it would be unfair to cheat the boy. "Gary Danfort was a special kind of man."

"Tell me about how he saved your life."

"Sure," Ryder answered and chuckled, then he talked nonstop for thirty minutes, relaying story after story about his exploits with Gary Danfort. They both laughed a couple of times and Ryder was surprised by how good he felt. In fact, he'd never missed Gary more than he did that minute, talking to the other man's eight-year-old son. Ryder expected the kind of raw emotional pain that came when he thought of his former partner, but instead he experienced a cleansing of sorts that would have been difficult to put into words.

When he'd finished, Jason's wide brows knit together, forming a ledge over his deep brown eyes. He looked as if his eager mind had soaked in every word, like a dry sponge sipping up spilled water.

"Mom told me he was a hero," Jason commented, when Ryder had finished, "but I never knew exactly what he did."

"You're going to be just like him someday," Ryder told the youth, and was rewarded with the widest grin he'd ever seen.

"The man who killed my dad is in prison," Jason

added, unexpectedly, "but Mom said I should try not to hate him because the only person that would end up hurting is me."

Ryder wished he could be as generous in spirit. "Your mother is a wise woman."

"She's hardly home anymore the way she used to be," Jason added, and released an elongated sigh. "She bought a business last year and it takes up all her time. She's only home afternoons and nights now, and when she is, she's pooped."

Ryder frowned. He remembered when he'd heard about Lynn buying the franchise, and thought it would be good for her. "What does she do there?" He assumed she'd taken over the management, but not an actual teaching position.

"She makes fat ladies skinny."

"I see." Once more Ryder was forced to swallow a chuckle. "And how does she manage that?"

Jason pointed a finger at the sky and vigorously shook it three times. "Exercise. Exercise. Exercise."

Unable to hold it inside any longer, Ryder laughed aloud.

"It's not really funny," Jason said. "These ladies are serious and so is Mom."

"It's not that, son."

Faintly, in the distance, Ryder heard Lynn calling Jason's name. The youngster perked up immediately. "I've got to go. I bet it's time to eat. Are you going to sit with us? Mom forgot all about the picnic until Michelle reminded her. We were supposed to bring potato salad, but Mom picked some up at the deli. It's not as good as what she usually makes, but it tastes okay. We brought along hot dogs and mustard and pickles my Grandma put up last summer and a bunch of other stuff, too. You don't have to worry about not bringing any food because we've got plenty. You can stay, can't you?"

Four

"I don't like this one bit," Jason muttered from the back eat of the five-year-old Honda Civic.

"To be honest, I'm not overly pleased myself," Lynn returned, tightening her grip on the steering wheel. Jason was so outraged at the prospect of spending his summer with a bunch of preschoolers that he'd refused to be in the front seat with her. But where her son chose to sit was the least of Lynn's worries.

"I'm too old to be in a day-care center."

"You're too young to stay by yourself."

"Then how come Michelle gets to stay with the Morrises?"

"We've been over this a hundred times, Jason. Michelle is staying with Mrs. Morris until I can find someplace permanent for her."

"What's the matter with Janice? She may be a little ditzy, but she was all right."

"How many times do I have to remind you that I can't trust the three of you alone together? You know why as well as I do."

"But, Mom, I can handle Janice."

"That's the problem!"

"Why can't I stay with Brad?"

"His mom works, too."

"But why can't I go where he goes?"

"I tried to get you into the day camp, but it's full. Your name's on a waiting list, and as soon as there's an opening you can switch over there."

"I can't believe you're doing this to me," Jason muttered disparagingly. He crossed his arms over his chest and sulked.

"Jason, I'm your mother. Trust me, I don't like it any better than you, but there doesn't seem to be any other solution. Maybe later in the summer a better idea will present itself, but for now, you're going to the Peter Pan Day-care Center."

"The Peter Pan Day-care Center?" Jason cried and bounced his head against the back of the seat. "I suppose you want me to call the teacher Tinker Bell."

"Don't be cute."

"If Dad were here, this wouldn't be happening."

Jason might as well have punched her in the stomach; his words had the same effect. The pain rippled out from her abdomen, each circle growing wider and more encompassing until the ache reached her heart and centered its strength there. Since Jason had met Ryder, he'd used every opportunity to bring up his father—and Ryder. But using Gary against her was unfair.

"Well your father *isn't* here," Lynn returned sternly, "and I've got to do what I think is best."

"Putting me in with a bunch of little kids is the best thing for me?" Jason cried, his voice filled with righteous indignation. "I'm not a baby anymore, Mom."

"Third grade isn't exactly high school."

"I can't believe my own mother is doing this to me," her son grumbled, sounding as though she'd turned traitor on him and was selling him into a life of slavery.

"Will you stop laying on the guilt," Lynn cried. "I feel bad enough as it is."

"If you felt that bad, you'd find a place with a different name. I bet Edward Norton's mother would never have done anything like this to him."

"Jason!"

"Peter Pan, Mom?"

"Think positive…you could teach the other boys your Super Hero games."

"Right," he said, but his voice lacked any enthusiasm.

After Lynn had left a tight-mouthed Jason at the day-care center, she drove to her salon. This last week hadn't been her best. If matters had been shaky before the precinct picnic, they were worse now. One of her instructors had quit, leaving Lynn to fill in until a replacement could be hired and trained. The night before she hadn't gotten home until after six and both kids were tired, hungry and cranky—an unpleasant combination. If that wasn't bad enough, Jason had been bringing up Ryder's name every afternoon like clockwork until Lynn was thoroughly sick of hearing about the man. She had trouble enough dismissing Ryder from her mind without Jason constantly talking about him. He repeated word for word what Ryder had told him about his father and the reason Ryder couldn't stay and eat with them the day of the picnic.

Lynn was smart enough to realize that it wasn't Jason's chatter that disturbed her. It was the fact that her son mentioned Ryder's name in such a reverent whisper, as though he were speaking of the Incredible Hulk himself. Lynn's feelings toward Ryder were still so muddled and unclear, she wasn't sure she could identify them. Even if she could, there wasn't time to do anything about them. What had really confused her was his dinner invitation. It had been more than a surprise—it had been a shock. As much of a jolt as seeing him again had been. She felt girlish and immature and uncertain of everything. After Gary's death, she'd faltered for a while, and staggered under the weight of shock and grief. It had taken her a long while to root herself once more, and find purpose for her and the children. But those few minutes with Ryder had knocked her off balance more than anything else since Gary's funeral.

The only thing they had in common anymore was their love for Gary. Ryder may have suggested getting together for dinner, but Lynn was convinced it had been a token offer. He was probably as surprised at himself for even suggesting it. He hadn't contacted her since, and she was grateful.

By noon, the same day she'd dropped Jason off at Peter Pan's, Lynn was exhausted. She was working at her desk, nibbling her lunch, when her assistant stuck her head in the door.

"A Mr. Matthews is here to see you. Should I send him in?"

The pen Lynn was holding slipped from her fingers and rolled across the desktop. She caught it just before it fell off the edge and onto the floor.

"Mr. Matthews?"

"Yes," Gloria answered, and wiggled her eyebrows expressively. "He's cute, too. Real cute. He's got a voice so husky it could pull a sled."

"Ah…" Lynn tried to laugh at her employee's joke

while glancing frantically around the room, seeking an excuse, any excuse, to send Ryder away. None presented itself. It was one thing to talk to Ryder at Green Lake where there were blue skies and lots of people. But it was another matter entirely to sit across her desk from him, when she was wearing pink leotards and a sleeveless top.

"Lynn, what about Mr. Matthews?"

"Sure, go ahead and send him in."

"A wise decision," Gloria whispered, and pushed open the door so Ryder could step inside.

He walked into her tiny office, and his presence seemed to stretch out and fill every corner and crevice in the room.

Lynn stood, her heart pounding as fast and hard as a piston in a clogged engine. "Hello, Ryder. What can I do for you?" She hoped her voice sounded more confident than she felt.

"Hello, Lynn. I've got the afternoon free and since I was in the neighborhood, I thought I'd stop and see if you could have lunch with me."

This second invitation surprised her as much as his first one had. She twisted around and pointed to her unopened yogurt and a rye crisp that was only half gone. "As you can see, I've already eaten."

"That doesn't look like much of a lunch to me."

"I wouldn't dare bring a hamburger in here," she said, forcing a smile. "I'd be mobbed."

Ryder chuckled and pulled out a chair.

Reluctantly, Lynn sat, too.

"I hadn't heard from you." He spoke first, looking strong and confident. His mouth twisted into a slow, sensual smile that told her he'd been waiting for her call.

A simple smile caused her stomach to knot.

"I was hoping you'd get in touch with me," he added.

Lynn blinked, wondering if she was missing something. "I was supposed to contact you?"

Ryder nodded. "You were going to consider going out to dinner with me."

Lynn's eyes widened involuntarily. "No, as I remember, I said I didn't have the time and that I felt it was better for us to leave matters between us the way they were."

"I asked you to dinner; I didn't suggest an affair."

Extending her lower lip, Lynn released a breath that was strong enough to ruffle her bangs. "Ryder...you've been gone three years. You were Gary's best friend; you were *my* friend, too, but my life is different now."

"So different you can't indulge in one evening's entertainment?"

"Yes...I mean, no." Even now Lynn wasn't exactly sure why she felt she had to refuse his offer. Something elemental, a protective device she'd acquired since becoming a widow, slid securely into place. "I can't," she answered after a brief hesitation, her voice strong and determined.

"Why not?"

"Ryder, this is crazy. I'm not anything like the women you used to date. I think of you as a friend and a brother...not that way."

"I see."

It was obvious from how he looked at her that he didn't. "But more importantly," she felt obliged to add, "you don't owe me this."

"*Owe* you this?" The smile vanished, replaced with

a piercing dark gaze that would intimidate the strongest personality.

"It's been three years now, and you seem to feel—"

"You amaze me the way you assume you know what I'm thinking," he said and stood, bracing his hands against the edge of the desk. "This time you're wrong."

His face was only a few inches from hers, and, although she tried not to look at him, his gaze dragged hers back to his. She braced herself, for *what* she didn't know—a clash of wills, she supposed. Instead she found herself sinking into the control and power she found in his eyes. It was like innocently walking into quicksand. It demanded all her strength to pull herself free. She was so weak when she managed to look away that she was trembling.

"Will you or won't you go to lunch with me?" Ryder asked.

He could have been asking about the weather for the casual way in which he spoke, but Lynn noted his voice had acquired a different quality. And yet his words weren't heavy or deep or sharp. She blinked, not sure what was happening to her or if her mind was playing games with her. What she saw and heard in Ryder was *purpose*. He wanted something from her and he wasn't about to give up until he achieved it.

"I…"

"Lunch with an old friend isn't so much to ask."

Lynn braced herself and kept her tone as even as possible, belying the jittery, unstable feeling inside her. "Ryder…I have my own life now. I just don't have the time to dig up the past, and, unfortunately, all we have in common anymore is Gary."

He said nothing, and his silence was more profound

than the most heated argument. Lynn knew Ryder, knew him well, or at least she had at one time. He was intelligent and perceptive, and she prayed he could make sense of her jumbled thoughts even if she couldn't.

"I'll give you more time—since you seem to need it," he said, after what felt like the longest moment of her life.

Lynn nodded, her throat dry.

With that, Ryder Matthews turned and walked out of her office, but Lynn had the feeling he was coming back. She frowned and absently reached for her yogurt.

"Michelle," Lynn called, standing in front of the stove. "Call Jason home for dinner, would you?"

"Where is he?"

"Brad's...I think." She turned off the burner and opened the cupboard to take down the dinner plates. As a peace offering to her disgruntled son, Lynn was fixing his favorite meal. Tacos, with homemade banana cream pie for dessert.

Michelle finished making the phone call. "Brad's mom says he isn't there."

Lynn paused, distinctly remembering Jason telling her he was going to play at Brad's house. "Try the Sawyers' place then." Jason was sure to be there.

Michelle reached for the phone and hung up a minute later. "He's not there, either."

"He isn't in the yard, is he?"

"No," Michelle was quick to confirm. "I already checked there. Personally I think he needs to be taught a lesson. We should just sit down and eat without him. He knew you were cooking dinner, and if he chooses to disappear, then let him go without."

"I planned tacos tonight just for him."

"All the better."

"Michelle, we're talking about an eight-year-old boy here."

"A *spoiled* eight-year-old boy."

Both Michelle and Jason were always so eager to see the other disciplined. Lynn prayed this was a stage her children were going through, because she found it downright irritating.

"Dinner's an effort to smooth his ruffled feathers for putting him in the day-care center. I don't want to use it against him."

"I'll see if he's at the Simons's," Michelle offered on the tail end of a frustrated sigh.

From the way her daughter walked toward the phone, Lynn could tell that her daughter heartily disapproved of her parenting techniques.

"While you're calling I'll check upstairs and see if he's there," she offered. It would be just like Jason to lie down and fall asleep while everyone was frantically searching for him.

The first thing Lynn noticed was that his bed was made and his room picked up. That in itself was a shock since she'd often claimed his room was a death trap and only the Hulk himself would be brave enough to venture inside.

The note propped against his pillow caught her eye and she walked over to it. The few words seemed to leap off the paper and cut off her oxygen supply. Lynn read them nonstop twice. Her knees went so weak she had to reach out and grip the headboard to keep from falling.

"Jason isn't at the Simons's, either," she told Michelle as calmly as possible, once she returned to the kitchen.

"I know," Michelle said, impatiently. "I just got off the phone with Scott's mother. If you aren't going to take dinner away from him, I sincerely hope you punish him for this. I'm hungry, you know."

Lynn pulled out a chair and sat down. Her mind was whirling and she felt sick to her stomach.

"Where could that little brat be?"

"I...don't know," Lynn said, and her voice came out sounding like a rusty door hinge.

Michelle swung around, her eyes curious. With a trembling hand, Lynn handed her Jason's note.

"He's run away?" Michelle cried and her voice cracked. "My baby brother has run away?"

Five

The first thing Lynn did was phone the police station. Certainly they could tell her what to do in instances such as this. Although Lieutenant Anderson, the officer who answered her frantic call, was reassuring, he told her that until Jason had been missing twenty-four hours, there wasn't anything the authorities could do.

"Did he actually claim he was running away?" The lieutenant asked sympathetically.

Lynn's fingers tightened around Jason's carefully lettered note. "Not exactly...he said that I wouldn't need to worry about him anymore and that he could take care of himself."

Lieutenant Anderson's hesitation told Lynn everything she wanted to know. "I'm sorry, Mrs. Danfort, but there isn't anything more I can do."

"But he's only eight years old." Her voice wobbled as she struggled to hold back the fear. Lynn's imagination was tormenting her every minute that Jason was missing. Surely the men who had worked with Gary would be willing to do something to help her. Anything.

"I'm sure your son will be back before nightfall," the officer offered.

Lynn wasn't nearly as convinced. "But anything could happen to Jason in twenty-four hours' time. He's upset and angry...he could get into a car with a stranger...isn't there someone you could phone?"

Again the man hesitated. "I'll give the officers on patrol a description and ask them to keep an eye out for him."

Lynn sighed, grateful for that much. She wasn't sure Lieutenant Anderson would have been willing to do even that if he hadn't known Gary. "Thank you. I want you to know how much I appreciate this."

"No problem, Mrs. Danfort, but when you find Jason, call me."

"Yes," Lynn promised. "Right away." Her fingers felt like blocks of ice when she replaced the receiver. The chill extended down her arm and stopped at her heart. Lieutenant Anderson sounded so confident, as though eight-year-old boys ran away from home every day of the week. His attitude gave her the impression that as soon as Jason got hungry he would have a change of heart and head home. Maybe so, but it was a dark, cruel world out there and the thought of her son facing it alone frightened Lynn beyond anything else.

"Well?" Michelle asked, studying her mother once she'd finished talking to the police. "Are they forming a search party?"

Lynn shook her head. "Not yet."

"You mean they aren't going to bring in bloodhounds?"

"No."

"Oh, I guess they're right. Searchlights and helicopters will work much better since it's getting so close to nighttime."

"There aren't going to be any searchlights, or any helicopters."

"Good grief," the preteen shouted, obviously growing more agitated by the minute. "Exactly *what* are the authorities planning to do to find my baby brother?"

Darn little, but Lynn couldn't tell her daughter that. "The lieutenant promised to give Jason's description to the officers who are patrolling our area."

"That's it? That's the extent of their plans!" Michelle wore a shocked look.

Worry was clawing away at Lynn's insides.

"Mom," Michelle cried, "what are you going to do?"

Lynn wasn't sure. "I...I don't know." The lump in her throat felt as large as a Texas grapefruit as she desperately tried to force her mind into some type of positive action.

"Shouldn't we call someone?" Michelle suggested, tears brightening her eyes. "I could kill him, I could just kill Jason for this."

"It's the Peter Pan Day-care Center," Lynn said in a strangled voice that was barely above a whisper. He'd hated the idea from the very first, but she'd been forced to enroll him in a center that wasn't geared to a boy his age. There hadn't been anyplace else with openings.

Michelle's gaze was incredulous. "He wouldn't go there!"

Lynn stared at her daughter, wondering at Michelle's farfetched reasoning. The day-care center would be the last place Jason would think to hide. "Of course he wouldn't...don't be silly." Lynn's sense of panic was growing stronger each minute. "What about his friends?"

"I've already called everyone in the neighborhood," Michelle reasoned, rubbing her palms together and pacing the kitchen like a caged beast.

"What about Danny Thompson?" Lynn whispered, remembering a boy from school whom Jason had been thick friends with several weeks before school had been dismissed earlier in the month.

Michelle gnawed on her lower lip. "Nope, the Thompsons are on vacation, remember?"

Lynn vaguely did. "Michelle, think," she pleaded. "Where would he go?"

The girl shook her head, then shrugged her shoulders. "I swear to you, Mom, if you don't spank him for this, I will."

"Let's worry about punishing him once we find him." Although the need to shake some sense into her son *did* carry a strong appeal, Lynn kept her thoughts to herself.

"Uncle Ryder," Michelle shouted as though she'd just invented pizza. "I bet you anything, Jason contacted Ryder. Don't you remember…every other word out of his mouth for the past week has been Ryder this and Ryder that. He's been talking about him every day since the picnic."

"But Jason doesn't have any way of contacting Ryder," Lynn countered. "He doesn't know his phone number."

"Who says?"

Now that she thought about it, maybe Ryder *had* given Jason his phone number, but Lynn was sure Jason would have mentioned it earlier if Ryder had. He would have repeated every conversation at length, Lynn was convinced of that. No, Jason didn't have any way of getting in touch with Ryder—at least that she knew about.

"Mom, call Uncle Ryder," Michelle pleaded.

"But—"

"Mom, please, he could be our only hope!"

Ryder picked up the TV controller and absently flipped stations. Television really didn't interest him. Neither did dinner. His meeting with Lynn at noon hadn't gone well and he blamed himself. Lynn wasn't the same woman he remembered—for that matter, he wasn't the same man either. She'd changed, matured, grown. In the past three years, she'd learned to deal effectively with the blows life had dealt her. She was competent and confident and stronger than he would ever have believed. That had pleased and surprised him. He'd been foolish to picture himself as a knight in shining armor, rushing to Seattle to rescue her from an unknown fate. Lynn didn't need anyone hurrying to her aid. She was doing just fine all on her own.

Another problem that Ryder had only now fully understood was that Lynn had always looked upon him as an endearing older brother. He knew she considered the thought of the two of them romantically involved as absurd. She seemed to find the thought of them kissing as downright incestuous. He supposed that was a natural response, after all, since they'd never viewed each other beyond good friends while Gary was alive.

Gary.

The role his former partner had played in his and Lynn's relationship presented an additional insight. Ryder had failed to realize that Gary had been the cohesive person in their friendship. Ryder had been Gary's partner and friend and Lynn had just been Gary's wife—at first. They'd eventually become fast friends as well, but Ryder was beginning to understand that, without Gary, that friendship had changed for Lynn. His three-year absence hadn't helped, either.

Ryder slouched back against the sofa and rubbed his hand across his face. He was expecting too much, too soon. All he had to do was give Lynn more time, and make himself available to her and the kids. He would invent excuses to drop by, win Lynn over little by little, until she was as comfortable with him as she had been in the old days. When the time was right he would hold and kiss her, Ryder mused. All he needed now was patience.

An idea started to form...a good one. A smile bounced from his eyes to his mouth, curving up the corners of his lips. Without realizing what he was doing, he stood and moved into the kitchen, unexpectedly ravenous. His hand was on the refrigerator when the telephone rang.

"Ryder," Lynn said, trying to control the anxiety in her voice. "I'm sorry to bother you..."

"Lynn, what is it?"

The alarm in Ryder's voice told her that no amount of fabricated poise was going to disguise the terror that had gripped her soul. She closed her eyes and slumped against the kitchen wall in an effort to compose herself before she started explaining Jason's note.

"Here," Michelle said, ripping the telephone out of her mother's hand. "Let me do the talking."

Lynn wasn't given an opportunity to protest.

"Uncle Ryder, this is Michelle," the youngster stated in a crisp, clear voice. "If you care anything at all about your godson then I suggest you get over here right away. Jason is missing and God only knows what's happened to him. He could be dead. Mother's in a panic, and frankly I'm upset myself." With that she replaced the receiver with a resounding force.

"Michelle," Lynn groaned. "That was a terrible thing to do to Ryder. He won't know what to think."

"What is there to think?" she demanded with irrefutable logic. "Jason's missing, we're worrying ourselves sick. Uncle Ryder is possibly the only man alive we know who can tell us what we should be doing to find that little monster."

"It still wasn't fair to frighten him like that," Lynn argued, reaching for the phone. She punched out his number a second time and let it ring ten times before she hung up.

"He isn't going to answer the stupid phone," Michelle stated the obvious. "Honestly, Mom, Ryder really cares about Jason and me."

That bit of dialogue threw Lynn for a spiraling loop. "How do you know that? Good heavens, you haven't seen him in years. I'm surprised you even remember him."

"Sure I do. Ryder always sends us nice Christmas gifts and he makes sure we hear from him on our birthdays."

"He's your godfather."

"I know. But I remember him from before..." She paused and a soft smile produced a dimple in both cheeks. "He used to sit me in his lap and tell me that I was going to grow up to be a princess someday. And if

I was lucky, and he used to tell me that he was certain that I was very lucky, then I was going to be as pretty as my mommy."

"He told you that?"

Michelle nodded. "He used to make me laugh by telling me silly jokes, too." She hesitated and grinned. "I remember once that he told me that you can lead a horse to water but you can't teach him to do a side stroke. I love Ryder. I'm glad he's back. It's almost like..." She paused and dropped her gaze, her expression sobering.

"Like what, honey?"

"Like the way things were before Dad died."

Michelle's words had a peculiar effect upon Lynn. She flinched as if stepping back to avoid an unexpected blow. Everything had been different since Gary's death. It was as if part of her had been waiting to wake up and discover the last three years had all been a nightmare. And yet so many positive things had happened in her life. She'd discovered herself, accepted her weaknesses, conquered numerous fears. On the negative side of Gary's death, she'd come to view the years she was married as idealistic, and that was a mistake. Her marriage hadn't been a stroll through Camelot, and it was wrong to compare every man she dated to Gary. Over the time he'd been gone, she'd found it increasingly difficult to imagine another man fitting into her and the children's lives. She wasn't a carefree adult any longer. The ability to flirt and play cute were long gone. But if she was different, and she was, then so were men. Lynn hadn't been kidding when she told Toni Morris that the dating world was a jungle.

"I think I hear Ryder now," Michelle announced and

raced out of the kitchen toward the front door. "Don't worry, if anyone can find Jason, he can."

Michelle was gone even before Lynn could stop her. The fact was, Lynn had trouble slowing down her own pace. She reached the door just in time to watch Michelle hurl herself into Ryder's arms and burst into flamboyant tears.

Ryder looked shocked by the preteen's emotional outburst. His gaze flew across the yard to Lynn who was standing on the front porch. One of her hands was braced against the wide support beam and the other hung limply at her side. In another time and place she would have wanted him to hold and reassure her too... but not now. She had to be strong, had to believe Jason would be found no worse for wear and everything was going to be all right. God wouldn't be so cruel that he would take both her husband and her son from her.

Ryder gently patted Michelle's back, and the tender way in which he spoke to the girl brought involuntary tears into Lynn's eyes. She looked away rather than let him know she was so close to weeping herself.

With one arm wrapped around Michelle's waist, Ryder led her to the top of the porch where Lynn was waiting.

"I can't seem to make much sense out of Michelle's story," he told Lynn. "Perhaps you'd better tell me what's going on with Jason."

Lynn opened her mouth to do exactly that, but when she started to speak, her voice cracked. Tears burned for release, tears she could barely control.

"He...I'm afraid Jason's decided to run away," she said and handed him her son's farewell note.

Six

Ryder took the creased note Lynn handed him and read the few short lines. "What did he take with him?"

Lynn's eyes rounded at the unexpected question. "I…I didn't think to check."

"Uncle Ryder, the police aren't doing anything to find Jason," Michelle informed him between loud sniffles. "No bloodhounds. No helicopter. No searchlights. Nothing."

"He'll need to be missing twenty-four hours before they get involved."

"I talked to Lou Anderson," Lynn explained, leading Ryder into the house and up the stairs to Jason's bedroom. "He's a lieutenant now and he was kind enough to give a description of Jason to the patrol officers, but I don't know if that'll do much good."

"It's something." Ryder paused just inside the bedroom door, surveying the room. "Did he pack any clothes?"

Systematically Lynn opened and closed her son's drawers, one after the other, until she'd finished with the chest. She couldn't see that he'd taken anything with him.

"I can tell you right now, he didn't bother with clean underwear," Michelle said with smug look. "If he brought anything it'd be those silly army things he treasures so much. He lives in those disgusting things. Mom practically has to wrestle him to the ground to get him to take 'em off so she can wash them."

Ryder looked to Lynn, who nodded.

"Just a minute," Michelle cried, "I just thought of something." Following that announcement, she raced down the stairs.

"Are you all right?" Ryder asked Lynn in the same tender voice he'd used earlier with Michelle. She didn't know how to deal with this gentle, caring concern. Part of her wanted to lean on him and let him absorb some of this dreadful fear that attacked her common sense like fiery darts. Lou Anderson was probably right: Jason would be home as soon as he got hungry. But then there was the off chance that her son had stumbled into real trouble.

"I don't know what I feel," she answered and lifted her hand to brush aside a stray lock of hair. To add to her dismay, she noted that her fingers were trembling. "I blame myself for this, Ryder. This is the first summer I haven't been home with the kids and it's been a disaster from the start. I don't know how other single parents manage home and a job. There've been so many problems."

Ryder motioned for Lynn to sit on the edge of Jason's mattress and when she did, he sat beside her.

"I didn't have any choice," Lynn continued, staring straight ahead at the wall and the life-size poster of her son's idol, Edward Norton as the Incredible Hulk. "I had to enroll Jason in the Peter Pan Day-care Center. I couldn't leave Michelle and Jason by themselves."

"I take it Jason isn't overly fond of Peter Pan's?"

"He hates it." She pinched her lips together as she remembered the martyred look he'd given her when she'd gone to pick him up that afternoon. It was enough to melt the hardest heart. "He...he would hardly talk to me on the way home. He claimed they made him eat tapioca pudding with a bunch of four-year-olds...his pride was shattered."

Ryder placed his arm over Lynn's shoulder and caressed the length of her upper arm in slow, even strokes that gently soothed her. The weight of his body, so close to her own, felt incredibly strong and confident. Without realizing what she was doing, she relaxed and had to fight the urge to rest her head against his shoulder.

"I've tried so hard to be a good mother, Ryder. I knew he was going to hate it there. I was trying to make it up to him by cooking his favorite dinner. He loves tacos and banana cream pie...I should have known that wouldn't be enough to appease him."

"You *are* a good mother, Lynn, don't be so hard on yourself."

"It's not only Jason running away," she admitted with a wobbly sigh. "The way he idolizes Super Heroes concerns me. That boy lives in a dream world in which he's the hero. Toni Morris told me it's a stage all little boys go through, but I can't help worrying. I can't help thinking—"

A breathless Michelle hurled herself into the room, interrupting Lynn. "I should have known," she announced dramatically. "The Oreos and a bunch of other goodies are missing, including a brand-new box of Cap'n Crunch cereal."

"He wouldn't think to take a sweater, but food didn't escape his notice," Lynn pointed out to Ryder.

"That thief took off with my fruit nuggets," an outraged Michelle continued.

"Your what?" Ryder's brow puckered with the question, obviously not understanding the significance.

"Fruit nuggets," Michelle repeated and slapped her hands against her sides in outrage. "Mother kindly explain!"

"It's a dried, gooey form of cherries, grapes, strawberries and other fruit that look like gumdrops."

"Ah."

"They were mine. Mom bought them for me and Jason knew it. That boy isn't any better than a…a…" Apparently Michelle couldn't think of anything low enough to compare him to. With her hands braced against her hips, the girl looked as outraged as if Jason had walked away with the national treasury stuffed into his pockets. A public hanging would be too good for him.

Ryder stood. "I think I've gleaned enough to know where he might be."

Apparently Ryder knew something Lynn didn't.

"Where?" Michelle demanded, noticeably eager to get her hands on her brother and her fruit nuggets while there was still time.

"I imagine he's taken along his backpack and his sleeping bag as well."

Michelle tossed open the closet door and peered inside. "Yup, both are missing."

Lynn leaped up and looked for herself. Sure enough, both were conspicuously absent.

"We've already phoned everyone in the entire neighborhood," Michelle advised Ryder. "I can guarantee you he isn't with any friends who live around here."

"I didn't think he would be."

"You'll call?" Lynn leaned against the closet door, her eyes wide and appealing.

"Every half hour, in case that boy's got the sense he was born with and decides to come home on his own. Otherwise I'll keep looking until he's found." His low voice was filled with an unwavering determination.

That lent Lynn some badly needed confidence. For the first time since finding Jason's note, Lynn felt a glimmer of reassurance.

"Ryder." The sound of his name vibrated in the air. He stopped abruptly and turned to her. Lynn held out her hand and grasped his fingers, squeezing them as hard as she could. "Thank you," she said in a strangled whisper. "I…didn't know what to do or who to call."

He brushed his fingertips across her cheek in the briefest of touches. It was the touch of a man who would walk through hell to bring Jason back home. A shiver of awareness skidded down Lynn's spine and she managed a weak smile.

"Ryder will find him," Michelle murmured after he'd left. "I know he will."

"I do, too," Lynn answered.

The wooded area behind the local park was the logical place for Ryder to begin his search. From his experience earlier with his godson, Ryder remembered how much the boy loved exploring. He probably had a fort all prepared for this little exercise, and had thought most matters through before leaving home.

He quickly located several well-traveled paths that led deep into the thicket.

Within a matter of minutes, Ryder stumbled upon a fallen tree with a Star Wars sleeping bag securely tucked beneath a shelter that had been carefully dug out. A canteen rested beside that. Ryder checked the contents and when he discovered granulated cereal, he knew he'd found his prey.

All he had to do now was wait.

That didn't take long. About five minutes later, Jason came traipsing through the woods with a confidence his military hero would have envied. He stopped abruptly when he saw Ryder, his young face tightening.

"If you're here to take me home, I'm not going."

"Okay," Ryder agreed with an aloof shrug.

"You mean you aren't going to make me go back?"

Ryder shook his head. "Not unless that's what you want, and it's obvious to me that you don't." He straightened, stuck the tips of his fingers into his jeans pockets, and glanced around the campsite Jason had so carefully built. "Nice place you've got here."

Jason's eager grin revealed his pride. "Thanks. I'd offer you something to eat, but I don't know how long my food supply is going to last."

Once more Ryder shrugged and made a show of patting his stomach. "Don't worry about it, I'm saving my appetite for tacos and banana cream pie."

Jason's gaze shot up so fast it was a wonder he didn't dislocate his neck. "Tacos? Banana cream pie?"

"Smelled delicious, too."

Looking disconcerted, Jason swallowed and Ryder

could have sworn the boy's mouth had started to water. In a gallant effort to disguise his distress, Jason walked over to the tree trunk and hopped onto the smooth bark. "I didn't want to have to run away like this, but Mom forced my hand."

"Peter Pan did it, right?"

"How'd you know?"

"Your mom told me."

"I suppose she sent you here."

"In a manner of speaking," Ryder answered smoothly. "She was pretty worried."

"I told her not to in my note," Jason fired back defensively. "Gee whiz, you'd think I couldn't take care of myself or something. That's the whole problem, Ryder, Mom treats me like I'm a little kid."

Ryder cast his eyes to the ground in order to hide his smile before Jason saw it. To his way of thinking an eight-year-old was a kid!

"I was planning to move back home as soon as school started, and the way I figure it, that's only six weeks. I've got to if I'm going to play with the Rockets."

"The Rockets?"

"My soccer team—we took first place last year. I made more goals than anyone, but Mom says it's a team sport and I can't take all the credit even though I worked the hardest and scored the most."

Feigning a pose of nonchalance, Ryder leaned against the fallen oak and crossed his arms and legs. "So Peter Pan's is the pits?"

"You wouldn't believe how bad it is. Half the time I was afraid some old lady was going to check me to see if I'd wet my pants."

"That bad?"

"Worse. It's unfair because Michelle gets to go over to her friend's house, but Mom sticks me in some kiddy factory." Jason drew a fruit nugget out of his pocket and popped it into his mouth, aggressively chewing it. "Mom's real nice and for a sister there are times when Michelle isn't half bad. The problem, the way I see it, is that I'm surrounded by women who can't understand a man like me."

"I've had the same trouble myself," Ryder confided.

His godson looked impressed. "I thought as much. You were wearing a tortured look the day I saw you at the lake."

"A tortured look?"

"Yeah, that's what I heard Mom say on the phone once. She was talking to Mrs. Morris about a man she'd gone out to dinner with and she said that and something else about him roaming the moors with Heathcliff… whatever that means."

Despite his effort not to, Ryder chuckled.

"Later, I asked Mom what she meant and she said that he frowned a lot. You were frowning, too."

Ryder supposed that he *had* been scowling that day. There'd been a good deal on his mind, not the least of which was finding a way to approach Lynn after three long years. He couldn't stroll up to a woman after that length of time and casually announce he was in love with her.

"I wanted to go to day camp with Brad—he's my best buddy—they do neat stuff like horseback riding and field trips, but Mom checked it out and they're already full up." He reached for another fruit nugget, paused and stared at it in the palm of his hand. "I don't suppose the banana cream pie was homemade?"

"It looked to me like it was."

Jason licked his lips. "I wonder if there were any leftovers?"

"Oh, I'm sure there are. No one felt much like eating. Your mother was too upset and Michelle was crying."

"Michelle cried because of *me*?" Jason looked astounded. "But I took her fruit nuggets. Oh, I get it," he said, nodding vigorously. "She didn't know it yet."

"She noticed that first thing; there was something about the Oreos and some Cap'n Crunch cereal missing, too, now that I think about it."

"I have to eat, you know. I left Michelle the shredded wheat."

Ryder examined the end of his fingernails, pausing to clean beneath a couple before adding, "Don't worry, Michelle understands."

"Then why was she crying?"

"I don't completely understand it myself. She was sobbing so hard it was difficult to understand her, but from what I could gather, she was afraid something terrible could happen to you."

Jason lowered his gaze and rubbed his hands over the thigh of his army pants. "A drunk shouted at me, but I ran away from him…he didn't follow me, though, I made sure of that."

"I see."

Jason hesitated. "He might have seen which way I headed, though."

"That's a possibility," Ryder agreed.

Jason looked distinctly uncomfortable. "So you're sure Mom's all right."

"No, I can't say that she is. Your mother's a strong

woman and it takes a lot to upset her, but you've managed to do that, son."

The boy's gaze plunged. "I suppose I should go home then...just so Mom won't worry."

"That sounds like a good idea to me. But before you do, I think we should have a talk—man to man."

Every minute that Ryder was gone felt like a lifetime to Lynn. She couldn't sit still, couldn't stay in one room, but paced between several. Not knowing what more she could do, she phoned everyone in the neighborhood and asked them to keep an eye out for Jason, although Michelle had already talked to all of Jason's friends. When she'd finished with that, she wandered back into her son's bedroom, but became so depressed and worried that she soon left.

Lynn was in the laundry room cleaning a cupboard when she heard Michelle's muffled cry. "Mom, Mom."

Dropping the rag, and rushing into the kitchen, Lynn discovered her daughter pointing to the inside of the junk drawer, tears raining down her face.

"What is it?"

"Jason left me a note," she sobbed. "He told me he was sorry for taking my fruit nuggets, but he needed them to live. He saved me all the grape ones...they're my favorite."

Lynn felt like bursting into tears herself.

"Ryder's going to find him."

Michelle had repeated those same words no less than fifteen times in the past hour. He hadn't phoned, which caused Lynn to be all the more nervous.

"I know." But the longer Ryder was gone, the less

confident Lynn grew. Within an hour, she'd been re-
duced to cleaning cupboards.

Both Lynn and Michelle heard the car door slam
from the driveway. Like a homing pigeon, Michelle flew
to the living room window and pushed aside the drape.

"It's Jason and Ryder."

Lynn felt the weight of a hundred years lift from her
shoulders. "Thank God," she whispered.

Seven

Jason walked into the house, his chin tucked so low against his shoulder that Lynn could see the crown of his head.

"Hello, Jason," she said, clenching her hands tightly together in front of her.

"Hi, Mom. Hi, Michelle."

Jason's voice was so low, Lynn had to strain to hear him speak.

Michelle sniffled loudly in a blatant effort to let her brother know how greatly he'd wronged her. She crossed her arms in an act of defiance, then whirled around, unwilling to face him or forgive him.

Ryder's hand rested on Jason's shoulder. "He was camping in the woods behind the park."

"The woods...behind the park," Lynn repeated, hardly able to believe what she was hearing. Even now the nightmares continued to ricochet off the edges of her mind. All the tragic could-have-beens pounded against her temple with agonizing force. If something had happened to Jason while he was hiding there, it could have been weeks before he was found.

"I believe Jason has something he'd like to say to you," Ryder continued.

The boy cleared his throat. "I'm real sorry for the worry I caused you, Mom."

Michelle whimpered softly.

"You, too, Michelle."

Somewhat appeased, the girl slowly turned to face her brother, apparently amenable now to entertain thoughts of mercy.

"I promise I won't run away or hide or do anything like this ever again, and if I do, you can burn my army clothes and tear up my poster of the Hulk." Having made such a gallant offer seemed to have drained Jason's energy bank. He paused, looked up at Ryder, who patted the boy's shoulder reassuringly and then continued. "I don't like that Peter Pan Day-care place, but I'm willing to stick it out until I go back to school. Next year we'll know to sign me up for day camp with Brad at the beginning of the summer so I can be with my best friend."

The knot in Lynn's throat felt as if it would choke her. The emotion that had blistered her soul demanded release. Heavy tears filled her eyes as she nodded, blurring her vision. Moisture ran down the side of her face and she held out her arms to her son.

Jason ran into them, his small body hurled against hers with enough force to knock her a step backward. He buried his face in her stomach and held on to her with such might that breathing was nearly impossible.

Michelle waited until Jason had finished hugging Lynn before she wrapped her arms around him in a rare display of affection. "You deserve the spanking of your life for this," she declared in high-pitched righteousness, "but I'm so glad you're back, I'm willing to let bygones be bygones...this once."

Jason tossed her a grateful glance. "Here," he said, digging his hands into his pockets. "I still got some of your fruit nuggets left."

Michelle looked down at the gooey, melting fruit pieces in his palm that had bits of grass and dirt stuck to them, wrinkled her nose and shook her head. "You can go ahead and eat them."

Jason was noticeably surprised. "Gee, thanks." He stuffed the entire handful into his mouth and chewed until a multicolored line of juice crept out of the corner of his lip. He abruptly wiped it aside with the sleeve of his shirt.

Michelle cringed. "You are so disgusting."

"What'd I do?" He asked and smeared more of the sugary fruit juice across his cheek.

Rolling her eyes, Michelle pointed toward the kitchen. "Go wash your hands and face before you touch something."

The pair disappeared and Lynn was left standing alone with Ryder. "I don't know how I can ever thank you," she told him. "I was so close to falling to pieces. When I found Jason's note it was like acid had burned a hole straight through me. I...I can bear just about anything but losing either of my children." She wiped the moisture from her cheekbones and tried to smile, failing. "I don't know how you guessed where he was hiding, but I'll always be grateful."

"I was here for you this time," he whispered.

"Oh, Ryder, don't blame yourself for the past. Please."

"I'm not. I went away because I had to, but I'm here

now and if you've got a problem, I want to be the first one you call."

Lynn wasn't sure she understood his reasoning. He'd walked away from her when she'd needed him most and calmly strolled back into her life three years later, looking to rescue her. For the most part, Lynn didn't need anyone to save her, she'd managed nicely on her own. She was proud of her accomplishments, and rightly so. In the time since Gary's death, she'd come a long way with little more than occasional parental advice. If Ryder thought he could leap into her life, wearing a red cape and blue tights, then he was several years too late. She was about to explain that to him as subtly and gently as possible, when Jason stuck his head around the kitchen door.

"Can I have a taco and some pie?"

Between her relief that her son was all right and calling Lieutenant Anderson to tell him he'd been found, Lynn had completely forgotten dinner. "Ah...sure." She tossed a glance at Ryder. "Have you eaten?"

He grinned and shook his head.

"Then please join us. It's the least we can do to thank you."

Ryder followed her into the kitchen and while Lynn brought out the grated cheese, cubed tomatoes and picante sauce, Ryder helped Michelle and Jason set the table.

The easy friendship between Ryder and the kids amazed Lynn. It was as if he'd never been away. They joked and laughed together so naturally that she found it only a little short of amazing. Lynn didn't know of any male, other than the children's grandfather, that the kids seemed more at ease with.

With Jason safely home, the terrible tension had evaporated and dinner proved to be a fun, enjoyable meal. Lynn was convinced the reason Jason loved tacos so much was that he could make a mess without getting corrected for eating like a pig. Bits of fried hamburger, cheese and lettuce circled the area where he was eating. Blithely unaware, Jason downed three huge tacos and took seconds of pie.

"I'm a growing boy, you know," he told Lynn when he delivered his clean plate to the kitchen counter.

The phone rang and Michelle leaped upon it as if answering it before the second ring was a matter of life or death. "It's Marcy," she announced, pressing the receiver to her shoulder. "Can I go over to her house? She got a new pair of jeans she wants me to see."

Lynn twisted around to look at the wall clock. "All right, but be back by eight."

"Mom, that's only a half hour."

"It's eight or not at all."

"All right, all right."

Jason yawned, covering his mouth with his palm, and after clearing the table, plopped himself down in front of the television. The next time Lynn glanced in his direction, her son was sound asleep.

"How about some coffee?" she asked Ryder.

"That sounds good."

He quickly loaded the dinner dishes into the dishwasher while Lynn started the coffee.

Lynn carried two steaming mugs into the living room where Ryder was waiting. He was standing in front of the television where a framed photograph of Gary rested. He turned, looking almost guilty, when she entered the room. He walked over to her to take one mug from her hand.

Her gaze skimmed across the photo of her late husband and back to Ryder. From the disconcerted look he wore, she knew he didn't want to discuss Gary, and she decided not to press the issue.

Smiling, she motioned for him to sit. He sat in the recliner and she took a seat on the sofa, slipping off her sandals and curling her feet beneath her.

"Well, this has certainly been an eventful day," she said, heaving a giant sigh. Rarely had any day been fuller or more traumatic. She'd effectively dealt with all the problems at work and had come home and faced even bigger ones there.

Ryder took a sip of the hot coffee. "It's been a good day for me. I'd forgotten how much I love Seattle. It feels right to be back here."

"It's good to have you." Lynn didn't realize how much she meant that until the words had already slipped from her lips. Ryder had always been a special kind of friend. For years she and Gary and Ryder had been thicker than thieves. Ryder was the brother Gary never had, and they were the best of friends. So Lynn's relationship with Ryder had fallen neatly into place because of his close association with her husband.

"I'm glad to be back, too." The color of Ryder's eyes intensified as his gaze held hers.

He dragged his look away with a reluctance she could feel all the way from the other side of the room. The undercurrents between them were so powerful that Lynn feared if she waded into anything beyond polite conversation, she would be pulled under and drown.

"Seattle's changed, though," he commented in a

voice that was slightly husky. "I hardly recognized the downtown area for all the new construction."

"I saw from your business card that your office is on University Street. How does it feel to be a white-collar worker?" Her gaze moved from Gary's photo to Ryder.

"I don't know if I'll ever get used to wearing a tie every day. I'm more comfortable in Levi's than in a suit, but I suppose that'll come in time."

Lynn smiled, and talked about the many changes happening in the Seattle area. She was pleased that some of the old camaraderie between her and Ryder had returned. When Gary and Ryder had been partners, the three of them had often sat and chatted over a pot of coffee or a pitcher of beer. They'd camped together, hiked together, taken trips to Reno together. They attended concerts, cheered on the Seattle Seahawks and taken skiing classes together. More often than not they'd been a threesome, but every now and again, Ryder would include his latest love interest. Gary and Lynn had delighted in baiting Ryder about how short his "interest span" was when it came to any one woman. He'd responded to their teasing with good-natured humor. He liked to joke, saying he was trying to find someone who was as good a sport as Lynn but was not having any luck.

The three of them were comfortable together—there wasn't any need for pretense. When Michelle was born, Ryder had been her first visitor, arriving at the hospital even before the birth. When Gary and Lynn had asked him to be their daughter's godfather, Ryder's eyes had shone with pride. He was as excited as Gary, carrying pictures of his goddaughter in his wallet and showing them to anyone who would stand still long enough to look. The case was the same with Jason. Ryder had been a natural with the kids, as good as Gary and just as patient and loving. Both Michelle and Jason had grown up with Ryder as a large part of their lives.

Then Gary had died and Ryder had abruptly moved away. Not only had Lynn lost her husband, but in one fell swoop, her two best friends as well.

Ryder must have read the confusion and doubt in her face because he started to frown. The television drew his gaze and his scowl deepened. He hesitated and then blurted out. "I had to leave in order to keep my sanity."

"Ryder, please, I understand. You don't need to explain."

"No, I don't think you do. Let me explain it one last time and then that'll be the end of it. My staying, continuing to be a part of your and the kids' lives would have been a constant reminder of Gary. Every time you looked at me, the memories would have been there slapping you in the face. You needed time to deal with your grief and I had to separate myself from you to get a grip on my own. Perhaps if I hadn't been with him that night…if the circumstances had been different, then the possibility of my remaining in Seattle would have been stronger. But I *was* there and it changed both our lives."

It was possible that Ryder was right, but Lynn didn't know anymore. She didn't want to think about the past and Ryder obviously found it equally painful.

"I'd been considering going back to law school even before…Gary died," Ryder confessed. "I think I may have even mentioned it at one point. I'd dropped out of graduate school in order to enter the academy because I wanted to make a more direct contribution to society. The idea of working with people, helping them, upholding law and order strongly appealed to me. At the time I couldn't see myself stuck away in some law office."

"You think you wasted your time on the force?" That would have surprised Lynn since she'd always assumed Ryder had loved his job as much as Gary had.

He shook his head. "I don't regret it at all. I saw where my effectiveness in a courtroom could be enhanced with my knowledge of police work. My parents had set aside a trust fund for me in case I *did* decide I wanted to go back to school. That had long been an option for me."

"And now you've achieved your goal," Lynn said and sipped her coffee. "I'm proud of you...you were always one to go after something when you wanted it. Gary was the same way. I think that's one reason you two were always such close friends—you were actually quite a bit alike."

"You share some of those character traits yourself."

He held himself rigid, refusing to relax. Their conversation was making him all the more uncomfortable, Lynn noted, and she knew all her talk about Gary was the cause.

"Tell me about Slender, Too."

She smiled at the question, knowing it was a blatant attempt to change the subject. She let him. "I've had the salon for about ten months. Buying that franchise was the scariest thing I've ever done, and I've managed to make a living with it, but it hasn't been easy."

"The kids seem to have adjusted to you working outside the home."

Lynn supposed they had, but the going hadn't been easy. Perhaps if she'd worked outside the home earlier in their lives Michelle and Jason might have adapted better. But they were accustomed to having her there when they needed her. The day-care problems this summer were a good example of how their lives had changed since she'd bought the business.

"If you run into any more problems, I want you to call me," he said, and straightened. He uncrossed his long legs and leaned forward, resting his elbows on his thighs.

"Ryder, I appreciate the offer, but there are few things I can't handle anymore."

"But there are some?"

She hesitated. After what had happened with Jason that evening, she didn't have a whole lot to brag about. "A few things every now and then."

"So call me and I'll do what I can to help straighten those things out."

"Ryder, honestly, you're beginning to sound like you want to be my fairy godfather."

He chuckled, but the sound quickly faded. "The last thing I want is for you to see me as an indulgent uncle."

His face and voice were fervent. It was the same expression he'd given her when they'd met at the precinct picnic, and she found it as disconcerting now as she had then.

Lynn was standing before she had a reason to be. Her mind searched for a logical excuse for why she'd found it necessary to bolt to her feet. The undercurrents tugging at her grew stronger. "Would you like some more coffee?" she asked, then her gaze rested on his still full mug.

"No, thanks."

Refilling her own mug justified the question, although hers was no closer to being empty than Ryder's, but she needed an excuse in order to escape.

Moving into the kitchen, she stood in front of the coffeepot. Lynn heard Ryder walk over and stand behind her. The warmth and proximity of his body were a distraction she chose to ignore.

He rested his hands on her shoulders and stroked her arms in a reassuring motion. "The past few years have been hard on you, haven't they?"

Lynn's hands were shaking as she lifted the glass pot and refilled her mug. "I've managed." Dear sweet heaven, she mused, could that rickety, wobbly voice really be hers? Ryder may have said something more, Lynn didn't know. It took everything within her not to be conscious of the strength of his broad chest, which was pressing against her back. Perspiration beaded her upper lip and although she would have liked to blame it on the heat, the day had actually been cloudy with the temperature in the low seventies.

"Lynn, turn around."

Reluctantly she did what he asked, all the while conscious of how close they were.

With a deliberate action, Ryder removed the mug from her fingers and set it aside. Lynn felt as if she were in a daze, hypnotized and immobile. Anytime else, with anyone else, she would have demanded to know the other person's intentions. But not with Ryder.

She knew what he wanted.

That knowledge would have troubled her except that she was honest enough to admit she wanted it, too.

He placed his hands on her shoulders once more, and his touch so confused her senses that voicing her thoughts became impossible. He slowly glided his fingers over her face, down her cheek to her neck. He reached for the French braid, which fell down the middle of her back, and pulled the strands of hair free, easing his hands through it. His gentle stroke was that of a lover, appreciating a woman's beauty.

Lynn's breath jammed in her throat and her heart started beating like a rampaging herd of buffalo. She refused to look up at him, concentrating instead on the buttons of his shirt because it was safe to look there.

"Lynn."

The demand in his voice was unmistakable. She had to glance up, had to meet his eyes. When she did, she couldn't stop staring at him. They were so close she could see every line in his rugged features. His nostrils flared slightly and the action excited her more than his touch had. Sexual excitement and longing, which had been dormant for years, filled her. The feelings felt foreign and yet perfectly natural.

He lowered his lips to hers.

Slowly, moving as though directed by Ryder's thoughts, hypnotized by what she witnessed in his eyes, Lynn moved in his arms, going up on her tiptoes, raising one hand to clench his shoulder for support.

He brushed his mouth against hers, softly, tenderly, in a butterfly kiss that teased and tantalized her. Her lips trembled at the swell of pure sensation. A soft rasping breath escaped, but Lynn didn't know if it came from her or Ryder. Her eyes were closed, blocking out reality, excluding everything but this incredible whitecap of sensation that had lapped over her. She wanted to deny these sensations, but it was more than she was capable of doing in that moment—more than Ryder would allow.

Still trembling, Lynn repositioned her upper body,

hoping to escape his arms. She soon realized her mistake as the softness of her breasts grazed the hard wall of his chest.

Ryder's breath caught. While once she'd sought to move away, now her arms slid around his neck.

He kissed her then, the way a starving man samples his first bite of food. His lips caressed, tasted and, savored her mouth until they were both breathless. Gasping, Lynn met his ravishing hunger with her own powerful need. She was shaking so hard that if he were to release her, she was convinced she would collapse onto the floor.

Passion built between them until Lynn felt as though her entire body had been seared.

His mouth left hers to slide across her cheek to her ear. An involuntary moan escaped as he nibbled her lobe.

"How I've dreamed of holding you like this," he murmured, his voice husky and low. His breath felt warm and moist against her skin.

The front door slammed and the sound reverberated around the kitchen like a ricocheting bullet. Lynn broke away from Ryder so fast that she would have tumbled to the floor if he hadn't secured her shoulders. Once he was assured that she was stable, he released her, dropping his hands to his sides.

"I'm back," Michelle announced, racing into the kitchen with the fervor of a summer squall.

For some obscure reason, Lynn felt it essential to reach for her coffee. She took a sip and in the process nearly spilled the entire contents down her front.

Michelle stopped abruptly and looked from Ryder

to her mother and then back to Ryder. "I'm not interrupting anything, am I?"

"No...of course not," Lynn said quickly. The words stumbled over her tongue like rocks crashing off the edge of a cliff and bouncing against the hillside on the long tumble downward.

"Your mother and I would like a few minutes alone," Ryder inserted, staring straight through Lynn.

"Oh, sure."

Michelle had turned and started to walk out of the room when Lynn cried. "No...don't go...it's not necessary." She knew she was contradicting Ryder, but now in the harsh light of reality, she felt ashamed by the way she'd succumbed to his kissing. She awkwardly struggled to rebraid her hair.

Michelle was noticeably confused. Her gaze jerked from her mother back to Ryder. "I wanted to show Marcy my magazine. We were going to go up to my room. That's all right, isn't it? She's asking her mom now if she can come over here."

It took Lynn a full minute to decide. With Michelle gone, she would have to face Ryder alone and she didn't know if she could bear to look him in the eye. She'd behaved like a love-starved creature, giving in to him in ways that made her blush all the way to the marrow of her bones. She'd clung to him, kissed him with an abandon that made her feel weak at the memory.

"Mom?"

"Ah...sure, that's fine."

Michelle gave her an odd look. "Are you all right?"

"Of course," she answered in a falsely cheerful voice.

"You look all pale, like you did when you came downstairs with Jason's note." The girl's gaze narrowed.

"He hasn't run away again, has he? That little brat...I knew I was being too generous to forgive him so easily."

"He fell asleep in front of the television," Ryder answered for her. "I don't think you'll have any more problems with him running off."

"It's a good thing you talked to him, Ryder. Someone had to. Mom tries, but she's much too easy on that boy. Mothers tend to be too softhearted."

The doorbell chimed and Michelle brightened. "That's Marcy now."

She ran to answer the door, and rather than face Ryder, Lynn walked away from him and into the family room where Jason lay curled up on the sofa, sound asleep.

"Jason," she whispered, nudging him gently. "Wake up, honey."

"He's dog-tired," Ryder said when Jason grumbled and rolled over in an effort to ignore his mother's voice. "Let him sleep."

"I will once I get him upstairs," she said. Her heart began to pound against her ribs in slow, painful thuds. It took all the courage she could muster just to look in Ryder's direction.

"Here," Ryder said, stepping in front of her. With strength she could only envy, he lifted the sleeping boy into his arms and headed for the staircase.

Jason flung his arms out and lifted his head. He opened his eyes just enough to look up and assess what was happening.

"Your mother wants you upstairs," Ryder explained.

Jason nodded, then closed his eyes, content to let Ryder carry him. That in itself told Lynn how exhausted her son was. From what she'd learned over dinner,

Jason had been planning his escape for several days. The boy probably hadn't had a decent sleep in two or three nights.

Lynn walked up the stairs behind the two; all the while her heart was hammering with trepidation. Once Jason was tucked into his bed, her excuses would have run out and she would be forced to face Ryder. It wasn't likely that she was going to be able to avoid him. She could try to lure Michelle and her friend into the kitchen, but Lynn wasn't likely to interest them in coming downstairs when there was a teen magazine clenched in their hot little hands.

Ryder set Jason on the edge of his mattress and peeled off the boy's shirt.

"He should probably take a bath."

"Ah, Mom," Jason grumbled, and yawned loud enough to wake people in three states. "I promise I'll take one in the morning." He made a gallant effort to keep his head up, but it lobbed to the side as if it had suddenly become too heavy for him to support.

"A bath in the morning," Lynn muttered under her breath. "Those are famous last words if I ever heard them."

Ryder shared a grin with her and the simple action went a long way toward easing some of the tension that was crippling her.

Next Ryder took off Jason's tennis shoes. A pile of dirt fell to the floor as the first sneaker was removed from the boy's foot.

"If Michelle were here, she'd be screaming, 'oh, yuck.'" Lynn joked in an effort to ease more of the tension.

Soon Jason was in his pajamas. He didn't hesitate in

the least before climbing between the sheets. He curled up in a tight ball, wrapping his arms around his pillow as though it were a long lost friend and they'd just recently been reunited.

"He won't wake up till morning," Ryder said, and gently smoothed the hair at the top of her son's head.

"Do you want any more coffee?" Lynn asked, on her way out of the bedroom.

"No."

She was so grateful she actually sighed with relief. Maybe he would decide to go home and give her the space she needed to think. Her thoughts were like murky waters and had clouded her reasoning ability. Kissing Ryder had been curious enough, but to become a wanton in his arms was something else entirely.

He waited until they were back in the kitchen before he spoke. "I don't want coffee or dessert. You know what I want." His voice was so low and seductive that just the sound of it caused tiny goose bumps to break out over her arms.

"Ryder…" She meant to protest, to say something— anything that would put an end to this madness. But Ryder didn't give her the opportunity. Before she could object, he turned her into his arms. Any opposition she'd felt earlier disappeared, like snow melting under an August sun, the minute he reached for her.

Ryder's arms closed convulsively around her waist.

"Please…don't."

"I've waited too long to go back now."

Lynn didn't understand any of what was happening, but when Ryder reached for her, she couldn't find it within herself to resist. His mouth swooped down on hers, his kiss possessive and hard, and yet incredibly soft.. Against every dictate of her will, Lynn lifted her arms to encircle his neck, and shamelessly gave herself over to his kiss.

Ryder groaned.

Lynn whimpered.

He kissed her again and again with a thoroughness that left her shivering, as if in a single minute he wanted to make up to her for all the years they'd been apart.

"No," she cried. "Please…no more." She twisted her face away from him and buried it in his shoulder.

"Lynn…"

"I…think you should go home now."

"Not until we've talked."

"But we're not talking now and I don't know what's happening between us. I need time to think. Please… just go. We'll talk, I promise, but later." Lynn had never felt more unsettled about anything in her life.

He hesitated. He gently stroked her hair as though he had to keep touching her. "It's too soon, isn't it?"

"Yes," she cried. She didn't know if that were true, but was willing to leap upon any excuse.

Slowly, as though it was causing him pain to do so, Ryder dropped his arms and stepped away from her.

A chill descended upon her as he moved away and she lifted her arms, cradling them around her waist.

"I'll be back, you know," he whispered. "And next time, I won't be willing to listen to any excuses."

Eight

"This is a rare treat," Toni Morris said when Lynn slid into the booth across from her in the seafood restaurant close to Lynn's salon. "It's been months since we last had lunch together."

Lynn's smile was noticeably absent as she picked up the menu and glanced over the day's specials. She decided quickly upon a Crab Louie and spent the next several moments adjusting the linen napkin on her lap.

"Well," Toni said, propping her elbows atop the table and lacing her fingers, "are you going to come right out and tell me why you arranged this meeting or are you going to keep me in suspense for half the meal?"

Lynn should have known Toni would see through this invite ruight away. "What makes you think there's something I want to talk about?"

Toni grinned, the simple action denting dimples in both cheeks. The thing Lynn found amazing about this former policewoman was her ability to be both tough and tender. She could look someone in the eye, cut them to the quick with her honesty and then heal them with a smile.

"You mean other than the fact you phoned me at ten-thirty last night suggesting we meet?"

Lynn's gaze darted past her friend. "It was a bit late, wasn't it?"

"Don't worry, you didn't get me out of bed."

The waitress came to take their order and Lynn was given a few minutes respite. She'd wanted to gradually introduce the subject of Ryder, but her friend wasn't going to allow that, which was probably best. Left to her own devices, Lynn was likely to avoid anything that had to do with the man until the last ten minutes of their lunch.

"Ryder came by last night," she said in as normal a tone as she could manage. "Actually I phoned him, desperate because Jason had run away and I thought he might have contacted Ryder."

"Jason did *what*?"

"You heard me…he hates Peter Pan's so much that he decided to live in the woods behind the park until soccer practice started the first week of September and then come home."

Momentarily speechless, Toni shook her head and reached for a breadstick. "That child amazes even me."

"Because I was desperate, I called Ryder and he found Jason for me."

"How?"

"Heaven only knows. I called him because…well because Jason mentioned Ryder's name every ten seconds after they met at the precinct picnic and I thought Ryder might know where Jason was hiding. Actually Michelle had insisted. By the time he arrived I was a candidate for the loony bin."

"I don't blame you. Good grief, Lynn, you should have let me know."

"There wasn't anything you could have done. I called the station and talked to Lou Anderson. You know him, don't you?"

"Yes, yes, go on—how did Ryder know where to find Jason?"

"It was a matter of simple deduction. Unfortunately I was in too much of a panic to think straight. Ryder arrived, asked several pertinent questions and used simple logic. Once Ryder went looking for him, Jason was home within the hour."

"Thank God." Toni expelled a tight sigh. "That boy is something else."

"Tell me about it." Lynn lowered her gaze and nervously smoothed an already creaseless napkin. "Ryder stayed for dinner and later we talked and…" A lump of nervous anticipation blocked her throat. It was one thing to tell her friend that Ryder had kissed her and another to admit how strongly she'd reacted to it.

"And what? For heaven's sake, woman, spit it out."

Despite everything, Lynn laughed.

"You want me to help you out?" Toni joked. "Ryder came over, found Jason, stayed for dinner and the two of you talked. Okay, let's go from there. Knowing you both the way I do, I'd guess that Ryder kissed you and you went into a tizzy."

Lynn nearly swallowed her glass of ice tea whole because Toni was so close to the truth. "How'd you know?"

Toni waved a bread stick like a band leader wielding a baton. "Let's just say I'm not the only one able to deduce matters from the evidence presented me."

Shaken, Lynn stared at her friend, wondering how much more Toni had guessed. She looked amazingly pleased by what had happened, as though she'd orchestrated the entire event herself.

"But Ryder isn't the first man to kiss you in the past three years." Toni's curious smile deepened, causing the edges of her mouth to quiver slightly.

"No, he isn't," Lynn admitted, "but he's the first one who's made me feel again. He appears to want to make up to me for the years he was away, insisting I call him when I stumble into any roadblocks. He doesn't seem to understand that I've changed and when something bothersome crops up, I prefer to find my own solutions."

"He's changed, too, you know."

"But I fear his concern for me and the kids is motivated by guilt."

"The kiss, too?"

"I...I don't know," Lynn answered, wavering. "He came by the salon yesterday, wanting to take me to lunch. I turned him down."

"Why?"

"For the same reasons I didn't want to have dinner with him when he suggested it at the picnic."

"Which are?"

"Oh, Toni, stop. You know as well as I do that I just don't have time right now for a social life. Good grief I probably shouldn't even be taking a whole hour for lunch today. This summer's been hectic at the salon, I can't seem to find good permanent help. The new girl phoned in and said she wouldn't be able to make her shift—she didn't even bother to give me an excuse. I think she'd rather be at the beach. I suspect the only reason she took the job in the first place was to tone up her muscles and get paid for it at the same time. It's been one problem after another for the past three weeks."

Toni's eyes grew serious. "Those are all excuses not to see Ryder and you know it."

"It isn't!"

"Ryder loves you..."

"We're friends—that's all. If he feels anything toward me it's rooted in his relationship with Gary. He helped me yesterday when Jason disappeared, like an older brother would help a younger sister."

"Is that the way he kissed you? Like a brother?"

Toni's words whooshed the argument out of Lynn like hot air from a balloon and with it went all pretense. "No, and that's what concerns me most."

"In other words, it felt good."

"*Too* good," she admitted in a tight whisper. "Much too good."

Their salads arrived and Lynn looked down at the lettuce covered with fresh crab meat and realized her appetite had vanished. She picked up her fork, but after a couple of moments, set it back down again. When she looked up, she noticed that Toni was watching her, her friend's eyes revealing her concern.

"It isn't the end of the world to like it when a man kisses you," Toni said with perfect logic. "If the truth be known, I've been worried about you lately. You've been so involved with Slender, Too, working far harder than you should have to, in addition to keeping up with the kids and the house. Something's going to have to give soon."

"Like my sanity?" Lynn tossed out the words jokingly, but actually she wasn't so far off base. It was the only rational way she could explain what had happened between her and Ryder. For the past year, she'd been dating occasionally, but no one had made her feel the way Ryder did. It had been months since a man had touched her. Months since she'd allowed her body to feel anything sexual. Just the memory of the way Ryder's hands had felt against her shoulders and back, the way he'd run his long, strong fingers through her hair, caused a rush of sensation shooting all the way down to her toes.

"Ryder cares about you and the kids," Toni said, still looking thoughtful and disturbed.

Lynn didn't want to hear that, not because she didn't believe it, but for the other reasons. "He thinks he can leap into my life after three years as if…as if nothing had ever happened."

"I don't think that's his intention."

"Well, I do!" Lynn flared. Toni chose to ignore her short temper, Lynn noted, and took a bite of her salad before answering. "Then what do you think?"

"I can only guess at what Ryder intends. If it bothers you so much, why don't you ask him?"

Toni's question hung between them like a tight rope walker, suspended in midair.

"But one word of warning, my friend," she added softly, "be prepared for the answer."

"What do you mean by that?"

"Just that I know you both. Ryder didn't come back here by accident—he planned it."

"Of course he did. He was accepted into a law firm in Seattle. He's familiar with the courts here and police procedure. It only makes sense that he'd want to set up practice in this area."

"Yes, it *does* make sense, but for other reasons, too."

"Right," Lynn answered defiantly. "He seems to think I need to be saved from myself and I find that both insulting and irritating. His whole attitude suggests I've bungled my family's lives for the past three years, and that everything's going to be better now that he's back. Well, I've got news for Ryder Matthews. *Big news.* I got along without him then and I can do it now."

Toni didn't say anything for several tortuous moments. "Don't you think you're confusing two separate issues?"

"No." Lynn answered without giving the question adequate thought. "He was a friend—a good one, and he feels a certain amount of guilt over Gary's death. If Ryder came back for any specific reason, it was to purge himself from that."

Toni arched her finely penciled brows. "I see. Then you have all the answers."

Not quite, but Lynn wasn't sure she was ready to admit as much. "I think I do."

"Then Ryder's task is going to be more difficult than he imagined."

"What do you mean?"

Toni glanced at her watch and sighed. "Listen, I'd like to stay and talk, but I promised to meet Joe. He wants to look at lawn mowers during his break." She offered Lynn a cocky smile and murmured, "From the sounds of it, you've got everything figured out, anyway."

"I...I don't know that I do." That was more difficult to admit than Lynn cared to think about. She knew Ryder, she knew herself, but they'd both changed.

"You'll figure everything out—just give yourself time." Toni set her napkin beside her plate and reached for the tab, studying it before retrieving her wallet. "I will make one suggestion, though."

"Sure."

"The next time Ryder stops by, ask him why he moved back to Seattle. You might be surprised by the answer." Following that, she scooted out of the seat and was gone.

By the time Lynn returned to the salon, she was more confused than ever. She'd wanted to talk out her feelings to Toni, but something had gone awry. It took her a while to realize what. Secretly Lynn had wanted Toni to tell her that kissing Ryder was all wrong. She'd hoped her friend would explain that she and Ryder had marched neglectfully into an uncharted area in a relationship that was best left alone. Unfortunately, Toni hadn't. Instead her friend had thrown questions at her Lynn didn't want to answer.

Lynn was forced to acknowledge that whatever her relationship had been with Ryder before he moved to Boston, it had now been altered. That much had been obvious from the minute she saw him at the picnic. Only it had taken time for Lynn to recognize that. She and Ryder weren't going to slip back into those old familiar roles, although Lynn would have been content to do so.

With her not-so-subtle questions, Toni kept insisting Lynn own up to her own feelings, which at the moment were difficult to decipher. Okay, so Ryder's kiss had affected her. She would figure out why and that should be the end of it.

Sharon walked into the office almost as soon as Lynn arrived. "Carrie phoned after you left. She won't be able to come in today."

Lynn groaned inwardly. "Is she sick?"

"She claims she was up half the night with some flu bug."

Lynn slouched down into her chair and released a frustrated sigh. "Great."

"Do you want to toss a coin and see which one of us stays until eight?"

Lynn was touched by her assistant's generosity. "No, I'll do it."

"What about Michelle and Jason?"

Lynn shrugged, there wasn't anything else to do. "I'll pick them up at four. They'll just have to stay here with me until closing time."

Sharon chuckled. "Jason's going to love that. Can't you just see him down here with his camouflage gear, waving at all these women in fancy tights?"

"I'll keep him busy drawing pictures in my office." That was optimistic thinking in action.

Sharon regarded her silently for a long moment. "You're sure? I can probably make arrangements with my sitter, if you want."

"No, I'll do it. Thanks anyway." It was her business and she was the one responsible. Besides, Sharon had stayed late one night this week already and Lynn couldn't ask that of her a second time.

"Okay, if you're sure." Sharon looked doubtful.

"I am. Were there any other calls?"

"Yeah, that guy with the husky voice phoned ten minutes after you left. He asked that you return his call and gave me the number. It's on your desk."

So Ryder had contacted her at lunchtime—somehow Lynn had expected he would.

"Anything else happen?"

"Not much. There were two or three more calls; I left the messages on your desk."

"Thanks, Sharon."

"No problem, it's what you pay me for."

Lynn sorted through the pink slips that were on top of her desk. She found it interesting that Sharon would specifically mention Ryder's call, but none of the others—except Carrie's.

From dealing with Ryder in the past, Lynn knew if she didn't return his call, he would keep trying until she answered. It was best to deal with him when she was the most prepared. Besides, she already knew what he wanted—he'd told her so himself when he'd left her the night before. He wanted to talk. Well, she didn't and she planned on telling him as much.

With resolve straightening her backbone, Lynn punched out his telephone number and waited. A secretary answered, her voice cool and efficient, conjuring up pictures of someone young and attractive. A pang of jealousy speared its way through Lynn. She found the emotion completely ridiculous. Ryder could be working with Miss Universe for all she cared.

"Ryder Matthews."

"Ryder, it's Lynn. I got the message that you called."

"Yes. I checked out a couple of day camps and found one in your area with an opening. Ever hear of Camp Puyallup?"

Lynn was so astonished it took her a full moment to find her breath. "Of course I have. It's the camp Jason wanted to attend, but they were full…I checked it out myself. Jason's friend Brad goes there."

"There's an opening now if Jason's interested."

"But…we're on their waiting list, we were told it

wasn't likely that he'd get in this summer. How did you manage it?"

Ryder hesitated as if he didn't want to admit something. "I phoned first thing this morning and was able to pull a few strings."

Lynn didn't know whether she should be furious or overjoyed. She knew how *Jason* would react, however, Her son would be in seventh heaven at the thought of escaping Peter Pan's. Lynn supposed she should be grateful Ryder had intervened on her behalf, but she didn't like him stepping into her life and "pulling strings." She could find her own solutions. All right, this day-care problem with Jason had been a thorn in her side and her son's as well.

"Jason will be pleased." It took an incredible amount of discipline to tell Ryder that much, although she tried to let him know in the cool way in which she spoke that she didn't appreciate what he'd done.

The ensuing silence was loud enough to create a sonic boom.

"I didn't mean to offend you." It was apparent from the clipped way in which he released his words that Ryder was upset. "I was only trying to help, Lynn."

"I know." She closed her eyes and let out a ragged sigh. It would be ridiculous to punish Jason because of her foolish pride. He was miserable at the center where he attended now and Camp Puyallup would be perfect for him.

"The camp director wanted to meet Jason tonight. Could you stop by with him for a few minutes after work?"

Lynn felt like weeping. "I can't…not tonight." As it was, her schedule was going to be exceptionally tight.

She would barely have time to pick up Jason and Michelle and be back at the salon in time to lead Carrie's four-thirty aerobics class.

"You can't take Jason! Why not?"

"I've got to work late. In fact, I was going to bring the kids down here with me."

"For how long?"

"Until closing."

"Which is?"

"Eight." It sounded like an eternity to Lynn. She could just see herself leading a dance aerobics class and trying to keep Jason out of mischief all at the same time. Tonight was going to be "one of those nights."

"Then I'll take Jason down myself," Ryder offered. "In fact, I'll pick up both kids; we'll make a night of it. I'll treat them to dinner and a movie afterward."

"Ryder, no. That isn't necessary."

"You'd rather have both kids down there with you? They'll be bored stiff."

Lynn didn't have any argument. Ryder was right. Given the choice between going to dinner and a movie with Ryder and staying holed up in her office, Lynn knew who the kids would want to spend the evening with. And she couldn't blame them.

"Well?"

"I...suppose that would be all right. I'll call Peter Pan's and tell them you'll be by to pick up Jason. Michelle's spending the day with Marcy...you met her last night."

"What time will you be home?"

"As soon after eight as I can manage."

Another silence followed, and Lynn was convinced Ryder was debating on whether to say something about the long hours she was putting in. She was grateful when he didn't.

"I'll have the kids home about that time."

"It's good of you to do this, Ryder. I appreciate it."

She could feel his smile all the way through the telephone line. "That wasn't so hard, was it?" he asked in a light teasing voice that was mellow enough to melt her insides.

It was apparent that he hadn't a clue as to how difficult it had been.

Ryder set down the phone and grinned lazily. He leaned back in his swivel chair and cupped his hands behind his head, satisfied by this unexpected turn of events. He was going to see Lynn again far sooner than he'd anticipated and that pleased him immeasurably.

Lynn had amazed him on two accounts. The first and foremost had been the way in which she'd responded to his kiss the night before. The plain and simple truth was that for the past six months, Ryder had been living on the edge. His biggest fear was that Lynn was going to meet another man and fall in love before he could get back to Seattle. He hadn't been eating properly—nor had he been sleeping well. There were so many hurdles to leap when it came to loving Lynn that fear had crowded his heart and his mind.

But holding and kissing her had sent him sailing over the first series of obstacles without a problem. She couldn't have responded to him the way she did without feeling something—and it wasn't anything remotely related to a brotherly affection. She'd wanted him. Ryder could feel it in his bones.

He hadn't been able to sleep for long hours afterward. Every time he closed his eyes, he imagined tasting her sweet mouth. If she'd wanted him to make love to her, and Ryder knew she did, it only touched the surface of the desire he'd experienced for her. By the time he arrived back at his apartment, his whole body had ached with need.

Months ago, when Ryder had first realized he was in love with Lynn, his first fleeting reaction was that it was wrong to feel the way he did. The best thing was for him to stay out of her life and let her find happiness elsewhere. It didn't take him much time to realize he couldn't allow that to happen. Like it or not Lynn was a part of him, and releasing her to love another man would be like chopping off his own arm. He could have managed it, but he would have gone through the remainder of his life aching his loss. Last night had confirmed that he'd made the right decision to woo Lynn. She was going to love him and the knowledge was enough to make him want to stand on top of his desk and shout for joy.

The second way in which Lynn had surprised him was how promptly she'd returned his phone call. It was almost as if she'd been eager to talk to him. Unfortunately, Ryder knew otherwise. He'd heard it in the sound of her voice, the minute he'd picked up the phone. She'd wanted to deal with his call and be done with it. Under different circumstances, Ryder would have been prepared for a two- or three-day wait before she contacted him. He didn't have time to delay and would have phoned her again until he reached her, but she'd surprised him first. Ryder didn't doubt that Lynn had been frustrated and confused over their encounter in her kitchen the night before. Talking to him would be the last thing she wanted to do, but she'd taken the initiative and he was proud of her.

Over the years, Ryder had learned to cherish his independence, and he could well appreciate Lynn's needs in that area. But darn it all, she couldn't manage everything on her own. It was time she set aside her pride and accept his willingness to lend her a helping hand.

She needed him just as much as he needed her.

Dropping his arms, Ryder briefly closed his eyes and let the tide of love for Lynn and the kids ebb over him. Things were going to work out just fine...just fine indeed.

Nine

Silence yawned through the living room when Lynn let herself into the house. Exhausted, she looped her purse on the doorknob to the entryway closet and walked directly into the kitchen. Usually she led two aerobics classes in a single workday, but on this one, she'd been forced to do four twenty-minute dance sessions. Every muscle in her weary body was loudly voicing its objection to the strenuous activity.

Lynn groaned when she stepped into the kitchen, rotating her neck to ease the stiffness there. The place was a disaster. As an experiment, Lynn had given Michelle a key to the house so her daughter could come and go as she pleased.

That was a mistake. From the looks of it, Michelle had decided to bake something. Now that she thought about it, she vaguely remembered Michelle phoning to ask permission to mix dough for chocolate-chip cookies. The entire conversation remained blurry in Lynn's mind, but from what she recalled, the actual baking part would take place at Marcy's house.

A fine dusting of flour littered the countertops like

frost on a winter's morning. The sugar bowl was open and chocolate chips were scattered from one end of the kitchen to the other.

Lynn popped a chocolate morsel into her mouth and let it melt on her tongue. It tasted incredibly good. She was beyond hungry—she'd barely touched her crab salad at lunch and it was hours past dinnertime.

It was after she'd finished wiping down the counters that Lynn found her daughter's note, promising to clean up the kitchen once she got home. Tiny print at the bottom of the page informed Lynn that her daughter had hidden her share of the cookies from Jason, they were somewhere safe in the house and Michelle would get one for her when she was home from the movie.

Opening the freezer door, Lynn found a frozen entree, and after reading the cooking directions, set it inside the microwave.

Seven minutes sounded like an eternity as she plopped herself down in the living room, removed her shoes and stretched her feet on top of the ottoman. If she could only close her eyes for a moment and rest... for just a minute.

Indistinctly, as if it were coming from a great distance, she heard the timer on the microwave beep. She didn't have the energy to move.

"Mom."

Lynn bolted awake, her feet dropping to the floor with a thunderous thud.

"Mom, guess what?" Jason flew into the room at the speed of a charging elephant, carrying with him—of all things—a stuffed furry basketball. "Ryder took me over to Camp Puyallup and I met everyone and they said I could join their troop. Brad and me are going to be partners tomorrow. Isn't that the greatest thing since… since hand grenades?"

Lynn managed to smile through her brain fog. "That's…wonderful, Jason."

"It's more than great…it's hell good."

"Hell good?"

"That's what everyone says when something is stupendous," Michelle informed her mother.

"I see." Lynn rubbed a hand over her face to wipe the sleep out of her eyes, hoping the action would unclog her mind. When she looked up Ryder was standing there, staring down on her. He was impossibly handsome and when he grinned, deep grooves formed at the sides of his mouth. Lynn felt as if the sun had come out and bathed her in its warm light. His smile was designed to disarm her and, to her chagrin, he succeeded. She smiled back despite her best intentions to cool things between them. She hated to admit, even to herself, how powerless she felt when she was around Ryder. It frightened her, and oddly enough, excited her all at the same time.

"Hi," he said, in that low, husky voice of his. "You look exhausted."

Lynn met his gaze steadily, refusing to allow herself to be sucked into his male charm, and knowing it would do little good to resist. She felt like she was swimming upstream against a raging current, battling for every inch of progress.

"Ryder took us out for Chinese food," Jason announced, plopping himself down on the ottoman in front of his mother. "And then—"

"I want to tell," Michelle cried impatiently. "You already told her about dinner."

"But *I* won the basketball. I should be the one to tell her."

"There was a carnival with rides and everything in the parking lot at the Fred Meyer store," Michelle announced, spitting the words out so fast they fell on top of each other. She ignored her brother's dirty look and continued, "We stopped there and Ryder let us go on all the rides we wanted."

"I won this." Jason held out a furry orange ball, beaming proudly.

"With a little help from Ryder." Michelle's singsong voice prompted the truth.

"Okay, okay, Ryder got down most of the pins, but I knocked some over all by myself."

"Congratulations, son." Lynn couldn't remember the last time Jason had looked so happy. His eyes shone with it and, for the first time in recent memory, he wasn't wearing his army clothes. Lynn didn't know what Ryder had said or done to get him to change, but whatever it was had worked better than anything she'd been able to come up with. A twinge of resentment shot through her, which she stifled. Her thoughts were petty, and she was angry with herself for being so small-minded.

"I got a mirror with Beyonce's profile sketched on it," Michelle announced, smugly holding it up for her mother's inspection.

A flash of her own image reflected back at her and caused Lynn to cringe. She looked dreadful—

"Yeah, but you didn't win that." Jason chimed in, interrupting her thoughts. It seemed he wanted to be sure his mother was aware no skill had been involved in obtaining Michelle's mirror.

"Actually Ryder was kind enough to buy it for me," Michelle answered in a disdainfully prim voice meant to put her obnoxious brother firmly in place.

"I want to show Brad my basketball," Jason said, turning his back on his sister. "Can I go over there…it isn't even dark yet."

Oh, the joys of summer, Lynn mused. It was almost nine and almost as light as it had been at three that afternoon.

"Marcy loves Beyonce. I want to run over to her house, too, can I?"

Lynn took one look at her children's eager expressions and nodded. Both vanished, leaving Ryder and Lynn alone in their wake. To her dismay, her empty stomach growled and Lynn flattened her hand over her abdomen.

"When was the last time you ate anything?" Ryder asked. His eyes blazed at her as though she'd committed some hideous crime and he was about to arrest her.

Lynn regarded him with a trace of irritation. "Noon. Listen, Ryder, I appreciate you taking the kids for me tonight. It's obvious they had the time of their lives, but I'm a big girl, I can take care of myself. I've even managed to feed myself a time or two."

"Not while working twelve-hour shifts."

"How much time I put in with my own salon is none of your business."

A frown darkened his features and as if to completely discredit her, her stomach growled again, this time loud enough to stir the cat who was sleeping on the back of the sofa.

"Come on," he said, "let's get you some dinner before you pass out."

"I can take care of myself."

"Then do it!"

With quick, efficient movements, Lynn marched into the kitchen and pulled the TV dinner out of the microwave. Whirling around to face him, she yanked open the silverware drawer and jerked out a fork.

"You can't eat that garbage." Ryder contemptuously regarded her meal, wrinkling up his nose as if he found the very smell of it offensive.

"I most certainly *can* eat this…just watch me." Before he could argue with her, she stabbed her fork into watery mashed potatoes. They tasted like liquid paper and she nearly gagged, but she managed to swallow the bite and pretend it was nectar from the gods.

"Lynn, stop being so incredibly stubborn and throw that thing out before it makes you sick." He removed the plastic carton from her hands.

Lynn grabbed it back before he could place it in the garbage. "Stop telling me what to do."

"Okay, I apologize. Now throw that out and cook yourself something decent. You can't work that many hours and treat your body this way."

"Since when have you become an expert on *my* body?" she yelled, growing more furious by the minute.

"Since last night," he yelled back.

Their eyes met in a defiant clash of wills. His were dark and narrowed and hers wide and furious. From the way the grooves at the edges of his mouth whitened, Lynn knew he was having trouble keeping a rein on his temper. For some obscure reason, that bit of insight pleased Lynn. It pleased her so much she had to resist the urge to laugh. He was clearly determined to bend her will to his no matter what it cost. And she was equally determined not to. Most anyone else would have been intimidated by his fierce gaze, but she wasn't. She knew Ryder well—besides, the stakes were far too high.

When he turned away and started sorting through her refrigerator, Lynn laughed out loud. "Just exactly what do you think you're doing?"

He ignored her completely.

Lynn slapped her hands against her sides and groaned. "Good grief, Ryder, don't you see how ridiculous this is? The two of us aren't any better than Michelle and Jason."

He set several items on top of the counter, then started searching through her cupboards until he found a frying pan.

"You're wasting your time," she told him, as he peeled off slices of bacon and placed them in the skillet.

"No, I'm not."

Lynn found the entire episode highly amusing. "If you think I'm going to eat that, you're sadly mistaken."

He didn't rise to her bait.

As if to prove her point, she took another bite of the atrocious entree, choking down a rubbery piece of meat that was floating in something that resembled gravy.

The distinctive odor of frying bacon filled the kitchen, slowly waltzing around Lynn, wafting under her nose and causing her mouth to water. She downed another bite of mashed potatoes, nearly gulping in an effort to force the tasteless mass down her throat.

For all the attention Ryder was giving her, she might as well have been invisible.

"You're wasting your time, Ryder," she told him a second time, angry that he was ignoring her.

He cut a tomato into incredibly thin slices and

stacked them in a neat pile. Next he buttered the bread, added just the right amount of salad dressing and then started building the sandwich with thick layers of bacon, lettuce and tomato.

"I'll end up giving that to the cat," she warned.

He folded the bread together, placed the BLT— Lynn's favorite kind of sandwich—on a plate and poured her a tall, cold glass of milk. Next he carried both the glass and the plate to the table and pulled out a chair for her, silently demanding that she sit down and eat.

"I told you it was a waste of time," she said, crossing her arms and purposely directing her nose in the opposite direction.

"Lynn," he coaxed softly, "come and eat."

"No." A lesser woman would have succumbed, but she was beyond reason. More than a silly sandwich was at stake; Ryder was challenging her pride.

Apparently he was prepared for her argument because he marched back to her. He settled his hands on her shoulders and tightened them just a little so she felt his fingers firmly against her flesh, but not painfully. She was conscious of an odd sensation that surged through her blood, an awareness, an exhilaration as if she'd been frozen for years and years and was only now beginning to melt.

"Sit down and eat."

She shook her head.

"My goodness, you're stubborn."

She gave him a saucy grin, hoping to mock him. She realized her mistake almost immediately—Ryder wasn't a man to be scorned. Harsh lines formed around his mouth and between his eyebrows and fire blazed from his eyes. Lynn had to do something and quick.

"Just who do you think you are?" she flared, attacking him, taking the offense rather than being forced into a defensive position. "You have no right—absolutely none—to tell me what to do."

Ryder's hold tightened on her shoulders and Lynn realized an instant later that she'd made her second tactical error. But this time she was too late to do anything about it.

"I'll tell you what gives me the right," he growled. "This." Before she knew what was happening, his mouth was on hers—his lips hard and compelling and so hot she felt singed all the way to her toes. He kissed her with a fierceness that claimed her breath. Her eyes were shut tightly and to her further humiliation, low growling sounds rose from the back of her throat that only seemed to encourage him. Lynn tried to resist—she honestly tried. Her mind scrambled with a hundred reasons why she should free herself, but it was useless. Beyond impossible. While her head was screaming at her to put an end to this madness, she slid her arms around his neck, clinging to him. She burrowed her fingers through the thick, dark hair at the back of his head, and her tongue darted in and out of his mouth in a game of cat and mouse.

Ryder slid his moist lips from hers to the scented hollow of her neck. Lynn drew in several deep, wobbly breaths in a reckless effort to regain her composure. She had melted so completely in Ryder's arms that he would have to peel her off.

"Lynn."

His harsh intake of breath gave her little satisfaction. He, too, had apparently been just as affected by their kissing.

"Yes?" Her own voice was low and gravelly.

"Why do you find it so necessary to argue with me?"

"I...I don't know."

"You're so hungry you're almost sick with it, and still you won't eat. Why?"

She shook her head, not bothering to mention that she'd cooked the frozen dinner and had every intention of suffering through that—would have, in fact, if he hadn't insisted on cooking her something else. But instead of arguing, she moved her head just a little and opened her mouth against his throat, kissing it. She felt his body tense and smiled, loving the exhilarating sensation of power the action provided her.

"I'm always cranky when I get overly hungry," she explained.

Ryder chuckled, but the sound of his amusement was tainted with chagrin. "Next time, I'll remember that."

Lynn wasn't sure she wanted him to, not when she enjoyed his methods of persuasion so much.

"Will you eat the sandwich now?"

Lynn didn't even have to think about it. "All right."

Ryder released her, and she meekly sat down at the table. She had just taken her first bite when Michelle and Marcy strolled into the kitchen.

"Hi Mom, hi, Ryder." She pulled out a chair, twisted it around and plopped herself down. "Have you told Mom about Wild Waves yet?" The question was directed to Ryder.

He frowned. "Not yet."

"What about Wild Waves?" Lynn inquired, almost afraid to ask. The water park was in the south end of

Seattle and a popular recreation spot. Machine produced waves and huge slides attracted large crowds.

Michelle grinned from ear to ear in a smile that would dazzle the sun. "Ryder's taking the three of us to the park Saturday. We're going to take a whole day off and have fun like a real family, isn't that right?"

Lynn could feel the heat building up in her cheeks. Not only was Ryder dictating what she ate, but now he apparently meant to take control of her whole life.

"Michelle," Ryder said, glancing at the girl. "Maybe it would be best if you gave your mother and me some time alone."

Ten

Ryder waited until Michelle and her friend had vacated the kitchen. Lynn was irate. Her eyes flashed fire at him, but that was nothing new. She'd been in a foul mood from the moment he walked into the house with the kids. By heaven the woman could be stubborn—Ryder hadn't realized how obstinate until recently. Couldn't she see that he was only trying to help her? From the way she was acting, one would assume he'd committed some terrible crime against women's rights. From what the kids had told him, Lynn hadn't had a full day off in months, but apparently suggesting a fun outing was paramount to being a male chauvinist pig. Especially on the heels of their showdown over the sandwich.

All Ryder had wanted Lynn to do was take care of herself, and surely that wasn't so terrible. As for this Wild Waves thing, she needed a day to relax, but from the way her narrowed eyes were spitting fireballs at him, she fully intended to argue with him about this, too.

"What's this about taking Saturday off and going

to Wild Waves?" Lynn demanded when he didn't immediately explain.

"I thought it might be a fun thing to do."

"I assumed you were working in a law office and understood minor things like making a living and responsibility? Obviously you think I'm independently wealthy."

"You know that's not true." He tried not to respond in like anger, but to remain coolheaded and reasonable. Apparently the food hadn't had enough time to defuse her bad mood.

"Then you assume that it's no problem for me to flutter in and out of the salon at will? Besides, the lawyers that *I* know work at least six-day weeks."

"My schedule isn't like that, and you know it." For now his workload was light. But it wouldn't always be that way. He wanted to take advantage of the summer months as best he could, using this time to court Lynn and spend time with Michelle and Jason.

"How could I possibly know anything about your schedule?" she demanded. "You show up at my place at noon, wanting to take me to lunch. Then the next thing I know, you're telling me you have Saturday free to laze away in some park." She finished the sandwich, stood and carried the empty plate to the sink, then turned to face him, her back braced against the kitchen counter. "Well, I can't take time off when I feel like it. Saturday isn't free for me and I have no intention of taking it off—I'm short-staffed as it is."

He shrugged, accepting her decision. There was little else he could do, although his disappointment was keen. "Then don't worry about it. I'll be happy to take the kids myself."

Her mouth was already open, the argument dying on her lips. "But—"

"Lynn, I thought Wild Waves was something you might enjoy as well."

"You should never have mentioned my coming in front of the kids. Now they're going to be disappointed."

He mulled that over, then nodded. "You're right." But Michelle and Jason had complained that all their mother ever did was work, suggesting a family outing had slipped out without him giving the matter the proper thought. A day completely free of worry and commitment sounded like just the thing for Lynn. Michelle and Jason both claimed she worked too hard, and Ryder was witness to the fact himself. She was driving herself toward a nervous breakdown, putting in ten- and twelve-hour days, skipping meals, and it didn't look as though she was sleeping well, either.

Ryder longed to wrap her in his arms and protect her. But holding Lynn when she was in this mood was like trying to kiss a porcupine. He could feel her bristle the minute Michelle had innocently mentioned the outing. Kissing her into submission wasn't going to work a second time. In fact, Ryder felt a bit guilty about having used that technique earlier, but she'd angered him so much that holding her had been his only weapon against her stubborn pride. For some obscure reason, he'd managed to convince himself he could control the passion between them. Wrong. The minute her sweet tongue had started teasing him, he'd been on the brink of lifting her into his arms and hauling her up those stairs. The only thing that had stopped him was the thought of Michelle and Jason bursting in on them.

Thank heaven he had enough common sense to cut the kissing off when he did.

The time had come to wake up and smell the coffee. When it came to his feelings for Lynn, Ryder was playing with a lit stick of dynamite and the sooner he owned up to the fact, the better. Who did he think he was, anyway? Superman? He couldn't kiss her like that and not pay the consequences. Just the memory of the way her silky, soft body had moved against him was enough to make his mouth go dry. He'd waited all these months to claim her as his own, he could wait a little longer. When they *did* make love, and that was inevitable, the timing would be right, and not the result of some heated argument.

"Don't misunderstand me, I'd enjoy a day off," Lynn admitted with some reluctance, "but I just can't."

"I understand," Ryder returned, although he had trouble accepting it. He walked over to her side and placed his hands on her forearms. She stiffened, which frustrated him all the more. He dropped his arms, not wanting to force another confrontation. The day would come, he assured himself, when she would welcome his touch. For now, she was frightened and confused and in need of a good deal of patience.

"Hi Mom, hi Ryder." Jason stepped into the kitchen, set his basketball on the tabletop and leaned forward. "What's happening?"

"Nothing much," Lynn said and set her plate and glass in the dishwasher.

"You ask Mom about Wild Waves?" The question was directed to Ryder.

"She has to work, son."

Disappointment flashed from his eyes and the smile

he'd been wearing folded over into a deeply set frown. "We can still go, can't we?"

"If it's all right with your mother."

"Of course it's all right," Lynn answered eagerly, as though to make up for the fact she wouldn't be with them.

Jason nodded, but none of the excitement returned. "We had a good time tonight. Ryder let me go on as many of the rides as I wanted and when that sissy Michelle was afraid to try the hammer, he went with me."

"A man's got to do what a man's got to do," Lynn joked and when she glanced in Ryder's direction, he grinned. "I'm pleased you had such a good time. I hope you remembered to properly thank Ryder."

"Of course I did." Jason pulled out a chair and folded his arms over the top of the stuffed basketball, his look thoughtful. "You took us to Wild Waves once, Mom, don't you remember? But that was when you were home. You used to do a lot of things with Michelle and me before you went to work with those fat ladies…but you don't do much of that anymore."

"I need to make a living, honey."

"I suppose," Jason returned with an elongated sigh. "But sometimes I think we were better off when we were poor."

"Jason," Lynn argued, staring at her son incredulously, as though she couldn't believe her own ears. "That's not true."

She cast Ryder a sideways glance as if she felt it was important for him to believe her. He smiled, telling her that he did.

"I'll be able to take you to Wild Waves another time."

"But when?" Jason cried. "You're always telling me

about all the great things we're going to do some day and they never happen."

"Jason, you're being completely unreasonable. Why...look at what we've done this summer."

"What? What have we done this summer, Mom?"

It was apparent that Lynn was searching her memory and was surprised to discover she'd spent far less time with her children than she realized. Her expression became a study in parental guilt. Her energy level was frayed to the edges as it was, and although Ryder had intended to stay out of the discussion, he stepped to Lynn's side and slipped his arm around her shoulder, hoping to lend her his strength. She didn't appreciate the action and he dropped his arm almost immediately.

"The only place we've gone *all* summer is to the precinct picnic," Jason told her righteously.

"I think it's time for bed, Jason, don't you?" Ryder suggested. "You've got a big day at camp tomorrow."

His eyes widened and his grin blossomed, spreading from ear to ear. "Right. Do you want me to tell Marcy it's time to go home, Mom?"

Lynn shook her head. "I'll do that. Now up to bed, young man."

"Okay." He walked over and kissed her cheek, then looked at Ryder and rolled his eyes. "Women expect that kind of thing," he explained, as if it were important for Ryder to understand that he didn't take to kissing girls.

"I know."

With that, Jason traipsed up the stairs and into his room. Lynn stood with her arms folded, staring after her son as though she couldn't quite believe what had just transpired. "He always has an excuse for staying up late. I can't remember the last time he didn't argue with me over bedtime."

With Lynn so exhausted, Ryder realized it was time he left. He didn't want to go, but what he longed for wasn't important right now—Lynn's health was.

"It's time I thought about heading home." He was a bit disappointed when she didn't suggest he stay longer, and mildly annoyed when she didn't so much as walk him to the door. It was all too obvious that she was glad to be rid of him, and that dented his pride. He'd come a long way with Lynn in a short amount of time, but miles of uncharted road stretched before him. At least when he kissed her, he had her attention. That small piece of information helped ease his mind as he climbed inside his car and drove off.

The following afternoon, Lynn sat at her desk, expelled a deep breath and reached for the phone. She couldn't delay calling Ryder any longer. Her finger jabbed out the number of his office as if to punish the phone for making this conversation necessary. Silly as it sounded, Lynn preferred contacting him at Crestron and Powers. It was less personal than calling him at his apartment. She fingered his business card until the honey-voiced secretary came on the line and efficiently announced the name of the firm. Whoever she was, this woman with the peaches-and-cream voice, Lynn didn't like her.

"Could I have Ryder Matthews's office please?"

"May I ask who's calling?"

It was on the tip of Lynn's tongue to demand to know just how many women Ryder had phoning him, but she realized in the nick of time how ridiculous that would have sounded. That thought alone was enough to prove that she'd made the right decision—she *needed* a day off.

"Lynn Danfort," she answered after a moment. "If he's busy, he can return the call."

"I'll put you through," the woman purred, and Lynn resisted the urge to make a face.

"Lynn, this is a pleasant surprise." Ryder came on the line almost immediately. "What can I do for you?"

Lynn dragged herself away from her thoughts. "Ryder, hello." She felt so foolish now. "It's about Wild Waves on Saturday. I...I was wondering if it would be all right if I *did* decide to tag along." There—that hadn't been so bad. Ryder was a gracious man—he'd never given her reason to think otherwise.

"That would be great. I'd love to have you."

"I talked with my assistant, Sharon, and she said that she'd cover for me." Lynn wouldn't mention what else Sharon had said. The woman seemed to think Lynn was a first-class idiot to turn down an outing with Ryder Matthews. *Any* outing, even if it included Michelle and Jason. For her part, including the kids was the only way Lynn would agree to see Ryder. When it came to dealing with her late husband's best friend, she was more confused than ever. She'd thought to avoid him as much as possible. That had been her intention after he'd asked her out that first day at the precinct picnic and then later when he'd come to the salon. She'd refused him both times. But circumstances seemed to keep tossing them together.

Lynn would have liked to blame Ryder for everything that had happened, but she couldn't even salvage her pride with that. And when he'd kissed her, it had been like setting a match to a firecracker, her response was that explosive. Every time Ryder came close to her, Lynn had been left indelibly marked. In the beginning she'd tried to pass her reaction off to the fact she'd been without a man for a long time. She'd dated a bit in the past couple of years, but no one else had been able to elicit the feeling Ryder had—no one except Gary, and that frightened her.

"I'd thought we'd make a full day of it and leave about ten-thirty."

"That sounds fine to me." Sleeping in sounded glorious. "I'll pack us a picnic lunch."

"Bring lots of suntan lotion and plenty of towels."

"Right." Her enthusiasm level increased just talking about the outing. It'd been so long since she'd spent a carefree day lazing in the sun.

"I'm really looking forward to this, Ryder."

He sighed and a wealth of satisfaction hummed through the wire. "Good."

After a few words of farewell, Lynn replaced the telephone receiver, but her hand lingered on the headset. For some obscure reason she couldn't explain or understand, she had the feeling everything was going to change between her and Ryder because of this outing.

Eleven

"Mom, look!"

Lynn and about thirteen other women turned in the direction of the young voice, glancing toward the water where the youngsters were bobbing up and down on the swirling waves. It took Lynn a couple of seconds to realize the boy's voice hadn't belonged to Jason.

The minute the four of them had arrived at Wild Waves, Jason had hit the water like the marines attacking Normandy beach and had yet to come out almost two hours later. Every now and again, Lynn saw him sitting atop his brightly colored tube, riding the swelling waters as if he were master of the seas. To say he loved the waterworks park would be an understatement.

Michelle, on the other hand, had spent an hour fixing her hair before Ryder had arrived. When Lynn had been silly enough to mention that all that mousse would be wasted once she got wet, Michelle had given her a look that suggested Lynn was brain dead. Later Michelle explained that she was styling her hair in case she happened to run into someone she knew. This "someone" was obviously a boy.

"It couldn't be a more perfect day had we planned it," Lynn told Ryder, who was lying back on the blanket, his face turned to the sun, his eyes closed. He'd recently walked out of the pool and his lean muscular length glistened in the bright golden light.

"I *did* plan it," he joked. "I told the person in charge of weather that we needed sunshine today. One word from me and it was arranged."

"It seems I've underestimated your influence." Her voice was teasing, but she couldn't disguise her pleasure. Ryder had been right; she needed this, far more than she'd been willing to admit. "Do you have anything else arranged that I should know about?"

A slow, easy smile worked its way across his face. "As a matter of fact, I do, but I'm saving that for later." He opened his eyes and looked up at her, his grin devilish and filled with boyish charm. "I suggest you be prepared."

"For what?"

He giggled his eyebrows up and down several times.

Despite the effort not to, Lynn laughed. It felt so good to throw caution to the wind and leave her worries behind her at least for this one day. She hadn't so much as called Sharon to see how things were going at the salon. If there were problems, she didn't want to know about them. It was amazing how comfortable it felt to bury her head in the sand—or in this case, the water.

"Mom, I'm starved."

This time the voice was unmistakably Jason's. Lynn twisted around and found her son wading out of the deep blue water, his inner tube under one arm and a snorkel in the other.

Lynn straightened and reached for the picnic basket,

and small cooler which were loaded with goodies. She brought out a turkey sandwich and a cold can of soda.

Jason fell to his knees and automatically reached for the soda. "Gee, this is fun. Did you see the wave I just took?"

"I…can't say that I did," Lynn admitted. She set out the potato chips and fresh fruit—seedless grapes were Jason's favorite, and she'd packed several large bunches.

"Where's Michelle?" Ryder asked, looking toward the slide area.

"The last time I saw her, she was talking to some guy," Jason told him in a disgruntled voice. "She's hardly been in the water all day. I asked her about it and she got all huffy and told me to get lost. Personally, I think she's afraid of getting her hair wet." He said this with a sigh and a meaningful shrug as if to suggest Lynn arrange intensive counseling for her oldest child. Between bites, Jason added. "I don't think I'll ever understand girls."

"I gave up trying years ago," Ryder admitted.

"Then why do we have anything to do with them?" Her son was completely serious. "Jason! What a thing to ask."

"*You're* all right, Mom," he was quick to assure her. "It's all the others. Look at Michelle—here we are at the neatest water place in the whole world and she's afraid to go in past her knees because she's doesn't want to splash her hair. It's ridiculous, don't you think?"

"No," Lynn shot back. Michelle was at an age when maintaining her looks was important to her. That was all part of growing up. Within a few years, Jason was sure to experience the same level of conscientiousness. She was sure he wouldn't find it quite so silly then.

"If you'll notice, your mother hasn't spent much time in the water, either," Ryder pointed out. He sat up and shot Lynn a mischievous grin.

"You're worried about your hair, too?" Jason cried as though he couldn't believe his ears. "My own mother!"

"Not exactly."

"Then how come you've only been in the pool a little bit?"

It was more a matter of crowd control. When Lynn first arrived, she'd taken out an inflated raft and had been quickly overpowered by what seemed like several thousand kids, each one eager to ride the waves. All those thrashing bodies had gotten in her way. She simply needed more space.

"Mom?" Jason asked, a second time. "Explain yourself."

Lynn laughed. "There are too many kids out there."

"Too many kids," Jason repeated, stunned.

"I go in and cool off when I get too hot, but other than that I prefer to lie in the sun and perfect my tan."

It looked as though Jason was about to make another derogatory comment referring to her wanting a golden tan. To divert his attention, she took out a package of potato chips and handed them to him. Her tactic worked, and within a minute the boy was too busy wolfing down his lunch to care how much time she spent in the water. As soon as he'd finished eating, he was off again, eager to return to his fun.

Kneeling in front of the picnic basket, Lynn closed the lid and picked up the discarded bits of litter left over from her son's lunch.

"You're getting sun-burned," Ryder commented wryly.

She paused and glanced down at her arm, but didn't notice any appreciable difference.

"You'd better put on some sunscreen before you get burned." He reached for her hand, lifting her arm as if to examine it. "Let me put it on for you."

"No," she returned automatically. All day she'd taken pains to avoid any type of physical contact with Ryder, even the most innocent of touches. The thought of him sliding his hands up and down her shoulders and over her back was enough to flash huge red warning lights inside her head. This was something to be avoided at any cost.

"Lynn, you're being silly. You aren't used to all this sun."

"I'm fine," she said, fighting the tingling awareness of his fingers holding on to hers. She couldn't allow herself to get too close to Ryder, fearing the power he had to control her body's responses. She tugged at her hand, wanting to free herself before she sought a deeper contact. But Ryder wouldn't release her. Instead he lifted her hand to his mouth and pressed a soft, lingering kiss to its back. His tongue flickered out, moistening the tender skin there. Lynn's heart leaped into her throat at the sensual contact. His eyes, staring at her over her wrist, seemed to convey a thousand words. There were emotions he had yet to verbalize, matters she wasn't prepared to accept. Lynn found herself mesmerized by his dark brown eyes; she couldn't have pulled away had her life depended on it. The world she'd so carefully constructed since Ryder's absence was about to crumple at her feet and yet she dared to linger. Her heart was pounding so hard, she thought it might damage her rib cage.

She managed to pull her gaze from his, dropping it, but to her dismay, she encountered the crisp curling hairs and the hard muscles of his chest. The overwhelming desire to run her fingers through those dark hairs was akin to a physical blow. Ryder's uneven breathing told her he was equally affected by her merest touch. If anything, that increased Lynn's already heightened awareness of him and their situation. With an incredible surge of inner strength, she pulled away and stood abruptly—so abruptly, she nearly stumbled.

"I...think I'll go in the pool for a little bit," she said in a voice that trembled.

Lynn couldn't get away fast enough.

Ryder watched Lynn go with an overpowering sense of frustration. He'd tried being patient with her; he'd taken pains to make this outing as relaxed as possible. From the minute he'd arrived at the house, Ryder recognized that Lynn had carefully chosen to play the role of a good friend. It was obvious that she didn't want to experience the things he made her feel. Apparently she wanted to pretend they'd never kissed, and ignore the fact she'd come to life in his arms. Not once, but twice. It had been difficult, but Ryder had played along, falling into her scheme—for her sake, certainly not because that was the way he wanted it. All along, his intention had been to give Lynn the time she needed to relax and enjoy herself. He didn't want to spoil it by making emotional demands on her. Any kind of demands.

But she was driving him crazy. She'd worn a demure one-piece swimsuit, although he was certain she owned more than one bikini. But the modest suit did little to disguise her magnificent body. If anything, it boldly emphasized every luscious curve of her womanly shape. He hadn't thought it was possible to desire her any more than he already did, but watching her move in that swimsuit came close to driving him crazy.

Ryder's fingers ached with the need to caress her. When he'd reached for her hand, he felt her involuntary reaction to his touch. She'd shivered slightly. The ache in him increased with the memory and he drew a deep breath in an effort to minimize his body's response. The problem was she was so beautiful, with her wind tousled hair and her sweet face devoid of any makeup. There wasn't a woman alive who could compete with her.

Now, like a frightened rabbit, she was running away from him. His instinct was to reach out and grab her, keep her at his side, demand that she listen to all the love he had stored up in his heart for her. But he couldn't do that, couldn't express all this emotion that burned within his chest. To do so could frighten her into running blindly into the night and if he let that happen, he might never be able to catch her.

Patience, he told himself, repeating the word over and over in his mind.

Lynn's escape into the water had nothing to do with the sun. She'd gone swimming in an effort to cool down from being so close to Ryder. His touch, although light and impersonal, could be compared to falling into a lava bed, Lynn mused. She felt the heat rising in her all the way from the soles of her feet, sweeping through her body like a brushfire out of control. The only thing left for her to do was flee. There weren't nearly as many kids in the water as there had been earlier. She waded out until she was waist deep and still she didn't feel any of the cooling effect she sought. She went deeper and deeper until she had no choice but to dip her head beneath the water's churning surface. The liquid seemed to sizzle against her red-hot face. Dear heaven, if only she knew what was happening to her.

She swam underwater until her lungs felt as though they were about to burst. Breaking the surface, she drew in huge gulps of oxygen and brushed the long, wet strands of hair away from her face with both hands.

"Jason would be proud of you." The voice was all too familiar.

"Ryder." She opened her eyes and issued his name on a husky murmur, surprised that he'd been able to find her in the huge pool.

"Lynn, don't keep running from me," his low voice pleaded with her.

Her eyes rounded and she stared at him so long she forgot to breathe. She opened her mouth to deny the fact she was trying to escape, but found she couldn't force the lie.

"Watch out."

Even before the words had completely left his mouth, Lynn was caught in a giant swell of water. Her feet flew out from under her and she was tossed about as easily as a leaf floating in an autumn breeze. A strong pair of hands slipped around her waist and righted her. Led by instinct, she reached out and held on.

Lynn and Ryder broke the surface together, clinging to each other.

"Are you all right?"

"Fine," she said automatically, not pausing to check otherwise.

"I didn't see it coming until the wave was on top of us."

He continued to hold her, bringing her so close to his body that Lynn was amazed the brief span of water between them wasn't boiling and spitting. She'd felt so strongly drawn to Ryder. In that moment, she had as much power to resist him as a stickpin would have against a magnet. Her hands were braced against the sides of his neck and she realized, too late, that she'd reached blindly for him, sensing she would be utterly safe in his arms.

Wordlessly he bent toward her, ever so slightly, and she began to stroke his neck, slipping her hands down the water-slickened muscles of his shoulders, reveling in the strength she sensed beneath her fingertips.

She was unsure of the exact moment it had happened, but a warm, reeling awareness took control of her will, leaving her almost giddy in its wake. Without her knowing exactly how he'd managed to do it, Ryder wrapped his arms fully around her, pressing her to the long, hard length of him. She trembled, fitting snugly into his embrace, powerfully aware of the place where his fingers touched her skin. A tingling sensation spread out from his hands in rippling waves that flooded every cell of her body. Swamped with countless emotions, Lynn didn't know which one to respond to first. Confused, flustered and so completely lost in awareness, she buried her face in the hollow of his neck while she struggled within herself. She drew in several deep, shaking breaths, hoping those would help to clear her head.

While he held her firmly around her waist, he combed her hair away from her face in a slow, soothing action. "I'm never going to leave you again," he whispered. "I couldn't bear it a second time."

Lynn longed to tell him it wasn't his leaving that had confused her so much as his coming back. Her fuddled brain tried to formulate the words, but the thoughts cluttered in her mind. She couldn't think while he continued with his gentle caress. She gasped softly in protest when he slipped his hand from her hair down to her shoulders and back.

She opened her mouth and instantly became aware of his chest hair. The curly, dark hairs had fascinated her earlier and she now realized how close they were to her mouth. Common sense was highly overrated, Lynn decided recklessly, and let her tongue investigate the throbbing hollow of his neck. He tasted like salt and water, pleasant beyond belief. Her mouth opened further, hungrily exploring his skin as if he were a delectable feast, as indeed he was.

"Lynn." Her name was ground out between his teeth.

She ignored the plea in his voice. This was what he wanted, why he'd swum out to find her. It was what she'd longed for all day and had tried desperately to avoid.

She continued pressing kisses up the strong cord of his neck, lapping him with her tongue, and giving him tiny love bites.

He tightened his arms around her. He was moving, carrying her through the water, but Lynn hardly noticed. When she happened to glance up, she noted that he'd found a secluded corner away from the rush of swimmers. She kissed the edge of his mouth to voice her approval. She nipped his earlobe, loving the way his body tensed with the action. He braced his feet farther apart as though expecting an assault.

Lynn gave him one.

She took his earlobe into her mouth, her tongue fluttering in and around, sucking, tasting, nibbling. A sense of hot pleasure flashed through her at the way his pulse exploded against her chest.

He groaned once, softly, and the sound excited her more than anything she'd ever known. He wove his fingers into her hair and she heard his harsh, ragged breath as he gently pulled her away from him. Lynn wasn't given more than a second to catch her breath before he took her mouth with a greed that defied anything she'd ever experienced.

Another wave assaulted them, but Lynn couldn't have cared less and apparently neither did Ryder. They were swept off their feet, tossed and rolled and still they relentlessly clung to each other. When they broke the surface, Ryder helped them back into a standing position. Briefly they broke apart, but he wouldn't allow it for long and kissed her again with a ravenous passion; he seemed to want to devour her whole. Lynn responded with everything that was in her. Her mouth opened to him like the sun coaxing open a flower bud. Lynn thought she would die from pure bliss. He lifted her against his body, holding on to her as if her life were at stake. As her body slipped intimately over his, he groaned anew. "Oh, Lynn."

Her arms were completely around his neck, her fingers digging mindlessly into his tense shoulder muscles. "I know," she cried. "This isn't the time or the place." They were in a public place, although she doubted that anyone had noticed them.

For All My Tomorrows

"I want you," he growled into her ear.

She smiled and rubbed her foot down the back of his thigh. "Tell me you want me, too. I need to hear it."

What seemed like an eternity passed before she was willing to admit it. Why it should be so difficult to tell him what couldn't be any more obvious was beyond her comprehension.

"Lynn…"

"Yes," she groaned. "Yes, I want you."

He expelled his breath, then leaned his forehead against hers. "I don't dare kiss you," he whispered. "I'm afraid I won't be able to stop."

"I…feel the same way."

"I want to touch you so much. I swear there isn't a place on my whole body that isn't aching. If this is the flu, then it's the worst case I've ever had."

Lynn grinned and lightly brushed her lips over his mouth, needing to touch him, ignoring the consequences. "I'll have you know, Ryder Matthews, it's not very flattering to be compared to the flu."

"I don't suppose you'd care to being likened to the bubonic plague then, either?"

"That's even worse." Lynn was teasing him, but she was experiencing the same level of frustration. "Should we get out of the water?" she suggested next, looking for a means of easing this self-inflicted torture.

Ryder grinned. "I don't think we…I dare."

"Do you want to swim?"

"No," he growled. "I want to make love to you."

Having him say it so bluntly had a curious effect upon Lynn. The blood drained out of her face and she felt weak and shaky. Ryder must have noticed because his eyes searched her face, his love-thirsty eyes drinking from her.

"Certainly that doesn't shock you?" he asked gently.

"No," she lowered her gaze and took in a calming breath before explaining. "It's just that…it's been a long time for me. I feel like a virgin all over again. I suppose that sounds crazy considering the fact I was married several years and bore two children."

"When it comes to you, I *am* crazy."

Her eyes flew to him. "You are?"

He nodded. "But, Lynn, I already know how very good it's going to be for us."

Lynn did, too. After years of living without a husband, years in which she denied feeling anything sexual, she experienced an awesome passion building within her, like a volcano threatening to explode.

She couldn't keep her hands still. She stroked and caressed his face, loving the feel of his hard jaw, the gentle rasp of his beard and the moist heat of his mouth. When she couldn't hold back any longer, she nuzzled his throat, licking him with the fever that burned within her.

He kissed her again as though he'd been waiting years and was starving for the taste of her. "When?" she rasped when his mouth slid from hers. "Ryder, oh, please tell me when." She couldn't believe she was being so forward.

He went still. "When? What do you mean *when*?"

With her hands braced on each side of his jaw, she continued her loving assault. "I want to know how long it will be before we make love. Tonight?" She was shaking so badly that if Ryder hadn't been holding on to her she would have sank to the bottom of the pool. "Oh, no," she groaned, "what about the kids? We're going to have to be so careful." Her lips slid across his cheek and lightly brushed over his lips, darting her tongue in and out of his mouth. "Your place would be better. I think—"

"Lynn…"

"I'm not on the pill, either…I hadn't counted on anything like this…ever. What should we do?"

He tensed. "Why?"

"Oh, Ryder, please, think about it. There are going to be problems with this…minor ones, but we can solve them, I know we can." Once more she angled her mouth over his, feeding him with soft, nibbling kisses, feeding herself, unable to get enough of him. "First of all, I don't think it would be a good idea for Michelle and Jason to know what we're doing. They're young and impressionable and I—"

"Lynn, stop," he interrupted, his voice controlled enough for her to grow still.

Slowly she raised her head. It took her a couple of moments to realize how serious he was. She didn't understand. Some of the excitement and happiness drained from her. "What's wrong?"

"I want to know why you want to make love." he asked her, his gaze never wavering from her face.

"Why?" she repeated, stunned. "Do you always ask a woman that kind of question?" She didn't know what was happening, but whatever it was confused her.

"I know what your body is feeling, trust me, love, I feel it, too. All I want you to do is give me one good reason why you're doing this."

"You know the answer to that." She loosened her hold from around his neck and braced her hands against his shoulders, feeling incredibly foolish now.

"I don't know the answer."

"Well…"

"Because it feels good?" he offered.

She leaped on that excuse and nodded eagerly. "Yes."

He closed his eyes as though she'd lashed out at him and when he opened them again an emotion she couldn't decipher flickered there.

"That's not enough for me," he told her with heavy reluctance. "I wish it was, but it isn't."

"Why isn't it?" she cried. It was enough for her…at least it had been until a few moments ago. She couldn't understand why Ryder was being so unreasonable. One minute he was whispering how much he wanted to make love to her and the next he was making her sound heartless and mercenary.

"I'm not looking for a woman to make me 'feel good.'"

He started to say more, but Lynn wouldn't let him, she dropped her arms and stepped back from him. Water lapped against her and when a large wave came on them, she rode it without a problem.

"If this is a joke, I'm not the least bit amused." Her intention was to sound sarcastic and flippant, but her voice broke. She jerked her chin a notch higher.

"Lynn, please," Ryder whispered, "don't look at me like that."

In response, she twisted away from him, feeling hurt and rejected. Only a minute before she'd come right out and admitted that there hadn't been anyone since Gary. Ryder knew she wasn't…loose, and yet he made her feel callous and coldhearted as if she made this type of arrangement with every man she felt the least bit attracted to.

"I don't know what you want from me," she murmured.

Several moments passed before he answered her, and when he did, his voice was filled with resignation. "No, I don't suppose you do. But you'll figure it out soon enough, and when you do I'll be waiting." That said, he swam away with clean, hard strokes.

Lynn watched him go and noted that he seemed to want to punish the water for what had just happened between them.

Exhausted, Ryder continued to pump his arms until his muscles quivvered and ached. He was as far away from Lynn as it was possible to get in the crowded swimming area. There wasn't any need to push himself further.

He loved Lynn, wanted her more than he'd ever longed for anything in his life. She'd wanted him, too. She was on fire for him. He hadn't dared to dream she would feel this strongly for him. But he didn't want a physical relationship with her that wasn't rooted in commitment. Her talk about keeping their affair a secret from the kids had been bad enough, but dragging up the subject of birth control was more than he could take. In the blink of an eye, he'd gone from aroused and eager to confused and irritated. He didn't want a casual affair with Lynn. He was looking for more from her than a few stolen moments together to ease the explosive physical need they felt for each other.

He wanted her, all right, but on his own terms. When they made love, there wouldn't be any questions left unanswered, nor would there be any secrets.

Soon enough, she would know what he wanted. Lynn

was too smart not to figure it out. He pleaded with heaven to make it soon because he couldn't take much more of this.

Lynn dried herself off with a thick beach towel, then reached for a light cotton blouse. Her fingers didn't want to cooperate and buttoning it seemed to take a half a lifetime. She was confused and angry and frustrated and excited. Each emotion demanded attention, and in response she ignored them all, making busywork around their picnic site. She folded the towels, and laid out the wet ones to dry, then she picked up a few pieces of litter. When she'd finished, she lay down on her stomach on the blanket and tried to sleep. Naturally that was impossible, but Ryder didn't need to know that. When he returned, she wanted him to think she'd simply forgotten what had happened in the water, and she'd put the entire incident behind her.

She heard him about ten minutes later and forcibly closed her eyes. He reached for a towel, that much she was able to ascertain by the sounds coming from behind her. Then she heard the cooler open and a soda can being opened. That was followed by the unmistakable rustle of him peeling the wrapping off a sandwich.

She frowned, marveling that he was able to overlook what had happened in the pool and sit down and eat. Her stomach was in turmoil and food was the last thing she cared about now.

When she couldn't stand it any longer, Lynn rolled onto her back. Shading her eyes with her forearm, she stared up to discover Michelle sitting at the picnic table.

"Hi, Mom. I thought you were asleep."

"Hi," Lynn greeted, feeling chagrined.

"This sure is a lot of fun. I've met some really awesome...people."

Lynn grinned, knowing exactly which sex these "people" probably were. "I'm glad, sweetie." She hadn't finished speaking when Ryder strolled up and reached for his towel, wiping the water from his face.

"I'm going back to my friends, now," Michelle said and stuffed the rest of her sandwich back inside the wicker basket.

"I'll be back in an hour," Michelle called and was off.

"Bye," Lynn called after her daughter, dreading the confrontation with Ryder more than anything she could remember. So much depended on what he was about to say.

Slowly he dropped the towel away from his face and gazed directly at her. "Are you all right?"

"Sure," she answered with a hysterical little laugh. "Why shouldn't I be?"

Twelve

A week passed and Ryder was amazed at all the ways Lynn invented in order to avoid him. She seemed absolutely determined to forget he existed. It would've been comical if Ryder didn't love her so much and long to put matters right between them. He knew beyond doubt the reason she was doing back flips in an effort to escape him. In the full light of reason, when her head wasn't muddled with passion and need, Lynn was probably thoroughly ashamed of their wanton behavior in the pool. Ryder had been delighted by her ready response. Her kisses had been ravenous, undisciplined and carnal. Every time Ryder thought about the way she blossomed in his arms, he trembled with aftershocks. The memory was like standing too close to an incinerator—he burned with a need she'd created in him.

Ryder cursed himself now for rejecting her offer to make love…for refusing himself. But he sought more than the release her body could give him, wanted more than to become Lynn's lover.

He yearned for her heart.

The realization had left him perplexed, and in some

ways stunned him. Earlier—before the incident at
the water park—he would gladly have accepted what
she'd so guilelessly offered him. She didn't love him,
he realized, but she would soon enough. When it came
right down to it, he didn't need the words. He loved her
enough for the both of them.

But something powerful and deeply rooted within
his conscience had stopped him from making love to
Lynn, some sentiment he had yet to name. All he did
know was that sleeping with her wouldn't be enough
to satisfy him.

If Ryder was bewildered by the extent of his emotional need for Lynn, it was nothing compared to what
she seemed to be experiencing. He hungered to talk to
her, but when he'd phoned her at the salon and later at
the house, she'd asked, both times, that a message be
taken and then hadn't bothered to return his calls. He'd
tried twice more, but on each occasion, she'd come up
with a convenient excuse to avoid talking to him.

He'd gone so far as to stop in at her salon only to be
told that she was too busy to see to him then. He was
told that if he would be willing to wait a couple of hours,
she would try to squeeze him in, but there weren't any
guarantees. Frustrated and angry, he'd quickly left.

Next, Ryder phoned Michelle and Jason and took
them to a movie, thinking he would surely see Lynn
when he dropped them off at the house. But she'd exas-
perated him once more. When he'd gone to pick them
up, Michelle had explained that they needed to be taken
to Toni Morris's after the movie. His frustration had
reached its peak that night.

Since Lynn seemed to require more time to sort out
what was happening between them, Ryder reluctantly

decided to give it to her. When she was ready, she would contact him. But there was a limit to his patience and it was fast running out.

Lynn parked her car outside Toni Morris's house and sat quietly for a couple of minutes, gathering her nerve before talking to her friend. Toni wouldn't let her pussyfoot around the issue, and Lynn knew that. She trusted Toni's insights, and sought her wisdom now.

Lynn's nervous fingers tightened around the steering wheel and she released her breath on a swell of anxiety and defeat.

"Lynn," Toni greeted, when she answered the door. "This is a pleasant surprise. Come in."

Lynn nervously brushed the hair from her forehead. "Have you got a minute? I mean if this is a bad time I could come back later."

Toni laughed. "I was looking for a reason not to mow the lawn. I should thank you for stopping by unexpectedly like this. At least I'll have an excuse when Joe gets home."

Lynn made a gallant effort to smile, followed Toni into the kitchen and nodded when the former policewoman motioned toward the coffeepot.

"So how are things developing with Ryder?"

Lynn nearly choked on the hot coffee. Leave it to Toni to cut through the small talk.

"Fine…he's been wonderful to the kids."

"I'm talking about *you* and Ryder," Toni pressed.

"Fine," she answered quickly…too quickly, calling herself the coward she was.

"I see." The two words were riddled with sarcasm. Toni pulled out the chair opposite Lynn and sat down.

The air seemed to crackle with tension until Toni added, "How much longer are you planning to avoid him?"

Lynn's jaw flopped open. "How'd...you know?"

Toni's answering smile was fleeting. "Michelle made some comment about not knowing why Ryder had to drop the two of them off at my place when you were supposed to be home. And frankly, you didn't do a good job of avoiding me that night, either."

"Why is it everything I do is so transparent?" Lynn asked, throwing her hands into the air. She felt like a witless adolescent.

"It's not as bad as you think," Toni answered with a saucy grin. "I know you, that's all." Toni took a couple of seconds to stir sugar into her coffee. "When was the last time you saw Ryder?"

"It's been over two weeks now."

"Did you argue?"

Lynn dropped her gaze so fast, she feared she'd strained her neck muscles. "In...a manner of speaking. He tried to call me several times, and stopped by the salon once, but I...I was busy."

Toni snickered softly at that bit of information. "When was the last time you heard from him?"

"Nine days ago."

"And you're ready to deal with whatever is happening?"

Lynn nodded. She'd been ready for almost a week, but Ryder hadn't contacted her. It was as if he'd dropped off the face of the earth. The first few days after their outing, she would have preferred death to confronting Ryder. Now she felt lost and terribly lonely without his friendship. Noise violated her from every direction, but the silence was killing her. In the past week, Lynn had been short-tempered with the kids, restless and uneasy at work. It was as though she'd walked into a giant void. Nothing felt right anymore. Nothing felt good.

"He's waiting for you to come to him."

The thought immobilized Lynn. She froze, the coffee cup raised halfway to her mouth. It was one thing to be willing to talk to Ryder, but to contact him herself demanded a special kind of courage. If she knew what to say, and how to say it, it would help matters considerably, but all she could think about was how much heat there'd been in the way she'd kissed him and pleaded with him to make love to her.

Just the memory of that afternoon was enough to raise her body's temperature by several degrees. She'd practically begged Ryder to make love to her. She'd thought that was what he'd wanted, too, but then he'd told her that wasn't enough. The way he'd acted led her to believe she'd insulted him. She couldn't understand that, either. Ryder had admitted he wanted her, and yet he'd been totally unreasonable. When she'd brought up Michelle and Jason and the need for some form of birth control, he'd backed away as if she'd slapped him.

"Well?" Toni demanded.

"You think I should be the one to call him?"

"That's why you're here isn't it?"

"I…I don't know." She set down the mug and wiped a hand over her face, feeling tense and ill at ease. "Ryder makes me feel again and, Toni, that frightens me. Just thinking about him causes me to get all nervous and hyper. I wish he'd never come back and, in the same moment, I thank God he did. I'm so scared."

"Why?"

"If I knew that I wouldn't be sitting here with my

knees knocking," Lynn cried, irritated by the way her friend continued to toss questions at her. "I don't like the way I feel around Ryder. I was comfortable the way things were before."

"You were miserable."

"I wasn't."

Toni's responding grin was off center. "That's not the story I got the day of the precinct picnic. You told me how you weren't sleeping well and how restless you'd become over the past several months."

Lynn tried to argue, but knew it was useless. Toni was right. Leaning back in her chair, her friend reached for the telephone receiver on the kitchen wall and handed it to Lynn. "Go ahead. I'll conveniently disappear and you can talk to your heart's content.

"But—"

"I hear the lawn calling to me now," Toni joked. She braced her hands against the table's edge and scooted back her seat. "I'm out of here."

"Toni, please, I don't know what to say."

"You'll think of something."

As it turned out, Lynn didn't need to come up with anything brilliant to start the conversation. Ryder was out of the office and when she tried his apartment, she got voice mail. She left a message on it, hating the way her voice wavered and pitched when she was trying so hard to sound cheerful and happy as though she'd contacted him every day of the week. She could only imagine what Ryder would think when he listened to it. Given the chance she would have gladly called back and erased the message, but it wasn't possible.

Toni glanced up expectantly and turned off the mower when Lynn came out of the house.

"He wasn't at the office or at his apartment," Lynn explained. "I...left a message so stop looking at me like I'm some kind of coward."

"If the shoe fits, my friend..." Toni laughed.

It was almost midnight and Ryder still hadn't returned her call. Hours before Lynn had given up expecting to hear from him. She was getting a taste of her own medicine and the flavor was definitely bitter. Depression settled over her shoulders like a heavy homemade quilt. Ryder was through with her and she had no one to blame but herself.

Forcing her attention away from the clock, Lynn focused on the ledger that was spread across the kitchen table. She tightened her fingers around the pencil until it threatened to snap in half. She'd gone over these figures so many times that the numbers had started to bleed together. No matter how many different ways she tried, nothing added up the way it should. Maintaining her own books for Slender, Too shouldn't be this complicated. She'd taken bookkeeping in high school and was familiar with the double-entry system, and yet... like everything else this summer, nothing was working out the way she planned.

Okay, so she'd blown it with Ryder. The disappointment was keen, but she'd suffered through disappointment before. It hurt, but it wasn't fatal. In many ways she was grateful to him. He'd waltzed into her life at a critical moment. She'd worked so hard in the past three years, seeking contentment in her children and her job, paying the price and never questioning the cost. In a few short weeks, Ryder had done something no other man had been able to do in a long time. He'd awakened her to the fact that she was a woman—a warm, generous woman made to feel and love. Since Gary's death, she'd done everything within her power to ignore that part of herself.

The sound of the front door opening caught her by surprise. Lynn leaped to her feet and met Ryder in the entryway. The sight of him bolted her to the floor.

"I would have knocked, but I didn't think you'd open the door once you saw it was me," he accused her, his voice filled with cynicism.

"That's not true—" She glanced up the stairs, grateful that Michelle and Jason were sound asleep.

"I doubt that," he shouted. "You've done everything you could to avoid me in the past two weeks and I'm fed up with it."

"There's no reason to shout." He'd been drinking, but he wasn't anywhere close to being drunk. He knew exactly what he was saying and doing, but that didn't reassure her any.

"I happen to feel there is. How much longer do you plan to bury your head in the sand?"

"If you think you can stand here and insult me, then let me assure you, you'd be doing us both a favor if you left."

"You can forget that."

Lynn refused to answer him. She whirled around and returned to the kitchen. She seated herself at the table and reached for the calculator. To her dismay, Ryder followed her inside.

He stood there silently for several moments, then twisted the ledger around and ran his gaze down the pale green sheet. "What's this?"

"The books for the salon. Not that it's any of your business."

"It's almost midnight."

"I'm well aware of the time, thank you," Lynn answered primly.

"Why are you working on those?"

She couldn't very well admit that she hadn't been able to sleep…hadn't even tried because she was mooning over her relationship with him. Working on balancing her books helped keep her mind off how she'd messed everything up between them.

"I'm not leaving until you answer me," Ryder demanded.

"I enjoy doing my own books."

He sniggered at that. "Sure you do. It's midnight."

"I…couldn't sleep."

"Why not?"

"That's none of your business." At all costs, she avoided looking in his direction.

"You don't need to answer that," he told her crisply. "I already know. You were thinking about me, weren't you? Regretting our day together and how you'd moved your body over mine in the water. You're wishing now you hadn't been so blatant in your wants. You're thinking that maybe I would have made love to you if you'd been a little more subtle."

His arrogance nettled her beyond belief. "Of all the nerve! You're vulgar, Ryder."

"Do you honestly believe I didn't know how much you wanted me?"

"Stop it," she cried, feeling her cheeks fill with flaming color.

"Honey, you wanted me so badly you practically burned me alive. I'm still smoldering two weeks later."

A husky denial burned on her lips. She *had* wanted him, but she would never admit it. Not now, when he was throwing the matter in her face, forcing her to deal with her body's response to him. Lynn preferred to forget the entire incident and go on with their relationship as though nothing had happened. But from the way he was looking at her, she realized the likelihood of that happening was slim.

Ryder turned her around, secured her jaw with one hand and lowered his mouth to hers.

Lynn struggled, but all her efforts only succeeded in exhausting her strength. When flinging her arms against his hard chest, and arching her back didn't help, she pressed her lips firmly together. When she relaxed ever so slightly, he outlined the shape of her lips with the tip of his tongue until her moans of anger and outrage became soft gasps of bliss. Finally, without any force from him, her mouth parted, and she gave herself over to his kiss.

"That's the way, Lynn," he praised her. "Enjoy it, love, enjoy it. Be honest, to yourself and to me."

His words were all the encouragement she needed. She folded her arms around his neck and without her being certain how he managed it, he lifted her from the chair and seated himself, setting her in his lap.

He broke off the kiss and his breath was warm and moist as it drifted over her upturned face. He smelled of expensive whiskey and she realized that was what she'd been tasting and loving. He didn't need to apply any pressure for her to welcome him a second time..

His breathing was as rapid and as unsteady as her

own when Ryder finished kissing her. With his gaze holding hers, he worked at the buttons of her shirt. His fingers were trembling. "You wanted this the other day, too, and I wanted to give it to you."

Too late, Lynn realized his intent. "Ryder, please don't," she begged. "I don't like it when you touch me. We shouldn't be doing this—"

He ignored her small cry of protest, obviously recognizing her lie, and pushed the shirt from her shoulders. Her intention had been to tell him to stop, to deny the incredible sensations that washed over her like a tidal wave. He wanted her to own up to her feelings, and still she held back, furious with him for forcing her to confront her emotions and even more furious with herself for wanting him so much.

"You wanted me to do this the other day, didn't you?" he whispered, coaxing the truth from her.

Lynn refused to answer him.

"Didn't you?" he demanded a second time.

"No," she lied, denying him the satisfaction of the truth.

His eyes filled with disappointment, but he wouldn't be denied and it showed in the look he gave her. "Somehow, I don't believe you."

It wasn't until he spoke and his moist breath settled over her that Lynn whimpered.

"You want something more now too, don't you?" he asked her softly, then added, "I'll give it to you, Lynn, all you have to do is be honest with me."

She would die before she would tell him what she was feeling.

He must have seen the determination in her eyes because he laughed softly and tormented her with kisses up and down the side of her neck until she was squirming and rolling her head from side to side.

"Please," she begged, when she couldn't bear it any longer.

"Please what?"

She moaned.

"Ask me, Lynn." His own voice contained a thread of pleading.

"No," she whimpered her refusal.

"That's not what I want to hear. Do you want me, Lynn? Do you?"

"Yes, Ryder . . . yes." A sob tore through her throat while he poised his mouth over hers.

Thirteen

Somehow Ryder was able to move away from Lynn. He walked over to the kitchen sink, braced his hot hands against the cool ledge and closed his eyes to the torment that racked him. He hadn't wanted to push her like that, but he needed to force her to take responsibility for her own desires. She was an expert at avoiding her feelings. Every cell of his own body demanded release, every fiber of his being sought completion with her, but he couldn't allow himself to give in to his baser instincts. Not like this. Not now.

He'd been a fool to come to her this way. An angry fool. His actions may have caused him to lose the only woman he'd ever loved. Ever would love.

"Are you angry with me again?" Lynn asked, in a voice that trembled with distress.

Her soft pleading stabbed through his soul. Slowly he turned to face Lynn. "No."

She'd fastened her blouse, but her eyes were filled with despair and longing. Ryder tightened his hands into fists of resolve. "I shouldn't have come here tonight. If anyone deserves an apology, it's you. I had no right to say and do those things to you."

Slowly Lynn lowered her gaze. "You were right about me not being able to sleep because I was thinking of you. I spent half the night hoping you'd answer my call."

"Answer your call?"

Her face shot upward. "You mean you didn't get my message? I left you a voice mail."

Defeated, Ryder rubbed a hand across his weary face. All this hopelessness, this overwhelming sense of frustration could have been eliminated if he'd gone home when he was finished at the office the way he should have. Instead he'd walked along the Seattle waterfront, depressed and discouraged. Later he'd sat in some uptown bar and found courage at the bottom of a bottle. He felt sick with himself now. He'd come to Lynn for all the wrong reasons, intent on forcing her to accept her feelings for him—whatever they were.

Frustration filled his mouth. He couldn't look at her, didn't dare for fear of what he would see in her eyes. The only thing left to do was leave, and pray she would find it in her heart to forgive him.

He started for the front door when she called him.

"Ryder?"

He stopped, as though waiting for her instructions. He felt completely at her mercy. If she were to tell him to stay out of her life, he would have no recourse but to do as she asked. His intent had been to crush her, to bend her to his will. His higher intentions couldn't overcome his actions. When he remembered the way he'd tormented her, there could be no forgiveness. None.

He heard the sound of her chair as she stood. Still he

didn't move, couldn't have even if the fate of the entire world rested on his actions.

She placed a hand on his elbow, then abruptly dropped it. "I was wondering…" Her voice was little more than a whisper. "I know it's probably more than what you want, but…"

"Yes," he coaxed, almost afraid to hope.

"Would it be all right, if the two of us…you and me started dating?"

Ryder turned, his heart ready to burst with the generosity of the second chance she was offering him. For a long moment, all they did was stare at each other. Lynn was the first to look away.

His sigh of relief had a wounded quality. When he'd kissed and held her, his actions hadn't been completely prompted by love and concern the way he'd wanted to believe—the way she deserved. He'd trampled on her heart, dealing her emotions a crippling blow and all in the name of his stupid pride. "I should never have come," he told her, his face dark with self-anger.

"I'm glad you did."

"You're glad?" He couldn't believe what he was hearing.

"I'm such a coward, Ryder, in so many ways."

Lynn a coward! She was possibly the most fearless woman he'd ever known. "No, honey, that's not true. I've been pushing you too hard and it hasn't worked. I just don't know what to do anymore."

She raised her gaze to his and looked straight at him. Her eyes were wide and filled with incredible longing. Ryder felt his knees weaken. If he were to press the issue, they would probably end up making love be-

fore the night was over. Clearly, it was what they both
wanted.

"I think dating is a great idea," he said. "We'll get
reacquainted with each other the way other couples
do." His words were more abrupt than he'd intended,
but he had to turn his thoughts around before he and
Lynn landed in bed and wondered how they'd gotten
there so soon.

Lynn nodded.

"Can you go out with me tomorrow night? Dinner?
Dancing? Anything you want."

"Dinner would be fine."

Her smile trembled on her lips and it took everything
within him not to lean down and taste her once more.
Briefly he wondered if a lifetime of her special brand
of kisses would ever be enough to satisfy him. Somehow he doubted it.

"Do you want some coffee before you leave?"

Her offer surprised him and his look must have said
as much.

"There's a pot already made," she explained. "I don't
think it would be a good idea for you to drive when
you've been drinking."

His actions had been sobering enough, but he
couldn't refuse the excuse to be with her longer. "I'll
take a cup—thanks for the offer."

She seemed almost glad as she moved out of the
entry and back inside the kitchen. He joined her there
and watched as she brought down two ceramic mugs
and filled them both.

Ryder sat at the table and his gaze fell upon the ledger. He frowned once more. "Are you having problems?"

She nodded, sitting across from him. "Something's off. I can't get this sheet to balance for the life of me."

"Put it away," he suggested. "The mistake will be easier to find in the morning."

"That's what I thought yesterday."

For a long moment, Ryder resisted asking her, but he couldn't bear not knowing. "How long have you been struggling over this?"

"A week now," she admitted with some reluctance.

"Do you always do your own books?"

"I have from the beginning." A sense of pride lit up her eyes. "I like to keep my hands on every aspect of my business. It means a great deal to me."

"I don't suppose you've ever thought of hiring an accountant to balance your books," he made the suggestion lightly, although it troubled him to have Lynn drive herself to the edge, complicating her life with details others could handle far more efficiently.

"No."

Her answer was hot and automatic. He was treading on thin ice, and knew it, but still he couldn't keep himself from stepping out further. Lynn was stretching her endurance—there wasn't any need to push herself this way. He was doing them both a disservice to stand by and say nothing.

"A good accountant would save you countless hours of frustration."

"I prefer to do my own books, thank you. Besides, hiring a bookkeeper would be much too expensive."

Ryder bit his tongue to keep from telling her that she should at least check it out. She was wasting needless energy when an accountant could balance her books within a couple of hours, in addition to advising her about local and federal taxes, plus payroll.

"Slender, Too, is mine, Ryder. I handle my business affairs the way I want."

He raised both of his hands in surrender, backing off. It bothered him that Lynn was so prickly about taking his advice. He was only looking to help her, but it was obvious she didn't want him butting into her business. In the years since he'd been away, Lynn had gained a fierce independence and seemed to want to prove how capable she was at doing everything on her own. He didn't doubt that, but he fervently wished she were more open to suggestions.

Ryder gulped down the coffee. "What time tomorrow?"

"Does seven work for you?"

"That's fine."

He stood, and when he did, Lynn joined him. She walked him to the front door and stepped into his arms as though she'd been doing it half her life. He kissed her goodbye, making sure the kiss would last him until the following night.

"Hi, Mom." Michelle bounced herself down on top of the queen-size mattress in the master bedroom where Lynn was dressing. "So you're going out to dinner with Ryder?"

Methodically, Lynn finished fastening the tiny pearl buttons to her silk blouse. "I already told you that."

"Yeah, I know."

"Then why the comment now?" Lynn knew she was being defensive, but she couldn't help it. All day she'd been looking forward to this evening with Ryder and at the same time dreading it. They couldn't seem to be in the same room together without a type of spontaneous combustion exploding between them. "I thought you liked Ryder."

"I love him. He's been great. This summer would have been a real drag without him."

Lynn wasn't convinced she could accept that. "But you're not sure how you feel about the two of us going out...is that it?"

"I know how *I* feel and so does Jason. In fact, the two of us were talking and we decided—"

"What?" Lynn asked when her daughter stopped abruptly.

Michelle looked mildly shaken. "Never mind."

"Michelle, I want to know what you and your brother were talking about, especially if it concerns me and Ryder."

"It's nothing. Really."

"Michelle," her voice lowered to a threatening cadence.

"Mom, I'm sorry, I can't tell you. Jason and I made a pact. I didn't want to go as far as to swear on my own life, but you know Jason. He's into this Incredible Hulk stuff so thick that he didn't give me any choice but to do what he said military style. Did you know commandos force their men to sign everything in fresh blood?"

Lynn managed to swallow a smile. "Did he make you do that?"

"He wanted to, but I refused. But he *did* manage to swear me to secrecy...so I can't say a word of what we talked about and decided."

"I understand."

Michelle heaved a giant sigh. "I will tell you this

much, though," she admitted in a soft whisper. "Both Jason and I are real glad that you're going out to dinner with Ryder, even if it does mean we have to have a baby-sitter—which is completely unnecessary, you know?"

Lynn didn't. "The babysitter is for Jason's benefit, but don't tell him that, okay?"

"Okay," Michelle agreed, placated.

"And I'm pleased to hear you don't object to my going out with Ryder."

"Actually it isn't any real surprise after the day at Wild Waves."

Heat suffused Lynn's face until she was sure her color would rival a peeled beet's. It would have been too much to hope Michelle and Jason didn't notice the electricity between her and Ryder that afternoon.

The doorbell sounded from downstairs.

"I'll get it," Michelle cried, flying off the bed. "I think it must be Ryder."

Lynn knew it had to be. With her daughter gone, she took a couple of extra moments to check her appearance in the mirror. Only partially satisfied, she flattened her hands down the front of her outfit. Her heart was ramming against her ribs in anticipation. Ryder hadn't said where they would be dining and she prayed she'd dressed appropriately.

He was waiting for her at the bottom of the stairs, and when she started down the staircase, his eyes went directly to her. Dressed carefully in a stylish suit and tie, he'd never looked more handsome.

"Lynn." He made her name a caress. "You look lovely."

"Thank you." Lynn noticed the way Michelle poked

her younger brother with her elbow. The two children looked at each other and nodded approvingly.

"Don't worry about coming home early," Michelle told Ryder excitedly. "Jason and I are watching videos and then going to bed early. Isn't that right, Jason?"

"Right." He offered Ryder a crisp military salute. "Sir," he added in afterthought.

A smile crowded Ryder's mouth and the edges of his lips quivered slightly. "At ease."

Jason dropped his arm and nodded. "Be sure to stay out as long as you want. Michelle and I want you to… there's no need to hurry home on our account."

While Ryder talked to her two kids, Lynn moved into the kitchen and gave a few instructions to the sitter. Ryder joined Lynn a couple of moments later with the phone number to the restaurant where they would be dining.

After a few choice instructions to the kids, Lynn reached for her purse and a light sweater. Ryder's hand, at the small of her back, directed her to his car, which was parked in front of the house. He held open the passenger door for her, and directed his gaze to her mouth. She thought he might want to kiss her and was mildly disappointed when he didn't. It wasn't until Lynn snapped her seat belt into place and she noticed Michelle and Jason studying her from the living-room window, that she understood Ryder's hesitancy.

They traveled the first five minutes in silence. "I've been thinking about you all day," Lynn spoke first, wishing she didn't feel like such a dunce in Ryder's company.

"I can't remember when I've looked forward to an

evening more," he answered. He reached for her hand, raised it to his lips and kissed her fingertips.

The simple kiss went through her like an electric shock. Lynn sucked in her breath and bit into the soft flesh of her inner cheek. He entered the freeway and headed south toward Tacoma. "There's a new seafood restaurant someone was telling me about. I thought we'd try it."

Lynn folded her fingers around the strap of her purse, which rested in her lap. "I suppose you remember how much I love lobster."

"This place is said to serve huge portions."

Lynn couldn't help smiling. She remembered once when the three of them had gone out for dinner and she'd ordered lobster, but when her meal arrived, she'd been outraged at how tiny her serving had been. Disappointed, Lynn had muttered that it should be illegal to kill anything that small.

"We had so many good times, didn't we?" she asked casually.

Ryder nodded, but she noted that he didn't embellish on any memories. She didn't blame Ryder, because talking about the good times with Gary would put a damper on their evening. They'd both loved him so much and nothing could be said that would wipe out the past.

"I had a busy day today," she tried next.

"Oh? Did another of your employees phone in sick?"

"No...I took time off this afternoon to call an accountant."

Ryder's gaze flew from the roadway to Lynn.

"Don't get excited," she said, "my attitude was rotten. The only reason I contacted him was to prove how wrong you were. I knew an accountant would cost me an arm and a leg and I couldn't possibly afford one."

"And?"

"And...he actually sounded quite reasonable so I took everything in to him and we talked. What takes me two days to accomplish, he can do in about twenty minutes. Everything's done online these days. I wasn't keen on having him keep my books overnight...I'm always needing to write a check for one reason or another, but he doesn't need it. He makes copies of my ledger pages, assigned each account a number so that all I need do is write that figure on each check. It's so simple I could hardly believe it."

"Expensive?"

"Not at all. I should have done this in the beginning. He's helping me with my quarterly taxes, too, and with other things I didn't even know that I should be doing." She expelled a deep sigh when she finished.

"That wasn't so hard was it?"

"What?"

"Telling me you hired an accountant."

"No, it wasn't. You were right, Ryder, and I'm grateful you said something, although I'm sure my attitude last night didn't make it easy."

If he longed to remind her how difficult she had made it, he didn't, and Lynn was pleased. Ryder was a rare kind of man. More rare than she'd realized.

The restaurant was situated on Commencement Bay and they were seated by the window, which offered a spectacular view of the water. Sailboats with their boldly hued spinnakers floated past, adding dashes of bright color to the evening horizon. After their shaky beginning, Lynn was surprised at how easily they fell into conversation. Ryder told her about an important case he'd been assigned, listing the details for her, without using names, of course. As they were talking, Lynn noticed several women glancing toward them, their looks envious. She couldn't blame them, Ryder was incredibly handsome.

By the time they were served their dinner a band had started to play in the background. The music seemed to wrap itself around Lynn like a steel cable. She set her fork aside and briefly closed her eyes.

"I remember how much you like to dance."

"And I remember how much you don't."

His grin was filled with wry humor. "Right now, I'd use any excuse to hold you."

She lowered her gaze. "Oh, Ryder, don't say things like that."

"Why not?"

Lynn lowered her eyes. She didn't know how to tell him that it wasn't necessary. He didn't need to invent a reason to take her in his arms. She would go there willingly, happily. All he ever had to do was ask.

When the waiter carried away their plates, Ryder stood and offered her his hand. Lynn accepted it and when they reached the edges of the crowded dance floor, she felt as though she floated into his embrace. Ryder wrapped one arm around her waist and Lynn tucked the side of her head against his jaw, cherishing the feel of his hands, which were so gently securing her to him. She rarely danced anymore—and yet it was as though she'd been partners with Ryder all her life. She fit into his arms as if she'd been handpicked for the position.

"You feel good against me," Ryder whispered close

to her ear, and the tremble in his voice said far more than his words.

Lynn closed her eyes and nodded. He felt incredibly good, too. Warm, vital, alive and male...so very male. The music whirled around her like an early morning mist, touching her, caressing her soul with velvet.

The song ended and reluctantly, Lynn dropped her arms. "Thank you, Ryder." She started to move away, appreciating the generosity of him dancing with her once, but he caught her hand, stopping her.

"If you're willing to risk me stepping on your toes a second time, I'm game for another song."

She smiled up at him shyly and nodded. The music hadn't even started when she reached up and folded her arms around his neck.

"The last time you held me like this, we were in the water," Ryder whispered against her hair, his breath heavy. "It was torture then, too." He moved ever so slightly and she followed his lead. Her thighs slid intimately against his. Although her skirt and his pants barred her from experiencing the smooth satiny feel of their bare legs rubbing together, it didn't seem to matter—the sensation was there.

Ryder tightened his grip around her waist, pressing her stomach provocatively against his own. Her breasts were flattened over his torso and her body throbbed with the seductive movements of the impossibly slow dance.

"Lynn," he whispered her name in soft agony. "Either we get off this floor now or we're doomed to spend the rest of the night here."

Once outside, the evening air felt cool against her flushed cheeks. "I could have danced all night," she said with a meaningful sigh, chancing a look in his direction. Almost from the moment they'd stepped on the dance floor, it had been apparent that Ryder was distinctly uncomfortable holding her that intimately in such a public place.

Ryder groaned at her light teasing and shook his head. "You're a wicked woman, Lynn Danfort."

She grinned. "Nice of you to say so."

The ride back to Seattle was accomplished in companionable silence. Ryder held her hand as though he needed to feel her close. Lynn experienced the same need, and at the same time she found it essential to root herself in reality.

Ryder exited off the freeway, but instead of heading in the direction of her house, he pulled onto a side street, turned off the engine and braced both hands against the steering wheel.

"What's wrong?"

Ryder expelled his breath forcefully. "I don't know where to go."

Lynn frowned. "I don't understand."

"If I take you back to your place, Michelle and Jason will be all over us."

"Yes," she agreed, "they will."

"But if I take you to my apartment we're going to end up making love. There won't be any way either of us is going to be able to stop." He paused and looked at her, studying her as if expecting her to deny the obvious. "I'm right, aren't I?"

Lynn nearly swallowed her tongue, seeking a way to deny the truth, but she couldn't meet his gaze and lie. "Yes," she admitted in a choked whisper.

Silence seemed to throb between them.

"I'm ready to explode anytime I get near you." Inhaling a slow, silent sigh, Ryder reached for her, taking her by the shoulders. He stared at her for a long moment, then cupped her chin in one hand and tilted back her head as he pressed his mouth over hers. His kiss was filled with hunger, passion and heat…such unbelievable heat. If a man could make love with his mouth, Ryder did so with that one kiss.

They broke apart, breathless. Feeling spineless, Lynn slumped against him and laid her cheek on his chest. No kiss had ever affected her more and she wondered if Ryder felt anything close to what she was experiencing.

"See what I mean," he whispered.

She nodded.

Ryder kissed her again, although she was sure he hadn't wanted to…at least not there on the dark street with cars buzzing past them.

Lynn laced her fingers through his hair, exalting in the feel of his mouth loving hers. He broke off the kiss and pressed his forehead against hers, taking in huge breaths as though to gain control of his needs.

Lynn felt as though she were about to incinerate. Ryder could do all this to her with a single kiss. She couldn't begin to imagine what would happen if they were to go to bed together. She trembled at the thought.

"Are you cold?" Ryder asked, rubbing his hands up and down the length of her arms.

"No. I'm burning up."

"Me, too. Sitting anywhere close to you I come away scorched."

"I'm sorry," she breathed.

"I'm not."

"You're not?"

"No, it tells me how good it's going to be for us."

Lynn frowned, not knowing how to comment. Ryder utterly confused her. They couldn't get close to each other without threatening to ignite anything within a half-mile radius. And yet whenever the subject of making love came up, Ryder tensed and withdrew from her.

"We can't go on like this." He moved his hands over her throat and chest. Everywhere his fingers grazed her, Lynn tingled.

"What are we going to do?" she asked, on a husky whisper, hardly able to speak.

"The only thing we can." Whatever he suggested had to be better than this agony. She was about to melt at his feet.

"You aren't going to like it," he said, straightening, his look serious.

"What?"

"I think we should get married. The sooner the better."

Fourteen

"Married," Lynn echoed, stunned. "Married?"

He looked past her, refusing to meet her startled gaze. "I know this must come as something of a surprise. I didn't mean to blurt it out like this, but honestly, Lynn, I don't see any other way around it."

"I—"

"I love you. I love Michelle and Jason and they love me. I want the four of us to be a family...a real family. At night, when I crawl into bed, I want you at my side to love me and ease this ache of loneliness. When I'm old and gray, there's no one I'd rather have at my side."

"Oh, Ryder..." Her voice trailed off and she lowered her eyes. He was offering her the sun and the moon. Huge salty tears formed in the corners of her eyes.

He kissed her—a long, sensual kiss. When they broke apart, Lynn pressed the back of her head against the seat, closed her eyes and took in several calming breaths.

"Let's get out of here."

The only response she was capable of giving him was a weak nod. He started the engine and zoomed through the streets at breakneck speed as if he couldn't get her away from there fast enough. Lynn had no idea where he was driving. Her mind was whirling. Marriage. Ryder was offering her marriage because he couldn't see any way around it. Yet he claimed he loved her... loved the kids.

The biggest problem that Lynn faced was her feelings for Ryder. She hadn't had time to analyze what was happening between them. If he was looking to rescue her, she didn't need that. Nor did she want to negate any lingering guilt he was suffering over Gary's death.

Yet in her heart she loved Ryder...she always had. However, her feelings for him were deeply rooted in friendship from years past when she, Ryder and Gary had spent so much time together. In the years since Ryder had been away, her love for him had gone dormant. But now that he was back, it was as if he'd never left, although her love had been transformed from that between a sister for a brother to that between a woman and a man. Everything was magically different and had been from the moment he'd first kissed her. Her whole world had changed drastically.

"You don't seem to have much to say," he commented, his voice gruff. "Lynn, listen, I don't mean to rush you. When we started out tonight, I had no intention of proposing, but it seemed the right thing to do."

"In the heat of the moment?"

"No!"

"It isn't necessary, you know."

"What? Marrying you?"

"Yes." She couldn't believe she was admitting something like this. She'd held on to her virtue with steel manacles with every other man she'd dated, but one touch from Ryder and she'd never felt more alive. It was as if her whole body had been hibernating for three long years, and suddenly every cell had sprung to life.

"It's what I want."

Lynn couldn't understand why. His brief affairs had been legendary, but he didn't seem to want a short-term commitment from her. And from the dark scowl that covered his face, she realized he was offering her all or nothing.

"I'm not looking for an affair with you, Lynn."

That message had come through loud and clear the day at the waterworks park. "But, Ryder—"

"Do you or do you not want to get married?" The question was sharp with impatience.

Lynn squared her shoulders. "I'm not looking for anyone to rescue me."

His laugh was short and sarcastic. "You're telling me? Every time I so much as try, you bite my head off and calmly take control."

"And if you think you owe me something because of what happened to Gary—"

"Gary has nothing to do with this." Once more his words were sharp and abrupt.

Lynn gnawed on her bottom lip. Indecision boiled inside her. No clear direction presented itself.

"Are you going to marry me and put us both out of this misery?"

His voice was tender and warm, scattering Lynn's objections before she had a chance to assemble them. "I...think so." She would be a fool to turn him down and equally foolish to agree. She felt like laughing and crying at once. Good grief, what was she doing?

Ryder stepped on the brake, reached for her and

kissed her soundly, ravaging her mouth. "I'll take that as a yes, then."

Lynn's mind was spinning. "We need to talk, though, don't you think?"

"Fine. A week from Saturday, okay?"

"You want to wait that long to talk?"

He cast her an astonished glance. "No, get married."

"So soon?" she gasped.

Ryder frowned. "As far as I'm concerned, it's a week longer than I want to wait. I'm going out of my head wanting you this way." He turned off the familiar thoroughfare and headed toward her house, easing the car into the driveway, out of sight of the house and hidden from the neighbors.

The engine had barely had time to stop humming before Ryder reached for her, closing his arms convulsively around her shoulders. Lynn wordlessly lifted her face to him, reaching out to him, parting her lips, shamelessly inviting his kiss. It was hot and possessive.

"Invite me inside," he muttered, nibbling on the edges of her lips.

"The kids?"

"We'll send them to bed."

She nodded, eager for his touch.

As it happened, both Michelle and Jason were upstairs asleep. Lynn paid the babysitter and walked the teenager to the door. She stood on the porch until the neighbor girl was safely inside her own house. By the time Lynn returned to the kitchen, Ryder was brewing a pot of coffee.

"I don't want that," she told him, slipping her arms around his middle, feeling brazen. When she accepted his proposal, she'd experienced a release of sorts. She was taking a chance marrying Ryder, but then life was full of them, and living dangerously entailed a good deal of excitement.

"You don't want any coffee?"

"Nope." She skillfully dealt with the buttons of his shirt. Once it was opened, she rubbed her palms up his firm chest, reveling in the feel of his nakedness.

Ryder's hands were equally busy. Their bodies were on fire for each other as they explored, beseeched and promised all at the same time.

"Say it," Ryder growled hoarsely. "I need to hear you say it."

At the moment, she would have agreed to verbalize anything he wanted. "What?" she asked, bewildered. "I'll marry you? I already said I would. Next week, tomorrow. Tonight, if you want."

"Not that." He kissed her repeatedly, slipping his hands down her backside.

She whimpered softly. "Ryder, what?"

"Tell me you love me. I need to hear the words…I need to know what you feel for me."

With her hands braced against the curve of his neck, she paused and slowly lifted her head. Her hungry gaze met his, and she was astonished at the uneasiness she saw there. He didn't know. He honestly didn't know.

Tenderness tore through her. This was a man who had often been recognized for his determination and arrogance. A man bold and persistent, volatile and tenacious. Yet he'd made himself vulnerable to her, opened himself up, exposed his inner self in a way she had never dreamed possible.

She slipped her hands up his neck and laced her fingers through his hair. His eyes held her, watching her, loving her. Tears boiled beneath the surface of her eyes.

"Lynn?"

She cocked her head at an angle to his mouth and slowly, patiently kissed him. He groaned, securing her against him.

"I love you," she told him when she'd finished the kiss. "I love you," she repeated obligingly when she witnessed a flicker of doubt flash into his gaze. "For now…for always."

"Lynn," he cried, and buried his face in her neck, crushing her in his embrace. "I need you so much."

Lynn doubted that she'd ever heard any words more beautiful in her life.

Lynn hardly slept that night and woke early the next morning, feeling rummy and out of sorts. A woman in love, a woman who had agreed to marry a man she'd loved and admired, shouldn't be feeling like this.

When the first light of dawn peeled across a cranky sky, Lynn climbed out of bed and stumbled into the kitchen for coffee.

By all rights, she should be the happiest woman alive. Between kisses and the building enthusiasm for this marriage, she'd agreed to a wedding date less than ten days away, although she couldn't understand the rush. But Ryder had been insistent and she couldn't find it in her heart to delay the ceremony any longer than he wanted. Yet she couldn't understand why he felt the need to bulldoze her into marriage.

Ryder had left her in the early morning hours when she'd been high on his love. She'd watched him leave and had reluctantly gone to bed. It was then that this melancholy mood had settled over her.

Their time together had been splurged on kisses and promises. They'd only brushed over the truly important issues. There were so many things that needed to be settled. Slender, Too, was a big concern. She didn't want to give up her business and she feared Ryder might insist upon certain changes. If he did, there could be problems. The children worried her, too. They loved Ryder, but he'd always played the role of an indulgent uncle with them. A father...stepfather was something entirely different, and she would personally feel more comfortable having him ease into that role instead of being thrust upon Michelle and Jason unexpectedly this way.

"Mom." Jason stood just inside the kitchen, looking surprised to see her. "What are you doing up so early?"

"Thinking," she answered with a smile. She held out her arms for a hug. He gave her one, although reluctantly. It was on her mind to tell him the Incredible Hulk hugged his mother, but she let the thought slide.

As for her answer to his question, he seemed to find the fact that she'd gotten up early to "think" acceptable. He dragged a chair across the kitchen floor, stood on it and opened the cupboard above the refrigerator, bringing down a cereal box. He then proceeded to pour himself a huge bowl.

"I thought we were out of Cap'n Crunch cereal?"

"That's what I wanted Michelle to think," he whispered. "A girl can't appreciate the finer qualities this cereal has to offer a man."

"So you've been holding out on her?"

He hesitated. "If that's the way you want to think of it."

At another time, Lynn would have scolded her son for his selfishness. Instead she decided to forego the lecture, determined to buy two boxes of the kids' favorite cereal the next time she went grocery shopping. That would settle that problem.

"So how'd the date go with Ryder?" Jason asked, carrying the impossibly full bowl over to the table and plopping himself down beside her.

"It...was nice."

"Nice?" Jason repeated, crunching his cereal at breakneck speed.

"Jason, please, don't talk with your mouth full."

"Sorry." He wiped the sleeve of his green camouflage pajamas across his mouth. "So you had a good time?"

"We had a very nice time."

"You like Ryder real well, don't you?" He paused and studied her, his dark brown eyes wide and curious.

"Yes..."

"Good," he said and nodded once, profoundly.

"Why is that good?"

His gaze darted across the room, skirting her probing one. "Because."

That didn't explain a whole lot. She was about to comment when Michelle appeared, looking sleepy and cross. "Good morning, sweetheart," Lynn greeted.

Michelle grunted in reply, walked past her mother and brother, crisscrossed her legs, plopped herself down in front of the sink and opened the cupboard. Lynn leaned backward in her chair to watch what her daughter was doing and nearly laughed out loud when Michelle extracted a box of Cap'n Crunch cereal from behind the pipes.

Jason's mouth dropped open. "She's been holding out on me," he fumed, glaring at his mother. "Aren't you going to say something?"

Lynn glanced from one child to the other and slowly shook her head. "No way—I'm staying out of this one."

Jason slouched forward, and muttered something under his breath about what kind of mother had God assigned him, anyway!

By midmorning, Lynn had come to a decision. She would agree to marry Ryder, but to do so within ten days was impossible. She would insist they set the date several weeks in the future, possibly in three or four months. Marriage was what they both wanted, but she couldn't understand Ryder's need to rush into a relationship this important. They had the rest of their lives to spend together, and lots of questions that needed to be answered before sealing their vows.

A niggling fear kept cropping up in the back of Lynn's mind. From the first day he'd returned, Ryder had resisted discussing Gary. Anytime Gary's name was mentioned, Ryder found a way to change the subject.

Although he'd assured her otherwise, Lynn couldn't dismiss the fear that Ryder was marrying her and taking on the responsibility of raising Michelle and Jason out of some kind of warped idea of duty to her dead husband. She honestly didn't believe that was the case, but the thought troubled her and she wanted the issue cleared.

At noon, she took the time to phone Ryder. She frowned when the honey-voiced receptionist answered.

Whoever she was, the woman was efficient, and Lynn was connected with Ryder's office immediately.

"Lynn." Ryder sounded pleased to hear from her.

"Hi," she managed to swallow the question about the age of the receptionist. She was behaving like a jealous fool. Simply because the woman's voice sounded like black velvet didn't mean she looked like a beauty queen. "Would it be possible for you to stop over at the house tonight?"

"Of course. Any reason?"

"I...I think we have several things to discuss, don't you?"

He chuckled softly. "We don't seem to be able to do much of that, do we?"

Lynn blushed and whispered. "No, but I think we should try."

"I'll be out of here at about three. Do you want me to pick up Michelle and Jason for you?"

The way things were looking at the salon, that might be a good idea. "If you don't mind."

"I don't," he assured her.

"I'll be done around six."

"The kids and I'll be waiting for you," he paused. "Everything's all right, isn't it?"

Lynn couldn't see stirring up trouble over the phone. "Of course."

"We're going to have a good life, Lynn. A very good life."

Lynn didn't doubt Ryder, but she had her fears and she wanted them laid to rest. A lengthy engagement wouldn't hurt either of them.

By the time she arrived at the house, Ryder's car was parked out front. She pulled into the driveway and had no sooner climbed out of the driver's side when both kids and Ryder appeared.

"Why didn't you tell us?" Michelle cried, bouncing up and down with excitement.

"Tell you what, honey?" Ryder would know better than to say anything to the kids about their wedding plans. The task was for her and her alone. Nonetheless, she frowned, wondering.

She slapped her hands against her thighs. "About you and Ryder getting married next week. Mom, this is just wonderful."

Lynn's narrowed gaze flew to Ryder.

"I told you this would happen," Jason told his sister with a look of untainted righteousness. "Even when you wouldn't sign the pact in blood, it worked. They're getting married just the way we want them to."

Fifteen

"Ryder," Lynn whispered angrily. "What have you done?"

"We called and talked to the pastor," Michelle informed her mother with a cheerful grin. "He said next Saturday is fine with him, and then Ryder called the florist. You're really going to love all the roses and stuff."

Jason examined a caterpillar he was holding in the palm of his hand. "Grandma sounded surprised, though, don't you think, Michelle?"

"You've talked to your grandparents?"

"I know they're supposed to be on vacation, but I figured you'd want them to know. They're packing up the motor home and driving back to Seattle right away."

"Oh, dear." Lynn slumped against the side of her car.

"You're happy, aren't you, Mom?"

"I…"

"I think we may be moving too fast for your mother, but I didn't want to give her a chance to change her mind." Ryder's eyes reached out and gently caressed Lynn.

"She's not going to back out," Michelle quickly assured him. "We won't let her."

"I...I think Ryder and I've got several issues we need to settle first, though," she said through clenched teeth.

"Aren't you going to give her the ring?" Jason asked, tugging at Ryder's sleeve. Her son turned toward Lynn. "It's been in his family for seventy years. This is the engagement ring his grandfather gave his grandmother and his father his mother. I think this may mean you're going to have babies, right?"

Lynn opened her mouth, but she didn't know how to answer Jason. The subject of children was one in a long list she had yet to discuss with Ryder.

"I wouldn't mind a brother," Jason informed her, "but I don't know what I'd do with another sister. I wouldn't suppose there's any way you could order me a brother?"

"Jason," Michelle demanded, jerking him away. "Can't you see Mom and Ryder need time alone? He wants to give her the ring."

"I'm going to watch. It isn't every day a kid gets to see this kind of mushy stuff." The eight-year-old yanked his elbow from his sister's grasp and refused to budge. "Ryder's marrying us, too—we should get to see this if we want."

"I'd like more children." Ryder's dark eyes continued to hold Lynn's, his gaze filled with tenderness.

The word *more* was her undoing. Ryder honestly loved Michelle and Jason, as though he had actually fathered them. In the future she need never doubt that his actions weren't prompted by genuine concern for their welfare.

"Are you going to tell her about us moving into another house?" Michelle questioned.

"Another house?" Infuriated, Lynn swerved toward

her daughter. She felt as if every aspect of her life had been taken over. "Do you have any *other* surprises for me?"

"I think I'd better do the talking now," Ryder said with a halting smile. His hand at the small of Lynn's back directed her toward the front door, although Lynn tried to free herself. Rushing her into marriage was one thing, but making these kind of arrangements was going too far. Worlds too far. Her mind was whirling with outrage.

"Ryder, just what is going on?" She whirled around the instant she was inside the door. "You've contacted my parents in Minnesota, you've talked to the pastor and ordered flowers—"

"You object?"

"You're darn right I do." She was fighting like mad to quell her anger. The last thing she wanted was for her children to witness what she planned to say to him. Furious, now she was nearly foaming at the mouth. But Michelle and Jason worshiped the man and if she was going to have a heated argument with him, she would rather they were out of hearing distance. Besides, knowing her children, they would probably side with Ryder!

"I was only trying to help."

"You weren't," she shouted, unable to stop herself. "You're forcing me into this wedding and I don't like it."

Jason scooted a chair from the kitchen, twisted it around and straddled it as if it were a wild bronco. He propped his chin in his hands, his gaze shifting from Ryder to his mother and then back again.

"Jason, I need to talk to Ryder…alone."

"Sure." But he didn't budge.

"I think your mother wants you to leave, son," Ryder explained a minute later.

"Oh." Jason hopped off the chair, looking mildly chagrined. "Michelle told me you were going to fight, but she said that's something moms and dads do all the time and there wasn't any need to worry."

"There's nothing to be concerned about."

Ryder answered the youngster when Lynn didn't. As far as she was concerned, there was *plenty* to be worried about. She waited until Jason had vacated the entryway.

"The whole thing's off," she announced, her hands slicing the air like an umpire making a call, his decision final.

It took a minute for Ryder to react. "All right, if that's what you want."

It wasn't entirely, but Lynn wasn't going to be rail-roaded into marriage.

She opened her mouth to tell him exactly how furious she was, but he turned his back to her and calmly stated, "Then we'll just have to live in sin."

"What?" she exploded.

"With the way things are between us now, you don't honestly expect us to stay out of the bedroom? We can try—we've done it so far, but my restraint is at its limit. You're probably stronger than me."

"I…" She looked over her shoulder to make sure Jason wasn't spying on them. "That's the least of my concerns. We're talking about blending our lives together. There are going to be . . . difficulties."

"Like what?" He turned back to face her, hands in his pockets, the picture of nonchalance.

"Like…the kids. They love you now because you take them places, buy them things. You're like Santa

Claus and the Easter Bunny all rolled into one wonderful person. But how are they going to feel when you start disciplining them?"

"That's something we're going to have to work out, isn't it?"

"In time, right."

"You mean you won't marry me if the kids balk when I send them to bed and they don't want to go?"

Lynn folded her arms tightly around her stomach. "I didn't suggest that…quit twisting everything I say to suit your own purpose."

"I'm only answering your questions. I don't understand the problem with the kids. They know I love them, they trust me to be fair. What's going to change if we get married?"

"What about children? Jason started asking me about a baby brother and I didn't know how to answer him."

"Do you want more children?"

"I think so…if you do."

"I do. That settles that. Is there anything else?"

"What about Slender, Too? I've put a lot of time and effort into building it up and I don't want to walk away from it now."

"You're asking me if I'm going to object if you keep working? Not in the least. That's your business and you have a right to be proud of what you've accomplished. I'm not going to take that away from you."

The hot wind that had buoyed the sails of her outrage started to slacken. What had once threatened to be a hurricane force diminished to a gentle breeze.

"But I don't want you to overdo it," Ryder warned. "When we decide it's time for you to get pregnant, I'd like you to consider taking time off to properly take care of yourself and the baby, but I'll leave that up to you."

Lynn blinked and nodded. "Naturally I'd want to do that."

"I love you, Lynn. I want you for my wife."

She stared at him mesmerized as he straightened and walked toward her. He was impossible to resist when he was looking at her with his eyes filled with such love. The only thing Lynn had to quell at the moment was the impulse to fall into his arms.

"You're going to marry me, aren't you?" he asked on a husky murmur. "It's what we both want, but yet you keep fighting it. Why?"

"I'm afraid," she admitted.

"I frighten you that much?"

"Not you," she countered.

"What then?"

Now that she had the opportunity to voice her objections, she found them garbled and twisted in her mind. If she were to mention Gary's name, he would tell her how silly she was being in the same way that he'd assured her about everything else.

"Gary…"

Ryder frowned. "What about him?"

"You loved him?"

"You know I did."

As always when she mentioned Gary's name, Ryder tensed, but she had to know. "You're not marrying me out of a sense of duty, are you?"

His face twisted into a glower as if he resented her insinuating as much. "No," he answered abruptly. "I already told you I've dealt with the guilt of what happened. Loving you is completely separate from Gary's death."

"I...I had to be sure."

He reached for her, hauling her into his arms, his mouth seeking hers. She met his lips eagerly, returning the passion until she was weak and clinging. Because he'd turned her mind around so completely, she was frustrated they couldn't be married any sooner.

"You're going to marry me." This time it was a statement, not a question.

Lynn lowered her gaze and nodded. Heaven help her for being such a fool, but she loved this man. He was offering her a slice of paradise and it wasn't in her to refuse.

"Michelle." Jason cried and popped up from behind the living-room sofa. "It's working out just great."

Lynn slumped forward, securing her forehead against Ryder's chest. "He was listening the whole time."

"Hurry and come downstairs," Jason yelled. "We don't have anything to worry about...they're getting married just the way you said. We're going to be a real family in no time."

"Do you take this man to be your lawfully wedded husband?" Pastor Teed asked Lynn.

She stared up at Ryder, who was standing so confidently beside her, and felt her insides go soft, and her heart began to pound unnaturally hard. She was about to make a giant leap into a whole new life. She stood tall and proud, but on the inside she was a mass of quivering nerves.

"Lynn," the pastor prompted softly.

"I do," she returned, certain that she was doing the right thing.

Ryder smiled at her and although the man of God continued speaking, Lynn barely heard what he was saying. When Pastor Teed informed Ryder that he could kiss the bride, he did so gently, as if she were the most priceless piece of porcelain in the world and he feared breaking her. Silly tears gathered in the corners of her eyes. She had never expected to find such happiness and love a second time—she'd given up trying. Yet here she was standing before God and man, pledging her life to Ryder.

The reception was an intimate affair with only a handful of friends. Her parents were there, and Toni Morris, who was busy serving cake and coffee. Lynn's mother and father looked happy and proud. They knew Ryder from before and were pleased with her choice.

Michelle and Jason mingled with the guests, telling everyone who would listen how they'd known all along that their mother was going to marry Ryder.

All too soon the reception came to a close, and it was time for Lynn to change out of the pale silk dress she'd worn for the wedding ceremony and into one more suitable for traveling.

Toni Morris wiped a stray tear from her cheek and hugged Lynn after she'd changed outfits. It was unlike Toni to be demonstrative and Lynn hugged her friend back, squeezing her tightly.

"I'm happy for you, Lynn. Ryder loves you, don't ever doubt that."

Lynn nodded, grateful for all the moral support Toni had given her over the years, although she found her friend's words mildly disturbing. There wasn't any reason for her to doubt Ryder's love.

"You've got everything?" Toni asked.

"Yes. I've been through the list a dozen times."

"Your parents are keeping Michelle and Jason for the week."

"God bless parents," Lynn whispered, raising her eyes toward the heavens.

"Your suitcase is packed and ready."

Lynn grinned, it was packed all right, but Toni made it sound as though she was on her way to the maternity ward instead of her honeymoon.

"Work?"

"Sharon's the acting manager. If anything drastic happens, she has your phone number."

"Great." Toni hugged her once more. "Have a wonderful honeymoon, Mrs. Matthews."

Lynn giggled, reaching for her suitcase. "I intend to."

Sixteen

As bold as she'd been earlier in their courtship, Lynn felt like a blushing bride when she met Ryder in front of the reception hall at the country club.

"Bye, Mom," Michelle cried, hugging her mother tightly around the waist. "You'll bring me something back from Hawaii, won't you?"

"Of course."

In front of an audience, Jason wasn't as keen about showing his affection. He offered his mother his hand to shake, and Lynn politely shook it, then hugged him anyway.

"I'll bring you back something, too," she assured him before he could ask.

"Do you think you could find me a shark's jaw?"

Lynn cringed and nodded, knowing Jason would be delighted with the grisly bone. "I'll see what I can do."

Her mother and father stepped forward and Lynn gave them each a warm embrace, grateful, as always, for their unfailing love and support.

No more than a minute later, Lynn and Ryder were in his car on the way to a hotel close to the airport. Their flight was scheduled to leave for Honolulu early the following morning. Ryder had arranged for them to spend their first night in the honeymoon suite.

He reached for her hand and raised it to his mouth, kissing her fingertips. "You're a beautiful bride, Mrs. Matthews."

"Thank you." Once more she felt soft color flush into her cheeks. She was trembling and grateful that Ryder was too preoccupied with the traffic to notice her nervousness. There had only been one lover in her life and fears crowded the edges of her mind that she wouldn't be the kind of woman Ryder needed in bed. She would have preferred it if their lovemaking had happened more…naturally. She felt timid and shy and awkward with this man she had just married. It was right for them to wait, Lynn realized that much, but doubts confronted her at every turn. Not if she'd done the right thing by marrying Ryder, but if she was woman enough to satisfy him.

While Ryder registered them at the hotel desk, Lynn looked toward the four-star restaurant where several couples were dining by candlelight and champagne music. Ryder joined her a moment later.

"Hungry?"

She nodded eagerly, looking for a way to delay their lovemaking. She was being silly, she knew that, but she couldn't seem to shake her nervousness.

"We can order dinner from room service," Ryder suggested.

"Would you mind if we ate at the restaurant…here?" she asked quickly.

Ryder looked disappointed, but agreed.

Lynn ordered two glasses of wine with her meal

and showed more interest in the chardonnay than the shrimp stuffed sole. She lingered over dessert, ignoring the fact that Ryder preferred not to order any and glanced at his watch two or three times while she leisurely nibbled away at hers.

"There's nothing to worry about, you know," he whispered, after the waiter refilled her coffee cup for the third time.

Her head shot upward, her eyes round. "What...do you mean?"

"You know what I'm talking about."

"Ryder...my stomach feels like a nest of red ants are building a whole new colony in there. My palms are sweaty and I feel like an inexperienced girl. I want to make love with you so much it frightens me and yet I'm terrified of doing so."

"Honey, come on. There's only one way to face something like this."

"Maybe we should wait until we get to Hawaii... that's the real start of our honeymoon."

"Lynn, you're being ridiculous." He paid the bill and with his hand under her elbow, directing her, he led her to the elevator.

The whole way up to the twentieth floor, Lynn's mind floundered, seeking excuses. Never in a thousand years would she have believed she could be this anxious over something she'd been wanting for weeks. For heaven's sake, she'd practically seduced Ryder that day in the water.

Her husband opened the room and pushed open the door. He lifted her into his arms and, disregarding her protests, carried her into the opulent suite. Gently he set her back on the thick carpeting. Their suitcases were waiting for them on the floor next to the bed, but her gaze refused to go as far as the king-size mattress.

"Oh, look, they show movies," she said cheerfully, as though watching the latest release would be the highlight of this trip.

"We're going to take things nice and slow, Lynn. There won't be any time for movies."

She nodded, realizing how incredibly absurd she must have sounded.

Reaching for her, Ryder took her shoulders between his hands and drew her against him. "I love you."

"I love you, too." Lynn tried to smile, she honestly tried, but she failed utterly. Moistening her lips, she lifted her arms, bracing her hands against his chest. The heavy beat of his heart seemed to thunder against her palms and did little to reassure her.

"There's magic between us," he told her in a warm whisper. "I recognized it the first time we kissed."

Lynn had, too. She stared into his tanned, lean face, loving him all the more for his patience. He smiled at her so gently, so tenderly, the way a child does when petting a newborn kitten. Lynn felt the worst of the tension ease out of her stiff body.

He kissed her, lightly, making no demands on her, then pulled away, studying her. "That wasn't so terrible, was it?"

She shut her eyes. "I'm being foolish."

"No, you're not," he countered and kissed her again, more deeply this time, although he continued to hold her as though she were delicate and could easily break.

The taste of his mouth over hers was an awakening for Lynn, and as a brilliantly colored marigold does to the morning sun, Lynn opened to Ryder, flowering, seeking his warmth and love. There was nothing to be afraid of with this man. Nothing. The memory of his touch, the sound and taste of his lovemaking filled her mind. Thread by thread, the thoughts unwove her hesitation.

Ryder's gaze moved over her face. "Feeling better now?"

Lynn nodded. "Isn't it a little warm in here?" Before he could answer, she reached up and started unfastening the buttons of his starched white shirt.

"Now that you mention it, yes." Eagerly he shucked his suit coat and let it fall heedlessly to the floor. Lynn smiled to herself, knowing how unlike Ryder it was to be messy or disorganized.

He reached for the zipper at the back of her dress, easing it down, slowly, cautiously as though he expected her to bolt and run from him at any time. His shirtfront was open and Lynn lifted her palms to his bare chest. His skin was hot to the touch and she longed to feel the kinky soft hairs matted there, against her face.

Ryder lifted his hands to her neck, easing the material of her dress over her shoulders and down her torso, past her hips. It disrupted her momentarily to step out of it and do away with her slip, bra and her other underthings, but they were disposed of soon enough.

She lifted her hands back to his chest. The need to taste him dominated her thoughts and she ran the tip of her tongue in a meandering path across his chest, savoring the hot, salty flavor of him.

Ryder shuddered and closed his arms around her waist, tugging her against his naked torso. She wrapped her arms around his neck, clinging to him, busying her fingers in the thick, dark hair at his nape. As she brushed her body against his, she could feel the gentle rasp of his body hair against her.

"Oh, Ryder," she whispered in rapturous awe.

Somehow he moved them onto the bed, laying above her, lowering himself just enough to brush his chest over her nakedness, tantalizing her. "Does that feel good, love?"

"Oh, yes…very good."

Ryder's mouth found hers in a kiss that was hard, hot and coaxing. He kissed her with a fierceness that robbed her of her breath and caused the blood to pound through her veins. She willingly parted her lips and arched her back until her tingling breasts encountered the hard, hairy wall of his chest once more.

"Ryder," she moaned, "I want you so much."

"Not yet, love."

Desire for him rocked through her until she was certain if he didn't take her soon, her bones would melt, longing for him the way she did. Her heart was pounding harder than it had at any other time in her life. Each staccato beat's echo was magnified a hundredfold in her ears.

His lips continued to torture her until the yearning was so potent she thought she would die from wanting him. It saturated every cell of her being and she lifted his head, and raised her mouth to his, longing to show him with her kiss how eager she was to be his wife. All her nervous reserve was gone, evaporating under his tender ministrations.

"Oh…please," she begged.

Lynn tangled her fingers in his hair and he dropped forward enough for her to plant a wild kiss on his lips. She gloried in the way his body trembled above hers.

"Lynn…oh, Lynn," he cried out. When they'd finished making love Lynn was replete, utterly enraptured by sensation.

They slept in each other's arms, and when she awoke the room was filled with dark shadows of night. She felt wonderful and, raising herself up on her elbow, she watched her husband's face, relaxed now in sleep. Ryder looked almost boyish and the surge of love that rocked through her brought a rush of tears to her eyes.

Slipping out of the sheet, she moved into the bathroom and ran water for a bath, luxuriating in the hot liquid.

"Lynn?" A thread of panic filled his voice.

"I'm in here." She climbed out of the tub and reached for a towel, holding it against her front.

Ryder stumbled into the room, looking mussed and sleepy, but he paused and relaxed when he saw her. "You're beautiful, Mrs. Matthews," he said, leaning against the door.

"I didn't mean to wake you."

"I'm glad you did."

"You are?"

He took a step toward her and gently pulled away the towel she was holding against her water-slickened body. "You're even more beautiful now."

Lynn lowered her head.

"You doubt me?"

"No," she told him softly. "Telling me that only assures me how much you really *do* love me." When she glanced at him, she read the confusion in his eyes. "I'm over thirty, Ryder, and I've borne two children…they've left their marks on my body. I'm not going to win any beauty pageants."

Instead of arguing, Ryder reached for her, folding her in his embrace. He led her back into the bedroom. "There isn't a woman on this earth more beautiful to me than you." His voice shook with sincerity.

Back in the bedroom, he sat on the edge of the mattress and pulled her down into his lap. He lifted his hands to her hair and tugged it loose from the carefully braided French roll the hairdresser had spent so long creating for her wedding. The length fell down the middle of her back. Ryder parted it over her shoulder and the dark length hung loosely, nearly covering her shoulders.

He paused and seemed to stop breathing as he lifted it away from her head with widespread fingers, letting the softness flow through his hands like spilled coffee. "I've dreamed of you kissing me with your hair falling over my face."

With her hands at his shoulders, she gently pressed him back against the mattress, securing him there. He watched her with curious eyes as she positioned herself above her husband.

Slowly, very slowly, she leaned forward, letting her hair fall over him. But Ryder surprised her even more by raising his head and clamping his hands at each side of her waist. Lynn whimpered with the explosive desire that pitched through her.

"Oh, Lynn," he breathed "Oh, baby, you haven't got a clue what you do to me."

Lynn smiled softly to herself. Actually she had a very good idea of what she did to him.Ryder scooted his chair away from his desk. He should be going over a brief, but his mind refused to focus on the case he was studying. Instead, his thoughts drifted to his wife.

They'd been married for several weeks now and it was as if they'd always been together. Every time he thought about Lynn his throat filled with such strong emotion that he could hardly breathe. He couldn't get enough of her and her special brand of lovemaking. Every time he felt her body, all soft and athletic beside him, it affected him. He had to have her. Sometimes once a night wasn't enough. Lynn seemed as eager as he was for this side of their marriage and that pleased him immeasurably. He would reach for her and she would come into his arms with an enthusiasm that caused his blood to boil.

Loving and craving Lynn the way he did frightened him. He'd never expected to experience this deep a commitment in his life. The need he felt just to know she was close clawed at him and the thought of losing her was enough to drive him over the edge of sanity.

He glanced at his watch, troubled by his thoughts. Lynn would be home by now. He decided to read the brief that night. With that decided, he shoved the papers inside his briefcase and headed out of the office.

Lynn's car was parked in the driveway when he pulled up in front of the house and he exhaled sharply.

"You're home early," she greeted, when he stepped into the kitchen. She wore an apron around her waist and was slicing thin strips of beef for their dinner.

"Where are Michelle and Jason?" he asked, and slipped his arms around her waist, nuzzling her neck.

"Michelle's helping Janice baby-sit and will be home at five-thirty, and Jason's at soccer practice."

"Good." He unknotted the apron strings and let it drop to the kitchen floor.

"Ryder?"

Next, he fiddled with the buttons on her blouse, peeling it open with an excitement that caused his hands to shake. Ryder had only meant to touch her, but the minute his hands experienced the silky softness of her skin he knew there was no stopping him. A melting sort of ecstasy grew within him that would be satisfied only by making love to Lynn.

"Now?" she breathed the question.

He answered her with an ardent kiss.

"Dinner's going to be late," she whispered.

"We'll order pizza," he answered, leading her toward the stairs.

Lynn giggled. "Ryder, we're too old for this! We can't keep this up and live beyond forty."

"Talk for yourself, woman."

"Married life certainly seems to suit you," Toni commented over lunch a few days later.

The lunch was Toni's treat. But Lynn wasn't fooled; her friend wanted to gloat. When Lynn had announced to Toni that she was marrying Ryder, Toni had asked what took her so long to figure out why Ryder had come back to Seattle.

"I'm so much in love I can hardly stand it," Lynn admitted almost shyly. "It's funny really…I'd given up dating. As far as I could see the world was filled with… I don't know."

"I think the term you used earlier this summer was warthogs."

Lynn smiled. "That about says it. Ryder came into my life when I least expected to fall in love again."

"I'd like to say I told you so, but Joe wouldn't let me say one word to you about Ryder loving you."

Lynn would have doubted her friend, anyway.

"Everything's working out with the kids?"

"It's too good to be true. They turn to him just as if he were their father. From day one they've both been on their best behavior."

"You don't expect that to last, do you?"

"No. Ryder knows that, too."

"Now what's this I hear about you buying a new house?"

Lynn focused her attention on the chef salad and slowly exhaled, hoping her friend didn't notice her hesitation. "Ryder wants to move."

"Is that so difficult to understand?"

It wasn't, but Lynn still had trouble letting go of the house. She'd lived in that colonial since shortly after she and Gary were married. Both children had been born while they lived there. The house was filled with happy memories of a life she treasured and revered. It was convenient to the salon and shopping. The school was only a few blocks away and the neighbors were good friends. At Ryder's insistence, they'd looked at several new homes, but Lynn couldn't find one that suited her.

"Is it?" Toni pressed.

"I can't seem to find anything I like."

"And Ryder?"

"He's found several he thinks we'll fit into nicely. We're leaning toward a five-bedroom place a couple of miles from where we live now."

"Five bedrooms?" Toni gasped, mocking Lynn with her eyes.

"Ryder wants one for a den."

"And later one for the baby?"

Lynn blushed. "There isn't going to be any baby for a year or more, so get that snide look off your face."

"But not from lack of trying, if what I see in your face is true. Good grief Lynn, it isn't any wonder Ryder's got circles under his eyes and you walk around wearing that silly grin."

"Toni, stop it, you're embarrassing me." But she *was* wearing a smile these days, a contented one, and nothing seemed to dampen her good spirits.

"How's the salon doing?"

Lynn shrugged. "Good. I've got a membership campaign in the works. I'm training a couple of new girls who seem to be working out nicely—no pun intended. Things couldn't be better."

"And Ryder doesn't object to you spending so much time at the salon?"

Lynn shrugged. There wasn't any reason for him to complain. She was home every night, usually before he was. He did offer a suggestion or two, which she'd taken into consideration. He liked to know what was going on in her business and she enjoyed sharing that part of her life with him.

"I hope you're not going to kill yourself over this membership campaign," Toni said with a sigh. "I know you and it's difficult for you to delegate responsibility. You can't do everything yourself, so don't make the mistake of trying."

The two chatted for several minutes more, then parted. Lynn went back to the salon, checked in with Sharon, then took the rest of the afternoon off, stopping at a couple of stores on the way home to do errands.

On impulse, she bought a negligee, wondering how long she would be able to keep it on once she modeled it for Ryder.

The house was quiet when she unlocked the door.

Once inside the entryway, she turned, feeling that something wasn't right, but couldn't put her finger on it. She looked around, but didn't notice anything different. Ryder was still at the office and both kids were in school. She set down the grocery bags and placed the milk inside the refrigerator.

"Hi, Mom." Jason shouted as he came through the front door. The screen door slammed in his wake. "What's for snack?"

"Milk and—"

"Are we having pizza for dinner again tonight?"

Lynn tried to hide a smile. "Why?"

"Joey wants to come over for dinner if we are. He said he didn't know anyone in the whole world who had pizza four nights in a row."

"Actually I thought I'd serve spaghetti and meatballs tonight. Is that all right?"

"Sure," he shrugged and reached for an apple. "I'm going outside, okay?"

"What about your homework?"

"I don't have any and if I did, I'd do it after dinner."

Lynn walked him to the front door and again was assailed with the fact that something was out of place. She turned and strolled through the living room, paused, and turned around.

Her gaze fell on the television and she gasped. Gary's picture, which had rested there for over three years was gone. She whirled around and looked at the fireplace. *All* the pictures of him were missing from there, too. Only the ones of her and Michelle and Jason remained.

There was only one person who would have removed them, and that was Ryder.

Lynn knew it was time for a talk.

Seventeen

"Hi, Mom," Michelle greeted when Lynn walked in the house the following week. Lynn had yet to confront Ryder about the missing photos of Gary. She was afraid, she suspected. Still it troubled her greatly. Her daughter's gaze was glued to the television where a popular rock group was crooning out the unintelligible words to a top-ten hit.

Lynn ripped the sweatband from her forehead and hurried toward the kitchen, tossing her purse on the counter and rubbing the pain in the small of her back. "Where're Ryder and Jason?"

"Soccer practice."

Lynn heaved a sigh of relief—she should have remembered that. This was the third night in a row that she was late getting out of the salon and she'd been worried about confronting Ryder. He hadn't said anything about the extra hours she was putting in, but she knew it bothered him.

"What's for dinner?" Michelle yelled. "I'm starved."

Lynn rubbed her hand over her face and sighed. "I don't know yet."

"Mom...is it going to be another one of those nights?"

Lynn paused. "What do you mean by that?"

"The only time we have a decent meal anymore is when Ryder orders out."

Lynn wanted to argue, but she hadn't a leg to stand on, as the old saying went. Things had been hectic at Slender, Too, since the first of the month. Lynn had started a membership campaign with local newspaper and radio advertisement. The response had been greater than she'd dared to hope, but consequently she was left to deal with a ton of paperwork plus individual exercise programs to calculate for her newest customers. To complicate matters, Lynn had come up with the brilliant idea of hanging a star from the salon ceiling for every inch lost in the month of September. It sounded like such a good suggestion at the time. But her fingers ached from working with scissors and the salon was quickly beginning to resemble another planet.

"How does bacon, eggs and pancakes sound?" Lynn asked her daughter, forcing some enthusiasm into her voice.

"Like something you should serve for breakfast."

"Sometimes a breakfast meal can be fun at dinnertime." Rooting through the refrigerator didn't offer her any other suggestions. The shelves were bare. What leftovers there were had long been eaten.

"How about tacos?"

Jason would love that, and Lynn sighed her regret. "I don't have any hamburger thawed out."

"Use the microwave...what have you got in the freezer, anyway?"

"Bacon and that's it." Lynn had been so busy over

the weekend that she hadn't had time to buy groceries. It was already Wednesday and she still hadn't gotten to the market.

"You mean to tell me all we've got is bacon?"

"I'm sorry," she snapped, "I'll get to the store tomorrow."

"That's what you said last night."

The front door banged open and Jason stormed inside like a Texas whirlwind. "I scored two goals and made an assist and Mr. Lawson said I did the best ever."

Lynn hugged her son and brushed the sweat-heavy hair from his flushed brow. "That's great."

"Ryder's going to be the assistant coach now."

Lynn's gaze found her husband's. "I didn't know you played soccer."

"He doesn't," Jason answered automatically, dismissing that detail as minor. "I have to teach him."

"But…" Lynn was about to question Ryder about the unexpectedness of his offer, when Jason jerked open the refrigerator and groaned.

"You haven't got any pop yet?"

"I…didn't get a chance to get to the store."

Jason wailed in protest. "Mom, you promised. I'm dying of thirst…you don't honestly expect me to drink *water*, do you?"

"I didn't promise. I told you I'd *try* to get to the store," she barked, feeling pressured and angry. "Why do I have to be the one to do everything around here? I work, too, you know. If I lazed around some luxurious office all day reading court papers then I'd probably have more time for other things, too." Lynn couldn't believe what she was saying, how unfair she was being, but once she got started, she couldn't seem to stop.

Ryder was the one having fun with her children while she was stuck in her office cutting out stupid gold stars. Tears filled her eyes and when she wiped them aside, she found Michelle, Jason and Ryder all staring at her in stunned silence.

Both children stood frozen, their eyes wide with shock and horror. Ryder's gaze was spitting and angry, but outwardly, at least, he remained calm.

"I think your mother and I need some time alone," he told Michelle and Jason, his hands on their shoulders. Gently he guided them toward the stairs. There was a quick exchange of whispers before Ryder returned to the kitchen.

"That's it, Lynn," he told her when he returned.

She slammed a package of microwave-thawed bacon on the counter. "All right, I shouldn't have said that. I apologize." Her hands were furiously at work trying to peel the thick slices of meat apart and place them in the frying pan.

"That's not good enough." He took a step closer.

"Don't accept my apology, then." She refused to look at him, fearing she would burst into tears if she did. The ache in the small of her back intensified.

"It's been weeks since we returned from Hawaii. At first everything was wonderful, but it's been a nightmare ever since."

"How can you say that?" she cried. She'd been trying so hard to be a good wife to him. Not once had she turned him down when he wanted to make love... and heaven knew that was every night. She kept the house spotless, managed the laundry and everything else that kept the house running smoothly. Okay, she hadn't gotten groceries in a few days, but that was only a minor thing.

"For the past two weeks, you fly in here after six, throw something together for dinner and then collapse."

"I work hard." She felt like weeping, tears churned just below the surface and the knot forming in her throat was large enough to choke her. No one seemed to appreciate all she did—they simply took it for granted that she could keep up with everything. Well, she couldn't.

"We all work hard—Michelle and Jason, too, in their own way. I just don't like what you're doing to yourself and everyone close to you."

Ryder wasn't the only one with complaints. She had a few of her own. She hadn't even mentioned anything about Gary's pictures being missing. Nor had she said anything about how she felt Ryder was trying to buy Michelle's and Jason's love. He couldn't seem to do enough for them. This latest thing—agreeing to help coach Jason's soccer team when he knew next to nothing about the sport was a perfect example.

"You're exhausted," he complained. "Look at you. You can hardly stand, you're so tired. You keep driving yourself and pretty soon you're going to crack. I can't allow that, Lynn. You're too important to us."

"If you didn't keep me up half the night with your lusty demands, then I might get a decent night's sleep."

Ryder's face drained of color. Lynn had never seen a man look more furious. His eyes were as cold as glaciers and when they narrowed on her, she realized she'd stepped over the line of his patience.

"Come here, Lynn," he demanded in a voice that would have shattered diamonds.

"No."

He took the bacon out of her hand so fast that Lynn whirled around and gasped. The meat fell to the floor with a slapping sound that seemed to echo around the kitchen.

"Now look what you've done," she cried, backing away from him.

He cornered her against the counter, pinning her there with the full length of his body. Lynn glared at him, her chin raised, her eyes spitting with defiance. Tears continued to sting her eyes, but she would die before she let them fall.

"So it's my 'lusty demands' that are responsible for keeping you up all night?"

"Yes," she cried.

"Then it's all my fault that you're so cranky and unreasonable."

She nodded, knowing it was a lie, but too proud to admit it. "You force me night after night. If I'm exhausted it's because of you…"

To her surprise, Ryder laughed at her. She knew she was being unreasonable and ridiculous, but he'd made her so angry and lashing out at him helped ease her frustration. But when he found her words humorous, that infuriated her all the more.

"You're lying to yourself if you believe that. You want to make love as much as I do, even more."

"No," she insisted, shaking her head.

"Oh, yes, you do."

He kissed her then, his lips moist and seductive. Her traitorous body sprang to life, responding to him the way a child does to praise. Soon her gasps of anger became tiny moans of pleasure.

"Stop it, Ryder," she cried when he broke off the

kiss, pushing at him, wanting out of his arms before she begged him to make love to her.

"Why?"

"I don't like it."

"Oh, but you do," he returned with supreme arrogance; his eyes continued to laugh at her. "Do you really want me to show you how much you like it?"

"No." She pushed again at his shoulders once more.

He smiled and kissed her again. Within seconds every part of her was throbbing.

Lynn swallowed a weak groan and sank her teeth into her bottom lip when Ryder caught her earlobe between his lips and tugged on it. "I don't suppose you like this, either?"

"No." Her hands fell lifelessly to her sides. Even a token protest was more than she could muster.

"I thought not," he returned in a husky murmur..

Lynn was convinced it was a miracle she didn't sink to the floor. Every fiber of her being was alive and singing, demanding the release he'd made so remarkably familiar to her.

He slipped his hand to her backside, dragging her even closer until they were glued together.

"Want me?"

She nodded, her whole body weak with longing.

He rewarded her with a kiss that liquified anything that was left of her defenses.

"That's too bad," he whispered, his own voice shaking. She opened her eyes slowly and discovered him staring at her, his gaze clouded with passion. "I want you, too, but you need your rest."

It took a moment for his words to sink in to her consciousness and when they did, she wanted to cry out in frustration. it felt as if she'd suffered a blow to her midsection. She scooted past him and brushed the hair from her flushed face. With deliberate movements, she picked up the bacon off the floor, her hands shaking so badly it was a wonder she could manage that.

Ryder slowly moved away from her. "I'll go get us something for dinner," he told her in a voice that was filled with strain. "Take a hot bath and go to bed. You're exhausted—I'll take care of everything here."

"You don't need to do that, Ryder. I'll fix dinner."

His answering sigh was filled with defeat. "Do what you want, then."

The sound of the front door closing sounded like thunder. Lynn stretched out her hand and grabbed hold of the counter, needing it to remain upright.

"Can we come down now?" Jason called from the top of the stairs.

"Sure." It took effort to keep her voice from pitching and wobbling.

"Where'd Ryder go?" Michelle wanted to know when she joined her mother in the kitchen. She looked around suspiciously as though she expected to find him hiding under the table.

"He…he's going to bring us back something to eat."

"I wish he'd taken me with him," Jason said, whining just a little. "We haven't had hamburgers in a long time and I was hoping for a little variety."

"Ryder didn't need to leave," Michelle pointed out. "He could've ordered pizza. We haven't had that in a while either—not like we used to when you first came back from Hawaii. What's he bringing us?"

"I don't know." Lynn turned back to the sink, not

wanting her children to know how close she was to bursting into tears.

"I thought you guys were going to have a big fight," Michelle said, "We listened, but we didn't even hear you shout."

"We...didn't. I think I'll go up and take a shower if you two don't need me."

"Sure, Mom, go ahead."

She raced up the stairs, undressed and turned on the water spigots. Tears scalded her cheeks as she heaved in giant gulps of oxygen. The water didn't ease any of the ache she was experiencing, but then she'd known it wouldn't. When she was finished, she dressed in her pajamas and stood at the top of the stairs.

"Michelle, would you tell Ryder when he gets back that I'm tired and I've decided to go to bed?"

"Okay," she answered with some reluctance.

"But, Mom, it's not even seven," Jason objected.

"I'm really exhausted tonight," she said and turned away to swallow a sob. "He'll understand."

Since that was exactly where he'd sent her, she doubted that Ryder would object. Although she listened for him, Ryder didn't come upstairs until several hours later. Lynn had snoozed off and on for most of the evening, but she was instantly awake the minute Ryder entered the bedroom. The illuminated dial on the clock radio revealed it was after eleven.

He didn't turn on the light, but she heard him undressing in the dark, taking pains to be quiet.

"I'm awake," she whispered. "Do you want to talk?"

"Not particularly."

If her mood had improved, his hadn't. Sullen silence filled the room.

"I'll stop on my way home tomorrow night and buy groceries," she offered a couple of minutes later, regretting the things she'd said and done and looking for a way to show him how sorry she was.

"While I was out earlier, I picked up a few essentials, so there's no rush." Ryder lifted the sheets and climbed into the bed, staying as far away from her as space would allow.

"I promise I'll do it tomorrow."

"Before or after you put in a ten-hour day?"

Lynn let that comment slide. "It's this membership campaign. You know it won't be like this every week, I promise. By the end of the month things will have settled back to normal."

He bunched up the pillow and rolled onto his side, presenting her with a clear view of his back.

More tortuous seconds passed.

"I'm sorry for the things I said earlier—none of them were true." She tried again, feeling more wretched by the minute, desperate to repair the damage her pride had inflicted.

He didn't respond and she felt a growing desolation. "Ryder, I love you so much, please don't do this…I can't bear it."

She felt him stiffen as though a battle were raging within him. It seemed like an eternity passed before he shifted his weight and turned onto his back. Lynn eagerly scooted into his arms, looping her arm around his waist and burying her face between his shoulder and his neck. It felt like coming home after being away a long while, his arms a shelter from the worst storms. Only this hurricane had been one of her own making.

"You can't go on like this," he whispered into her

hair, tenderly brushing it away from her face. "I refuse to let you do this to yourself, to your family."

She could only agree. "I've been doing a lot of thinking, between catnaps tonight," she admitted. "I think I understand what's been happening with Slender, Too, the last few months, and why I've pushed myself the way I have."

"You do?"

Lynn nodded. "The first couple of years after Gary was gone, I floundered terribly. Everything in my life was dictated by other people while I struggled for some kind of control. Bit by bit, I gained my independence in small ways. When I was ready to really break free and soar on my own, I bought the franchise. It was the first time in my life that I'd invested in something that was completely mine. I was the one in charge. Slender, Too, was a tiny piece of life that I could govern and the success or failure rested entirely on my shoulders. That first sample of accomplishment was powerful and the taste of independence addictive. I've clung on to it, refusing to let go of even the most mundane aspects of the business, despite the fact that the children didn't have as much attention as they'd wanted. I needed the time for *me*."

"But you're willing to now?"

"Yes, I have to, because I've learned how important my family is in my life. And…"

"Yes?"

"You did that, Ryder."

Then he kissed her until her heart was pounding out of control. "Ah, Lynn, you know exactly what to say to turn my head."

She giggled, loving the feel of his hands as they sought her.

"I want to change things, Ryder, but I'm not sure I know how."

"What you need is a manager to take some of the responsibility off your shoulders."

"But I still want to maintain some control," she inserted, knowing the role of observer would never satisfy her.

"You will have, honey, just not all the hours. Try it out and see how it works."

She nodded, knowing he was right, but still having trouble admitting it—she always *did* have problems owning up to that.

He closed his arms more securely around her. "About what happened in the kitchen," he murmured, flicking his tongue over her ear, nibbling on her lobe.

"Yes?"

Ryder's hand lifted her breast. "Don't you think it's time we finished what we started?"

Eighteen

"Ryder," Lynn purred, utterly content. She slid her bare leg seductively down his much longer one and toyed with the soft hairs at his nape. She was resting on her back and he was lying on his stomach with his hand draped over her middle. "I love you."

"Hmm...I know." He raised himself up on one elbow and kissed her in a leisurely exercise. "But if anyone should complain about being kept awake nights, it's me."

"Very funny." She rubbed her hands over his back, pausing at the dip below his waist, then hesitated. "I want to talk to you about something important."

He caught her lower lip between his teeth and sucked gently. "What?"

"Gary."

Ryder went completely still. She felt his breath lodge in his throat and his body tense. "Why?"

"Because every time I mention his name, you freeze up and change the subject."

His mouth descended over hers while he rooted through her long hair as though to punish her for bringing Gary's name into their conversation. Lynn gave a painful yelp and he relaxed his grip and lifted his head. His lungs made a soft rustling sound. "That's because I don't want to talk about him."

She smiled gently, and whispered, "I guessed as much, but, Ryder, I don't think that's healthy." Except for their initial discussion at the picnic, from the time he'd returned from Boston, Ryder had gone to great lengths to avoid talking about his best friend.

Again and again he'd assured Lynn that his love for her had nothing to do with what had happened to Gary or any guilt associated with the tragedy of his death. Perhaps because she'd wanted to believe it so badly, she'd held on to the assumption. But lately little things had started to add up and she didn't like the sum total she was seeing. Tonight seemed to be the one to settle their qualms. This problem with Gary was important and she wanted to lay it to rest.

"He's dead, Lynn."

"But that shouldn't mean—"

"You're my wife now."

"I'm not contesting that."

"It's a good thing." He tried the playful approach in an effort to beset her, planting kisses on the edges of her mouth in a teasing game that would have easily turned her mind an hour earlier.

"Ryder, please," she begged.

He emitted a low guttural sound and chuckled. "I love it when you say that."

"You're impossible!"

He slipped his gaze his down her stomach and the amusement drained from his eyes.

Emotion flickered through them as he eased himself up and over her. "You're doing it again," she said, stopping him.

"I plan to do it every day of our married life."

"Ryder…"

"I want a baby," he announced without warning. "I know we agreed to wait, but I need to get you pregnant now. Tonight. Right now. I can't wait a minute more to feel my son moving inside you."

The plea that came into his voice was almost desperate. "I've thought about it a good deal this past month. Living with Michelle and Jason has taught me so much," he continued, holding her gaze. "I often wondered what kind of a father I'd be. I've even worried about it, but now I know I'm going to love having children."

"Oh, Ryder." She was eager, too, but a little afraid.

His face, poised above her own, filled with wonder. His jaw was clenched tight, but not with anger—some other emotion, restraint, she decided. His eyes shone with more vulnerability than she had ever seen in him. Just gazing up at this man she had married, and her heart felt as if it would burst.

"I remember how you had morning sickness with Michelle and Jason. I only want one baby…just one," he said, and laid his hand against her cheek, rubbing his thumb over her lower lip. "But promise me you'll throw out those damn birth control pills."

Tears gathered in the corners of her eyes as she nodded. "Ryder, I love you. I'll give you a dozen children if that's what you want."

"Oh Lynn, will I ever get enough of you?"

"I sincerely hope not." She twisted around, so that she was on her stomach, and reached for the knot behind her head that would unravel the long plait of hair.

Ryder watched her movements with wide-eyed wonder, as though he couldn't believe what she was preparing to do. Coming to a kneeling position, she pressed his shoulders back against the mattress before staddling him.

It wasn't until Lynn was dressing the following morning that she discovered Gary's uniform hat and badge were missing. She'd kept them stored on the shelf above the closet in their bedroom, carefully packed away in a box she planned to give Jason when he turned eighteen.

She paused, uncertain. Removing Gary's photo from the living room was one thing, but for Ryder to take away something that was a part of her son's inheritance was another. After a short search, she found Gary's photos and several other items stored in the garage, tucked away in a secluded corner.

Lynn exhaled sharply, remembering how she'd tried to talk to Ryder about Gary just the night before. But Ryder had done it to her again. Now that she gave the matter thought, Lynn realized that Michelle and Jason rarely mentioned their deceased father anymore, either. They, too, had apparently sensed Ryder's uneasiness over the subject and had eliminated Gary's name from casual conversation.

Following that episode with the missing hat and badge, Lynn was more determined than ever to have this out with Ryder. It was paramount that they discuss Gary and the role he now played in their lives. Ryder seemed to want to shove him aside and pretend he'd never existed. The only reason she could figure why he would do something like that wasn't one she was eager to face. If Ryder continued to carry a burden of guilt over Gary's death, then she could never be fully certain of his motive for marrying her and taking on the responsibility of raising Michelle and Jason.

She loved him. The children loved him. Ryder had made certain of that. He'd done everything humanly possible to garner their affection. He spoiled Michelle and Jason, taking his duty as stepfather far beyond what anyone would have expected. In analyzing the situation, Lynn realized it was as if Ryder was trying to make up to them for all the years they'd gone without a father figure.

The knot in her stomach twisted into a tighter knot.

When it came to proving his devotion to her, Ryder had seemed determined to be the model husband. He brought her gifts, made love to her frequently, and spoiled her in much the same way he did the children, as if he needed to compensate her for the loss of Gary.

A week passed, and although Lynn tried twice more to talk about her dead husband, Ryder wouldn't allow it. He was never abrupt or angry in his efforts to avoid the subject, but firmly subtle. She would carefully plan the discussion, wait for a quiet moment, usually after Michelle and Jason were in bed, and fifteen minutes later she would marvel at just how skillful Ryder's methods were of dodging the issue.

The problem was that they were both so busy. Ryder's caseload was increasing, which meant he left for work earlier and arrived home later. On her end, Lynn had offered the job of manager, with an appropriate increase in salary, to her assistant, Sharon. Her employee seemed both pleased and surprised and had eagerly accepted the promotion. That same week, Lynn hired another new assistant and left her training in Sharon's capable hands.

Lynn was still needed at the salon, but much of the day-to-day responsibility fell onto Sharon, which surprisingly pleased Lynn. She thought she would miss the control, but her life was so full that it was a relief not to worry about Slender, Too along with everything else.

On Wednesday, Lynn decided to try once more to talk to Ryder. This time, she wouldn't be put off so easily.

"I'm going to lunch now," Sharon informed Lynn, sticking her head into the office. "Judy's taking the noon class, but this is her first time going solo, so you might want to keep an eye on her."

"Will do," Lynn answered with a smile. She was reviewing the work schedule, penciling in names and times for the following week.

Sharon left the door to the office ajar, and the upbeat melody for the aerobics class drifted into the room. Absently Lynn tapped her foot, but the action stopped abruptly as her eyes fell on the following Monday's date.

It was silly that such a minor thing would trouble her so—Gary's birthday—or what would have been his birthday. He would have been thirty-seven, only Gary would remain thirty-three forever.

The remainder of the day was melancholy. Lynn found herself pensive and blue. She wouldn't change her life from the way it was now—she had no regrets—but a certain sadness permeated her being. One she couldn't shake or fully understand.

She was home before the kids, which was unusual. She left the salon early, telling Sharon she had a headache.

"Mom, I'm going over to Marcy's. Okay?" Michelle asked ten minutes after she was in the door.

"That's fine, honey."

Jason was holding an apple and a banana in one hand and a box of graham crackers in the other. "Do we have any chocolate chip cookies left?" He must have noticed her frown because he added, "I'm a growing boy—I need my afternoon snack."

"Take the apple and a few of the crackers, I don't want you ruining your dinner."

"Oh, Mom."

He may not have agreed, but he willingly obeyed her.

The pork chops were ready for the oven and the house was quiet. The real-estate agent they'd been working with phoned to tell Lynn about a large colonial that had just come on the market.

"Would you like to make an appointment to see it this evening?"

Lynn's gaze scooted around the kitchen and family room, falling lovingly on each wall and each piece of furniture. She didn't want to move, she never had. Ryder had been the one who insisted they start looking for another home right away. The day they returned from their honeymoon, he'd contacted a realtor. At least Lynn had been able to convince him not to put their house on the market until they found something suitable.

"Mrs. Matthews?"

"Not tonight," she answered abruptly, realizing she'd left the woman hanging. "Perhaps tomorrow…I'm not feeling well." Considering her mood, that wasn't so far from the truth.

When she finished with the phone conversation, Lynn sat and covered her face with her hands. In the bottom drawer of the china cabinet was her and Gary's wedding album. She felt drawn to that. Reverently she removed the bulky book and folded back the cover and the first thick page as though turning something fragile. The picture of her and Gary, standing with their wedding party, both so young and so much in love, greeted her like an old friend.

Tears flooded Lynn's eyes. Tears she couldn't fully comprehend.

She loved Ryder...she loved Gary.

The front door opened and thinking it was one of the children, Lynn wiped the moisture from her cheek and forced a smile.

Instead Ryder sauntered into the room. It was hours before he was due home. "Did the realtor call to set an appointment for us to see that new house?"

"I...I told her we'd look at it another day," she answered abruptly, quickly closing the picture album.

Ryder frowned. "I called the salon, but Sharon told me you'd gone home because of a headache."

Feeling incredibly guilty, Lynn stood abruptly and moved in front of the table. "I'm fine." She rubbed her palms together in an agitated movement and stepped across the room, praying Ryder wouldn't notice the picture album.

Ryder hesitated. "You've been crying."

"Not really...something must have gotten into my eye."

"Lynn, what's wrong?"

"Nothing." She moved to the kitchen counter and brewed herself a cup of coffee, although she already had one. When she turned back, she found Ryder standing at the round oak table, his hand on the wedding portfolio. He lifted back the cover.

Watching him, Lynn wanted to cry out for him to stop, but she knew it wouldn't do any good. His narrowed gaze rested on the picture she had been studying. He seemed to stop breathing. She looked on helplessly as he clenched his jaw, but the action wasn't directed by anger. Somehow, she'd expected him to become irate, but the look on his face revealed far more pain than irritation.

"You're still in love with him, aren't you?"

Nineteen

"Yes," Lynn admitted. "I love Gary."

The blood drained from Ryder's face as though she'd physically punched him. After the initial shock, he wore a look that claimed he'd known it all along, and wasn't the least bit surprised.

"Ryder...I was married to the man for nine years. Michelle and Jason are his children. I'm not the kind of woman who can conveniently forget that. Yes, I love Gary and as much as you don't want to hear it, I'm not likely to ever forget him."

"Gary is dead."

"You're making it sound like I'm being unfaithful to you by remembering him. I can't pretend the man never existed and neither can you."

"Thinking about him is one thing, but do you have to moon over his pictures, grieving your terrible loss?"

"His death *was* a terrible loss," she cried, losing patience. "And I wasn't mooning!"

"I find you weeping while looking over pictures of your wedding to another man and you try to feed me some line about there being something in your eye. You don't even have to say it, I can tell you regret the fact we're married."

"I don't. How can you ever think such a thing?"

"You honestly expect me to answer that? How many other times have you taken out that wedding album and cried over Gary?"

"This is the first time…in months. I don't even remember the last time I felt like this. He was my husband, I have the right to look at these pictures and feel sad."

"Not when you're married to me."

"I will if I want," she cried defensively.

Ryder's mouth thinned. "I'm your husband, Lynn."

"I know that." His attitude was infuriating her more every minute.

"What possible reason would you have to drag out those old pictures and weep over him now?"

Lynn's hands knotted in defense, knowing Ryder wasn't going to like her answer. "It's his birthday."

Ryder took three abrupt steps away from her, halted and jerked his fingers through his hair. "The man is dead. He doesn't have birthdays."

"I'm well aware of that. But I can't forget the fact he lived and breathed and loved."

Ryder began pacing and seemed to mull over her words. "The loving part is the crux of the problem, isn't it?"

"Of course," she cried. "I know that bothers you, and I'm sorry, but I can't change the past anymore than I could raise Gary from the dead. He was an important part of my life and I don't plan on forgetting him because you can't bear the mention of his name."

Ryder went still as if a new thought had flashed into

his mind. His dark eyes hardened. "You blame me for his death, too, don't you? I'd always feared you would, and then I chose to overlook the obvious."

"Oh, Ryder, honestly," she whispered, wanting to weep, "I don't blame you. I never did—I couldn't have married you if there'd been doubt in my heart."

He shook his head, discounting her answer. "The revenge would be sweet. If you'd planned to torture me, you couldn't have chosen a more painful method."

"Stop talking like that. It's crazy—I love you. Hasn't the past month taught you that much?"

"I did this to myself," he murmured, defeated. "There's no one else to blame." He inhaled a long, slow breath, and continued thoughtfully. "I rushed you into the marriage, using every trick I could think of, and like a fool, I didn't even consider the fact you planned to hold on to Gary with both hands."

"I'm not holding on to Gary—you're being utterly ridiculous."

"Am I?"

The fight seemed to have died in him, Lynn noticed. He was resolved now, subdued, as if he'd lost the most important battle of his life.

"I honestly thought I could step into Michelle's and Jason's lives and fill the void left by Gary's death. Only there wasn't one. You've carried his image in your heart and on your lips all these years. They didn't need a father, not when the memory of Gary remained so strong. You made sure of that."

"Ryder…"

"You didn't need a husband, either."

"You're right," she cried, her patience gone. "I didn't *need* one, but I *wanted* you…"

"In bed."

"In my life," she cried. Tears of anger and frustration brimmed in her eyes and she wiped them aside, furious that she couldn't hold back the emotion.

His smile was unbelievably sad. "I knew you loved Gary in the beginning, but I thought once we were married that would change."

"Change?"

He ignored her question and walked over to the kitchen window, looking out onto the back patio, although Lynn felt certain he was blind to the glory of the late summer afternoon. "The realtor has taken us to look at how many houses now?"

He was jumping from one subject to another, without any logical reason that she could decipher. "What has that got to do with anything?"

"Ten homes? Fifteen? And yet you've never been able to find one you like. The house may be perfect for us, but you've always managed to come up with a convenient excuse why we shouldn't buy it."

"I—"

"Have you ever considered the reason all those homes didn't suit you? Why you've continued to drag your feet again and again? It's getting to the point now that you delay even setting up the appointment with the realtor."

She wanted to shout at him, tell him how wrong he was, but as far as the realtor went, she was guilty of everything he claimed. "I...oh, Ryder, I never *did* want to move. I'm trying, but there are so many happy memories associated with this place. I love it here, I'm comfortable."

"And I'm not."

She dipped her head and eased her breath out on a disheartened sigh. "I know."

"Gary's ghost is here, in every room, and he's haunted me from the minute we returned from Hawaii. Every time I walk through the front door, I feel his presence, every time I turn around, his face is looking at me, accusing me. I tried to ignore him, tried to pretend he wasn't there. I went so far as to remove his pictures and a few other things, thinking that would help, but it didn't."

Lynn wasn't sure what to say. She could understand his feelings, although that didn't help their situation any.

"But a new house isn't going to solve that, is it, Lynn?"

"How do you mean?"

"Gary's a part of you in the same way that he's a part of Michelle and Jason. We won't ever be able to escape him, because wherever you are, he'll be there, too."

She opened her mouth to deny that, then realized what he said was true.

"I notice you're not bothering to repudiate that fact."

Lynn drooped her head as the defeat worked its way through her tired limbs. "No, I don't think I can. You're right."

"I thought as much." If he experienced any elation at correctly deciphering her actions, it wasn't evident in his voice. What *did* come through was a heavy note of despair. "I can't continue to fool myself any longer and neither can you. Nothing's going to change."

"I don't understand why it should," she cried. "You're asking me to wipe out a decade of my life, and I find that unreasonable. It's just not going to happen."

"You don't need to tell me that, I figured it out already." He reached out and touched her, lightly grazing her cheek with his fingertips, his eyes filled with an agony of regret. "I won't take second place in your life, Lynn."

The action tugged at Lynn's heart and she caught his hand in her own, wanting to weep and beg him to understand. She managed to hold all the emotion boiling within her at bay; she longed to find the words that would reassure him, but was at a loss.

"I love you, Ryder."

He nodded, sadly. "But not enough."

With that he turned and slowly climbed the stairs.

Lynn followed him a couple of minutes later and was shocked to see him packing his suitcases.

"What are you doing?"

"Giving us both some needed space to think things out."

"But you're moving out. Why?" Tears gushed down her face—she didn't even try to hold them inside.

"I was wrong to have married you," Ryder said, busily filling his luggage, hardly stopping to look at her.

"Well, that's just wonderful," she cried and slumped onto the edge of the mattress. Her legs felt incredibly weak. "So you're going to walk out on me. It's getting to be a habit with you, Ryder. A bad habit. When the going gets tough, the tough move on, is that it? Where are you going this time? Europe? Do you think that'll be far enough away to forget?"

He whirled around. "You've already admitted you still love Gary, what else do you expect me to do?"

"I also admitted that I love *you*! Love me back, accept me for who I am—love Michelle and Jason. I want you to give me the child you've talked about so much, and build a good life with me and our children."

"And play second fiddle to a dead man? No thanks." He slammed the top closed on the first suitcase and reached for the second.

"Why are you doing this?" she cried.

He hesitated. "You already know the answer to that. There isn't any need to discuss it further."

Desperate now, Lynn scooted off the bed and walked over to the window. She closed her eyes and covered her mouth with her hand. "Aren't I even allowed to keep the memories?"

He didn't respond, which was answer enough.

"Can't I?" she tried again, tears drenching her face, dripping onto her chin. She brushed them off with the heel of her hand, and held her head high, the action dictated by an abundance of pride.

"Go ahead and leave me, Ryder. Walk out on me. I got along without you the first time, I'll do it again." She marched across the room to the closet and ripped his dress shirts off the hangers one by one in a disorderly fashion. "I wouldn't want you to forget anything," she sobbed. "Take it all."

He carelessly stuffed the pressed shirts in the bottom of the garment bag, paused and glance around. "I'll send someone for whatever else is left."

"Fine." She didn't dare look at him, for fear she would break down completely and beg him to stay. "Just be sure this is what you really want."

He hesitated, his gaze mirroring her own agony. "It isn't, but I think a separation will give us both time to sort through our feelings."

"How long? One year? Three? Or should we try to break a record this time?"

Ryder closed his eyes, as though her words were a physical assault. Lynn frantically wiped the moisture from her face. "I tried to talk to you about Gary," she sobbed. "You know, I tried, but you'd never let me. The minute I mentioned his name you did cartwheels in an effort to change the subject."

"The reason should have been obvious."

"If we'd been able to clear the air before...then maybe none of this would be necessary. But oh no, you insisted on sweeping everything under the carpet—ignore it and it'll go away. But Gary isn't going and neither am I!"

"I didn't want to hear what you were so bound and determined to tell me," he shouted. "In this instance, ignorance was bliss." He swung the suitcases off the mattress with such force it tugged the bedspread onto the floor.

Lynn righted it as though that was of the utmost importance.

Ryder left the bedroom, walking away from her with ground-devouring steps, as if he couldn't get away fast enough. Lynn remained in the bedroom, and flinched at the sound of the front door closing as it echoed up the stairway.

The silence that followed was as profound as it was deafening.

Lynn didn't know how long she stood there, immobile and numb. The floor seemed to sway and buckle under her feet and she lowered herself onto the edge of the bed, her fingers biting into the mattress.

The tears had dried against the flushed skin of her

cheeks long before she was composed enough to go downstairs and confront Michelle and Jason.

"When's dinner?" Jason asked as he barged in the front door a few minutes later with Michelle close behind him.

"I'm...just putting it on now." She quietly put the pork chops into the oven, all the time knowing she wouldn't be able to gag down a single bite of the evening meal.

"You haven't even started yet?"

"It's only five," Michelle said indignantly.

"I need something to carry me through," Jason cried. He opened the cookie jar and stuck in his hand. The bowl had been empty all week, but her son managed to gain a pawful of crumbs and took delight in licking them from his hand a finger at a time as he walked out of the kitchen.

"I don't suppose you thought to wash your hands before you did that?" Michelle commented, having gone to position herself in front of the television. "Aren't you going to tell him to wash, Mom? He could be bringing in germs that will infect us all."

"It would be like closing the gate after the horse gets loose," she said, doing her best to pretend everything was normal.

"When's Ryder getting home?" Jason asked, opening the refrigerator and peering inside.

"He's...going to be away on a business trip for a while," she said as nonchalantly as possible, trying to play down the fact he was missing without arousing their suspicions.

The door to the refrigerator closed with a bang. "When did he tell you this?"

She glanced at the clock. "An hour ago."

"How long is he going to be gone?" Jason asked anxiously. "What about soccer? What am I going to tell the coach when Ryder doesn't show up...I'm counting on him and so is everyone else. I play better when Ryder's there watching me."

"I...don't know what you should tell Mr. Lawson... tell him Ryder had to go out of town."

"He could have said something to us, don't you think?" Michelle said with a pout. "I need him to help me with math. We're dividing fractions and some of those problems are too hard for me and a simple calculator. I've got to have massive help."

"You can do it, Michelle, I'll be around to lend a hand."

"Thanks, but no thanks," she said, on a sarcastic note. "I remember the last time you decided to tutor me in fractions. I'm lucky I made it out of fifth grade."

"Why would Ryder leave on a business trip?" Jason wanted to know, his eyes curious. "I thought all his cases were in Seattle."

Lynn hated to lie to her children, but she didn't want to alarm them unnecessarily. She would tell them the truth, but not now when it was difficult enough for her to face.

The dinner was one of the best Lynn had fixed all week, but no one seemed to have much of an appetite.

"Ryder's coming back, isn't he, Mom?" Michelle whispered the question while Lynn removed their plates from the table. Jason was talking to Brad on the telephone.

"Of course he is," she returned with an encouraging grin that took all her reserve of strength. She didn't know what had prompted the question and prayed her daughter didn't notice the way her hands shook as she placed their dinner dishes in the dishwasher.

Michelle relaxed. "It's been good having a dad again."

"I know." It had been good having a husband, too. But Lynn had the crippling feeling that this problem with Ryder wasn't going to be settled overnight.

"Ryder's going to phone us, isn't he?" Jason asked, once he was finished talking to his friend. "Brad's father goes on business trips sometimes and he calls every night. Brad says it's really great because when his dad comes home, he brings him and his little sister gifts."

"I don't know if Ryder will have a chance to call," Lynn said, making busywork around the sink, scrubbing it extra hard. Her eyes blurred with fresh tears.

"He'll bring us back a present, won't he?"

"I...don't know that, either."

Jason uttered a disgruntled sound. "What's the use of having him go away, if he doesn't bring us back something?"

"Maybe he doesn't know he's supposed to," Michelle murmured thoughtfully. "He didn't have any kids until us. Maybe we should all write him and drop the hint. I'm sure he'd want to know what his duties are to me and Jason."

Lynn couldn't endure another minute of their exchange. Ryder claimed Gary's ghost filled their house and that their children held on to his memory. If Ryder were there to hear this conversation now, he would know how untrue that was.

The evening seemed to drag. Although Michelle claimed she didn't want Lynn's help with her math, after several minutes of grumbling over her assignment, she succumbed and took everything to her mother. When Lynn wasn't much help, Michelle suggested they call Lynn's accountant.

As expected, Jason put up a fuss about taking a bath, but that was normal. Lynn's patience was stretched to its limit. Jason must have known that because after voicing the usual arguments, he went upstairs and bathed in world-record time. Lynn wondered if he'd managed to get his entire body wet, but hadn't the fight in her to question him.

The kids were in their rooms when the front door opened.

"Ryder," Jason cried from the top of the stairs, racing into his arms. "What happened on your business trip? Did you know when you go away you're supposed to bring back presents for your kids? It's the expected thing."

"You're not supposed to blurt it out like that!" Michelle stormed. "You can be such a nerd, sometimes."

"Who's calling who a nerd?"

"Children, please," Lynn cried moving into the entryway. She sought Ryder's gaze, but he avoided meeting hers.

"How come you're home?" Michelle asked. "You haven't even been gone a single night."

"The plane was late," Ryder told her. He glanced at his watch. "Now go back upstairs, it's long past your bed time."

"Okay."

"Do we have to?"

"Yes, you do," Lynn answered for Ryder. "Good night to you both."

"You missed a great dinner," Jason added, hugging him one last time. "Mom cooked her special pork chops."

If pork chops would have kept Ryder home, Lynn would cook them every night.

"I'll see you in the morning," Jason said on the tail end of a yawn. "I hope you stay home...it's not right when you're gone."

Both Michelle and Jason had returned to their bedrooms before Ryder spoke. "I apologize for dropping in like this, but I forgot my briefcase. There are some papers I'll need in the morning, otherwise I wouldn't have troubled you."

Twenty

Ryder scooted past Lynn and retrieved his briefcase. Lynn stood frozen, her heart jackhammering against her rib cage, but she dared not move for fear she would break down and weep before he left.

Ryder returned, and paused in front of the door. "I take it you told the kids I was going away on a business trip?"

She nodded. "I probably shouldn't have lied, but I didn't know what else to say."

"That explanation is as good as any. Once they get used to the idea of me being gone, you can tell them the truth."

"Which is?"

"Which is," he repeated and drew in an unsteady breath, "I needed to get away for a while...to think things through."

"I'm sure they'll understand that readily enough." Her voice dipped sarcastically. "And what should I tell them you're thinking about? They'll ask me that, you know. Exactly what do you want me to tell them?"

"You know the answer to that," he snapped.

"I don't."

"I'm trying to decide if I can continue to live with a woman who's in love with another man."

Lynn crossed her arms over her middle to ward off a chill that descended over her like an October frost. "You make it sound so vile, as though I'm committing adultery by honoring Gary's memory."

"You do more than honor his memory, despite what we have, you won't let him go."

"No…" Her voice cracked, and she whirled around, unable to face him any longer. "I love you, Ryder, and it's going to break my heart to lose you, but I don't know what I can do to make things right for us."

He was silent for so long, Lynn wondered if he'd slipped out the door without her hearing him move, but she didn't turn around to investigate.

Suddenly the tension of the day overwhelmed her. Tears flooded her eyes and she sobbed so hard her shoulders shook violently.

A bedroom door opened upstairs. "Mom?"

"It's all right, Jason," Ryder answered.

"I can hear Mom crying." Her son started down the stairs, pausing halfway down. "She *is* crying."

Lynn wiped the moisture from her face as best she could. "I'm fine, honey."

"Ryder," Jason shouted. "Do something…hold her or kiss her or do that other stuff women like. You can't let her stand there like that, bawling her head off."

Ryder hesitated, then walked over to Lynn's side. He didn't want to touch her, she could feel his reluctance, but they both knew Jason wouldn't be appeased until he was assured his mother was receiving the comfort she needed. Ryder wrapped his arms around her and

Lynn buried her face in his shoulder, her arms hanging limply at her sides.

"You've got to hold on to him, too, Mom," Jason instructed impatiently.

Lynn complied, awkwardly. Her raised arms loosely circled Ryder's waist. Being this close to him demanded a steep fee and she quivered, wondering how she would ever adjust to a life where there wouldn't be someone to love her the way Ryder did. Her whole body felt as if it were trembling from the inside out.

"I don't think you should be taking this business trip," Jason announced, marching the rest of the way down the stairs, with a military crispness that would have pleased an Army officer.

Lynn backed out of Ryder's arms and made an effort to compose herself. "Honey, listen—"

"Ryder didn't say anything about going away on business trips when he married us."

"I'm sorry, son, but I have to leave." Ryder's own voice was dark and heavy.

"But we need you here. Mom tried not to show it, but Michelle and I noticed how miserable she was all night. She misses you a whole bunch already and you've only been gone a little while."

Ryder's gaze fell on Lynn and a weary sadness invaded his eyes.

"Michelle and I need you, too. Mom had to help Michelle with her math tonight and it didn't go very well."

"I'm sure your mother did just fine."

"Not according to Michelle," Jason murmured, tossing Lynn an apologetic glance. "I don't think Mom's into fractions."

"What are you guys talking about down there?" Michelle shouted testily. "I thought we were supposed to be in bed, asleep."

"Mom's crying," Jason shot back at his sister.

"I knew something like this was going to happen," Michelle blurted out and raced down the stairs like an avenging angel of mercy. "I hope you know this is all your fault, Ryder."

"Michelle," Lynn warned.

"Mom's been a basket case all night. How can you leave the woman who loves you alone like this?"

So much for the gallant effort she'd made to hide her distress from the kids. Knowing how woefully she'd failed, Lynn's lower lip quivered and she was forced to take in several deep breaths to hold back a fresh batch of tears. "Michelle and Jason, it's time for you to go back upstairs."

"Are you going to cry again?" Jason wanted reassurance before he returned to his bedroom.

Lynn shook her head, then realized she couldn't make that guarantee. "I'll try not to."

Michelle and Jason shared a meaningful glance and then by unspoken agreement, headed toward their bedrooms. Lynn stopped them at the foot of the stairs, hugging them separately, loving her children so much her heart felt as if it would burst with the weight of the emotion. Gary had given her these precious two and if there had been no other grounds than that, she would always love him. As it was there were so many reasons to love and remember Gary Danfort.

"You want a hug, too, Ryder?" Michelle asked, yawning out the question with her hand in front of her face.

He nodded, holding Michelle close. Lynn noted the way his eyes closed and his jaw tightened.

"Next time when you need to go away on business," Michelle murmured, "try to tell us sooner so we won't all feel so lonely without you. It's bad when you leave and we haven't had time to…" she paused, and dragged a huge breath through her lungs, "…prepare for it."

"You're not still going, are you?" Jason cried, shocked. "After all this?"

"Jason, to bed!" Lynn pointed up the stairs, her voice more solid.

"He made you cry and Michelle could flunk math, and Ryder is still going to catch that stupid plane, anyway? Doesn't he know he's got responsibilities…like taking out the garbage and helping coach soccer—"

"We're going to be just fine without Ryder," Lynn interrupted her son's outburst, but her voice lacked any real conviction.

"No, we won't!" Jason proclaimed under his breath. He paused and his eyes flashed with concern. "You'll be back in time for Saturday's game, won't you?"

"I'm not sure."

With that, Jason tossed his arms into the air. "What's the use of having a new dad if he can't come to my soccer games?"

"Jason!"

He muttered something unintelligible under his breath and vanished inside his bedroom.

Lynn straightened her shoulders and tried to offer Ryder a smile to make up for the disruption, but her mouth wouldn't cooperate. It was unlikely that Ryder even noticed since his gaze was centered on the empty hallway upstairs, from where both children had disappeared.

"They love you," Lynn told him softly, wondering if he fully understood how much.

Ryder nodded and reluctantly reached for his brief-case.

Lynn closed her eyes, unable to bear the pain of his leaving. It had been difficult enough the first time. The words to ask him to stay burned on the tip of her tongue, but she was forced to swallow them. The taste of acid filled her dry mouth.

Ryder hesitated in front of the door and then turned back to her. "I don't know that I can do it." Each word seemed to be painfully pulled from his heart, his voice strained and low.

Lynn bowed her head. "I don't know that I can let you."

"By all rights, you should throw me out of here, but I'd like to try to sort this out if we can. Let's reason this out."

Lynn felt her body go weak with relief, and led the way into the kitchen. She automatically put on a pot of coffee. Ryder stepped behind her, his hands resting lightly on her shoulders as if he needed to touch her.

"I didn't really need the briefcase," he admitted, "I was looking for a convenient excuse to come back and make things right, although heaven knows, I can't see any solution to this."

Lynn sucked part of her bottom lip with her teeth. It had cost Ryder a good deal of pride to be so honest and she was grateful.

When the coffee had finished dripping into the glass pot, she poured them each a mug and carried them to the table, where Ryder was waiting. She sat across from him.

Ryder cupped his hands around the steaming mug, his eyes downcast. "After what just happened with Michelle and Jason, I realize what a jealous fool I'm being. How can I feel resentful toward a man I loved…a man who's been dead for over three years?"

"But, Ryder you don't have any reason to be jealous of Gary."

Ryder looked away from her, refusing to meet her eyes. "Please let me finish, Lynn. It's not a pleasant emotion to have to admit to myself, let alone confess to you. I realized while I was driving around tonight that undiluted, hard-core jealousy was exactly what I was feeling."

"But, Ryder, I love you so much."

"I know that, too, but as damning as it sounds, I begrudge every minute of the life you shared with Gary." He stopped and ran his hand over his jaw as if the action would erase the guilt charted across the tight lines of his face. "Admitting it to you this way makes me feel like I've got to be the pettiest man alive. How can I even think like this? What kind of man am I to feel these things? I look around me and this crushing weight of shame is pressed upon me. I loved Gary—he was the best kind of police officer and human being I'm ever likely to know. He was everything that was good…honorable and generous…he was my friend and yet I'm harboring all these negative emotions toward him."

Lynn reached for Ryder's hand, intertwining their fingers. "You love Gary and you resent Gary…it isn't any wonder you haven't wanted to talk about him."

"If he hadn't died, I wouldn't have you and the kids and so there's an incredible amount of guilt involved as well." He sucked in a sigh and slowly shook his head as though the magnitude of his emotions was more than he could fully comprehend. "I honestly believed I'd dealt with all my feelings for him while I was in law school, but I can see now that you were right. I was sweeping all these painful emotions under a carpet, avoiding confronting them because I've been so confused. In fact, I'm still confused." The rugged lines in his face were testament enough to the turmoil churning inside his soul. "I packed my bags and was running away from you and the kids…that was so stupid, so illogical, I can't believe the thought so much as entered my mind. The only place in the world I want to be is with you and Michelle and Jason. My heart is here…my soul is here… there's no leaving, no running away."

Tears bled down the side of Lynn's face. Unable to maintain this distance from her husband any longer, she stood and walked around the table. Ryder scooted out his chair and lowered her into his lap, folding her in his embrace, sighing as her arms circled him.

"I've been doing some thinking tonight myself," Lynn told him, her throat thick with emotion. "And like you, I realize I've made a lot of mistakes. Looking over those wedding pictures was one of them…I can understand how you must have felt when you found me."

"Deep down inside, I know how completely unreasonable I'm being to ask you to forget Gary, but I can't seem to put that behind me."

"Can *you* forget him?" she asked quietly, cupping his face in her hands.

Ryder's mouth twisted with the question and Lynn could feel the tension in his taut body. "No," he admitted with a strangled breath. "And I'm not sure I want to."

"I can't either. You loved him. I loved him. Michelle and Jason loved him. We can't conveniently forget he lived and touched our lives. We can't pretend a part of him won't always be with us. You love Michelle and Jason—you have from the time they were born—they're a part of Gary, too."

"I know...I know." But that insight didn't seem to ease Ryder's distress. "Maybe we're going about this all wrong."

Lynn frowned. "How do you mean?"

His arms circled her waist and he pressed his forehead against her shoulder. "For the past few months, I've done everything I could to cast him from our lives. I've resented his intrusion into what I consider my family, but I've been wrong, because you and the kids are his family, too."

"Yes," she answered, not sure she was following his line of reasoning.

"I've tried everything within my power to make everyone forget him. You didn't. Michelle and Jason didn't. And neither did I."

Lynn nodded.

"I can't ignore him any longer, Lynn. If he were here now, we could sit down and talk this out. Man to man."

"But he isn't here."

For the first time that evening, Ryder smiled. "I think he is...not in any ghostly form or anything like that, but his spirit is here, his essence. He's a large part of Michelle and Jason...and a part of you."

"If Gary were here," she murmured, "and you could talk to him, what would you say?"

Ryder frowned thoughtfully. "I'm not sure. One thing I'd do is tell him how much I love you and explain that I know he felt the same deep commitment to you. I think he'd understand and approve of me marrying you." Some of the weary tautness left his limbs as soon as he'd voiced the thought.

"If Gary had handpicked the man to take his place in our lives, it would have been you."

Ryder relaxed even more with that. "I'd tell him how proud he'd be of his children, and of you," he paused to kiss her lightly.

Some of the strain eased from his eyes and Lynn leaned forward enough to plant a simple kiss on his lips. She ran her fingers through his hair, toying with it because she needed to keep touching and feeling him. "You know what we're doing, don't you?"

Ryder's responding glance confirmed that he didn't.

"We're inviting Gary's memory back into our lives, because excluding him would be futile."

"And wrong," Ryder added in a voice that trembled slightly.

They stared at each other, both sets of eyes glistening with unshed tears. Words weren't necessary now, they would have been superfluous at that moment. Lynn and Ryder had emptied their hearts of any emotion except the gift Gary Danfort had given them—each other.

Lynn wrapped her arms around Ryder's neck and hugged him close, cradling his head against her breast. "Don't you think it's time to unpack those bags?"

He was too busy toying with the front of her blouse. "I think it's time for other things, too."

"Sleep?"

"If you think you're going upstairs to rest, think again, woman."

Slowly their mouths merged, and when they kissed their hearts were open, free from the chains of the past, free to soar in their love.

* * * * *

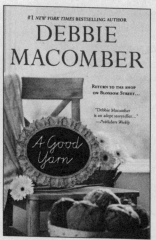

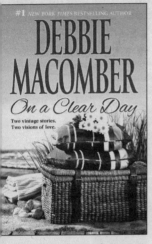

H BESTSELLING AUTHOR COLLECTION

TM

CLASSIC ROMANCES IN COLLECTIBLE VOLUMES

#1 *New York Times* Bestselling Author

SHERRYL WOODS

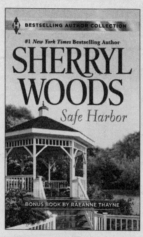

To Tina Harrington, the definition was simple: anyone she loved was part of her family. Including all the people—and animals—she'd invited into her home when they'd had nowhere else to go. She was their safe harbor, and they were hers. And she would protect them from whomever challenged their right to be a family—namely her new neighbor, the handsome and high-powered Drew Landry.

SAFE HARBOR

Available August 26, 2014, wherever books are sold.

**Plus, ENJOY the bonus story *A Cold Creek Homecoming*
RaeAnne Thayne, included in this 2-in-1 volume!**

REQUEST YOUR FREE BOOKS!

2 FREE NOVELS
FROM THE ROMANCE COLLECTION
PLUS 2 FREE GIFTS!

YES! Please send me 2 FREE novels from the Romance Collection and my 2 FREE gifts (gifts are worth about $10). After receiving them, if I don't wish to receive any more books, I can return the shipping statement marked "cancel." If I don't cancel, I will receive 4 brand-new novels every month and be billed just $6.24 per book in the U.S. or $6.74 per book in Canada. That's a savings of at least 22% off the cover price. It's quite a bargain! Shipping and handling is just 50¢ per book in the U.S. and 75¢ per book in Canada.* I understand that accepting the 2 free books and gifts places me under no obligation to buy anything. I can always return a shipment and cancel at any time. Even if I never buy another book, the two free books and gifts are mine to keep forever.

194/394 MDN F4XY

Name   (PLEASE PRINT)

Address   Apt. #

City   State/Prov.   Zip/Postal Code

Signature (if under 18, a parent or guardian must sign)

Mail to the Harlequin® Reader Service:
IN U.S.A.: P.O. Box 1867, Buffalo, NY 14240-1867
IN CANADA: P.O. Box 609, Fort Erie, Ontario L2A 5X3

Want to try two free books from another line?
Call 1-800-873-8635 or visit www.ReaderService.com.

* Terms and prices subject to change without notice. Prices do not include applicable taxes. Sales tax applicable in N.Y. Canadian residents will be charged applicable taxes. Offer not valid in Quebec. This offer is limited to one order per household. Not valid for current subscribers to the Romance Collection or the Romance/Suspense Collection. All orders subject to credit approval. Credit or debit balances in a customer's account(s) may be offset by any other outstanding balance owed by or to the customer. Please allow 4 to 6 weeks for delivery. Offer available while quantities last.

Your Privacy—The Harlequin® Reader Service is committed to protecting your privacy. Our Privacy Policy is available online at www.ReaderService.com or upon request from the Harlequin Reader Service.

We make a portion of our mailing list available to reputable third parties that offer products we believe may interest you. If you prefer that we not exchange your name with third parties, or if you wish to clarify or modify your communication preferences, please visit us at www.ReaderService.com/consumerchoice or write to us at Harlequin Reader Service Preference Service, P.O. Box 9062, Buffalo, NY 14269. Include your complete name and address.

ROM13R

DEBBIE MACOMBER

32988	OUT OF THE RAIN	___	$7.99 U.S.	___ $9.99 CAN.
32929	HANNAH'S LIST	___	$7.99 U.S.	___ $9.99 CAN.
32918	AN ENGAGEMENT IN SEATTLE	___	$7.99 U.S.	___ $9.99 CAN.
32911	THE MANNING SISTERS	___	$7.99 U.S.	___ $9.99 CAN.
32883	TWENTY WISHES	___	$7.99 U.S.	___ $9.99 CAN.
32858	HOME FOR THE HOLIDAYS	___	$7.99 U.S.	___ $9.99 CAN.
32828	ORCHARD VALLEY BRIDES	___	$7.99 U.S.	___ $9.99 CAN.
32798	ORCHARD VALLEY GROOMS	___	$7.99 U.S.	___ $9.99 CAN.
32783	THE MAN YOU'LL MARRY	___	$7.99 U.S.	___ $9.99 CAN.
32767	SUMMER ON BLOSSOM STREET	___	$7.99 U.S.	___ $9.99 CAN.
32743	THE SOONER THE BETTER	___	$7.99 U.S.	___ $9.99 CAN.
32702	FAIRY TALE WEDDINGS	___	$7.99 U.S.	___ $9.99 CAN.
32602	THE MANNING GROOMS	___	$7.99 U.S.	___ $7.99 CAN.
32569	ALWAYS DAKOTA	___	$7.99 U.S.	___ $7.99 CAN.
32474	THE MANNING BRIDES	___	$7.99 U.S.	___ $7.99 CAN.
32362	COUNTRY BRIDES	___	$7.99 U.S.	___ $9.50 CAN.
31580	MARRIAGE BETWEEN FRIENDS	___	$7.99 U.S.	___ $8.99 CAN.
31535	PROMISE, TEXAS	___	$7.99 U.S.	___ $8.99 CAN.
31458	CALL ME MRS. MIRACLE	___	$7.99 U.S.	___ $8.99 CAN.
31457	HEART OF TEXAS VOLUME 3	___	$7.99 U.S.	___ $8.99 CAN.
31441	HEART OF TEXAS VOLUME 2	___	$7.99 U.S.	___ $8.99 CAN.
31426	HEART OF TEXAS VOLUME 1	___	$7.99 U.S.	___ $9.99 CAN.
31424	MONTANA	___	$7.99 U.S.	___ $9.99 CAN.
31413	LOVE IN PLAIN SIGHT	___	$7.99 U.S.	___ $9.99 CAN.
31395	GLAD TIDINGS	___	$7.99 U.S.	___ $9.99 CAN.
31357	I LEFT MY HEART	___	$7.99 U.S.	___ $9.99 CAN.
31341	THE UNEXPECTED HUSBAND	___	$7.99 U.S.	___ $9.99 CAN.
31325	A TURN IN THE ROAD	___	$7.99 U.S.	___ $9.99 CAN.

(limited quantities available)

TOTAL AMOUNT	$ _____
POSTAGE & HANDLING	$ _____
($1.00 for 1 book, 50¢ for each additional)	
APPLICABLE TAXES*	$ _____
TOTAL PAYABLE	$ _____

(check or money order—please do not send cash)

To order, complete this form and send it, along with a check or money order for the total above, payable to Harlequin MIRA, to: **In the U.S.:** 3010 Walden Avenue, P.O. Box 9077, Buffalo, NY 14269-9077; **In Canada:** P.O. Box 636, Fort Erie, Ontario, L2A 5X3.

Name: _____

Address: _____ City: _____

State/Prov.: _____ Zip/Postal Code: _____

Account Number (if applicable): _____

075 CSAS

*New York residents remit applicable sales taxes.
*Canadian residents remit applicable GST and provincial taxes.

HARLEQUIN® MIRA®
™ www.Harlequin.com

MDM0614BL